THE DEAD ROOM

**Center Point
Large Print**

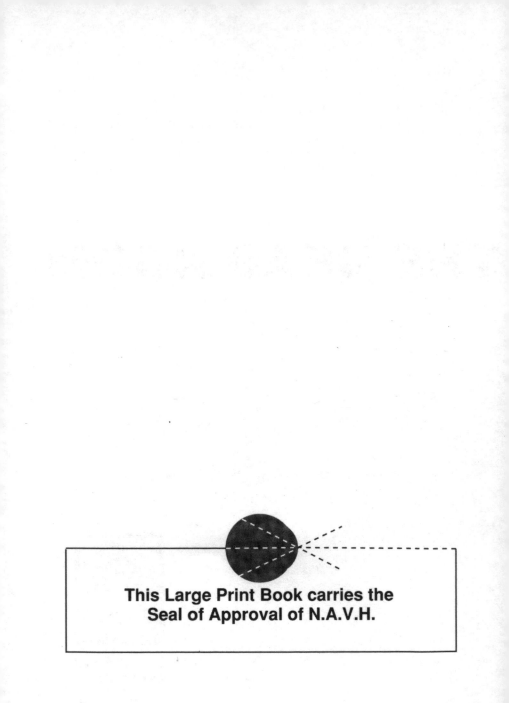

**This Large Print Book carries the
Seal of Approval of N.A.V.H.**

THE DEAD ROOM

HEATHER GRAHAM

CENTER POINT PUBLISHING
THORNDIKE, MAINE

This Center Point Large Print edition
is published in the year 2007 by arrangement with
Harlequin Enterprises Ltd.

The text of this Large Print edition is unabridged. In other
aspects, this book may vary from the original edition.
Printed in the United States of America.
Set in 16-point Times New Roman type.

ISBN-10: 1-58547-961-6
ISBN-13: 978-1-58547-961-0

Library of Congress Cataloging-in-Publication Data

Graham, Heather.
    The dead room / Heather Graham.--Center Point large print ed.
    p. cm.
    ISBN-13: 978-1-58547-961-0 (lib. bdg. : alk. paper)
    1. New York--Fiction. 2. Large type books. I. Title.

PS3557.R198D435 2007
813'.54--dc22

2006102866

For ITW,
CJ Lyons, Gayle Lynds, David Morrell and
M. Diane Vogt, who worked so very hard—and
pulled off the incredible. And for our fearless leader
Bob Levinson and the Killer Thriller Band—
F. Paul Wilson, John Lescroart, Michael Palmer (the
lyrics man!), Daniel Palmer, Nathan Walpow, Blake
Crouch, Dave Simms, Scott Nicholson, David Morrell (again) and Gayle Lynds (amazing triangle!).
And for my truly beautiful fellow Killerettes—
Harley Jane Kozak and Alex Sokoloff.
Deepest thanks to all.

PROLOGUE

The light was blinding.

For a moment it seemed as if nothing had existed before it, as if nothing could be greater than rising to meet it. It seemed to reach out with a sweet, alluring warmth. At the source there seemed to be beckoning shadows, but though Leslie MacIntyre could see nothing clearly, they seemed to offer comfort, as well, as if they were waiting to welcome her, to enfold her into their loving arms.

"Hey, you!"

The voice was husky, affectionate, yet strangely jarring. She looked up. It was Matt. She didn't know where they were, but so long as she and Matt Connolly were together, everything was all right.

They'd met when she'd been the new kid on the block. Though he was a few years older, he'd pulled her along in his wake and made her one of his crowd. He'd called her Rebel, but he'd done it in such a teasing tone that no one had ever been able to use it against her. He'd mocked her Southern accent, then announced that it was the most charming thing he'd ever heard. She'd practically worshipped him over the years, then—yes, she could admit it—lusted after him as they'd grown older. Strangely, it was a tragedy that had made her hopes and dreams come true, that had suddenly made him realize the girl he had befriended had grown up. And since then . . .

The years hadn't all been perfect. They'd been quite a thing once she'd graduated from high school, but their pride had sometimes gotten the best of them. One tempestuous blowup had led to a breakup, sending him to college in another state far to the south to play football, while she, still his Rebel, had stayed behind in Yankee territory, opting for NYU. Despite a year in the pros post-college, he'd gone on to journalism, while she had chosen urban archaeology, specializing in her own adopted home of New York. He had started in sports but gone on to world affairs, then come home to write a column about life and issues in New York City.

Back in New York, he had found her again—digging in the dirt, he joked. For months, they had both been cautious, dying to see each other, afraid of the intensity of the emotion that still roiled between them. One night he had simply shown up at her door at 3:00 a.m. and sanity flew to the wind. They'd immediately gotten engaged, and now they were planning a wedding.

Oddly enough, their lives together had added to both their careers. He'd done some of his very best pieces for the paper—a man's take on the modern wedding. Through Matt, Leslie had been drawn into conversation with a detective about an elderly man who had gone missing. She knew the area in Brooklyn where he had disappeared, which was filled with old subway tunnels. Asking the detective to humor her, she had led him to the place where the man had ended his days.

She'd felt almost as if she'd been beckoned to the site, though she argued with herself that knowledge and logic had brought her to the place. But now many detectives found her very interesting, and Matt had warned her that they were thinking about asking her to use her extraordinary knowledge of the city and its infrastructure to help with a new spate of disappearances. Matt himself was taking the matter very seriously and writing about it for the paper. People constantly disappeared in New York, of course. But these disappearances seemed to be linked. The missing were all women who lived on the streets. And they were all prostitutes.

Matt had pointed out that, throughout history, neither the police nor the populace had seemed to care about the fate of those who lived in the underbelly of society.

The moral majority never worried too much until it was threatened itself.

She could tell that Matt wanted her to get involved, though she seriously doubted she could be of any help. She wished she could, but she couldn't suddenly claim to be some kind of clairvoyant.

And she had her real work, which she believed was important, and which she loved.

And which had brought them here. *Here? Where exactly were they now?*

They'd started the evening in the newly renovated Hastings House, at a fund-raiser so the historical foundation that employed her could continue excavating the neighboring site. There was a field of architectural gold to be explored there, and her employer was thrilled to have such an eloquent columnist as Matt Connolly on their side while they battled a major construction company for the right to do research before everything was destroyed for the sake of a new high-rise.

But as for actually being with Matt tonight . . . They'd barely had a chance to say hello.

A number of representatives were there from the development company that had bought the surrounding property—trying to pretend that they were delighted to plan around the historical significance of the place—along with Greta Peterson, socialite and ambassador for the Historical Society, a few Broadway personalities, some local celebrities and more. Hank Smith, of megadeveloper Tyson, Smith and Tryon, had swooped down on Matt the minute they'd entered the place, hoping to sway Matt's opinion to the firm's side. There were police representatives, including Captain Ken Dryer, the charismatic department spokesman, Sergeant Robert Adair—who was in charge of the investigation into the missing prostitutes and was actually watching *her* with brooding contemplation most of the night—and politicians from the five boroughs.

She'd been across the room from Matt, exchanging pleasantries with a colleague.

She'd just excused herself to go to Matt and then . . . What?

He was hunkered down beside her now just as he had been when a football struck her in the head when they were playing in the streets so many years ago. He offered the same smile he'd given her then, full of interest and amusement toward most situations, a dry smile. Even a bit rueful, as if, in the end, there was little to do but mock himself.

"Matt," she murmured, frowning, wondering why she couldn't remember crossing the room to his side. And what was she doing on the floor? "You're here."

"Yeah, I'm here," he murmured. "For just this moment."

"Just this moment?" she queried. She wanted to reach out and touch his face. Damn, but he'd always been gorgeous. In a manly, rugged way, of course. Steady blue eyes, generous mouth, broad forehead, high cheekbones. Tall and in shape, he was the guy everyone would have hated if he hadn't been so damned decent. So men liked him, and women loved him.

Despite her confusion, she felt herself rise and turn toward the light. It had the most incredible power. She couldn't resist it. She felt that it offered release from pain, from doubt.

"No," Matt said softly as he caught her arm. Or was that just her imagination? She turned her attention back to him, confused. She could no longer hear the string quartet that had been playing that evening. From a far distant place, she thought she heard screams and chaos.

"Silly Rebel," he said softly, as he had so many

times when she was growing up. "You have to stay here. You can't go yet."

"Who's going to stop me, Matt Connolly?" she demanded. "You?"

"It's not your time," he said. "Leslie, there are things you need to do. You are *not* to follow the light," he said firmly.

"Hey, are you holding out on me?" she demanded lightly, looking around and seeing people getting up and moving single-file toward the light. "Matt, I'm with you. We're together. I have to get in line."

"We're all in line, in a way, from day one," he said very softly. "But not you, not now. You have to stay here. Some things are meant to be."

"Some things are meant to be?" she whispered.

"Some things are meant to be," he said firmly.

He squeezed her hand, and heat shot through her.

Then it felt as if she were jolted. As if they were interrupted.

"Hey!" a deep voice called. "This one is alive!"

It was as if she were watching a movie, but she was in it. There was a horrible scent in the air, as if something were burning. People were everywhere, running, shouting.

There had been an explosion, she thought. Someone had screamed something about gas, and then a blast had seemed to rock the world. Yes! She could remember it now, the feeling of being lifted, of flying . . . slamming hard against a wall. But . . . she wasn't lying against a wall.

She was looking down on a scene of absolute chaos. And she was in it. She was lying in a row of sleeping people. She couldn't recognize any of them. Matt . . . where was Matt? Emergency personnel were moving purposefully through the chaos, imposing order. The newly painted walls of the room were blackened and scorched. There had been a blast and a fire. Everything pointed to it.

And she hurt! Oh, God, she ached everywhere, she thought, back in her body, no longer looking down on the carnage. The scent of charred wood . . . worse, the scent of charred flesh, filled her nostrils.

Because the people she was aligned with were not sleeping.

They were dead.

She could see the open, glazed eyes of the woman beside her. Suddenly she realized that a man was hunkered down by her side. And it wasn't Matt.

"This one is alive!" the man yelled.

Of course I'm alive, she thought.

There was sudden confusion. People rushing over to her. More shouting.

"Quick, or we'll lose her! Her pulse is fading."

More people started rushing around her.

"Clear!"

There was a fire in her chest.

Every bone in her body seemed to be in raw agony. She knew she needed to open her eyes, to take a breath.

She blinked. The lights blazing all around her were the false and neon glitter of night.

"We've got her! She's back."

Then she was being lifted onto something soft and flat. She was dimly aware that someone was talking to the man at her side. Her vision of the scene around her suddenly seemed acute and agonizing.

There were four bodies against the wall. And one of them was Matt.

Then there was no light, no confusion. Just the horrible knowledge.

Matt was dead.

She started to scream. . . .

"Calm down," a medic said. "Please . . . You're alive, and we want to keep you that way."

Alive? Then Matt . . .

"Please, you've got to help Matt. He's alive. I was just talking to him. You've got to help him!"

She saw the distress in the medic's eyes.

"I'm so sorry . . ."

She was in the midst of hell on earth, she realized. *Matt . . .*

She was vaguely aware of a needle in her arm.

Then there was only darkness.

1

One year later

Leslie paused for a minute, looking skyward. What a beautiful evening it was. The sky couldn't have been a lovelier shade of violet. But then, the countryside in northern Virginia was some of the most beautiful in the world.

More so than ever before, at least to her.

In the past year, she had come to appreciate such simple thing as the colors of life. It had been such a strange year, filled with vividly conflicting emotions. The touch of the sun, the color of a dawn, seemed more intense than ever. The anguish of learning to live alone still interrupted the newfound beauty. Life had become doubly precious, except that she felt it was such an incredible gift that it should be shared . . . yet she was alive and Matt was dead.

The setting sun was beautiful, and the night breeze sweet and soft. With that thought in mind, she closed her eyes and felt the waning brush of day against her cheeks. The warmth was wonderful.

She sighed, then returned to work. She needed to hurry. The light would be gone soon.

Painstakingly, bit by bit, she brushed away the dust covering the recently revealed area. She removed the last few specks, and then . . .

Yes!

She continued to brush away the dirt from the skull fragment in the crevice, feeling a sense of jubilation. She couldn't be certain, of course, not absolutely, but it looked like they had discovered the old St. Mathias graveyard that Professor David Laymon had been certain was here. She eyed the skull for size and shape. Bones weren't her specialty. She knew objects, fabrics, even architecture, all the *things* that made up life, backward and forward. She knew bones only because she had come across them in her work so often.

The fragments of calico by the skull hinted at a type of hair decoration that fit perfectly with Laymon's belief that this section of the graveyard had been reserved for indentured servants, slaves and those who were simply too poor to pay for anything better.

"Brad!"

"Yeah?"

Brad Verdun, her good friend and colleague, was busy working a few yards away. As she waited for his attention, she took her tweezers and carefully collected the bits of fabric she had discovered; a lab analysis would verify her thoughts, she was certain, but every little shred needed to be preserved.

"Brad!"

"Yeah, yeah." At last he dusted his hands and rose, then walked to where she was working. He swore softly, shaking his head. "You were right. Again." He stared at her a little skeptically. "If I didn't know you so well, I just might agree with everyone else that you're psychic."

She smiled a little uneasily. "You would have chosen the same spot yourself," she assured him.

"Yeah, eventually." He looked across the work site, staring at the professor, who was down on his hands and knees about fifty yards away. "Well, princess of the past, announce your discovery. Give the old boy his thrill for the night."

"You tell him."

"You found the bones."

"We work together," she said modestly. "You were just a few feet away."

"You made the discovery."

"We came as a team, a package deal," she reminded him stubbornly.

"I won't take your credit."

"I want you to take the credit! Please?"

He sighed deeply. "All right, all right. I'll bring him over. But I won't lie."

"You're not lying if you say we found it as a team," she insisted.

He stared at her for a moment, then touched the top of her head with gentle affection. "Okay. You want to stay out of the limelight, kiddo, I'll do my best to help you. For a while, anyway." Like a brother, he stroked her cheek, giving her an encouraging smile.

"Thanks," she murmured softly.

"You're going to be okay. You're coming along just great," he said.

She nodded, looking down.

Was she? A year had gone by. She functioned, yes, but she continued to hurt every day. Work was good. Friends were good.

Nights were torture.

And life itself . . .

Was definitely different. That difference had become clear while she'd still been in the hospital after the explosion. If she hadn't happened to pick up a magazine and seen the article on Adam Harrison and Harrison Investigations . . .

Well, she would probably either be dead now—having scared herself into an early grave—or in a mental hospital. Adam Harrison and his team, especially Nikki Blackhawk, had undoubtedly saved both her life and her sanity. But that was information she shared with no one. Not Brad, and certainly not Professor Laymon.

She watched as Brad walked over to talk to Laymon. Brad was definitely a good guy, the best. If she'd had a brother, he couldn't have been better to her. Years ago, when they had first started working together, she'd known that he wanted more of a relationship, but no one was ever going to stand a chance against Matt. And in fact, he'd liked Matt so much himself that they'd all fallen into a great friendship. She hesitated, watching Brad, glad that nothing had changed, that he had kept a brotherly distance from her and given his full support without any indication that his affections could turn sexual. She knew she would never feel any differently about him; there came a point in life where someone was a friend and that would never change. Brad was tall, well muscled, patient, intelligent and fun. The perfect guy—for someone else. The great thing about their friendship was that they shared their love of what they did. Some of the first enjoyment she had felt since the explosion that had killed Matt had been because of Brad, because of the excitement in his dark and arresting eyes when they made a discovery.

In large part thanks to him, sometimes, she could even have fun these days, going for drinks or dinner after work. His presence kept other guys away, but if he wanted to start something up with someone else, she didn't get in the way.

They had worked well together before the accident.

Now she relied on him more than ever—even if she was the one who usually "saw" the past more clearly and homed in on a location with eerily perfect accuracy. Sometimes he eyed her almost warily, but when she shrugged, he let it alone.

She watched as Laymon listened to Brad. His face lit up as if the sun had risen again purely to shine down on him. He was up in a flash, hurrying to Leslie's side, shouting excitedly and bringing the rest of the team—teachers, students and volunteers—in his wake. "Watch where you walk," he cautioned. "We don't want all this work trampled." Hopping over one of the plastic lines set out to protect the dig and provide the grid that allowed them to map their finds, he seemed like a little kid, he was so happy.

He stared at Leslie, eyebrows raised questioningly, then looked down at the skull she'd uncovered before turning back to her again. A broad smile lit his worn features. He pushed his Ben Franklin bifocals up the bridge of his nose and scratched his white-bearded chin. If anyone had ever looked the part of a professor, it was David Laymon. "You've done it," he said.

"*We've* done it," she murmured.

"We'll uncover the rest of the skeleton in the morning,

then get it to the folks at the Smithsonian . . . right away, right away. It's too late to work anymore tonight, but we need to secure this area before we go, then get back to work first thing in the morning. From now on we'll need speed—and real care. Leslie, I could hug you. I *will* hug you!" He drew her to her feet, hugged her, then kissed her on the cheek. She was suffused with color, a blush staining her cheeks, as a burst of applause sounded from all around them.

"Hey, please," she protested. "We're all in on this, and Brad was the one to cordon off this particular area."

"Still, what a find," Professor Laymon murmured. "You'll need to speak to the press. This is big excitement for this area . . . for historians everywhere."

"Please," she said softly, firmly, "let Brad speak to the press. Better yet, the two of you can speak as a team."

Laymon frowned, looking mildly annoyed.

"Please," Leslie repeated firmly.

Laymon sighed deeply, looking at her with sorrow in his gray eyes. "You never used to be so shy," he said. "Okay, sorry, I understand. It's just that . . ." He shook his head. "I understand. Whatever you want. All right, I'll get the ball rolling for the press conference, and you stay here—grab some students to give you a hand—and make sure that the site is protected until we get back to it in the morning. I'm going to see to it that we get some police out here to keep an eye on things, too."

Leslie wasn't sure why anyone would want to disturb a paupers' cemetery, but she knew that plenty of digs had been compromised, even ruined, by intruders in the past. She assured Laymon that she would stand guard until they were battened down for the night.

He stared at her, letting out a sigh and shaking his head again as he walked away. Brad walked behind him. One of the grad students, a shapely redhead, hurried up alongside Brad, slipping an arm through his. Leslie decided that she would have to tease him about her later.

For a moment, she wondered what Brad said about her when he decided to get close to a woman. *Oh, my friend Leslie? Completely platonic. She was engaged, but there was a terrible accident. She almost died, and her fiancé was killed. Since then she's been having kind of a hard time, so I try to be there for her.* But it wasn't that long ago, just a year. . . .

Just a year.

She wondered if she would ever again feel that there was a perfect guy out there for. Right now, all she felt was . . .

Cold.

Just a year. A year since she had buried Matt. Buried her life . . .

With a shake, she forced her attention back to her work.

Despite her determination to call it an early night, she found herself dragged to a celebration dinner. They didn't opt for anything fancy—budget would always be important in field work—just a chain pancake house on the main highway. But when the group decided to go on to a local tavern for a few drinks, she at last managed to bow out.

She returned to the residence provided for those higher up in the echelon. She, Laymon, Brad and a few others were housed in a Colonial plantation that was now a charming bed-and-breakfast. Their hostess, a cheerful septuagenarian, rose with the rooster's crow, so she went to bed early. She happily saw them off each morning, and since she was a bit hard of hearing, she was also happy when they came in late at night, because she never heard a thing.

Very tired herself, but feeling a comforting sense of satisfaction, Leslie helped herself to a cup of hot tea from the well-stocked kitchen left open for the help-yourself pleasure of the guests. She took a seat before the large open hearth that dominated the room and sipped her tea from the comfort of the rocker to the left of the gently burning fire. Within a few minutes, she knew she was not alone.

She glanced slowly to her side, a smile curving her lips as she looked at the man who had joined her. He had a rounded stomach, emphasized by his plain black waistcoat and the bit of bleached cotton that protruded from his waistband right where it shouldn't. His wig was a bit messy, but in the style of his time, and the tricornered hat he wore sat perfectly atop it. His hose were thick, white and somewhat worn; his shoes bore handsome buckles. His cheeks were rosy, his eyes a bit dark and small beneath bushy brows. He looked at her and returned her smile with a sigh of satisfaction. "Well, now, it's good and done, eh?" he asked her.

She nodded. "And you mustn't worry, Reverend Donegal. It's true that some of the bones will be boxed and sent for analysis, but the people at the Smithsonian are very careful and reverent. They'll be returned, and we'll see to it that all the dead are reinterred with prayers and all the respect that's due them. And I believe that once the significance of what we've found here has been verified, the Park Service will have its way. A lovely memorial and a facsimile of the church will be built, and generations of visitors will be able to enjoy the beautiful countryside and learn about everything that happened here during both the Revolutionary and Civil Wars." Her smile turned slightly rueful. "I know you did a great deal to help refugees during the Revolutionary War, but this very house was a stop for escaping slaves during the days of the Underground Railroad. There was also a Civil War skirmish in the front yard here. It's amazing the place is still standing."

"Solid construction," Reverend Donegal said sternly. "Folks to care for her. Why, I remember, years and years ago, of course, when I came many a Sunday to this house for my tea following services . . . ah, lovely then, it was. So much excitement and fear. A new country." His eyes darkened, and he seemed troubled for a minute. "Pity . . . one war always leads to the next. It hurt me to be here . . . to see so many fine men die, North and South, believing in the same God. . . . Ah, well, never mind. There's always hope that man will learn from his mistakes." He paused, his old eyes clouding, and she knew he was looking back to his own time, firmly fixed in his mind.

Of course, she knew his story. He had worshipped the hostess of his very house from afar, always entirely circumspect, but enjoying every opportunity to be in her company. He had faithfully served his flock of parishioners; a good man. His one pleasure had been his Sunday tea. And so, one day, he had come here, had his tea . . . and then died of a heart attack in the arms of the woman he had secretly adored for so many years. Leslie had thought at first that he must have been a very sad ghost, seeking the love he hadn't allowed himself in life. But that hadn't been the case at all. She had discovered that he had been at peace with himself; that his distant and unrequited love for Mrs. Adella Baxter had in actuality been a pleasant fantasy but not one he had truly hoped to fulfill. He had enjoyed his life as a bachelor, administering to his flock. He had stayed all these years because he felt so many of his flock needed to be remembered. In short, he had wanted the graveyard found.

At first, he hadn't trusted her. He'd tried a dozen tricks, moving her brush around, locking her suitcase, hiding her keys. He hadn't expected her to see him, and he certainly hadn't expected her to get angry, yell at him and demand that they talk. Once they had, he'd become an absolute charmer. Through his eyes, she'd seen the house as it had been in his day. She'd experienced his passion as he'd spoken of what he and so many others had gone through to establish a new country; his fear that he might be hanged as a traitor— something that had been a distinct possibility many times during the brutal years of the Revolution. He was deeply disturbed that so few of the people who passed through the old house were aware of just how precarious the struggle for freedom had been. "You can't understand," he had told her. "We almost lost the war. In fact, it's a miracle that we won. And all those men who signed the Declaration of Independence? They would have been hanged! So many risked so much. Ah, well, God does show his will, against all odds."

Right now he seemed lost in thought.

"Thank you for your help," she said very softly to him.

He nodded, then wagged a finger at her. "I expect you to play fair, young lady. You see that the right thing is done by my people. Especially little Peg. You did find her grave, didn't you, right where I sent you?"

Leslie nodded, then stared at the fire for a moment, as lost in the past as he had been. It was strange. Before the blast, she'd had intuitions, like the one that had helped her find the homeless man. As if she could close her eyes and imagine something of a life now gone, then home in on it. Logic? Instinct? Something more? She couldn't have said. But now . . .

Now ghosts came into her life.

"I will see that Peg's story is told," she assured Reverend Donegal. She repeated what he had told her before about the girl. "Peg, aged ten, walked the ten miles from town through a pouring, freezing rain to bring the men from the county together when she knew an attack was coming. She rallied the local troops, and they successfully defended the river and the plantation here, all because of her bravery. She died of the fever that came on her that night, after her journey through the rain and cold and enemy lines. And after the war . . . well, people were poor. She was given the best burial they could manage."

He nodded in satisfaction. "A statue would be very nice. You will get someone to pay for a statue?"

"I'll pay for a statue of her myself, if need be," she assured him.

He looked at her indignantly. "A statue of *me!*" he declared. "Oh, well, of course, Peg must be honored, too, I suppose."

"You'll have a place when they rebuild the church, and Peg will be honored in the graveyard. How's that?" she said, glad she could smile.

He nodded, staring at the fire. "There's a chill in here," he said. "Ah, these old bones . . ."

"It *is* chilly tonight, but I don't think you're really feeling your old bones," she teased. She set her cup down and rose, walked to the fire and let it warm her hands. When she turned to speak to the reverend again, he was gone.

She sat back in her chair. In a little while she heard the others returning. It had grown late; she assumed they would head right up to their beds, but she sensed someone behind her, and this time she heard breathing.

She turned. Brad was there, just inside the doorway, staring at her.

"Hey," she said.

"Hey," he echoed, still staring at her.

"What?" she demanded.

"Laymon really didn't say anything to you yet?" he asked, looking surprised. "I thought he called you."

"About what?" she asked.

"They're researching another site in Lower Manhattan," he said.

She felt a streak of cold sweep along her spine, as if she'd been stroked by an icy sword. She looked at the fire, trying to speak perfectly calmly. "I'm sure that at any given time, someone is always digging somewhere in Lower Manhattan."

"This is going to be a major project." He was quiet for a minute. "Near Hastings House."

"Great," she murmured, still staring at the flames.

He hunkered down by her chair. "You know, only the one room was severely damaged. They've pretty much got the place back up and running now."

Her fingers tensed on the arms of her chair. "Glad to hear it."

"What happened there was a tragic accident, Leslie."

She stared at him—hard. "Yes, I do know that, Brad."

"The point is, you don't seem to get it, to understand what that means. I'm not trying to be brutal here, Leslie, but Matt died. You didn't."

She stared blankly back at him for several moments. "I almost died there."

"But you didn't."

"I know. And I'm grateful to be alive. I truly appreciate every day."

"It's time to go back."

"Time to go back?" she repeated.

"You need to accept the past, and move into the present and then into the future. No, you'll never forget Matt. But you have to accept that he's dead. You've been . . . well, kind of weird since it happened. Maybe you need to confront your memories."

Again, she stared at him.

Oh, Brad. You don't get it, do you? And I will never, ever explain, I can assure you of that.

"We still have work to do here," she said flatly.

He waved a hand in the air. "We're the pros—there are lots of worker bees. Thanks to you and your amazing instincts, all that's left is the grunt work. We can move on."

She shook her head.

"Listen, this new site is really important. . . . I know Laymon wants to talk to you about it. He's going back to lead the team, with or without you. With or without *us,*" Brad amended quickly.

28

Her nails dug into the arms of the chair. She stared at the flames. "I've made some promises here," she said.

He looked puzzled. "You made promises? To whom?"

"To myself. To see that people are honored, that bones are buried with the proper rites," she said.

"We'll tell Laymon, and he'll make sure it happens," Brad said. "It's not like we're leaving the country. With the way your reputation has grown, you can drop a word and people will hustle, you know that."

"Okay," she murmured.

"Laymon got the call when we were on the way to the tavern, and he talked about nothing else once we got there," Brad said softly. "New York City, Leslie! You know you love it."

"I can't go back."

"You *need* to go back."

"Brad . . ."

"Leslie, please."

She stared at him and saw the earnest plea in his eyes. She lowered her head quickly, not wanting him to read her thoughts.

Hastings House. It was fixed, repaired, reopened. Brought back to life again. But the dead . . . the dead couldn't be brought back to life . . . ?

And some of the dead had never left.

She lowered her head, biting her lower lip. It had started immediately. In the hospital, she'd thought she'd gone mad. There had been the horrible pain, the ache like the loss of a limb or half of her soul, knowing Matt was gone. The concussion, the bruising, the cuts, scrapes, burns . . .

Those had been nothing compared to the pain of losing Matt.

At first she had lived in a stage somewhere between consciousness and dreams. One night she'd awakened in the hospital morgue, drawn there by a man who had lost his wedding ring when they'd rolled him down. All he had wanted was to have his ring put back on his finger. But she hadn't known that, and she'd freaked. She was lucky she hadn't wound up in the psychiatric ward that night. Luckily for her, the next day she'd discovered an article in a news magazine about a man named Adam Harrison and the group of paranormal investigators who worked for him. No matter how the reporter had tried to trip him up, the man had come off as intelligent and well spoken, and not at all like a kook. She had started to shake, reading the article. She had called Harrison Investigations immediately, and, to her amazement, Adam Harrison himself had shown up in the hospital. They had talked then, and again when she had been released. It was as if she had instantly acquired not only a new best friend, one she felt she had known forever, but as if she'd gotten her father back, though her real father had been gone since she was a little girl.

She'd called Adam right away when she'd started talking to the ghostly Colonial churchman, and soon after, she'd noticed a couple in the crowd of visitors hanging around the site. They'd stood out, and eventually they'd introduced themselves as two of Harrison's employees. Brent and Nikki Blackhawk—he dark and strikingly handsome, his wife blond and beautiful—had gone back to the house with her and taught her how to become friends with the ghost, even chatted with him casually themselves. There really were others like her, she'd realized, and that meant she was sane.

"Leslie," Brad said softly, recalling her to the present. "I told Laymon I'd work the new dig, so I'll be there with you. You need to go back, to put the past to rest, to put the pain behind you."

She stared at him. Smiled slowly.

Brad didn't know about Adam Harrison, the Blackhawks, or that there were others like them to help her. Brad didn't know that it was thanks to Adam and his associates that she had been able to sit calmly in a Colonial kitchen, talking to a long-dead reverend, and that she could feel entirely sane as she did so.

But as to going back, facing her own ghosts . . . That was something else again, something she dreaded but something she needed to do.

Brad let out a soft sigh. "Okay, I'm sorry. Too soon," he said.

She stared back at him. "I didn't say that," she murmured quickly. "Maybe I *should* go back. I think . . . I think maybe I want to go back to Hastings House."

He hesitated. "I know you have an apartment in Brooklyn, but . . ." He stared, paused, then said quickly, on a single fast breath, "There are a few rooms available for the workers at Hastings House."

"What?"

Brad shook his head quickly. "I'm sorry. I shouldn't even have mentioned that."

"Who is this work for?" she demanded.

The Historical Society, of course. Greta will be the official liaison between the society, the contractors and the workers. And once again, it's Tyson, Smith and Tryon who bought and are developing the property. They've been legally blocked from building until the significance of the site is established and any necessary excavation is done. Laymon says they're taking it well, though, basking in their national publicity as good guys. But the lost time must be costing them a bundle. Anyway, the site is really close to Hastings House. It's in the next block, actually."

"And that's why they're offering the rooms at Hastings House?"

He shrugged. "I don't know why I even mentioned that, honestly. Hell, I have an apartment in the city, and you have your place in Brooklyn." He took a deep breath. "Of course, you lived there with Matt, so maybe you don't want to go back there. But I'm glad you're holding on to it. Real estate in your neighborhood is rising sky-high. Oh, God, I'm sorry. That didn't come out right. I'm stumbling all over here."

"It's all right, Brad."

"Yeah. Right." He tried to smile.

"I didn't even get to go to his funeral. I was in the

hospital," she murmured, staring at the flames.

Suddenly a massive ache seemed to tear through her heart.

Ghosts came to her, sought her out sometimes, asked for her help.

But not Matt.

The ghost she wanted to see, desperately longed to tell—one last time—how much she had loved him, how he had been her life, how he had filled the world with wonder with his simple presence . . . that ghost she never saw.

"I want to stay at Hastings House," she said.

He lowered his head. He was smiling, she realized. He was convinced that he had handled things just right, and that by talking about lodging, he had tricked her into deciding to go back.

Maybe he deserved his self-congratulations.

Or maybe it was just time for her to go back.

"You really want to stay there? You're serious?"

"Dead serious."

She stood, patting him on the shoulder as she started out. She paused in the hallway, looking back at him. "No pun intended," she said lightly, and offered him a dry grin. "You're right. I'm ready to go back. Excited to go back. Good night."

She left him, still down on his knees by the chair.

Excited? Dear God, she was a liar.

And yet . . .

It was true. She never would have thought of it her-self. Never would have woken up one morning

33

thinking, *Wow, I'd really love to head back to Hastings House.*

But now that she was going . . .

The past beckoned to her. She needed to come to terms with it.

She *had* to go back.

2

It was late. A strange time, Joe Connolly thought, to be having this meeting. The woman sitting nervously across from him was stunning, but she reminded him of a high-strung, inbred greyhound. She was excessively thin, and her long fingers were elegantly manicured and glittering with diamonds and other fine jewels. She had called that morning and set up this meeting. They were at the venue of her choice—a small Irish tavern off Wall Street. He would have expected her to suggest a private corner at an exclusive club, but perhaps she didn't want to be seen with a private investigator. For whatever reason, she had chosen O'Malley's, which was warm, small and inviting, a pub she had probably visited many a time in her youth.

She had originally come from humble stock, he knew. On her mother's side, she was second-generation Irish; her father, an O'Brien, came from a line of hard-working laborers who had arrived in the United States during the 1840s. Blood, sweat and muscle had taken him far in the trades, and thus their modest family fortune had begun and then risen to riches. Then Eileen O'Brien had married well, and she was now Mrs. Thomas Brideswell, widow of the late senator and construction magnate.

She thrust an eight-by-ten picture of a young woman across the table at him. He stared down at the likeness. Genevieve O'Brien looked back at him. Her eyes were huge and blue, and she was as slender as her aunt Eileen, with beautifully defined features. Her hair was dark, with an auburn sheen. The photographer had captured laughter, eagerness and the optimism of youth.

"How old is this picture?" Joe asked.

"It was taken about two and half years ago," Eileen said, and hesitated. With a weary sadness and a hunch of her shoulders, she looked down. "Just before her falling out with my brother and me."

Joe shook his head. "I'm sorry, I don't mean to press the issue, but I need to understand. If she left home voluntarily, and there was already an estrangement between you, what makes you so sure that something's happened to her?"

Eileen sighed deeply. "Donald died soon after she walked out of his house. She came back for his funeral. She wanted to keep her distance from me and what she called my ridiculous family devotion to a ridiculously dysfunctional family. I think she was upset that my brother died without the two of them ever having made their peace, but . . ." She lifted one of her bejeweled hands. "I suppose it was nasty growing up in my brother's household. There was a lot to be said for everything my father and grandfather accomplished, but it came at a price. Impossible expectations for their children. So much fault-finding when something was wrong." She shook her head, and Joe felt moved by her obvious distress. There was such a deep and underlying sadness in the woman, despite her reserve and elegance. She looked him in the face then. "Ever since my brother died, she's called me every two weeks. At least once, every two weeks. I haven't heard from her in over a month."

He leaned back, watching her. He had learned a lot in his years with the police force, and a lot more in the years since he had gone out on his own. Watching someone's face as they spoke was often as important as listening to the words that were said.

"Was there something said between you the last time you spoke that might have caused a greater rift?" he asked.

There was a very slight hesitation.

"No," she said.

She was lying.

"I need to know everything," he said firmly.

Again an elegant hand fluttered. "Well, there had been this awful article in one of those tabloids about the family," she said.

"And?" he prompted.

"She was convinced that her father wasn't her father."

"She bears a remarkable resemblance to you. I'm

36

assuming you and your brother must have looked quite a bit alike," he said.

"Exactly," Eileen said.

He waited. "What was the paper? When was the article printed?"

"You don't want to read that dreadful piece of garbage," she assured him.

"I need to read it. Mrs. Brideswell, I'm working in the dark here. Your niece is twenty-six. She's an adult. Adults who choose to disappear are allowed to do so. I have almost nothing to go on. You've given me first names and street names for a few acquaintances, and I have her work contacts—though she resigned from her job a month ago. That in itself could indicate that she planned to leave the city. I have addresses for a few of the places where you believe she hung out. You can't hold back on me. And when I find her—*if I find her*—I can't guarantee I can convince her to call you."

"No! You don't understand. I believe with my whole heart that if she could call me, she would."

Joe answered carefully. "Do you believe that your niece is dead, Mrs. Brideswell?"

Pain flashed across her features. "I don't know," she whispered. "I just . . . I know that she loved . . . loves me. No matter what came between us . . . Genevieve would call me. And if she's out there somewhere . . . crying for help, she's crying to me. Oh, my God, Mr. Connolly, I'll admit there were awful times in the family, times when she was sent away . . . we were so embarrassed by her activities! My brother was . . .

very strict. With reason, I suppose. My father taught us that we had to behave with propriety, or at least the appearance of it. But still . . . she loves me. And I know she needs me. I've had to admit to myself that she may be dead, but don't you understand? I have to know. And if she *has* become a victim of . . . of some misfortune, I have to see justice done for her before I die."

Joe wondered why she spoke so passionately about her own death; she couldn't be more than forty-something, and she could easily be mistaken for thirty-five.

"A victim of misfortune," Joe repeated, and asked flatly, "Do you suspect that she was murdered?"

Eileen inhaled deeply, and when she spoke, her words were bitter. "I've spoken to the police, Mr. Connolly, which of course you would imagine I had done. And I don't know if he warned you or not, but it was your old friend Sergeant Adair who suggested I call you, but not until after he gave me a speech about all the other disappearances that are perplexing him. I gather the police are trying to keep what's been going on with those prostitutes under wraps, though of course it's not working. People talk. And those disappearances have been going on for more than a year."

"But your niece wasn't a prostitute plying her trade downtown," he reminded her.

She waved a hand in the air. "I know. And we all know that plenty of people *not* involved in . . . in the trade disappear, as well. But I got the impression that Sergeant Adair sees some relationship between those disappearances and the fact that I haven't heard from Genevieve."

Joe was confused. He knew that Robert Adair was tearing his hair out over the continued disappearances of prostitutes in the downtown area. There were no clues, no trails of blood. The girls just disappeared, but the police knew they hadn't just moved on—unless they'd moved on without saying a word and leaving all their belongings behind. But what would the daughter of a millionaire have in common with a bunch of missing prostitutes?

"I think this remains a very sensitive area for the police. The women who've disappeared are adults. Adults have a right to move on in their lives."

Eileen stared at him, her eyes scorning his words. "We both know the truth."

She was right. It had begun over a year ago. A few months apart, two prostitutes had vanished, but since there had been no clues and no signs of foul play, little had been done when their friends reported them missing. Then a homeless transvestite known as the Mimic had disappeared. Then two more young women.

She leaned closer to him, her eyes still flashing. She might be rich, but she could be tough when she needed to. "The thing is, prostitutes murdered by their johns usually turn up somewhere. A homeless man who freezes to death is found on the pavement. But these girls disappeared off the streets without a trace—just like Genevieve. Do you think aliens are beaming these people up, Mr. Connolly? I don't. I think there is a serial killer at large in New York who knows how to dispose of bodies so they'll never be found. I thought it was disgraceful when I first heard about the disappearances and the apparent lack of concern on the part of our government on the local and even the state level. Now? I'm incensed. Don't get me wrong. I'm not angry with the poor cop just trying to work his beat. I'm furious that someone doesn't step in and say, 'These people count!' And now I haven't heard a word from Gen in so long, and every day I'm more and more worried, and though it doesn't seem that I have any power, I do have money."

"All right, let's look at this from the beginning. Your niece was a social worker, yes?"

"Yes, here in the city," Eileen murmured. "Up until a little more than a month ago. She found it terribly frustrating. . . ." She inhaled deeply. "And not just the job itself. In my family, we were supposed to make— or marry—money. Both my brother and I were terribly hard on Gen, and all she wanted to do was make life easier on those who didn't have the same advantages we did. The frustration and red tape got to her, as well, but . . . none of that's what matters now. This is the point, this is why I think there's a connection. She'd been working to help prostitutes in the same area where prostitutes have been disappearing into thin air. Don't you see? I'm sure she knew some of those missing girls!" Eileen herself seemed ready to explode at that moment.

"Do you know any particulars on why she quit her job?"

Eileen waved a slender, elegant hand in the air. "Irritation with the system. She wanted to get workfare programs going . . . she wanted to help some of the girls keep their children. She is really an extraordinary human being, Mr. Connolly. Oh, I am so frustrated. No one seems to believe that I *know* that something's really wrong. The police can't—or won't—do anything."

"I do understand your frustration," Joe told her, "but you have to understand that the police are seriously frustrated themselves. The point is, these are *disappearances*. There's nothing for them to go on. And the people who have disappeared—in this particular situation—have lived transient lifestyles, which makes it very hard, as well. They can question those closest to the victims—if that's what they are. They can question people up and down the streets where the victims were last seen. They've harassed known pimps to the point that their behavior borders on the illegal. But absolutely no one so far has seen anything to indicate foul play. Meanwhile, the police still have murders, rapes and robberies to deal with, crimes with sadly obvious victims. There's only so much they can do when they have no victims, no murder weapons, no blood trails, no evidence of any kind."

"Blood trails?" Eileen said, her eyes snapping. "They have to find out what's going on and stop it before we discover that we're in a *river* of blood! And before my niece is discovered lying dead somewhere. But they're not going to find out what's going on because, as you say, they have to deal with the blood they do see on the streets. I'm not calling our police incompetent. They try. Sergeant Adair has, I believe, been ordered to find the explanation for these disappearances, no matter what. They've searched Gen's apartment—if she disappeared by choice, she did so with only her purse and the clothes on her back, not even a good coat. They've been to her former office. They've tried to question people on the streets. Sadly, I know nothing about her real friends. Or if she was dating. The basics have been done. They've proved nothing. Except that she's gone, which I already knew. So I've hired you."

"I'll do my best."

"And you will find Genevieve," she said passionately. "Because you will make finding her your priority every single morning from the moment you open your eyes. I'll reward you highly."

He pocketed the picture. "You know my fee. I don't work to be rewarded highly. If I take a case on, it's part of my every waking moment until I have an answer. But I'll need your help at all times. Be ready to answer my calls," he warned her. "I need to assimilate all that I've learned from you tonight, then get busy on my own and see what else I can discover. But I'll need more help from you. I'll need everything. Everything you know, anything that occurs to you. And don't hold back on me. I'm in your employ. I'll

42

never repeat anything you tell me. Don't let any family embarrassment hold you back from being entirely truthful with me, do you understand, Mrs. Brideswell? I can't help you if you aren't completely honest with me. No amount of money will change that."

She nodded. Reaching down, she found her purse and produced a small notepad. "I've written down everything I know, what names and places I've heard . . . anything I can think of that might be some help." She produced a pen, scribbling down another notation. "I've added the publication I was talking about," she murmured. "That's it."

He accepted the notepad from her. "I'll do everything I can," he told her.

She picked up the teacup before her on the table, her eyes distant. She drank what must have been very cold tea by then.

"I'm very sorry about your cousin," she said softly.

"Thank you." The words took him by surprise, though he knew instantly what she meant.

"His death was a tremendous loss to the city, but for you, of course, it was very personal, and I extend my sincere condolences." Her eyes began to water. "I was there that night, you know," she murmured.

"I didn't know," he said.

"I learned later that Gen would have been interested in going. In retrospect, I'm glad I didn't know in time to invite her. She'd met a lot of people involved through the years. She had a lot of close contact with the police—being a social worker and all. And she knew Greta through me, of course."

Joe couldn't help himself. He leaned forward. "What do you remember about that night?"

"The lights, the music, the beautiful clothing, the glamour . . . I was in the entryway when the explosion occurred. They rounded us up and got us out immediately. I remember standing on the street and just being incredulous. I remember the sound of the sirens, the ambulances, the paramedics . . . and the body bags," she said. "I am so, so sorry."

"Thank you. Eileen, do you remember anything strange at all?" he pressed.

She gave him a pained smile. "You lost someone you loved, so you want there to be a reason, a better explanation than a gas explosion. No, I'm sorry. It's all a blur. I was chatting, there was a noise like thunder. Someone was screaming 'fire,' people were panicking . . . the cops came and we were all ushered out."

Joe nodded. *Just what had he been hoping for?*

"Thank you," he repeated.

Her eyes met his, and her words were desperate. "I have to find Genevieve, Mr. Connolly. Please help me."

Although her posture still seemed so regal and aloof, he reached across the table and laid his hand on hers. "I will do everything I can," he told her solemnly.

She almost smiled. And then she turned her palm up and gripped his hand in return. Her touch was strong, and as desperate as the sound of her voice.

They talked for a few minutes longer about Genevieve, and as the girl in the picture began to come to life for him, Joe began to make mental notes as to exactly where he would begin his investigation. First he would go over the basic police work. Then he would move on to where the police, by virtue of their sworn duty, could not go.

There were others in the house.

He knew that from the beginning.

At first it was only a vague sense of awareness. They paid him no mind, seemed not to see or recognize him, but even so, he was aware that he was not alone.

There was the woman in the kitchen, for one. She was always by the hearth, stirring something in what he imagined had been a pot over an open fire. She was pretty and young, and wore Colonial garb, including a little mobcap on her head. He wasn't sure if she had been an illicit mistress or a servant, but she hummed in a pretty voice as she stirred. Every so often she would suddenly straighten, her face pinching into a mask of pain. She would turn around, and her eyes would widen, and then she would fall . . . and fade away.

There was the soldier in the entry. He staggered into the house, mingled with the misty form of another individual. He would whisper something about a betrayal, and then he, too, would fall and fade away.

He didn't want to be one of them. He didn't want

to spend eternity standing by the hearth in the servants' pantry, laughing pleasantly, looking across the room . . . and then disappearing in the memory of an explosion.

After a while he realized that in addition to playing out their final moments over and over again, they did more. They recognized one another, though they might not have come from the same time. They mingled now and then.

While he . . .

He didn't need to worry about eternally haunting the servants' pantry. He couldn't even manage that much. He could only be . . . aware.

So why was he there? Just to ache? Just to yearn and fear constantly for the woman he had loved? Damn it. Not fair. He'd lived his life as a decent man.

Others had died with him, so where were they? He didn't have any sense of them whatsoever.

He saw the workmen. Heard them talk. Perhaps it should have been gratifying to have even that much contact with what had once been his world. To hear their anger that he should have died in such a stupid freak accident. They had respected and admired him. Nice to know, except that he was still dead.

Then came the day when the woman at the hearth turned to look at him at last. She even gave him a little smile. Maybe he was somehow real then. She walked over, and it felt as if she touched his cheek, like a sweet sister. "It takes time," she told him, and smiled again.

All he could whisper was "Why?"

She shrugged sadly. "Justice? Something that must be known? The man who murdered me walked free. Perhaps it's too late and the world will never know. So much time has passed. But it's not so horrible, really. Maybe we're here because we've more to learn?"

There was a comfort in her contact. Soon after, the soldier acknowledged him, too.

Then the burning question began in his mind. Why? There had to be a reason why he was here and the others who'd died that night weren't.

The question dominated his thoughts, filled him with the resolve to know the answer, to solve the mystery of what had happened.

Sometimes, though, he thought of Leslie. Good God, how he had loved her. . . .

It was late when the phone rang, but Leslie wasn't asleep. And, oddly enough, she knew immediately who it was.

"Hi, Nikki."

"You're getting good."

"Nothing to do with intuition or special gifts," Leslie said with a laugh. "It's late, but we've been on the news, and I knew that you're the one person who might be calling."

"How do you feel?"

"Great. I got to help find closure for people, in a weird sort of way."

"Exactly," Nikki said.

Leslie could picture Nikki. Slim and vivacious, with brilliant blue-green eyes. She led tours in New Orleans and loved history. She loved her city, too, and was working hard to bring tourism back to New Orleans. But she and Brent had taken time out to help Leslie adjust to life with the dead popping up now and then. What had seemed like a curse had almost become a gift with Nikki and Brent so serenely at her side.

"How's everything going in your neck of the woods?" Leslie asked.

"Step by step, but we're coming back. So many neighborhoods are still in need of total rebuilding, but we'll get there. And you? Everything all right?"

"Great. I think . . . I think we may have seen the last of the reverend."

"Ah. Well, bless his heart. So . . . I guess you're going to see to the details now? My history is a lot easier—I just talk about it. You spend hours brushing dust off yours."

Leslie wondered why she'd thought that Nikki already knew what she was about to do.

"Actually," she replied, "I'm going home."

"Home . . . ?"

"New York. I was born in the South, but New York's been home for a long time now. There's a new project there, a site near . . . near Hastings House, and I'm going to work on it."

"Are you ready?" Nikki asked flatly.

"Yes . . . No . . . Maybe."

"Then . . . ?"

"I'm not sure I'll never actually be ready. I think I just have to do it."

The phone line was silent for several seconds, and she knew that Nikki was carefully weighing her next words. "Leslie, you do know that although we've come to accept certain things and learned to use our abilities to a degree, we don't have all the answers. You're still fragile, whether you want to believe that or not. So be careful. And don't . . . don't let yourself get trapped in the past, in what was. You're here. You're alive."

"Nikki, thanks to you guys, I'm still sane and I appreciate living. It's just that . . . you know how you feel when you lose someone, like there were so many things you didn't get to say, and you want so desperately to know that everything is all right, and of course it isn't, because the person is dead . . . okay, now I do sound a little on the loopy side. But . . . I just wish I could say goodbye, you know?"

"You can't know that you'll get that chance, Leslie, even if you do go back. Matt Connolly was an exceptional man. He did a lot of good in his days on earth. He might, well . . . he might never be seen."

"I know that. I promise you, I'm not going home because I'm sure I'll see him if I do. I just know I have to go on. And this is a great opportunity."

"Want me to hop a plane on up?"

Leslie smiled. Some things were so strange. She'd had many friends when Matt had died. Nice people.

But she'd found that she had to push them away a bit. Politely, she hoped. It was just that she didn't really want to make their lives painful, and she didn't like people tiptoeing around her feelings. She hadn't been able to talk, really talk, to many people. But then Nikki had stepped into her life, and it had been as if she'd known her forever.

Of course, they both saw ghosts, as did Nikki's husband, Brent. Nikki always found it amusing that most people accepted his ability to communicate with the dead more easily than hers, simply because he had Dakota Sioux in his background. Apparently that made him a more spiritual soul in the eyes of the world.

"Leslie?"

"I'm okay. And I . . . I think I need to be alone a bit. But later, I'd love for you to visit. I'll show you New York as you've never seen it."

"Deal," Nikki said.

After a few more minutes of chat, they hung up.

Leslie lay in bed, awake. She was going home for all the right reasons, she assured herself. The work. The opportunity. And she just plain loved New York. She needed to be back.

Hell.

She was going home to try to find a way to reach Matt. . . .

Joe watched as Eileen settled into her chauffeur-driven sedan, refusing the offer of a ride with a thank-

50

you, though he wasn't really sure why. It was late, but this was New York. People were out at all hours, even though some areas, like this one, became much quieter.

When the car had disappeared into the easy flow of the late-night traffic, he found himself just walking down the street. He had always loved downtown. He was a New Yorker, born and bred in Brooklyn Heights, an area he loved. But downtown New York offered a history few people took the time to appreciate, since the city offered such a bustle of business, shopping and entertainment.

His walk took him down Broadway. He found himself feeling a strange sense of comfort as he walked by St. Paul's; even the old burial ground, a sign of the times gone by, gave him a sense of permanence and belonging. He loved St. Paul's, though it wasn't as grand as Trinity Church just down the road. St. Paul's was the only remaining church built before the Revolutionary War, a true Georgian masterpiece. Washington's pew was still there, along with displays honoring those who had worked tirelessly on the rescue efforts after 9/11, since the church lay in the shadows of the monumental tragedy. Drenched in history, yet still a place for modern man to find solace.

He kept walking, wondering at the age of some of the buildings, trying to discern what might really be old beneath a newer facade, his wanderings taking him by Fraunces Tavern and then down to the once-again newly restored Hastings House.

He had come here before, since that fateful night. Several times. And he never knew exactly why. Every time he felt the same searing and poignant ripple of pain. Four dead. Jerry Osbourne, police officer. Sally Rydell, socialite. Tom Burton, architect. And Matthew Connolly, brilliant journalist, a man whose words had the ability to create genuine change.

He'd been working out in Las Vegas when it had happened, on a cold case involving kidnapping, fraud and money laundering. The job had taken nearly a year, but it had paid extremely well. He'd managed to tie it all up shortly after he'd flown home for his cousin's funeral. He had never felt so numb in his life. When he'd gone to the hospital afterward, where Matt's fiancée, Leslie, had still been in intensive care, he had been grateful to discover that she spent most of her time unconscious. He hadn't known what to say to her. Because of the amount of time he spent out of the city, he'd never actually met her, except maybe once, when they'd been kids. He'd felt awkward, glad that he could leave a message saying he'd been there, equally glad to disappear.

Strange, growing up, he and Matt had seen each other only on family occasions. Matt had lived by Central Park; he had lived in Brooklyn Heights. Once it had seemed as if they were far apart. Maybe it was just the size of New York. Each neighborhood was complete unto itself. They'd always gotten along; as adults, even though real distance often came between them. They had actually become the best of friends.

Maybe it had been their shared passion for many of the same rights and ideals.

Matt had been a man of impeccable integrity. Many people would miss him. But for Joe, the loss was personal, and he still felt a helpless rage every time he thought about the stupidity of the way he'd died.

He had planned to return to the city after wrapping up of the Vegas thing and get to know Leslie and make plans with Matt. He would have been the best man at the wedding. Strange. He didn't know Leslie because of happenstance. They had simply never been in the same place at the same time, yet she was the closest living link to Matt.

It was amazing that she had survived the blast.

The force of the explosion had thrown her across the room, saving her from the flames. Then again, the dead had died on impact, according to the coroner; they hadn't had to face the agony of burning to death.

The blast had been investigated. Backward and forward and inside out. But in the end, there had been no explanation other than that there had been a gas buildup in the line. The innocent flicking of a furnace switch had caused a spark, which had triggered the explosion and the tragedy.

Hastings House was back now. It was open to the public, other than the private rooms in back, some of which were maintained as offices and others as accommodations for archaeologists working on historical sites around downtown. It seemed that these days, every construction project uncovered some remnant of the past, a clear illustration of the contrast between those dedicated to preservation and those dedicated to moving on. Hastings House had been a worthy project, he was sure. But he could never forget what had happened there, and he found himself turning quickly away for a moment to compose himself before looking back at the building. He couldn't help the bitterness that seemed to assail him every time he saw the house. He understood Eileen Brideswell, because it seemed to him, too, that pain was only endurable with knowledge or a conclusion; he realized that the rage that filled him each time he came here had more to do with his feelings of helplessness and failure than the natural pain of loss. He couldn't help but believe, no matter what conclusion the extensive investigations had led to, that something more had gone on here. That they had missed something.

That someone had gotten away with murder.

Had Matt been the target?

He'd done some investigating himself, hitting dead end after dead end. He was sure it was frustration that kept him coming back to stand here, impotently staring at the house.

People walked past him. Tourists, with their guidebooks out. He wondered if he should warn them that wandering around on their own wasn't such a great thing to be doing at that hour of the night.

A few teenagers walked by the house, and then a couple with two children somewhere around the age of ten. More tourists.

"Is it haunted?" the boy asked eagerly.

"Could be," the father said. "Patriots met here during the Revolutionary War, and others met here during the War of 1812. It was even a stop on the Underground Railroad during the Civil War. Lots of people could be haunting the place." The father winked.

His wife nudged him. "Don't go telling him that, Herbert," she said firmly, then dropped her voice to a whisper. "People died here just last year."

The father sighed. "Marina, we're seeing New York. Can't we just let the kids have some fun along with their education?"

"Fun?" the wife repeated icily.

"I'm sorry," the father said with a sigh.

Joe couldn't help himself. "Good evening," he said, approaching the group. "It's a little late. Not much open around here at this hour. Actually . . . nothing open. But bars."

The father puffed up. But the wife agreed.

"Yes," she murmured, staring at Joe a little suspiciously, then tugged at her husband's arm. "We should get back to the hotel."

"We only have two days here with the kids," the husband said.

"You might notice that the street is pretty deserted," Joe said politely.

"Are you a cop?" the wife asked.

"I was."

"I read in the newspaper that there have been unexplained disappearances in this area," the wife said.

"Are we prostitutes?" the husband hissed.

"I want to go," the wife insisted.

They moved on, looking back now and then to see that they weren't being followed.

"Catch a taxi down the block—they'll be going north," Joe called.

Then he put the house and its memories behind him and started down the street in the opposite direction, shrugging his shoulders, as if he could shrug away the feelings that seized him every time he came to Hastings House.

Strange. He felt as if the house itself were beckoning to him. As if something—some*one?*—inside was calling him back, unwilling to let him go.

He gritted his teeth and moved on. He wasn't given to fantasy. The real world was tough enough.

Still, he stopped halfway down the block and stared back at the house. Then, almost angrily, he moved on.

A house simply *could not* call out to him, as if asking for some kind of help. . . .

3

It was evening when they arrived at Hastings House. To the left there was a large pit, along with the partially demolished miniskyscraper that was being torn down to be replaced by a megabuilding. Downtown was coming back in a big way.

To the right—beyond a narrow expanse of grass, the only evidence that there had once been many residences in the area—stood an office building/apartment complex built in the 1940s. The sun was falling, and, if Leslie narrowed her vision, she could almost imagine what this very small spot in the world might have looked like in the past.

But then she began to hear the angry beeping of horns, the sudden blare of rap music, a shout, the click of heels on pavement . . . this was, after all, New York. Even on a lazy Sunday afternoon, this was the piece of granite where so many people had decided they had to live. The center of the universe, in the minds of so many. She smiled. With all its sins and dirt and mixture of good and evil, she loved the city. Rebel she might be, but she loved New York.

And it was good to be back.

"Hey!" the cabbie interjected, breaking her thoughts. With an accent only on the single syllable, she wasn't sure just what part of the world his speech denoted. "Somebody gonna pay me?"

"Oh, yes, right," Professor Laymon said. Leslie didn't even turn around. She felt Brad at her shoulder as she stared at Hastings House. *What would it offer up to her now? Now that she was who she was—now that she was changed?*

She felt Brad's hand on her shoulder. "It's a house," he said softly. "But if you're the least bit uneasy, there's no reason on earth for you to stay here."

She turned, smiling at him. "I want to stay here."

"It won't bring Matt back to life."

"I know," she said, looking back toward Hastings House.

The house was beautiful. Two stories high, and all the outer over-the-centuries additions had been ripped away and its facade had been restored to the Colonial-era style in which it had been originally built. Even downtown, there were few buildings to compare with it, other than St. Paul's Cathedral and Fraunces Tavern. It had been given a white-picket fence— higher than it would have been when the house was built, and even as the sun set, the alarm wires around it were visible. A sign on the gate advertised the house's historical importance, and announced visiting times and admission prices.

It looked just as it had the last time she had come here.

The damage from the blast and fire had been repaired.

And since it was Sunday, after five, there were no lingering tourists. The horn blasts and other street sounds seemed to come from far away. The house was quiet, as if it were resting.

As if it were expecting something.

Then the front door burst open, and Greta Peterson came hurrying down the walk to the gate. "Come in, come in. We've been waiting for you. Watching."

We?

Who the heck else was here? Leslie had hoped for a quiet night. No one would have understood, so she hadn't said anything, but she really wanted the house to herself.

Before she knew it, Greta, with all her warmth and enthusiasm, had reached her, hugged her, rested an arm around her shoulders and called out a greeting to Professor Laymon and Brad. Then Greta dragged her up the walk, saying, "Oh, Leslie, I'm so happy to see you. You look wonderful, dear. A bit too thin, but wonderful. I know that thin is in . . . but don't go losing your shape, young lady."

That from a rail-thin, hyper matron, Leslie thought dryly.

But Greta's warmth and enthusiasm were endearing. Then, as they neared the house, Leslie's heart sank.

Greta had apparently planned a welcome party. Thankfully, it appeared to be a small one. Sergeant Robert Adair—okay, she liked Robert and was delighted to see him—peeked out the doorway as they approached. Behind him, Hank Smith, from the development company, stepped into view, and then Ken Dryer, the attractive and articulate police spokesman, made an appearance.

"Leslie!" Robert called, smiling affectionately.

"Robert," she said with a smile, accepting a hug as the other men stood back.

"Hey, Les," Hank said, offering her a handshake.

Ken Dryer gave her a very proper hug before moving on to shake Brad's hand and ask about the weather in D.C. Then he started down the path to welcome the professor and collect Leslie's rolling suitcase from the sidewalk.

"Gorgeous as ever," Robert Adair whispered softly. "You okay?" he asked, taking her hands and looking at her with concern in his eyes.

"Fine," she assured him.

He kissed her cheek quickly. Robert was around fifty, she thought, a twenty-year veteran of the force. He worked out of One Police Plaza and wasn't assigned to a particular precinct. He was called a liaison officer and became involved with crimes that crossed precinct boundaries to affect multiple areas of the city—like the missing prostitutes—or that started garnering more than a mention in the newspapers.

Greta bustled past him to stand face-to-face with Leslie.

"We are delighted to see you, my dear. If you'd refused to come, everyone would have understood," she said. There was real concern in her soft gray eyes, the kind that made Leslie feel the ache inside again, but she needed to get past all that. And really, it had been sweet of Greta to find a special way to welcome her, Brad and Professor Layman on their arrival. Greta had been blessed to be born with not just the proverbial silver spoon in her mouth, but with a whole array of cutlery. Her ancestors had been fur traders on a par with the Astors. She was a born-and-bred New Yorker who truly loved her city and its history, and because of that ardent love, she was acknowledged as a major— if not *the* major—power in the field of restoration and archaeology.

"I love this city, and I'm privileged to be invited to

work this new find," Leslie told her cheerfully.

"We all are," Brad said quickly, then flushed. "Well, the professor *is* history, but Leslie and I are both very pleased to be respected enough to be asked back."

"Well, you're both not just talented," Ken Dryer said, "you love the city. You know the city."

"And it's so kind of you all to be here," Leslie said, smiling. "I thought the professor and Brad would be helping me settle in quietly, but it looks like we have a dinner party to attend." She tried to sound enthusiastic.

"Oh, just us and the caterers," Greta said. "I had to do something." Then she cut to the chase. "Oh, Leslie . . . do you really want to *stay* in the house? *Sleep* in it?"

Leslie smiled dryly. "I'm dying to stay here," she assured Greta.

"But you won't stay?" Greta asked Brad, sounding disapproving.

Brad shrugged, opting to answer lightly. "Sadly, Leslie has made it clear that she would prefer not to sleep with me."

Greta wasn't amused. She frowned.

"Sorry, just teasing," Brad said quickly. "I have an apartment in Manhattan. Leslie's place is out in Brooklyn, so it's more convenient for her to stay here," Brad said.

"I can walk right over to the dig," Leslie explained. She smiled, trying to put Greta at ease. "Honestly, Greta, I love this place. I don't blame what happened on a *house*. I want to be here."

Greta stared at Professor Laymon. "And you're not staying, either?" she demanded tartly.

Layman looked acutely uncomfortable. "Greta, we've talked, and this is Leslie's choice. I have a home here, too," he explained. He lifted his hands, the very image of brilliant but helpless.

Greta shook her head, her soft, short silver hair bobbing around her attractive face. "Oh, dear," she murmured, still unhappy. "There's no guard on duty, you know, except for when the house is open to the public. There's an alarm system, of course. State-of-the-art. But the Historical Society can't afford full-time security."

"A state-of-the-art alarm system is much better than what I have in Brooklyn," Leslie assured her. As Greta looked back at her, trying to smile, Leslie realized that the woman had set up the whole party just to keep her from being alone for as long as possible. She had to lower her head and smile. Then she lifted her eyes. "This place is fantastic. I loved it from the beginning. And I understand that the damage has been completely repaired, that you can't even tell that . . . that anything happened. So . . . how is the tourism thing going? Do a lot of people come see the place?"

"We actually had to have crowd control when it first reopened," Ken Dryer said. He smiled as he spoke. He always smiled. Wheaten-haired and handsome, like the boy next door all grown-up, with an ability to spin any situation, he was perfectly suited to his position, but Leslie always felt, despite how nice he had always been to her, that he was just a bit *oily,* as well. What his real thoughts were, she seldom knew. She had heard that he had political ambitions, and she was sure that on the political trail, he would charm an audience without ever really saying anything substantive about the issues.

"Crowd control?" Brad marveled.

Robert cleared his throat uneasily. "There's nothing like an . . . event to draw crowds."

Hank Smith groaned, taking Leslie by the arm. "What our good sergeant is trying to explain without words is that not only is this house a historical masterpiece, it has a modern-day tragedy to go with it. Unfortunately, tragedy brings people in droves. In the beginning, we had cops every day. The lines were around the block. That's slacked off some, but even so, eventually this place is going to pay for itself. Look, you've chosen to stay here, and I, for one, am not going to tiptoe around. You know that we were all affected by what happened, that we all felt a terrible loss—not as great as yours, but a terrible loss all the same—and if you want to be here, I say good for you. And that's not sucking up, that's God's honest truth. So, hey, can we eat now, Greta?"

"Of course, of course," Greta stuttered. "Come along to the dining room. Leslie, I've put you in the best bedroom. We'll get your bag up in a bit. One of these brawny fellows will be willing to serve as a . . . well, as a brawny fellow and take it up there for you."

"Hey, I can handle a suitcase," Leslie said.

"Yeah, and one of us can be a gentleman and take care of it, too," Brad told her. "Let's eat." He looked at his watch. She had a feeling that Brad had other plans for the evening and that a welcome-back dinner party hadn't been on his agenda.

Leslie . . .

She was thinner. She looked almost ethereal. He had never known such pain, such longing, as he felt seeing her there that night. He wanted to touch her so badly. He wanted to tell her that it was all right.

He wanted to tell her that Hank Smith was a dickhead. He laughed at himself. He hadn't known he disliked the developer so much. On the surface, the guy was a decent sort. Maybe he was too perfect. Tall, dark and slimy. His Armani suits were pressed to a T. Even his shoes were designer. He was a big man in town. Went to the right clubs. Ate at all the right places. Shook hands with the mayor. Hell, the guy even kissed babies' cheeks. He was a partner in Tyson, Smith, and Tryon, and he was the perfect representative whenever the firm had to deal with permits, public opinion and the laws of the state. But he just wasn't the kind of man other men liked. His lines were too smooth. He didn't kick back at a local bar to enjoy a good football game. Did that make him bad? No, just . . . a dickhead.

And there was Robert Adair, good old Robert, still looking like a bloodhound. Working tirelessly, always concerned, always in the middle of something tragic, criminal, sad . . .

Ken Dryer. He didn't like him any better than he liked Hank Smith. He never wore Armani. Instead, he was spotless in his police dress best. But then, Dryer had a tough job, speaking to the media, trying to assure New Yorkers that even under the worst circumstances, they were going to be all right. He supposed he should have more sympathy for the man, but he didn't. Dryer liked his job too much. Liked finding a way to put a spin on things that always made himself look good.

Greta . . . well, she loved history more than life itself. She was a good old broad, caring, genuine, which was hard, when you came from that much money.

Professor Laymon . . . he should get to know Greta better. They would make one hell of a couple.

Brad Verdun. He almost smiled. Would have smiled, if he'd had substance and could have. Once upon a time, he'd been jealous of Brad. Like Ken Dryer and Hank Smith, Brad loved the limelight. He was a good-looking dude, too. But he'd never had any cause to be jealous. To Leslie, Brad was a friend and colleague, someone with whom she worked well. They'd laughed about a few of his romantic fiascos together. But now . . .

His heart ached. Funny, he had no heart, but he could feel the pain. That was then, and this was now. He himself was gone.

He loved Leslie. Wanted her to have a life. Wanted her to find something as great as what they had shared. Really . . .

He just didn't want her falling for some asshole.

All right, so he'd gotten bitter. How the hell not?

Don't touch her, don't you dare touch her, he thought.

Then he amended that.

Don't hurt her, don't you dare hurt her. If you do, I'll . . .

He'd what? He couldn't even appear at will, could barely communicate with the others haunting the same space.

Don't hurt her, he prayed.

Hastings House wasn't huge. The entry was handsome, with the staircase off to the side to allow for a breeze to make its way all the way through the house. Leslie imagined that once those breezes had been plentiful; now, with the house surrounded by skyscrapers, the possibility was highly unlikely. There were two rooms to the right, two rooms to the left, and six bedrooms upstairs. The dining room was the second door on the left, and behind it was the one accommodation to the twenty-first century; the kitchen and huge back pantry were attached to the house by an arched passageway.

"Are you really all right?" Robert asked, coming alongside Leslie as they headed toward the dining room.

She squeezed his arm. "Really," she assured him.

Really, she repeated in her mind. *I just want you all to get out of my house.*

Her house?

It wasn't her house at all.

It was simply the house where Matt had died.

"So, Hank," Brad said as they filed into the dining room. "Your company made another historical discovery, huh? Must be hard. All that time and money invested—and now you have to stop work and wait for us to prowl around."

"Thankfully," Professor Laymon said, before Hank could reply, "the company doesn't try to hide what it comes across, Brad."

But Hank was grinning. "Do I mind losing money, Brad? Sure. But we get more promotional bucks out of this than you could begin to imagine."

As she took a chair at the period reproduction dining table, Leslie ignored the men and flashed a smile at Greta. They were eating on reproduction Dutch porcelain dishes, and fresh flowers graced the table. The minute she'd entered the house, she'd smelled the aroma of beef cooking, so she assumed they would be having a traditional old English pub roast.

"So, Hank, tell us more about the find," Brad said.

Hank looked a little surprised. "Professor Laymon has been given all the specifics."

"He's told us what he knows, but I'm curious. Why do you think you've discovered a working-class burial?"

Hank shrugged, taking his seat just as the caterers made their appearance, bringing the meal from the kitchen. A roast, whipped potatoes, greens, a tomato salad. Red wine. A very nice and very traditional meal.

"No one has turned vegetarian on me lately, have they?" Greta asked worriedly.

They all shook their heads as Hank started to answer Brad's question.

"Well, we haven't come across any coffins or bones—we're leaving that to you," he said, helping himself to the potatoes. "Gravy?" he asked. Ken Dryer passed over the gravy boat.

"What our first worker came across was a set of wooden teeth," Hank explained.

"Wooden teeth?" Leslie echoed.

"Just like the pair of George Washington's in the Smithsonian," Hank said.

"Poor people didn't generally have false teeth," Leslie said.

"They're very rough, and only preserved because they happened to have been wrapped in a scrap of tarp, like something a soldier might have had," Hank said. "I don't really know anything about this stuff, but that's what the first guy on the site, someone from the museum, said. Anyway, there was more. A few pieces of jewelry, costume stuff, and poor costume stuff at that. And a couple of tiny crosses—those were actually real silver. We stopped work right away, of course."

"Of course," Brad agreed. Leslie thought he sounded skeptical, but Brad de facto disliked anyone who worked for a development company.

"Then," Greta reminded Hank, "there were the records we found at the Morgan Library. Records that indicated a church had stood on the spot before it burned to the ground. At the time, this area was heavily populated with immigrant families, struggling to get by. Up the street, there was once a Catholic church. Down this way, there was another Episcopal church, not to mention Trinity and St. Paul's. Remember, everyone went to church in those days."

"Right, Greta. Anyway," Hank said, flashing a grin at Professor Laymon, "the decision was made that our good friend here should head the project, and all work has been stopped, the areas where the finds were made have been cordoned off, and you're all set to go. And—" he offered another of his broad smiles to Leslie "—we have two of the city's most esteemed archaeologists on the case, along with whatever hordes the professor cares to hire." He turned to Brad. "So do speak highly of us to the press, please."

Greta laughed softly; Leslie smiled. It seemed to her that Hank was honest enough, even if she didn't always trust developers herself.

"You know, construction workers need to make a living, too," Robert piped in.

"Right. Some of us poor slobs are just worker bees," Ken said.

"Yeah, poor Ken. You're just the average worker bee, right?" Leslie teased.

He laughed. "Okay, so, I'm a lucky, well-educated worker bee. Talk to Robert, here, though, if you're looking for a guy who has worked his ass off—sorry, Greta—to get somewhere, and despite all he's done, he's got a tough job, nowhere near enough respect and a lousy paycheck."

"Hey!" Robert protested.

"Oh, we cops are suddenly well paid?" Ken said.

"Could be worse," Robert told him.

Ken groaned.

"Besides, I doubt you intend to be a cop forever," Robert said.

"Do you have political aspirations?" Leslie asked, sipping her wine.

"Not this year, I assure you," Ken said. "Greta, this is absolutely delicious. Thank you so much for inviting me."

"Well," Greta said, waving a hand in the air, "we want Leslie to feel that the police are with her if she ever needs them, right?"

"Greta is really worried about you staying at the house alone," Robert told Leslie. He didn't add *and so am I*. He didn't need to. She could see it in his eyes.

"Hey, I know New York City. I'm street smart," Leslie assured them both.

"Anyone can need help," Robert said.

"Should I be afraid for some reason?" Leslie asked. "Do you know something I don't?"

"No," Robert said.

"Well, we still haven't gotten to the bottom of those local disappearances," Ken said.

"Leslie doesn't need to worry. She doesn't exactly fit the profile," Robert said.

"There's still been no break in the prostitute case?"

Leslie asked. "Is that what you're talking about?"

"No, no break," Ken said. He hesitated. "Matt had people concerned, but no one has picked up where he left off."

"Since Leslie is hardly likely to start walking the streets soliciting, I don't think she needs to worry too much about that," Greta announced. "I mean, personally. Of course we all need to worry in the larger sense."

"Maybe there's a modern-day Jack the Ripper out there," Brad offered.

"Jack the Ripper got his kicks by letting others discover the butchered bodies of his victims," Robert said sharply, then flushed, hearing his own tone. "Sorry, this is a real sore spot with me. We're just not getting anywhere. And whenever we think it might have stopped, we get another distant relative, hooker friend or embarrassed john down at the station, talking about a girl who's just vanished."

"Maybe they're just moving on," Brad suggested.

"I wish that were the case," Robert said. "I just don't believe it."

"Why aren't we finding any bodies, then?" Ken asked him.

"I don't know," Robert said. "I didn't mean to make you uneasy, Leslie," he added, turning to her.

"You didn't. I have a state-of-the-art alarm here, remember?" she asked, smiling.

But Robert still seemed disturbed as he stared at her. Shortly afterward, their dishes were removed and coffee was served, along with a delicious apple cobbler. As dessert was set down, Leslie decided that she was going to lighten the mood. "So . . . anything new and exciting going on in anyone's social life?" she asked.

Apparently it wasn't the right light question.

"What social life?" Ken asked. "Do you have one of those, Robert?"

"Sure, I'm here for dinner tonight," Robert said. "Thanks to this gracious lady," he added, reaching across the table and squeezing Greta's hand.

"Greta's whole life is social, but since she works so hard at it, she doesn't have an actual social life, either," Hank teased.

"Nonsense," Greta said. "I'm a happy woman. I love working for my causes, especially history. And you, Ken. You're at every social event."

"Ah, but is that a social life?" Ken asked.

"Sorry I asked," Leslie said.

Finally the coffee was cleared, the dining room and kitchen were immaculately cleaned, and all that was left was the aroma of the dinner that had been. Since everyone seemed reluctant to leave, Leslie decided that it was time to ask them to go.

She feigned a yawn. "Oh, sorry. Hey, we do start tomorrow morning, right, Professor?"

"Are you trying to kick us out?" Brad asked.

"I can't really kick you out. It isn't my house. But, yes, please leave. I need to go to bed," she told him, grinning.

Robert Adair looked at Brad. "I guess she's serious."

"Looks like," Brad agreed with a shrug.

There were a lot of goodbyes, with everyone making sure she had their numbers programmed into her cell phone and forcing her to promise that she would call right away if she needed anything.

Greta insisted on walking through the downstairs and making sure the caterers had cleaned up to her satisfaction and turned off all the appliances, and that the doors and windows were all locked. She explained the alarm and gave the code to Leslie, while the others hovered in the entryway. At last, even Greta was willing to admit that all was well.

"Now, tomorrow is Monday. The house opens at ten, so Melissa Turner arrives at around eight-thirty— she's in charge of ticket sales—and Tandy Goren and Jeff Green—the historical guides—usually get here a bit after. Melissa comes in and makes her coffee early. She's one of those people who likes to get to work ahead of schedule so she can take her time. She's a sweetheart—you'll love her. Just don't be startled when you hear voices early."

"I may already be gone," Leslie said. She looked at Laymon. "What time are we meeting at the site, Professor?"

"Take your time tomorrow. Ten will be fine," Professor Laymon said. "You know where it is?"

"Down the street. I don't think I can miss it." She smiled.

"Yes, well, just dial my cell if you don't see where

we are. I want to make my general assessment, then I'll get you and Brad going while I take care of hiring some grad students and start with the other what-have-yous."

She nodded, waiting anxiously for them to leave.

Ken Dryer brushed sandy hair from his forehead and took her hand. "I'm still a cop," he said huskily. "You know you can count on me if you need anything."

Let go of her hand, dickhead!

Ken frowned suddenly, then shrugged. "Call me."

"Thank you," she said.

Hank stepped forward. "Okay, I'm not a cop, but I'm always around if you need me, anyway." He kissed her cheek.

You are the dickhead of all dickheads!

Hank suddenly seemed to stumble. "Just let me know if you need me," he said.

Robert hugged her easily; Brad bussed her cheek. "See you tomorrow, kid."

Greta hugged her fiercely. Leslie felt as if she were about to leave on a safari into the deepest jungle. They were all so worried. And she couldn't possibly explain why she so badly wanted to stay in the house.

Alone.

At last the good-nights were ending. Robert Adair continued to look troubled. She kissed his cheek. "We'll have dinner soon, how's that?" she whispered to him.

That seemed to brighten him. He nodded.

"It's really good to see you back, Leslie," he said gravely.

"Back in New York. Back with us all," Ken Dryer added.

She smiled. "This is home," she murmured.

Finally they left and she was alone in the house.

She stood in the entry. She could still hear the street noises, muffled by the fence and the thick walls of the house. The sound of a horn, a shout, a car alarm. The usual.

She forced those noises into the background and tried to hear the house itself.

Nothing. Everything was quiet. Not even an old board creaked.

Hastings House had stood for more than two centuries. It had seen war, peace, life, love . . . and death. It had to be filled with a few spirits. It had been witness to a revolution, to a civil war that had torn a country apart. It had been there in 1812 when a fledgling nation had faced its first major confrontation following its independence. It had witnessed riots, the teeming disturbance of a world gone crazy in the caste war pitting old immigrants against new. World wars had come and gone, and the Cold War after them. It had survived the tragedy and trials of the twenty-first century.

There had to be spirits here. . . .

But she heard, sensed, nothing. The house was silent.

"Matt?" she whispered hopefully.

75

But there was no reply.

She closed her eyes, prayed, hoped, waited.

Nothing.

At last she went up to bed.

There are no rules, Nikki had told her once. No one really knew what lay beyond this world.

She lay awake as long as she could, still and expectant.

But nothing happened, and without even noticing the transition from wakefulness, she finally fell asleep.

4

At three in the morning, Joe was trolling the streets, driving slowly, looking for his one hooker in a veritable sea of them.

He'd started doing the basics immediately. Checking and double-checking the information Eileen had given him, making appointments, sending e-mails . . .

He'd read the magazine article several times over but had found nothing but an allusion to a long-ago rumor of an extramarital affair—not enough to make an intelligent grown woman go berserk, surely. The reporter was currently on assignment overseas, so there was no way to get hold of him to see how much he really knew.

Joe didn't think he was going to get much help from that quarter, anyway.

The secret to Genevieve's whereabouts was out here somewhere on the streets.

One of the notes Eileen had given him referred to a hooker Genevieve had tried to help in the course of her job and had actually spoken about to her aunt. *Didi Dancer.* Probably not the girl's real name, but . . .

Five foot four, huge breasts, tiny waist, liked to wear a skintight red skirt and leather jacket when she worked. Spiked heels. Her vanity was her hair, long and a rich, vibrant brown; she wouldn't be hard to spot.

He saw the woman and pulled over to the curb. She noticed that he was driving a Lexus, and he noted the hard smile that curved her lips as she walked over to the car. She leaned against it, arching her body suggestively as she did so.

"Hey," she said. Then her hard smile eased a bit. "So, good-looking, what are you up to tonight?"

"I'd like to talk to you," he said.

She had pretty features. Her skin was dry and taut, though. Too many cigarettes. Maybe—probably—too many less legal substances, as well. "Talk? Sure, honey, everyone wants to talk."

He smiled; her own grin deepened. "Hey," she said again, her voice growing husky. "You really are good-looking, sugar. Maybe we can work out a good deal—for talking."

"Honestly, I really do just want to talk, but I'll make it worth your while."

She tensed suddenly, started to straighten. "You're

77

fucking vice, aren't you? I haven't said a thing. You can't run me in."

She started to walk away, heels clicking sharply on the pavement.

He hopped quickly out of the car. "I swear to God, I'm not vice. And I *will* make it worth your while. You're, uh, Didi Dancer, right?" Man, what a ridiculous name.

She paused, then turned back, staring at him across the sidewalk.

"Who are you? *What* are you?" she asked suspiciously.

"I'm a private investigator. And I just need some help. I'm looking for a missing girl. Genevieve O'Brien."

A strange look washed over her face. Something containing caring and humanity.

Her voice still husky, she asked, "That pretty social worker?"

"Yes."

"I talked to the cops, you know."

"Will you talk to me?"

She hesitated. "All right," she said at last. "If you'll take me for a ride. That's a cool car."

"Thanks."

She crawled into the passenger seat, ran her hands over the soft leather, then looked at him.

"Where did you want to go?" he asked her.

"Just drive. Hey, let's take the FDR."

"All right."

He drove for several minutes, navigating the city streets to reach the highway, before she started to talk. "The police quizzed a lot of us about the missing hookers, you know. Strange. Well, not so strange. It was like it was all by rote. Questions they had to ask. They think we chose this life, that we deserve whatever happens to us." She shook her head, staring out the window. Then she looked back at him. "Can I smoke in here?" she asked him.

"If you can help me, you can light up a cigar," he told her.

She smiled, staring at him. "You are one handsome dude, you know? I should have known right off you weren't looking for a fuck. No, that's not true. You'd be amazed at the really good-looking young guys who just want sex without any emotional bullshit. Or kinky things, or sometimes not even all that kinky. Just things their wives won't do." She frowned. "You really aren't vice, right?"

"I swear, I'm not vice. I'll show you my ID."

"Oh, honey, anyone can fake ID," she said with a laugh. Then she sobered. "I wish I could help you."

"Try."

"Okay." She opened her window and lit a cigarette. Exhaling, she began. "Genevieve. The cops asked about her, too. Such a pretty name for such a pretty girl." She inhaled deeply, just air. At that moment she didn't even seem to realize she had a lit cigarette. "I have a daughter. They took her away. She's in foster care. Genevieve came to see me. I gave her a hard time at first. The girl looks like she ought to be posing for *Vogue* or something like that. And I heard from some of the other girls that she's really rich, too . . . but she was the real deal. She really wanted to help me. Us. I even got her together with some of the other girls one time. She was so sweet. She wanted to know about *our* dreams, can you imagine that? Like, did we plan on doing what we're doing forever? Was it just to pull in some money? She wanted to help us get real jobs that paid enough to survive here. Enough to get legit. To get our kids back," she said softly.

"When was the last time you saw her?" Joe asked.

"About a month ago."

Right around when she disappeared?

"Did she visit you? Were you at a restaurant . . . on the street, what and where?" Joe pursued quietly.

"We were right where you picked me up tonight," she told him. "She knew where to find me."

"Why was she looking for you?"

"She thought she might have a job for me." Didi inhaled on her cigarette, exhaled the smoke, then flicked the butt out the window and looked at him. "She wanted to know if I was seriously—really seriously—ready to change my lifestyle. If I wanted my daughter back bad enough to stay clean. Squeaky clean."

"And what did you tell her?"

She folded her hands in her lap and looked down at them. "I said yes."

He nodded. "But she never came back?"

80

"No."

"When and how did she leave you?"

"A car pulled up, and I could tell she knew the driver. She walked over to it, and it looked like she and the guy—I think it was a guy—it looked like they were kinda arguing. I couldn't hear what they said, but she looked pissed, you know? Then she waved at me and said she'd get back with me about the job."

"And then she got in the car?"

"Yes."

"What can you tell me about the car?"

"It was a dark sedan. Black, blue, something like that."

"By any wild chance, did you get the plate number?"

Didi shook her head. "I wasn't looking. I . . . I didn't notice anything more."

"You didn't watch her go, maybe wave as she drove off ?"

"No," Didi said softly, then looked at him. "Another car showed up. A regular of mine. I knew the guy; knew he was worth money. I forgot all about Genevieve then. I had to. I mean, I seriously would have taken her offer, and I would have stayed clean. But . . . well, I needed to eat in the meantime."

"Right," he murmured.

He drove her back to the curb where he had found her. After he slid the car into neutral, he pulled out a wad of bills.

"You don't owe me," she said.

"I told you I'd pay you to talk."

"It was about Genevieve. You don't owe me. I really hope that you find her. I pray sometimes that she's okay."

"Take the money, have some dinner. Give yourself a break."

She paused, looked into eyes, then took the money. "What makes you think I'm not just gonna buy some coke with it?"

"You might. I hope you don't."

She started to get out of the car. "You know, you're the only one who asked me that."

"Asked you what?"

"What I said to Genevieve. No one else cared if I meant to clean up or not. That was really nice of you."

"You could probably get yourself a real job, with or without Genevieve," he said.

"Yeah? I have great references. 'John Q. says I'm a great lay,'" she said dryly. She flushed, then dug into her small handbag. She produced a scrap of paper, a receipt from a coffee house, and scratched down a number. "If you think I can help you again, call me."

He accepted the paper. "Thank you. Are you sure you don't remember anything else about the car? Can you take a guess on the color?"

"Black. I think it was black," she said. Then she sighed. "I'm just not sure."

"Okay. Thank you. Really."

She touched his face, her eyes soft. "No, thank you, sweetie. You treated me nice. Real nice. And I'm serious. You call me." She gave him her dry smile once again. "And that wasn't a come-on. Good night."

She hopped out of the car.

He drove on down the street, past the site of the new dig. At night, it seemed huge, protected behind quickly rigged barbed wire. Hardly aware of what he was doing, he slid into a spot along the curb, stepped out of the car and started walking, making mental notes as he went.

Eileen Brideswell might just be right. Her niece had been working with prostitutes in the same area where a number of hookers had gone missing. She had been picked up by a dark, probably black, sedan off the street—in that same area. He needed Robert Adair's notes; he needed to know if any friends of the other missing girls had seen them getting into a dark sedan.

He kept walking, using the time as he often did to make sense of what he had learned.

He found himself standing in front of Hastings House once again, as if brought there by instinct.

Well, that was crazy as hell. What could Hastings House have to do with the disappearance of Genevieve O'Brien?

The place just bugged him, that was all. He couldn't shake the feeling that the blast had been intentional and Matt had been the intended target.

And that someone was getting away with murder.

He stood beneath the streetlight, staring at the house. It seemed to live and breathe; the old colonial windows were like eyes, the door like a mouth.

Unease filled him. Eileen Brideswell was right, he thought. Her niece *had* been the victim of foul play. Just as the prostitutes had been.

Someone was getting away with murder.

Just like at Hastings House.

At first Leslie slept deeply. Then, suddenly, she discovered that she was wide awake.

She glanced at her travel alarm on the Duncan Fife reproduction by her bed. Four in the morning. Much too early to get out of bed.

She plumped her pillow, but sleep wouldn't come. After half an hour she sighed and gave up. She slipped on a robe and went quietly downstairs.

So far, she hadn't gone into the room where the explosion had taken place. Was she ready for that?

Did she want to reach Matt?

In the entryway, she hesitated, then went into the first room off the entryway, now set up as a Colonial parlor. There was a love seat beneath the window, a table in the center of the room, a pianoforte to one side, and various chairs, along with a tea table. She stood there in the shadows and the diffuse glow cast by the security lights. "Hello?" she said softly.

But the room was just a room, an image of a past that might or might not have been exactly as it was represented now.

She walked through the connecting door to the dining room, thinking that last night was now just a moment in history, like everything else.

Then she walked through the kitchen and back to the servants' pantry.

The hearth had been rebuilt. She could almost imagine Matt standing by it the way he had that night. She could almost see herself nearby, held captive in a different conversation. In her mind's eye, she could almost see . . .

But the room was silent. Just a room.

"Not even a Colonial gentleman here, huh? The lady of the house?" she said aloud.

Just an empty room.

She walked back into the kitchen, found the coffeepot and the coffee, and thought that if the supplies belonged to Melissa, the ticket-seller, she would make a point of replacing them. She set a pot of coffee on to brew. Upstairs, in her room, which wasn't part of any tour, she had a television. She could sip coffee and watch an early-morning news show soon.

That settled, she hummed while she made coffee, thinking that she might turn and see a ghost at any time. But the coffee brewed, and she saw nothing. She found a large cup, filled it, added cream that she found in the artfully disguised refrigerator and headed back up the stairs.

She set her coffee down and turned on the television, then walked to the window and looked idly down at the street. Her heart stopped.

There was a man on the sidewalk, standing under the streetlight.

Matt.

She blinked. He was still there. As tall as Matt, standing the exact way that Matt stood. It had to be Matt.

The man looked up.

Good God, it was *Matt!*

She forgot that she was wearing nothing but a robe over a short nightgown. She almost forgot about the alarm as she raced downstairs toward the front door, but at the last minute she suddenly realized that a siren would go off and the police would be alerted if she didn't punch in the code. She hit the numbers hastily, then threw open the door and ran down the walk.

At the picket fence, she slowed and swore softly. The man was gone.

She wrapped her robe more tightly around her body. The street was so quiet now.

Dead, actually.

She opened the gate and looked anxiously down the street. Nothing in either direction. The man under the streetlight must have been a trick of her imagination.

But if it had *been Matt. . . . A ghost didn't have to run off down the street, so foolishly running around barefoot wouldn't do any good. But it probably hadn't been Matt; she had just wanted so badly to see him. . . .*

She let out a soft sigh. "Hello? Is anybody there?"

She felt a soft breeze touch her face, heard the sound of a distant horn and someone shouting "Taxi!"

The city never really slept. Not even down here, in the financial district.

"Hello?" she murmured again.

"Hi, yourself, lady."

She spun around. A filthy, toothless, long-haired bum was grinning as he stood behind her. "I mean, hello, *honey,*" he added.

She looked him up and down, trying not to wrinkle her nose in distaste or scream in shock.

"Uh, hi," she said. "Bye."

With a wave, she fled back through the gate, taking a minute to latch it behind herself, and up the steps. Inside the house, she locked the door and keyed in the alarm, making a mental note to herself to start being really careful or people really *would* start thinking she was crazy.

At nine o'clock on the nose, Joe Connolly was in the office of social services, speaking with the man who had been Genevieve's boss, a harried, irritable curmudgeon named Manny Yarborough who didn't seem inclined to be helpful.

"I've already had an officer in here, and I can't tell you anything else. The girl quit. Cleared out her desk and quit. That's it."

"No, that's not it. Did she say where she was going? Did she leave an address for her last check? Did she say that she'd be in to get it? May I see her desk, her work area, please?"

"You know what, mister? I'm a really busy man. We're always shorthanded around here, and Genevieve left us shorter. She didn't say anything. When I asked her not to leave that way, told her she had to work with the system and give notice, that she couldn't just quit, she just said, 'Watch me.' Then she grabbed her stuff and she walked. And you're crazy if you think I didn't put that desk right back to work the second she was out of this place. We need space, and we need help. This is New York!"

"I'll need whatever address you have on file, and I'd like to look at the desk anyway," Joe said firmly.

"You got a search warrant?"

"Why—do you think this is going to turn into a homicide investigation? I told you. I'm not a cop, I'm working for the family, a family that helps support the city charities, and I'm sure you know that. How about you give me a hand, please?"

The man looked at him in exasperation. "I'll get you what I had for a phone and an address, and you can ask Alice over there if she minds if you look at her desk."

Alice was young and looked uneasy. She seemed exceptionally kind, though, the type of person who was meant for her line of work. She was still idealistic. Her eyes were big and blue, and she must have heard the conversation, because she jumped out of her chair when Joe approached, eager to be of assistance. "I can go get some coffee or something if you want. I mean, I can get out of your way." She was thin, and a little like a nervous terrier.

"I'd really appreciate it if you could stay and tell me what I'm looking at," he told her, offering what he hoped was a reassuring smile.

"Sure."

Manny walked away, as if disgusted with the whole thing.

Joe sat at the desk.

"The bottom drawer is files," Alice offered. "I'll go through them with you."

He quickly discovered that Genevieve's work with the prostitutes seemed to have consumed her caseload, though, interestingly, she hadn't labeled them as prostitutes. She had listed the women as "Working temporary jobs" or "Seeking better opportunities." She had notes on all the children—babies, mostly—court documents listing when they had been taken by Children's Services and where they'd been placed, and little notes everywhere. He found the file for Didi Dancer. Her baby girl had been taken six months ago. Maybe Dancer was her real name after all, because the child was listed as Dianna Dancer. There was one note in Didi's file that wasn't clipped to the others. It read, *She has a chance. Go for the big guns.*

A second later, he heard a cough. He and Alice both looked up. Manny was back, scowling fiercely. "Mr. Connolly, here is the information I promised you. Now, I believe I've offered you every courtesy. We are an underpaid service here, and time is valuable."

"I haven't minded helping Mr. Connolly at all," Alice assured him, her eyes still innocently wide.

"Yes, but you are due in court on the Blalock case in thirty minutes."

"In thirty minutes?" Alice said with dismay. She

jumped up again. Joe decided she was more like a nervous hamster than a terrier. He stood, as well. As he rose, he palmed the scrap of paper with Genevieve's note. Later, he could always say he hadn't taken it on purpose.

He managed to whisper to Alice, "Can you copy the files for me?" he asked.

She looked delighted to be involved in a secret conspiracy against her boss. She nodded, eyes shining, a smile playing at her lips.

"Alice, time is passing here," Manny said.

"Thank you both," Joe said politely, adding, "I may be back."

Manny scowled.

Joe decided to retreat and fight another day. He extended a hand to Manny. "Thanks. I'm praying I'll find Miss O'Brien alive, and if I do, it will be in large part thanks to your help." What a load of bullshit. Still, he'd learned over the years. He was never obsequious—that would be too much; he would have to vomit on the spot. But being cordial to guys like this one usually made them feel awkward and sometimes even more willing to help in the future.

He extended a hand to Alice, as well, thanking her sincerely. She flushed and stuttered. "Y-you're very welcome. I loved Genevieve. We all did. Do, I mean."

"Yes, and now we all need to get back to work," Manny said.

Joe gave Alice a wink, and she smiled broadly. He left.

He had his cell phone out and was calling Robert Adair before he even left the building. Luck was with him. He didn't lose his signal in the elevator, and Robert answered immediately.

"I need to talk to you about Genevieve O'Brien and the missing prostitutes," he said.

"What?" Robert said.

"I said—"

"No, I heard you. But . . . Genevieve wasn't a prostitute."

"I know. Humor me," Joe said, quite sure that Robert had made the same connection he had but wasn't about to give anything away.

"All right. I'm at the site. Can you meet me here?"

"What site?"

"What do you mean, what site? The new dig site. The Big New York Dig, they're calling it." Robert was silent for a second, then added, "Down by Hastings House."

"I'll be there in a few," Joe said, and hung up.

Leslie was filthy, but she barely noticed and certainly didn't care. She was alive with the thrill of discovery that had been part of her chosen vocation from the very beginning. This place was an archaeological gold mine.

In a matter of hours they had laid out their grid, and Laymon had taken on a number of professionals, using all the people from the museum who were already involved and twenty grad students from local universities. People were down on their knees with small trowels and delicate brushes, while heavy machinery stood silently by. Thus far, they had found shoe buckles, belt buckles and fragments of jewelry.

Leslie was sure there would be lots more.

At first she hadn't known why she was drawn to a particular section of the grid. But then, as she dug and then dusted, she had looked up . . .

And seen the child.

She must have been about seven. She was hugging a handmade, unbleached muslin doll. Her hair was in a single braid. She was very thin, and her legs were slightly bowed. *Rickets,* Leslie thought. She had stared at the child for several seconds before she realized she was seeing someone none of the others could.

A ghost child.

She smiled, hoping no one noticed as she whispered, "Hello."

The little girl had huge brown eyes. She was dressed in a calico print dress and a spotless apron. She hugged the doll more tightly and mouthed back, "Hello. You can see me?"

"Yes."

"What did you say, Leslie?" Brad, just a few feet away but luckily with his back to her, asked.

"Uh, nothing. How are you doing?"

"Fine," he replied, then turned back to his work.

Leslie smiled at the child again. "What's your name?"

"Mary."

"Beautiful name," Leslie said.

"What did you say?" Brad demanded again.

"Nothing."

"You're talking to yourself again," Brad said with a sigh, staring at her.

"I'm just singing. It passes the time."

"Oh. Well . . . you can't carry a tune, you know."

"Thanks. I'll avoid karaoke clubs, then."

He made a grunting sound of irritation, rolled his eyes and went back to work.

She was afraid that Mary would be gone, but the ghostly child had remained. She was grinning. "I'm sure you sing just fine, miss."

"Thank you." She hesitated. "Are you lost?"

"I don't know where my mother is."

"Was she . . . sick?"

The little girl nodded gravely.

"And were you sick, too?"

She nodded and looked troubled. "I think my mother died. I think I came here with my father when she died. But I can't find her now."

"Do you think that her grave was here . . . right here, where I am now?"

The girl pointed a few feet away.

"I'll find her. When I do, Mary, they'll take her away for a bit. But . . . I'll find you, too. And I'll make sure, in the end, that they keep you together." She took a deep breath. "Mary . . . you know that you're . . ."

"I'm dead. Yes, I know. I just want my mother."

Despite herself and everything she knew, Leslie felt a terrible chill. The sun was bright. It was a beautiful day. She was glad she was surrounded by people. Real live people.

Brad was standing, dusting his hands on his khakis.

She made a face at him. "I think I'm going to move right over there. Want to give me a hand? We'll need to dig a bit."

"How do you know?"

"A hunch. Instinct. I don't know. But I want to try over there."

He looked both skeptical and annoyed, but he joined her nonetheless.

They began to work in silence. Leslie looked up, intending to smile and reassure the child again, but the little girl was gone.

She didn't know how long she worked, she was so absorbed in what she was doing. And then, at last, she hit a fragment of wood.

"Brad."

"What?"

"Look." She dusted the piece and handed it to him. "Coffin?" she asked softly.

"Let's keep going."

A minute later he let out a hoarse cry. He'd come across a piece so big it could actually be termed a board.

"We're on it," Leslie murmured.

"Delicately, delicately now . . . just the brushes, no matter how long it takes."

"Yeah, yeah, I know. How long have we worked together?"

He didn't even look up.

She found the first bone. A breastbone. They both stopped and looked at each other.

"Let's go a little farther," he whispered.

She nodded. They went back to work, meticulously, slowly. Her back ached, but she scarcely noticed the discomfort. Minutes passed. Eventually they revealed the skeletal remains of a woman. Bits and pieces of fabric had also survived the ravages of time and the worms of the grave. And a cross. A simple gold cross. Very tiny, a poor woman's treasure.

About to get up and summon the others, Leslie realized that they were already surrounded. Silently, and one by one, about twenty people, including Professor Laymon, Robert Adair and Hank Smith, had circled carefully around their position.

"Um, well, it's definitely a graveyard," Leslie said.

"We knew there was a church here. It's a churchyard. There will be lots of graves, and, with luck, they'll reveal volumes of new understanding about the area," Professor Laymon said, pleased.

Leslie wondered if Hank Smith felt happy. He shouldn't. This would put his project on hold for some time.

But Hank Smith was smooth, a man who had apparently learned never to give his true emotions away. His face revealed absolutely nothing of whatever he was feeling.

Laymon, however, looked as if he were about to have an orgasm.

"Oh. My. God," he breathed. He sounded like a Valley girl, Leslie thought with a smile. "All right, we'll need to get the photographers over here . . . and the news crews." He frowned. He didn't want anyone trampling on what he now considered to be *his* territory, but they could always use the publicity, and, anyway, there was no way *not* to allow the press at least some access, especially since it was the good PR that kept the developers happy. "Sergeant Adair, will you post a guard, please? And when we bring her up, I want her *in situ* . . . the dirt around her *and* beneath her."

Laymon definitely looked as if he belonged in a laboratory somewhere—or filming a mad scientist movie—Leslie thought. He was in a smudged white lab coat, his glasses were sitting halfway down his nose, and his hair was dusty and sticking out at odd angles. She smiled. The man certainly got into his work.

Hank Smith reached down to help her up the little incline from where she'd been digging. She hesitated, worrying about leaving Mary's mother alone.

"Leslie, come on up. I promise, you'll get to oversee as soon as the photographers are done," Laymon said.

She grinned at Hank Smith and accepted his hand, then found herself apologizing. He was wearing a suit that appeared to be the most haute of designer apparel, even if it had been designed for business. He looked like a million bucks in it. "I'm going to ruin your clothing. I'm a mess."

"You're a beautiful mess," he said politely, and grinned. "In fact, you can mess me up any time you like."

"Thanks," she murmured, unsure just how to take his words.

Brad had stepped up on his own; others were milling closer.

Leslie noted that Robert Adair had walked off. She frowned, trying to see where he had gotten to.

"Smile," Hank whispered to her, drawing her close. A reporter had arrived. Leslie found herself standing between Hank and Laymon, and the men slipped their arms around her quickly. A flash went off.

Great.

"Hey, Miss MacIntyre, you're getting famous for finding bones," a slender young newswoman called to her. "How did you find this lady?"

"The site was found for me," she returned.

"Want to escape?" Hank Smith whispered to her.

"Yes," she said. "Brad and Laymon can handle this."

"Miss MacIntyre—"

"Talk to my partner, please, I've got to get . . . uh . . ."

"Come on. There's a trailer right over there," Hank said. He waved a hand to the reporter. "Excuse us, please."

He led her firmly away from the crowd, maneuvering with a surprising expertise through the stakes and ropes that then divided the site until they reached the trailer, parked near the street. It had been put there originally for the convenience of the building crew, she realized as he ushered her in.

The trailer was light and bright, offering a work station, kitchenette and table. "Take a seat, relax. I can get you water, soda, iced tea. Even wine, beer . . ."

"Iced tea sounds really great."

He offered her a bottle and took one for himself, then crossed the trailer to open the plain cotton drapes. "I guess they'll be there for a bit." He let the drape fall. "Well." He sat across from her at the work station. "You really do have a nose for homing in on the past, don't you?"

"Seriously, the site was there. And all those other sections of the grid? We'll find more, believe me. I just happened to be in the right place at the right time, as they say."

"Sounds like you happen to be in the right place at the right time a lot," he said pleasantly. Then he hesitated. "I'm sorry, you were in the hospital a long time, not in the right place at all the night that . . . I'm sorry. I didn't mean to make you remember."

"It's all right. I never really forget."

"Hey, I'd love to hear about Virginia sometime."

"It's a great state."

"And you made a great find there."

"It was pretty exciting," she admitted.

"An old churchyard . . . and here you are, proving there's another old churchyard right here. I'd love to hear more about how you do it sometime. Maybe you'll go to lunch with me one day."

She started to protest, but he lifted a hand. "Look,

you're a bright and, let's face it, gorgeous woman, but I know you're not interested in dating. So I'm not asking you on a date. I'd just like to buy you lunch one of these days."

She nodded. "Yes, then. Someday you can take me to lunch."

"Since you won't date, maybe you can teach me more about figuring out women," he said, shaking his head in dramatic bewilderment.

"Hank, you're rich, important and a handsome guy," she said dryly. "I'm sure your life is full of women."

"Yes, full, but . . . which one is the right one?"

"I'm not sure I can help you with that. Hey, are you upset that we made the find? This has to be costing you, I know."

He shook his head. "Honestly, we can spin this so that every state in the union wants to see our bids when they have a project coming up. Some people get testy when a building is put on hold. I may think, 'Damn, how did we pick another blankety-blank historic site?' for a few minutes, but then I move on. The world is what it is. And yes, it runs on money, so I like money. But perception is important, and creating the perception that we're humanitarians, conservationists, is good business."

"Well, here's to your excellent spin-doctoring and perception, then. Cheers," she said, lifting her bottle of tea to his.

"Cheers. Though this should be champagne," he said.

"To tell you the truth, I like the taste of tea much better," she said.

"Are you a total teetotaler?" he asked with mock horror.

"Not at all. Just give me a good beer and a slice of pizza any day," she said.

"A down-home girl, huh?"

Hank was nice, she thought, but things were beginning to feel a little bit too chummy.

She rose and walked over to the window, looking out. She could see Robert Adair standing out on the sidewalk, on the other side of the fence, talking earnestly to a tall, light-haired man. Her heart began to thud. Tall and light-haired—like Matt. His head was bowed in concentration, as Matt's had so often been. He looked up. Matt's features. Not . . .

He said something to Robert, thanking him, she thought. Then he turned away.

"Hey!" she cried.

"What is it?" Hank demanded.

"That man . . . Excuse me, Hank, but I have to get to Robert. . . ." The trailer was narrow; she almost stumbled over him in her haste to get away.

"Leslie—"

"Thanks!" she called over her shoulder. "See you later."

She streaked across the site, avoiding the ropes and stakes of the grid out of habit. She headed straight for the fence.

But Robert was gone.

And the other man was gone, too.

As if he had never been.

As if he were . . .

A ghost.

5

That night, he came to her at last, but not as she could ever have expected.

It was late when she left the dig. Her hasty exit from the trailer had exposed her to the reporters again, and there had been more pictures to be taken. This time she posed with Brad. Inevitably, there had been questions about the events of last year, and even some unexpected concern about her health. She was grateful to realize, during the course of the questioning, that no one had mentioned that she had chosen to stay at Hastings House, so she was spared any inquiries on that score. Still, the whole thing seemed to take forever, and she was longing for a shower and solitude. She realized, however, that she had been given an opportunity to remind everyone that this had been a graveyard and the remains found here deserved to be treated with respect and consideration. "I'm hoping we can put some families back together again," she was able to say.

Finally it was over.

Laymon had ordered pizzas for everyone who wanted to stay, so, still dirty and very tired, they crowded into the trailer, ate and called it a day.

"I'll walk you home," Brad told her.

"I live down the block," she reminded him.

"I know. I'll walk you."

"I'm a New Yorker and can take care of myself," she reminded him.

He looked straight ahead. "I don't know. Matt always called you a rebel."

"You remember that?"

"Sure. But I want to walk you home just because . . . well, I don't care how street-smart you are. I'll see you in, and then I can stand on the curb and pray for a cab or just wander over to Broadway and get one. And thanks, by the way."

"For what?"

"You tossed all the press attention in my direction again."

"We're partners."

"Yeah, but you're the one who always knows where to dig. Anyway, the limelight finds you no matter what. The reporters love you. You're young and gorgeous, and you dig up the dead. That kind of thing fascinates people."

"I don't dig up the dead, I dig up history," she said.

He shrugged.

"And besides, you're young and gorgeous, too."

"Thanks for noticing," he told her, laughing.

She laughed, too, and they walked arm in arm to the house.

He saw her to the door and left her. The moment he was gone, she dialed Robert's number.

"Are you all right?" he asked immediately.

"I'm fine."

"Good. You home? Or at Hastings House, I mean."

"Yup."

"It was a zoo out there today. A good zoo, though."

"Sure. I guess. So . . . what's up?"

"Um . . . Robert . . ." She hesitated, trying to sound light. "You haven't started seeing ghosts, have you?"

"What?" He sounded astonished—and then worried again. "Leslie, what are you talking about?"

"Who was that man?"

"What man?"

"The one you were talking to."

"Leslie, I talked to dozens of men today."

"This afternoon. Out on the sidewalk near the site."

Did he hesitate for just a second? Was she imagining that he sounded suspicious when he answered?

"I think you know most of the people I talked to today. Hank, Dryer . . . maybe you saw me talking to him? Let's see, I talked with Brad a couple of times, with Laymon . . . a really cute grad student—but she was no man. Hmm. A not-so-cute grad student, some other cops, a P.I., a nosy businessman . . . a guy driving a double-parked limo. . . ."

"Okay, sorry. Never mind," Leslie said.

"You sure you're all right?"

"I'm great. Actually, I'm tired and filthy, but at least I'm not hungry—we had pizza. I'm sorry I bothered you, Robert. I'm going to clean up and go to bed. But enough about me. How are you doing?"

"I'm great. No, no, I'm not," he said, and she could hear the rueful humor in his voice. "Half the time I'm so frustrated I could scream, but then again, I'm an old cop, and I'm accustomed to that feeling. I'll tell you what. When I take you to dinner, I'll pour my heart out, how's that?"

"Sounds fine," she assured him.

"Good night, then. You call me if you need me. And ask me anything. Anytime."

"You're a doll. And you know I will. Thank you."

She clicked off, then stood in the entryway and looked around. The house was so quiet it seemed almost unnatural.

"Someone has to be here," she said aloud. But if they were, apparently they had no intention of showing themselves to her.

She went upstairs and showered. Afterward, drying her hair, she turned on the television. She'd no idea it had gotten quite so late, but the ten o'clock news was on. She got to see herself, Brad, Laymon, a few of the excited grad students and Dryer, who announced that the police were excited by the discovery, like everyone else, and that there would be a large police presence in the area. New York would be preserved for New Yorkers. The city wouldn't stand for vandalism or interference.

At last, with the television on, she fell asleep.

And that was when he came to her.

In dreams.

She slept, and he was there.

She knew that she dreamed, but the dreaming was sweet and real. She felt his presence as he spooned his body around her, just as they had so often slept when he was alive. His arms were around her, and she could feel the soft seduction of his breath against her nape. She smiled. "I knew that you would come. But—"

"Shh," he said softly.

He brushed his knuckles across her cheek, caressed the length of her back, stroked soothingly along her spine.

She turned into his arms, felt his kiss. Hungry, erotic, just as it had always been when they were apart for any length of time. A kiss that spoke volumes. Strong and powerful, liquid and ardent. His embrace was strong, reassuring, somehow gentle, like the power of his passion, and she slid into that embrace as if they had never been apart. She returned his kiss with the love that had lain dormant in the painful corridors of her heart ever since . . .

But she knew she was only dreaming.

She broke the kiss, lips moving the slightest distance away.

"I love you so much," he whispered.

"Why won't you come to me? Speak to me? Why has it taken you so long? Why can I only dream about you?" she whispered. "I see so many others. . . ."

"But I'm not like any of the others," he told her, and he smiled, that rakish, rueful smile. He was such a combination of assurance and humility.

"Matt . . ."

"Shh . . ."

And then his lips were against hers once again. So loving, so passionate.

As their lips locked, their hands bumped as they drew her nightgown over her head, both of them working to get the garment out of the way. And then she was against him, flesh against flesh, and he was warm and vital, hard muscle and taut sinew, his heartbeat thundering in rhythm with her own. She let her fingers play over his shoulders, slide down his back, clasp his buttocks. In turn, he drew her even closer, fitting her body to his own. It seemed as if they kissed forever, lips locked, bodies straining to be ever closer, as if they could crawl inside each other. She touched him . . . and touched him. . . .

It was sweet and aching and poignant.

And it was a dream. . . .

At last he pulled away, an apparition in her mind, but one that seemed so real. She met his eyes for a moment, the deep, dark, dazzling blue eyes that had so teased and loved her throughout most of her life. "Rebel," he breathed. "Damn, I've missed you."

She stroked a strand of hair away from his eyes.

"There really is no life without you," she murmured.

He shook his head. "Yes, there is. There has to be," he told her. And then his lips curved into that smile that always took her breath away. "But not tonight."

And then he began to make love to her, his lips caressing her flesh, tender, provocative. His fingertips danced along her arms, her collarbone, her breasts.

Delicate kisses followed, growing more forceful, teasing . . . the stroke of his tongue, the brush of his teeth, his lips . . . barely there, so that she strained toward him in search of sensation.

He moved against her, her wraith of the night, his flesh and vitality eliciting her own growing arousal. As intimate as he had always been, his kisses found her abdomen, the brush of his hair teasing her midriff. His hands moved down her inner thighs, spreading them wide as he lowered his head, leaving a whisper of sweet wet fire everywhere his mouth fell. She felt the spiraling ache of longing grow until it approached madness, and she strained against him, whispered his name, threaded her fingers through his hair. He made love to her with the hot wired tension of his body and the searing caress of his lips and tongue, until she was writhing and whispering and finally all but sobbing his name.

And then he rose above her again before driving into her with the passion she had never forgotten.

Her arms were locked around him, her hips rocking with his. His hands cradled her buttocks, pulling her against him, until it seemed they really had become one. She arched, quivered, her heart thundering as she strove to get even closer to him, soaring on a cloud of dreams and ecstasy. His mouth found hers again, melding against it just as she melded into him. He stroked and drove deeper, until the fire seemed to consume her. She wanted it go on forever, wanted to reach the promised climax, to know that shattering moment of completion once again. . . .

Finally it came. She cried out his name, shuddering as the world seemed to explode around her, within her. And she felt him, *felt him,* as he tensed, frame hard as steel, haunches taut and straining. She *heard* the hoarse cry that fell from his lips, felt him as he fell against her, drawing her fully into his arms once again, holding her.

"Matt?"

"Shh."

"But, Matt . . ."

His arms were still around her. His fingers smoothed back the dampness of her hair. "Sleep," he whispered. "Dream."

And there in his arms, she did.

In the morning, of course, she woke alone.

But the dream was fresh in her mind.

She lay in bed, staring at the ceiling. Maybe dreams were better than nothing, than the loss, the ache of loneliness, that never seemed to leave her.

Or maybe, as Brad had told her, she needed to come to terms with the past, to get on with her life.

She rose, showered and dressed for a day in the trenches in jeans, a blue denim shirt and sneakers. They were on to a treasure. But even the excitement of discovery seemed to lie dormant in her heart compared to the dream, which, she had to admit, had shaken her badly.

Downstairs, she was greeted by humming. Cheerful humming. *Perky,* cheerful humming. When she entered the kitchen, she got her first glance of Melissa Turner. The young woman was busy at the coffeepot. She had short brown hair and was a little on the stout side, comfortably dressed in serviceable deck shoes, a calf-length skirt and a white blouse. The tune she was humming was "Yankee Doodle."

She'd been running the water for the coffee, which was probably why she hadn't heard Leslie come down. When she turned, she jumped and screamed dramatically, staring with wide brown eyes at Leslie.

"I'm so sorry. I didn't mean to startle you," Leslie said.

"Startle me? You scared me out of ten years of life," Melissa replied. She had a death grip on the coffee urn. Probably a good thing. It might have crashed to the floor otherwise.

"But you're not a ghost," Melissa said, still staring.

Leslie shook her head, half smiling, half frowning. "No, I'm Leslie MacIntyre. Didn't they tell you? I'm staying here while I work on the new dig site. You were expecting a ghost?"

"No, they told me. I just forgot. And, well, I think this place *has* to be haunted."

"I see," Leslie murmured.

"Oh, Lord, I'm *so* sorry," Melissa said awkwardly. "I meant . . . ghosts from the Revolutionary War. The gang wars. Old ghosts."

"It's all right," Leslie said. Melissa was trying so hard and seemed so earnest that she almost laughed aloud. "It's a very historic house."

"Incredibly historic," Melissa agreed. "And you—you're an archaeologist," Melissa said, her tone filled with reverence.

"Yes. You'll see lots of them around here."

"Not of your caliber."

"I've had some luck," Leslie admitted.

"Luck? You're a mile above the rest."

"I've just had a few more years at it than some, that's all."

Melissa stared back at her, looking unconvinced.

"How about you finish making that coffee? I'd love a cup. And if you're the one buying the supplies, please let me chip in."

"I'd be happy to pay for your coffee," Melissa told her.

Leslie hesitated, certain the Historical Society wasn't paying the girl much. "Honestly, I'm happy to help out. I mean, you can't be making—"

"Oh, I make pure shit," Melissa said, then added quickly, "Oh, Lord, there I go again. I'm sorry. I should just thank God they pay me enough to live on. I'm not here for the money. I'm here because I want to be. I love this place. I'm fascinated by history, especially New York history."

"Then you should be an archaeologist."

"School," Melissa said, grimacing. "I can't afford it."

"Well . . . there's got to be a way. You know that old saying. 'Where's there's a will' and all that. I can help you work on it."

"You'd do that for me?" Melissa asked in awe.

"Sure. And lots of the stuff we do, we use volunteers. That is, if you want to do volunteer work, after all the hours you put in."

"I'd die!" Melissa said, then gasped. "I mean . . ."

"Melissa, it's all right," Leslie said, stepping past the girl as she realized she would have to finish making the coffee herself.

"Greta said that pretty soon she'll let me work one day a week as a guide. Thing is, the guides don't make any more than I do. The other guides are set for money. Tandy's husband makes a fortune. And Jeff Green is retired military, so he's got his pension. But I love the history of this place, and I swear, I'd work here for free if I could afford to."

"I'm sure we can figure things out so you don't have to do that," Leslie promised. "Now, do you use cream and sugar?"

Melissa stopped and flushed. "I guess I'm preaching to the choir," she said.

"It's fine. I think your enthusiasm's wonderful," Leslie assured her truthfully. She liked Melissa, loved her enthusiasm. She just had to get the girl to treat her like any other normal person.

"Can you imagine, though, everything that must have happened in this place? With all the battles, all the fires, can you believe that it never burned to the ground? Even a modern-day explosion . . . oh, God. Sorry. There I go again."

"Melissa, just relax. Please."

The coffee was finally ready. Leslie poured two cups as Melissa stepped anxiously to her side.

"They're all worried about you, you know."

"And they don't need to be."

"Everyone says you and Matt were like a fairy-tale couple. So in love and—oh, foot in mouth again."

"I love him very much, and I like being here because I can think about him. I'm fine. I'm coming—I've come to terms with losing him. It's okay if you talk about him—it's how we keep those we loved alive."

Melissa was silent for a moment as Leslie added cream to her coffee.

"Do you see him?" Melissa asked then.

"What?"

"They say that you . . . well, that you have some kind of ESP," Melissa said gravely.

"They're wrong," Leslie said. She wasn't lying, she told herself. It sure as hell wasn't ESP that she lived with every day.

"Really?" Melissa sounded disappointed.

"Sorry."

Melissa sighed and sipped her coffee. "Honestly . . . I'd dreamed of being here with you and finding out that the place is haunted by a soldier from the Revolution, someone who died for his country."

"Tell you what. If I do come across a ghost, I'll be sure to get a good story from him—or her."

Melissa flushed.

"Seriously, I'll look into it. There are some great stories associated with this house. Did you know it was an Underground Railroad stop on the way to Canada during the Civil War? And it doesn't stand all that far from where the slave market was set up in 1711 at the foot of Wall Street."

"It got its name because the Dutch really did build a wall there," Melissa said. "I know that because I'm going to be a guide, but I guess you know it, too, huh?"

"Well . . . yes," Leslie admitted as diplomatically as she could.

"I'm not scaring you away, am I?" Melissa asked.

"No," Leslie assured her. She glanced at her watch. "But I do have to get over to the site."

"Lucky you."

"Hey, we'll work on your future, okay? You've got the love and commitment, and those are the most important things."

"You think?"

"I do. But right now I need to get going."

"Don't you eat? Wow. That must be why you look like a twig."

"Doughnuts on the job," Leslie assured her.

"I wish I could eat doughnuts."

Leslie arched a brow, wondering if there was a right thing to say at such a moment. "Um, I had a bad year."

"I gain weight when I get depressed," Melissa said sadly.

"Maybe we can get together and invent special sugar-free doughnuts," Leslie suggested.

"Cool."

"Great. I'll see you tomorrow morning?"

"You bet. Unless you get home early tonight. Honestly, I haven't scared you into avoiding me, have I?" Melissa asked anxiously.

"No, I think you're very nice."

"Thanks!"

"Sure."

Leslie set down her cup and started out. Halfway along the hall toward the entryway, she stopped and stared. A man and woman in Colonial dress were entering, chatting with each other. They stopped and stared back at her.

"Hi." She strode forward, offering a hand. "I'm Leslie MacIntyre. You must be Tandy and Jeff."

"You got it. Hi," Tandy said. She had bright eyes, appeared to be a very attractive forty or so, and made a perfect Martha Washington. Her wig and hat fit well, and she looked completely authentic in the wide skirt and apron. The man was tall and lean, and also wore his wig naturally. They really could have been George and his missus.

"Miss MacIntyre, a pleasure," Jeff Green said.

"Thanks so much. I'm glad to get to meet you both, but I hope you'll excuse me. I'm running late."

"Of course. Hope we get to see more of you later," Jeff said.

"I hope so, too."

As she escaped, she could hear Jeff asking for coffee and Tandy excitedly asking Melissa what "Miss Mac-Intyre" was like and had they talked to any ghosts yet?

114

As she got closer to the site, she realized that hurrying was going to do her little good. Once again, there was a crowd around the gates. She wasn't even sure she wanted to press her way through it.

Reporters were in heavy evidence, and she found herself irritated. In a city like New York, there were a thousand things going on, so why were they all hanging around here? Then again, she supposed she should be glad that so many people seemed to have such an appreciation for the history of the city that history was making the news.

It was just that, despite what she'd told Melissa, she was tired of all the questions about Matt and how she herself was coping.

Well, she had chosen to come back here, so she had no right to complain. She straightened her shoulders and headed straight for the gate, where most of the throng was standing.

"Excuse me, I'm working here and I need to get through," she said, pushing her way past people.

Professor Laymon was standing in the middle of the dig, holding court in front of a group of journalists, with Brad at his side. She didn't want to steal anyone's thunder, but maybe it would be better to get the interest in her over and done with. She strode toward the two of them.

"It's Leslie MacIntyre," someone whispered as she passed, and the sound seemed to grow as others echoed her name.

"Hi," she said cheerfully when she reached the two

men. There was a nice police presence, she saw. People were being kept from trampling sacred ground.

"Miss MacIntyre, welcome back to New York," a man called. He had a notebook in his hand.

"Thanks."

"What's it like being back?" someone shouted.

"Is there a new man in your life?"

"How are you coping, being so close to Hastings House?"

"Have you been back inside?"

"I'm thrilled to be back in New York," she said, leaning toward Laymon's mike. "I think this is going to be a very important discovery, and . . . well, New York is my home."

"Hey, you found the body yesterday, right?"

"I happened upon the remains, yes. Along with my partner, Brad Verdun. Brad and I are both here under the guidance of Professor David Laymon. We're all very grateful to the city for inviting us to be part of this extraordinary project—and, of course, to the development company of Tyson, Smith and Tryon. There's Hank Smith now," she said, pointing him out. "It's thanks to his company that we have this opportunity. And thank you all for your interest, but now, please excuse us. We need to get back to work."

But the reporters weren't going away. Too bad. She had managed to speak, to be friendly—even to suck up to the developers, she thought wryly. But now she was done. She hurried away, leaving Professor Laymon and Brad to do the talking, but once again it seemed there was nowhere to go to but the trailer, so she strode toward it, hoping it had been left open.

It had. But once inside, she found herself frustrated once again, since she had none of her research materials with her to study. Then she noticed that someone had left the daily papers lying around, so she picked one up and started to flip through the local section. There was a large article on the dig, which she skimmed. Then she turned the page and found a picture of a very pretty young woman with wide eyes that seemed to defy the world. The caption read: Family Desperate to Find Missing Heiress Genevieve O'Brien.

She found herself reading the accompanying article with such keen interest that the time slipped away. Genevieve had been a social worker who had resigned her position shortly before her disappearance. She had worked long, hard and diligently for the underprivileged. She had last been seen on a street downtown, entering a dark sedan. Her family was offering a substantial reward for any information that led to her return.

Without thinking, she shut her eyes and let her fingers roam over the picture.

"Trying to communicate with the missing now?" a teasing voice asked.

Startled, her eyes flew open and focused on the door to the trailer. Hank Smith, as neatly and richly attired as ever, was standing there.

"A little tired, that's all," she murmured.

He shrugged, walking over to the little refrigerator and taking out a bottle of water. "Well, you never know. Our good friend Sergeant Adair may soon be asking for your help. In my opinion, the girl just got sick of her persnickety family and her grungy clients and moved on." She must not have been looking at him with much approval, because he quickly added, "Sorry, I know that sounded cold. But I've known a few addicts in my day. You can't help an addict who doesn't want to be helped. It's a waste of time and money, and I hate to waste money."

"I know the feeling," she said politely, wondering if he was less sanguine than he'd claimed about the consequences of delaying the project. "Is the press spectacle over?"

"They all went back to digging, and it seems they managed to drive the press off through boredom," Hank said, grinning. "Sorry, I know it's your thing. But to those of us without the patience . . . it's pretty damn dull." He smiled disarmingly to take the sting out of the words.

She stood, setting the paper aside. "Believe me, Hank, you're not the first person to say so." She grinned. "And thanks for the use of the trailer."

"No problem. And like I said, anytime you want to escape for lunch, you let me know."

"I will—thanks."

She left the trailer, eager to get back to work at last.

Within a few hours she had to admit that Hank wasn't the only one who would have found that day's work

118

incredibly boring. After the discovery of the first grave, Laymon was taking no chances. They weren't digging. They were dusting—from the surface all the way down. Meanwhile, the remains she had discovered the day before were being painstakingly lifted, surrounding dirt and debris included. She supervised until the precious bones were tenderly crated, and then she went to work with the others, remembering that there were more graves, and more pieces of the past, to find. The process, however, was indeed slow and tedious.

She noticed, each time she stretched to give her back a break, that Robert Adair was frequently prowling the scene. His interest, however, didn't exactly seem to be in the dig. She had the feeling that he was walking around the entire block where the dig was taking place and beyond. She wondered what he was up to and made a mental note to tell him that she would have dinner with him the following night.

At last she felt Brad's tap on her shoulder. "Have you noticed something?" he whispered teasingly.

"What?" she found herself whispering back.

"It's night. Even Laymon's given up. C'mon. I'll walk you back to Hastings House."

"Oh!" She looked up. They were alone in the fenced-in area. "Did Laymon say good-night?"

"Yes," Brad said with amusement. "I won't leave you here alone, Leslie, even if there is a police guard at the gate."

"Thank you. I'm actually in pain from stooping for too long," she told him.

He shook his head sadly. "One of these days you'll be a hunchback. Such a waste of youth and beauty."

"I'm glad you stopped me, thank you," she said, and laughed, looking down at her clothes as she stood. "I'm filthy. I can't wait to get home, shower and go to bed."

"What a wild child you are," Brad said.

"You're going out tonight?"

"I am."

"Well, I'm impressed. Have fun."

"You could come with me."

"Thanks, but no thanks."

"You *should* come with me. What if I wheedled?"

She laughed. "Thanks. Brad, but I'm beat."

"That's because you don't realize you'll be happy and awake if you go out."

"Honestly, I'm exhausted. And I promised Robert I'd go out to dinner with him tomorrow."

"Good man. Nice father figure."

"He's a friend."

"Trust me, he wants something from you, too."

"Maybe, but he's still a good friend."

Brad opened his mouth as if he were going to say something, but then he just shook his head. "When you want a wild night, you let me know. I can take you to all the coolest bars."

"I know you can. And if you pick up any of the wrong girls, I'll do my best to rescue you."

"Aw, shucks, thanks, sis."

He wrapped an arm around her shoulders, and they

trudged carefully from the site, stopping to say good-night to the officer on duty, who gave them a cheerful wave.

Brad saw her past the gate and up to the door. "Want me to check the place out?"

"I'm fine," Leslie assured him. "State-of-the-art alarm, remember? Anyway, some of the employees may still be around."

"Tandy and Jeff . . . well, they're all right. But Melissa . . ." He rolled his eyes.

"She's sweet."

"She's neurotic, but hey . . . you have fun."

"Thanks. Bed will be fun, after the amazing hysteria of a shower."

"All right then, baby, you're on your own. Luv ya—good night."

"Good night. Thanks."

She was glad to lock Brad out of the house.

There were always lights on—dim lights inside, brighter lights in the yard—and, of course, warnings about the alarm plastered rather unhistorically along the fence. She felt completely safe, and there was certainly no coming home, even at night, to be met by darkness. In fact, she had a clear view of the entryway and the hall.

And she was alone.

There were ghosts here.

There *had* to be ghosts here. Soldiers had died here during the Revolution, when the house had been used as a makeshift hospital. An escaping slave, mangled by dogs, had reached Hastings House, only to die moments after reaching safety. A girl, wounded in the riots of 1863, had lain on a couch in the long hallway and breathed her last.

There were lots of stories, but so far, none of the ghosts had decided to trust her, to make their presence known, to talk to her.

And certainly not Matt.

Except in her vividly passionate dreams.

She whistled softly as she headed for her room. Upstairs, she remembered that she hadn't eaten, but she didn't care. She was too tired to bother.

She warned herself that when she woke up in the middle of the night with her stomach growling, she was going to be sorry, but she ignored the warning. She was totally worn out, and not just from work.

As if she had been up all night, enjoying wickedly carnal sex . . .

She headed for the shower. Maybe after that she would feel revived enough to manage some food.

Or was she pathetically desperate to go to bed? To dream?

The water was deliciously hot, and she stood under it for a very long time. Emerging in a state that could only be described as squeaky clean, she crawled into her nightgown, turned on the television and realized ruefully that it was all of eight-thirty. She was going to bed very early. Pathetically early.

The better to dream, my dear.

No wonder Brad thought she needed to get a life.

And in fact, she agreed with him. Right after this dig.

Right after she came to terms with this house and Matt's death.

She wandered over to the window to look out onto the street.

Her heart seemed to stutter to a halt.

He was there again.

Matt?

No, that was impossible.

But there *was* a man standing beneath the streetlight.

Surely she was imagining him; her eyes must be playing tricks.

No. He was there.

She wasn't going to lose him this time.

She pushed away from the window as if she were a swimmer gaining impetus for a lap and went flying across the room, grabbing her robe in passing and flinging it on as she raced down the stairs. She hurried to the door, looking through the peephole as she fumbled with the alarm and the lock.

Dismay filled her heart. He was gone.

She threw the door open, ready to race out into the street, anyway.

Instead, she slammed against something rock hard. Flesh and blood. A wall of muscle. She looked up.

Matt!

No, this man was real. Breathing. Hot. Vital. Alive.

"Matt?" She couldn't keep from whispering the name.

"Not exactly," the man said.

Matt's voice. Matt's arms reaching out to steady her as she tried to speak. Opened her mouth.

Passed out cold.

6

Shit.

The woman was slim, but even "slim" made for considerable dead weight in Joe's arms. He lifted her, hoping she had disarmed the alarm so that a dozen cops wouldn't come bearing down on him any second.

Thankfully, there was lots of light as he carried her into the foyer. He strode straight to the daybed that flanked one wall and set her down on it. Luckily he'd been in the house before, when he'd come himself to examine the scene of the explosion, so he knew his way around. Once he'd set her down, he headed straight for the kitchen and a damp towel. A quick examination of the cupboards produced no sign of anything remotely alcoholic, so he poured a glass of water and hurried back with that and the towel. He knew he stood no chance of finding an ammonia pellet, so he hoped it was just the shock of seeing him that had made her faint, and that she would spring back quickly.

She did. Her face, beautiful and delicate, scrunched into a frown when the towel touched her forehead.

She opened her dazzling eyes wide as she stared at him, her sense of alarm returning. She braced her hands on the mattress as she strained away from him, her entire posture wary. "Matt?" she asked hesitantly, disbelievingly.

"Sorry, no," he said as soothingly as he could. "I'm not Matt, I'm Joe. We never met, but maybe you've heard of me? I'm Joe Connolly, Matt's cousin."

He couldn't identify the surge of emotion that washed through those glorious eyes as she stared at him. Finally a rueful smile curved her lips; rich, thick lashes fell over her eyes, and she managed a shaky laugh.

"My God. I'm so sorry. I'm not . . . I don't usually run around passing out or . . . I'm sorry." She produced a hand, and he took it. She had a firm grip. "I'm Leslie MacIntyre, and of course Matt talked about you all the time. I feel so foolish, but . . . the family resemblance is . . . amazing."

"Not really," he assured her. "Matt was . . . cuter," he offered with a grin. "Seriously, he had lighter hair. My eyes are green, his were blue. But I guess . . . we were about the same height. Both built like my grandfather . . . good old Irish brawn, I suppose. I don't think we were descended from the aristocracy. We were probably potato farmers." He was talking too much, something he didn't usually do, but she seemed in need of reassurance, no matter how quickly she appeared to be bouncing back.

At least she wasn't pretending not to stare at him.

She smiled, looking rueful once again. "I really am sorry."

"No, I'm sorry. I guess I forgot about the family

resemblance. Matt and I never saw it much, anyway." He stared back at her and grew serious. "A mutual friend, Robert Adair, told me you were staying here."

"Did he? He might have warned me about you," she said with a laugh.

"Well, he's known me forever, knew Matt forever . . . he probably doesn't really see the resemblance anymore."

She nodded. "Well, it's really great to meet you. At last."

"I went by the hospital," he said quietly. "You weren't conscious at the time."

She nodded, looking away at last. "I got your note. Honestly, I'm so embarrassed. I'm not really dressed, I've passed out on you . . . I assure you, Matt intended to marry an intelligent human being. I mean, that's what I usually am."

"No assurance needed," he said. "I shocked you. *I'm* really sorry."

They were very close, he suddenly realized, she half prone, he by her side. He must have been making her uncomfortable. He rose. "I just came by to say hello, but I see you're ready to go to bed." It was just past eight-thirty, he realized. Well, she worked hard. Digging all day must be exhausting. Anyway, lots of people went to bed early. *Eight-thirty?* "I'll get out of your hair. Though I would love to see you again, if you have time."

She smiled. "I'd make time for Matt's cousin, Joe," she said softly.

God, her smile was pure enchantment. He knew why Matt had been so in love.

"Great," he returned.

She was staring up at him again. "Have you been in Hastings House before?" she asked him.

"Yes." He shrugged. Why pussyfoot around? "I'm a private investigator. I had to come. I had to investigate the explosion for myself."

"And?"

"It appeared to have been an accident."

"Appeared?"

"The police investigated, the fire department investigated . . . a gas line exploded when someone turned up the heat."

The words hung between them. He wondered if she was thinking the same thing he was. *Accident? Or had the line been rigged, and had someone known and decided to turn up the heat at just the right time?*

"Greta was the hostess that night," she murmured.

He lifted his shoulders. "I think Greta would lie across the railroad tracks before she'd destroy a place of historic value."

Leslie lowered her head; Joe could tell that she agreed with him. He had learned over the years that the answers to many things could be surprising, but that was one headline he just didn't see. Wealthy Socialite Runs Amok, Destroys Historic House.

But someone else . . . ? That he could see.

Leslie looked up at him and flushed. She wondered if their thoughts had been running along the same

127

route. She stood suddenly. "Actually, it's ridiculously early. Want to give me a minute? I neglected to have dinner this evening, and I'm suddenly starving. Oh, sorry, you probably have plans."

"I'd love to take you to dinner."

"I wasn't suggesting . . . and I really wouldn't want you to change any plans on my behalf."

"I'd love to take you to dinner," he repeated.

She arched a brow, studying him.

"I don't have any plans."

"Great. Then . . . make yourself at home. Except," she added with a laugh, "watch out for the tourist no-no tapes."

"I wouldn't dream of sitting on an antique chair," he assured her. "I'll be in the kitchen, how's that? Fairly safe, right?"

"Absolutely. I'll be right down."

He watched her race up the stairs.

Matt had been a lucky man. Then again, Matt had deserved the best.

He wandered into the kitchen and helped himself to a glass of water. There was a plain wooden chair by the hearth. There was no fire burning, but he sat and stared into the darkened recess of the alcove anyway.

He smiled suddenly, glad that he had stopped by. Eileen Brideswell wouldn't be pleased, but he couldn't work every minute of every day, and he had thought of little but her missing niece since he had taken on the case. In fact, she had grown in his mind. He felt almost as if he knew her. He knew the idealism that had driven her, knew the passion with which she had worked.

He prayed that she wasn't dead. That she had, perhaps subconsciously, wanted to inflict some punishment on her aunt, the remaining bastion of a difficult family, so she had run off on impulse to take a breather up in Canada or down in Mexico.

But he didn't believe it. She hadn't used a single credit card. She hadn't written a check. No one had made either legal or illegal use of her social security number. The last person to have seen her—before she stepped into a dark sedan—was Didi Dancer, who had clearly liked her and seemed to have no reason to lie about what she'd seen.

He leaned back in the chair, shaking his head and turning his thoughts to tonight. He was glad to have met Leslie at last. She had taken his mind off his task and given him a much-needed break. But she came with baggage, too. Sorrow that they shared.

He needed a vacation, he decided. Tahiti was starting to sound awfully good.

He rose, walking into the servants' pantry, where the explosion had occurred.

He looked around at the repaired walls, the fresh paint, the furniture. He was no expert. He couldn't tell the difference between real period furniture and good reproductions. It was interesting, though, that the explosion had taken place here and the rest of the house had suffered very little damage.

Targeted.

He couldn't get that thought out of his mind.

He knew that Matt had been working on several things when he died. Because of Leslie, he had written about restoration efforts in the downtown area. His other focus at the time had been the prostitutes who were disappearing.

Had Matt been targeted because he was such a good investigative reporter? Because he had come too close to the truth? And yet, was the disappearance of the down-and-out really such an important issue that someone would kill because of it?

Sure. The abductor and presumed murderer. But how would he have managed access to Hastings House? And most people wouldn't know how to rig a gas explosion to look so convincingly like an accident.

Joe felt a strange draft. Enough to make him rub his arms to ward off the chill. "Matt," he said aloud, "I just don't like it. I swear, I *will* find out the truth."

He was talking to the air, he told himself in disgust.

And yet, he felt more determined than ever. There was no logical reason for it, but he didn't give a damn what the experts had said. Something about the accident scenario wasn't right.

"You were too good a man," he said softly. "Someone had to be after you."

There was no whisper of approval. Nothing.

"Hey."

He turned quickly. People didn't come up on him by surprise often. He must have been very deep in thought.

Or too busy talking to himself.

"I had a feeling I might find you here," she said.

He lifted a hand. "Sorry—talking to myself. I didn't hear you coming."

"I was watching your face. You don't believe it was an accident."

It was a statement, not a question.

"Maybe I have to find a reason," he said.

"I know. I've thought the same thing. Anyway, shall we go?" she asked.

She was wearing perfume. An elusive, soft scent. Her hair was long and swinging free, shimmering in the light. She was a bit too thin, but even thin, she had a nice shape. Smiling at him from the doorway, she was a vision. He felt a stirring and quickly tamped it down. Matt's girl. He had to be a friend, nothing more.

"What are you in the mood for?" he asked.

"Italian?"

"Sounds good to me. I know a great place in Little Italy, and my car is just around the corner. I was down here . . . looking around before I decided to stop by."

Her smile faded for a moment. "You're going to dig until you find the truth, aren't you?"

"Actually," he replied, "I've been hired to search for a missing girl right now."

"Oh?"

"She disappeared down here."

She frowned. "One of the prostitutes?"

"No. Come on. I'll tell you about it over dinner."

She smiled. "I don't believe you. You're going to dig."

"Hey, you're the one who digs for a living," he reminded her.

"But . . ."

"I looked into the explosion. I grilled every friend, acquaintance and total stranger who was here or knew someone here. Well, except for you," he added with a rueful grin. "There's no way to prove anything. The only answer anyone came up with was the combination of the gas line and happenstance."

She turned and started out, then hesitated and looked back, smiling. "I don't believe you're going to stop looking."

"Okay, for the sake of argument, let's say I'm not. But I'm Matt's cousin, so I can't help but think . . . well, I can't stop. Can't accept the obvious explanation. Because of him. That doesn't mean I know anything. Now come on. They do a great *francese* at this place. Veal or chicken—take your pick."

"Chicken. Can't help it, I avoid veal."

"Tell me you're not a vegetarian."

"Not unless chicken has become a vegetable."

He laughed. He'd sure as hell walked right into that one. Strangely, it wasn't at all awkward being with her. He liked her. He could see why Matt had loved her. But he had to remember that Matt had been engaged to her and tread carefully.

Joe. Good old Joe. The world's best cousin, practically a brother. He'd tried so hard to touch him. He had to let Joe know that it was okay.

Except that it wasn't okay. And he knew why, now that Joe had put it into words. It hadn't been a freak accident. He'd been murdered.

Why? Who would have killed so many so callously, just to get to him?

Joe would figure it out. Good old Joe.

Good old flesh-and-blood Joe.

And Leslie.

Leslie, who had thought Joe was him. Did they really look that much alike? Or, rather, had they once resembled each other so much? Maybe. Those closest seldom saw it.

Joe . . . and Leslie.

They were just going to dinner. And Joe was a good guy. Not slimy. So . . . He had to let her go. Not that dinner meant that anything was going on, at least not right away.

Besides, maybe they needed time together to discover the truth that had eluded them all.

The living and the dead.

They managed to secure an outside table. The street was closed to traffic, and the weather was unbelievably balmy, a promise that summer was coming. Joe had known Rudolfo, the owner and host, for years, and he was complimentary to Leslie without being smarmy. They had a bottle of his best Chianti and an antipasto of cheeses, meats and marinated vegetables almost immediately, and Leslie proved that she was definitely hungry. They both ordered the chicken *francese,* and then she sat back, her head cocked at an angle, and smiled.

"So tell me about your case. Is it the girl whose picture was in the paper?"

"Yes. Genevieve O'Brien."

"Do you think . . . ?"

"That she's alive?" he finished. "I don't know. I certainly don't believe she just took off without telling anyone. First things first—the police had done their homework. I went over it, and there's absolutely no sign of her turning up anywhere else."

Leslie considered that fact. "She's rich, right?"

"None of her funds have been touched."

"Scary," she said. "And sad," she murmured, lifting her wineglass and taking a sip. "I'm sure lots of people disappear and never show up again. I mean, think of the places people can dispose of bodies. Swamps, deserts . . . oceans."

"This is New York City," he said.

"Rivers, landfills, a city beneath the city."

He frowned, realizing that he hadn't really thought about that last possibility. He leaned back, staring at her. "Brilliant."

"Maybe not," she said. "I just happen to know that . . . well, there's a city beneath the city. In a lot of neighborhoods, the way that the streets have been built up, you can be in a basement looking out at what once was street level. And then there are old foundations, old tunnels . . . all kinds of unknown underground places. Plus, even though the city's mainly built on granite bedrock, loose earth shifts. I learned that looking for graves. In fact, in many old grave-yards, the coffins have shifted until there's actually nothing—or at least not the right something—beneath the headstones, and you're walking on graves no matter where you go. Over time, when the earth is soft, when there's rain, construction, vibrations from the subways . . . well, things shift."

"Creepy," he said.

She smiled, shaking her head. "Not if you're in my line of work."

Their food came. They chatted about the neighbor-hood for a while, about how so much of Little Italy was being absorbed by Chinatown, but that was New York for you, always changing. New groups of people came in on a daily basis. Some people liked it, some people continued to hate foreigners, even though they themselves had been the foreigners of a previous decade or century.

"This is a land of promise, but sometimes that scares people, so they ignore what bothers them, whatever messes up their pretty picture," he said. "That's one of the problems with the missing prostitutes. Getting people to care. A lot of the people have a tendency to think that women like that deserve what they get."

"Jack the Ripper went after prostitutes, and it was one of the biggest scandals in Victorian London," she pointed out.

"Because people were horrified by the gruesome brutality of the crimes. Here, people are just disappearing. No bodies, no horrifying details in the tabloids. And these days we're far more accustomed to serial killers—and so far, no one's even proved that we have one."

"Do you think that Genevieve O'Brien's disappearance is connected to the missing prostitutes?" she asked.

"The last person I've found who'll admit to seeing her is a prostitute. She was trying to help a lot of the working girls. Actually, I'm surprised Robert hasn't asked for your help yet. According to him, you have a gift for finding . . . people."

She sighed, setting down her fork. "Robert told you that?"

"I read it. This evening's paper has an article about you."

Her eyes widened. "No."

"Yes. You're credited with waltzing in and immediately making an important discovery at the dig. The reporter brought out the fact that you'd homed right in on a missing homeless man a couple of years ago."

She looked upset. "Damn."

"Well, do you have a special gift?" he asked teasingly.

She wasn't amused. In fact, she seemed to be even more irritated. "Logic," she said briefly. "I was told the man's habits and something about his past. He was found in an old subway tunnel. Simple deduction."

She had suddenly grown almost hostile, but he asked his next question, anyway. "But even before that . . . you were known for having an instinct for finding graves."

"A feel for history. Did you want coffee?"

The question was abrupt. He was intrigued, but he followed her lead and changed the subject. When Rudolfo came to ask how their dinner had been, Joe had a question for his old friend, too. "Rudolfo, could you use another waitress?"

Rudolfo looked back at him skeptically, then groaned.

"Well?"

"Actually, yes, I could use a waitress. A good one. A good girl."

"Can I send someone around to see you?" he asked.

"Send her next week. Monday. If I like her, she's hired. She's got to be a good girl."

"She will be, or I swear . . . I'll wash dishes for a week."

Rudolfo sniffed. "I have a very good dishwasher. The mechanical kind."

Joe grinned. "Okay, so I'll bus tables and man the steaming monster, how's that?"

Rudolfo pointed a finger at him. "You will work for me. Like a green immigrant. I'll work you hard."

"It's a deal."

Rudolfo sniffed and left them.

Leslie stared at Joe, smiling again. "You're going to get a prostitute to work here, aren't you? Do you do that often?"

"I believe in this woman," he said simply.

She touched his hand where it lay on the table. "We can try, but we can't always change the world, you know."

He felt a stirring, which he firmly banished. "Let's just say I'm doing this one for Genevieve," he told her.

She nodded, a small smile curving her lips. Her brilliant gaze met his. She did understand.

Lord, it would be easy to fall in love with this woman.

As Matt had.

Back at Hastings House, he walked her to the door. He was surprised when she walked in and left the door open, letting him follow. In the foyer, she turned to look at him. "I find it very hard to accept that what happened was an accident." She hesitated. "Matt was writing about the missing prostitutes, you know. Trying to arouse public awareness and sympathy. I'd really love to know more about the gas lines and how the explosion might have been rigged."

"Well, it's impossible to discover anything now," he said.

"Why?"

"Why?" he repeated, grimacing as he stared at her.

"Why?"

"Leslie, haven't you noticed? Everything in the house has been redone to work with electricity. There are no more gas lines."

"Oh," she said, flushing. "I hadn't noticed."

He frowned suddenly. "Leslie, don't go sharing your suspicions with everyone, all right?"

"I haven't, not exactly, but . . ."

"Please. Just don't."

"You're suspicious, too."

"And investigating is what I do for a living."

"But I can help."

"Oh?"

"I have . . . instincts, sometimes. Look, I just don't like to be laughed at, and I hate it when people call me the psychic. I'm not psychic. But I know . . . things, sometimes. Please, will you let me help? Even with your missing girl?"

He felt his heart pounding.

If it means spending time with you, you bet. Oh, you bet.

No, she was Matt's fiancée.

But Matt was . . .

Dead.

"Sure, we'll talk," he said. He extended his hand to shake hers good-night. All she needed was Matt's trusted cousin turning into a lech.

But damn, he was only flesh and blood.

Stop.

Forgive me, Matt. God help me, I'll keep my thoughts to myself.

"We'll talk," he repeated. "But if you want to help me, you have to promise you'll be careful about what you say—and what you do."

"Cross my heart," she swore with an enchanting smile.

"All right, then. Now," he said, glancing at his

watch—almost eleven. "I'm getting out of here. You can still get a good night's sleep."

"Sure. Thanks. How do I reach you?"

He gave her a card. "Call me anytime."

She smiled.

"What?"

"People seem to think I'm like a hothouse flower. I get that all the time, mostly because people are worried and want to take care of me. But . . . well, I *will* call you."

"Good night, then. Lock up."

"You bet."

"Set the alarm."

"Oh, yeah. It's state-of-the-art."

He forced himself not to look back as he exited the house.

Upstairs, television on, back in her nightgown, Leslie walked to the window, almost expecting to see a man leaning against the lamppost.

But he wasn't there.

She smiled. She felt better for having met Joe, though she still couldn't believe he had startled her so badly that she had passed out. But for a minute . . . just for a minute . . . she had thought Matt was back. In the flesh.

No, Matt was only in her dreams.

Was Joe right, though? That the explosion hadn't been an accident? The idea had certainly occurred to her time and time again that Matt had been targeted.

And what about Genevieve O'Brien? Could she possibly help Joe find her?

She was excited at the thought, though also a bit chastened by the thought that the only people she'd found to date had been dead.

"Hey," she commanded herself. "Get back to reality here. You still have work to do at the dig."

And she did. She was going to find Mary's grave, then see to it that mother and child were reburied together.

With that thought uppermost in her mind, she climbed into bed to watch the news. She saw her own face on the screen and watched in morbid fascination as a reporter came on to talk about her apparent ability to find bodies, an ability, the reporter claimed, that predated the death of her fiancé and her own terrible ordeal following the explosion at Hastings House.

Luckily, nothing was said about her living there now. People were still keeping mum on that subject.

As soon as the report was over, she found a station that was showing repeats of *Gilligan's Island* and watched the adventures of the seven castaways until she felt herself drifting off at last.

She turned off the television, then lay awake wondering whether Matt would come to her in her dreams again.

She kept opening her eyes, looking into the shadows, willing him to appear.

Nothing.

At last she drifted to sleep.

And then he came.

Once again, she knew she was asleep, that she was dreaming. But it didn't matter, because he was there. Long and hard and lean, as vital as he had been in life. He touched her, stroked her. She *felt* his fingers on her naked flesh, followed by the brush of his lips, as real as his kisses had ever been.

A caress down her spine . . .

Liquid fire on her breasts . . .

Pressure, thrusting, enfolding arms . . .

He whispered, "I love you so much, Leslie. . . . Oh, God, Leslie . . ."

She wanted the soaring, the hunger, the yearning . . . the passion, the tenderness and the volatility . . . to go on forever.

She was filled with the sweetest ache at the sheer intimacy that raged between them, at his natural physical grace. Together they strained, rocked, writhed together. She reveled in the hardness of his body, the shudder of his desire, the sudden explosion of his climax. . . .

And basked in his arms, eternally around her.

His breath was soft against her ear as he sighed in complete sexual satisfaction. She could still feel his body, molded to hers.

She moved in his arms, as she had done so many times before. When they'd lived together they had often kept different hours. He would come in once she was asleep, and slowly, seductively, awaken her by making love to her.

And they would sometimes whisper about their days afterward, lying replete in each other's arms, so it seemed the most natural thing in the world to talk to him now, even knowing it was only in her dreams.

"I met Joe today."

"Joe, huh? Good guy. Sad history, though."

"Oh?"

"He was madly in love with his high-school sweet-heart."

"And?"

"She died. Cancer."

"I'm sorry."

"I don't think he's ever given up the ghost."

The ghost.

"He's an interesting guy," she said.

"He is. He's great. Listen to him."

He nuzzled her neck, holding her more tightly.

"I thought he was you for a minute."

"Yeah? I guess we did look alike."

Then his lips found hers, and it started all over again.

It was her turn to whisper to him. "Matt, I love you so much. And I miss you so much, need you so much. . . ."

He drew back slightly, looking down at her. "You can't let yourself need me, Leslie."

"I always will."

"No," he whispered, and then his touch took over. "Forgive me, but I just need a little more time."

"Time?" she repeated.

He didn't reply. Not with words.

She awoke, the dream still so real in her mind, and found herself naked, her bed a rumpled disaster.

She swore softly, deeply embarrassed, even though she was alone.

She closed her eyes, shook her head, then opened her eyes and looked across the room. A soft gasp escaped her.

Matt was there.

Sitting in the wing chair by the fireplace.

"Here I am . . . but it's wrong. I shouldn't be here," he said.

"What?" Leslie murmured, so stunned that she could barely form the word.

"Sorry. Never mind. He's right, you know."

"What?"

"It wasn't an accident."

"Matt, talk to me, tell me what you know."

"I don't know anything. That's the problem."

She started to rise, tripped on the sheet, and by the time she untangled herself and looked toward the chair, he was gone as if he had never been.

As if their conversation had been nothing more than part of a desperate and wistful dream.

7

There was dust everywhere; Joe wasn't at all certain that he could have ascertained anything in the gray and vile-smelling room he entered. But he was pleased to be here, doubly pleased because Leslie had called him with such excitement and insisted that he come.

The police presence around the dig was larger than ever, and the press swell had grown to monstrous proportions. But Robert Adair had cut his way through the crowd to reach him, then created a path for the two of them to reach the site and climb down into the strange gaping hole. Despite the work lights, he had been totally disoriented when he'd first entered the underground room. It wasn't exactly the smell of death that had assailed his nostrils when he'd first managed to straighten up in the subterranean room, but more like something stale, the overwhelming odor of simple decay that had been closed up for too long.

"There you are!"

He was startled when Leslie rushed over and hugged him. She was barely recognizable, she was so covered in the dust of the past, but her eyes were bright in her smudged face. "Well?"

"You found a room," he said, feeling foolish for stating the obvious.

She laughed. He saw that Professor Laymon, Brad Verdun and a number of other workers were clustered at the far side of the room. They clearly understood the significance of the find far more that he did. They were talking excitedly and dusting at a wall.

"It's a crypt," she told him.

"A crypt?"

"There was a church here at one time, built in 1817,

to be exact," she told him. "A few years later, it burned to the ground in the fire that destroyed much of old New York. Other buildings went up on the site and were razed over the next century, and then, in the late 1930s, what we'd now call a miniskyscraper went up. That's what was just torn down. But this is it, the proof that we've made an amazing find. Look! This is where the priests and the wealthy were buried, not mixed with the poorer people buried in the church-yard. We've already found gold crucifixes and other High Episcopalian paraphernalia, and even a store-room of old books and documents. Isn't it great?" she demanded.

"Amazing," he told her. "And your . . ." He found himself lowering his voice. "Your *instinct* led you to it?"

She started laughing again, delighted, elated. "No, I leaned against what I thought was an embankment, and I fell through."

He had to appreciate the rueful humor in her eyes.

Professor Laymon let out an excited cry. "I can't believe it! It's a cache of sermons. There's a protected niche here . . . watch the bones," he warned, as eager workers surged forward.

"Congratulations," Joe said. "And thanks for getting me in here."

She was holding his hands, he realized, as if they were old friends. But then again, they did have a bond.

They had both loved Matt.

She pulled him closer, rising slightly on her toes to

146

whisper, "You had to see what I was talking about."

"I did?"

"The city under the city."

"And," he said softly, "you think that there might be a psycho kidnapping and killing prostitutes and then hiding the bodies in hidden crypts?" He didn't mean to sound as skeptical as he did, but she merely stared at him, amused.

"Maybe not crypts, but somewhere in the abandoned places under New York. Do you have any better answers?" she inquired.

"No. So let's start exploring underground."

She nodded, smiling. "I'm just about done here, anyway. So how was your day?"

He started to answer, and then decided not to bother. He'd spent the day retracing his steps. He'd gone back to Genevieve's apartment. He'd studied every little scrap of paper she'd left lying around, every note. He'd checked out her last doctor's appointment and her last dentist appointment. He'd visited the bars where she'd partied with friends, and all he'd found anywhere were people who spoke of her wistfully and with affection. He'd checked again for any evidence of her credit cards being used. Then he'd headed back to the street where Didi continued to ply her trade. She hadn't remembered anything else, and none of the other prostitutes she'd introduced him to had anything helpful to add, either, though they had all spoken admiringly of Genevieve. In the end, it still seemed he had hit his best stroke of luck when he first met

Didi—the last time anyone had seen Genevieve O'Brien had been when she had gotten into the dark sedan.

The highlight of the day, of course, had been telling Didi about the waitressing job he had arranged.

"Your friend would hire me?" she asked skeptically.

"Yes. Cut the makeup by half, wear something that covers you . . . you know the drill."

"You're taking a risk."

"Life is a risk."

"I owe you. I'll be there. And I won't let you down. Except now I won't have Genevieve to help me get my daughter back."

"Start with legitimate employment, huh?"

"Absolutely." She'd hugged him.

The low point of the day had been talking to Eileen Brideswell and telling her that, so far, he'd traced Genevieve to a street corner and a dark sedan, and no further.

"Leslie," Brad Verdun called excitedly. "Come look at these."

She turned at the sound of her name and was looking at him when he first noticed Joe. For a minute he went dead still. Maybe it was the light, but he seemed to turn parchment white. His lips formed a single word. *Matt.*

"Sorry, no. Joe Connolly, Matt's cousin," Joe said, walking carefully across the uneven floor and offering his hand.

"Wow." Verdun stared at him, openmouthed.

Laymon turned around then and gasped.

"Joseph Connolly," Joe repeated. "Matt's cousin." Did they all believe in ghosts? Hell, these people spent their lives working with the past and the dead.

"You're a dead ringer for him," Brad said, then winced. "Sorry."

"It's all right. Leslie asked me down here."

"Cool," Brad said. "She just never mentioned you, that's all."

Joe didn't reply. No need to say that they had just met.

Leslie came up behind him then. "I'm going to take off, let you guys deal with all this," she said.

Brad frowned. "Leslie, you must realize the significance—"

"Yes, and we'll be working in here for weeks," she said cheerfully. "And for the love of God, Brad, you deal with the reporters, huh?"

"You know I will."

"Come on," she said to Joe, taking his arm.

"Nice to meet you," he said, letting her drag him away. The other men just stared. Neither one replied.

Joe climbed out of the hole first, then reached back to help her. They were both covered in grime, but as he helped her out, he was surprised by the sound of applause coming from the street.

Beneath the dirt on her face, he saw her blanch. "It's all right. We'll get away," he said.

When she was standing, he turned to see Ken Dryer,

whom he knew from his own days on the force, coming toward them.

Despite the dirt everywhere, Dryer still managed to look impeccable in his dress uniform. He was the perfect spokesman—tall, dark and handsome, with a voice that would have done the old crooners proud. "Leslie, the reporters are all clamoring to talk to you."

"I fell into a hole. You tell them about it," she said.

"I can, but—" He broke off, staring at Joe. "Hey, Joe. What are you doing here?"

"Leslie called me."

"You two—oh, yeah . . . the Matt connection," he said.

Joe shrugged. "Right, the Matt connection."

"Ken, please help me get out of here today."

Ken stared at her, then shrugged and smiled. "I guess the rest of us are exhibitionists, huh? Brad and the professor love to talk. Even Hank has been giving them an earful, though his heart must be sinking. I'd say you're looking at a good year here, holding up the building process. Oh, well, they're going for public appeal, and this time, they'll be paying a price. Head for the trailer. I'll send an officer to lead you out the back gate in the fence."

"Thanks, Ken," she said, then took Joe's arm. "This way," she told him.

They headed for the trailer. He could hear the protest of the crowd, but then Dryer's smooth tones rose above it, followed a moment later by laughter.

They reached the trailer in safety. "Want water? A

soda?" she asked him as soon as they were inside.

"Water would be great."

She had barely supplied him with a plastic bottle before the door opened. In Joe's opinion, the man who entered could only be described as oily. "Hey, Leslie. I heard you needed some help escaping," he said.

Joe wasn't sure why, but he hated the guy the minute he heard those simple words. The man was talking as if it were his job to protect Leslie. His voice had a proprietorial tone, and he just didn't like it.

When the guy noticed him—how it had taken him so long, Joe didn't know, since he was a good six-three—he went dead still, gaping. Joe found himself enjoying it.

"Joseph Connolly," he said, offering a hand.

For a second the fellow looked horrified, as if he were about to collapse. "Hello, sorry . . . I . . . uh . . ."

"You didn't see a ghost. I'm Matt's cousin, and I'm just starting to realize how much he and I resembled each other."

"A lot." Hank looked at Leslie. In fact, he looked as if he'd like to come between the two of them.

"What do you think of the new discovery?" Joe asked politely.

"Incredible. Seems Leslie's luck is still holding."

"Just lack of coordination, I'm afraid," she said. "I fell through a wall."

"This will hold up building for a long time," Joe said easily. "How is the company going to deal with that?"

"We're going to go with the flow, celebrate history,"

Hank said. He grinned, and it seemed like an honest grin. "Every time those cameras roll, they're picking up the company logo."

"Still, you must be talking millions."

"And millions. Doesn't matter. Have you ever tried to buy an ad during the Superbowl?" Hank asked.

"Can't say I have."

"Good press is expensive." Hank touched Leslie's cheek. A little too familiarly, Joe thought, then told himself to shut up. What right did he have, after all? "When you can't beat trouble, you just have to deal," he said.

Leslie moved slightly away from him, and Joe could have sworn that her smile was false. "Hopefully, we're doing the city a favor."

"And our stockholders, too," Hank said.

The trailer door opened. "Police escort," a voice said cheerfully. A known voice.

"Robert!" Leslie said with pleasure.

Robert Adair came up the steps. Leslie gave him a hug, then apologized quickly. "I've just smudged you big time," she said.

"I can live with being smudged by you anytime," Robert said. "Hey there, Joe. So you two have—"

"Smudged each other already," Joe interrupted quickly. He didn't want Hank Smith knowing they had just met, though he wasn't sure why. Let them all think that he and Leslie had a past history as friends. He could protect her better that way.

Protect her? From what? Where had that thought

152

come from? What implication had there ever been that Leslie might be in danger?

"Let's get going. There's a gate in the fence in the back where I can get you out," Robert told them.

They followed him, and a few minutes later they emerged on the far side of the site. "You both need baths, you know. Otherwise, people will be stopping you in the street and offering you money."

"You think?" Leslie said. She laughed. "I've seen much worse on the streets of New York."

Robert studied her and rolled his eyes. "Okay, you've got a point. But you sure do look like you just climbed out of a hole in the mud."

"Okay, bath," Leslie agreed.

"Then dinner," Robert said.

"Dinner?" Joe cut in.

"Leslie promised to have dinner with me tonight. Want to come along? You can tell me where you're getting looking for the O'Brien girl."

Joe shrugged and looked at Leslie. "Deal?" he asked.

"Deal," she agreed.

She arrived home in time to see Hastings House in action. Melissa was handling tickets. Her smile was radiant when she saw Leslie. "Hi."

"Hi, yourself. How's it going?"

"Great. There are two tours going on now. Just wave to the guides on your way up to your room. Oh, and lock your door. We keep an eye on the tourists, but you never know when someone will go wandering off. By the way . . . you're really, uh, dirty."

"I know. Thanks," Leslie told her.

Jeff was with a group in the hall, explaining Colonial construction. He got wide-eyed when he saw her, so of course the ten or so people in his group stared at her, too. Jeff just gave her a nod and said, "One of our archaeologists, always busy at work."

She was grimy enough that she hoped she wouldn't be recognized from any recent articles or newscasts, and she gave a quick wave before hurrying up the stairs. She passed the second tour group in the upper hallway, where they were hearing about the house's history as part of the Underground Railroad.

She paused for a minute. She'd been aware of the history of the house for a very long time, but being reminded that it had been part of the Underground Railroad suddenly seemed to be important.

Why?

She realized she was just standing there, filthy. She hurried to her bedroom—locking the door behind her, as Melissa had warned. Then she leaned against it for a moment, staring at the rocker by the hearth. But it was empty.

Had he really been there this morning? Was he haunting Hastings House? Or had she just wished him there, just as she had wished him into her dreams? And had his comments come to her mind because she had actually been talking to the flesh-and-blood Joe, a man who believed that there had been foul play at the house?

"Matt?" she whispered.

But there was no answer. She showered and dressed, whimsically opting for a black velvet sheath that fit the changing weather. By the time she left her room the tours were over and the guides were gone.

Melissa was still there, though, in the small upstairs office, counting receipts and balancing her books. She whistled when Leslie walked by. "That's a knockout."

"Thanks."

"Off to a black-tie event?" Melissa asked.

"No. Dinner with friends."

"I heard about the crypt you discovered."

"Fell into."

Melissa sighed dreamily. "Think I could really volunteer to work with you?"

"You bet. I'll see to it."

"Thank you so much." Melissa frowned even as she spoke.

"What's the matter?"

"I . . . I've lost a twenty, I think."

"It's got to be there somewhere," Leslie said.

"Yes, but . . . oh, it's right here. I swear it wasn't here a minute ago," Melissa said, still frowning.

"Maybe something was on top of it."

Melissa grinned at her. "And maybe the ghosts are helping me out. You think?" she asked wistfully.

"Maybe."

The sound of knocking came from downstairs. "Good night, Melissa, I'll see you in the morning," Leslie told her.

"Right. Have a good time. Knock 'em dead." She blushed. "I mean, you look like a million."

"Thanks."

Joe was at the door. She forced herself to smile as she greeted him. He wasn't Matt; she knew that. They were different people, different personalities. But tonight, he reminded her so much of Matt as he'd looked last night. . . .

They even used the same aftershave.

But he looked good, dark blond hair newly washed, still damp, hard-cut rugged features, casual suede jacket. Tall and well muscled. His shoulders were a little broader than Matt's; maybe Matt had been a half inch taller.

"Is everything all right?" he asked, frowning.

"Of course. Where's Robert?"

"We're meeting him just down the street. Tonight, a good old American steakhouse."

She smiled. "Let's go."

When they reached the sidewalk, she found herself looking back. There sat the house—a picture-perfect Colonial. Around it, present-day Manhattan. Alive, wild, a little bit wicked, and still a place where people were just born, lived and died. The past and the present, interlocking. Countless stories above the ground. Countless stories below it. She closed her eyes. Not far away, theWorld Trade Towers had stood. So much tragedy. So much destruction. A certain sadness still permeated downtown, despite the fact that so much was up and running again. Somehow, centuries-old churches only blocks away had remained standing. History remembered, history lost.

It was an amazing city, and it was equally amazing the way the house stood where it did, with the modern world all around it. Every decade made a change, she reminded herself.

The house, she thought, was somehow a key to murder.

Matt's murder.

"What is it?" Joe asked.

"Nothing," she said quickly, forcing a smile. But it *was* something. Worlds colliding. Stories above the earth, stories below.

He tried to follow. Couldn't.

But just this morning, she had seen him. It hadn't lasted long, but she had seen him. Even so . . .

He had to let go.

No, he couldn't say goodbye. Not yet, not when he'd just learned to say hello. And now, because of Leslie, Joe was coming to the house. Joe had a sense that something wrong had happened there, and he was convinced that the truth needed to be told. Then . . .

He loved her, really loved her, and she deserved a long life and happiness, so then he would say goodbye.

"So . . . your mysterious sixth sense has struck again," Robert said, idly rubbing his thumb and forefinger over the beginning stubble of a gray beard.

"It had nothing to do with any sixth sense. I fell. Honest to God, I fell," Leslie said.

Robert shrugged disbelievingly. "Do you know how long Howard Carter looked for King Tut's tomb without finding it?"

"Robert," she protested, "it was pure dumb luck. And it's not even a total shock. City records indicated that the church had been there."

"Why don't you just get to it?" Joe asked Robert, amused. He sipped his beer, watching Leslie. They'd already ordered: steaks, potatoes and salads all around. Even Leslie had opted for a beer.

"Get to it?" Robert asked blandly.

"Come on. You know you want her to give you a hand."

Robert flushed. "No . . . no."

"Liar," Joe said with a laugh.

Robert's blush deepened. "All right. It's the missing prostitutes. After each disappearance we put men out on the street to ask a zillion questions that never have any answers. Mostly, we scratch our heads. Then the furor dies down and I'm left with a bunch of useless information that does me no good the next time. All in all, if I'm right and the cases are associated, we're talking about twelve missing women. In every case, they've just vanished off the street." He looked across the table at Joe. "Including the one who wasn't a hooker—Genevieve O'Brien."

Leslie looked at Joe. "The woman you're searching for," she said.

"I have to agree with Robert," he said. "At first, I wasn't sure, but the more I found out about just how involved she was with those women, the more sense it seemed to make. The best lead I have is that she stepped into a dark sedan. On the same street where half those girls worked."

"Strange," Leslie murmured awkwardly. "And you haven't found any bodies."

"No bodies. No blood. No sign of a struggle. Nothing," Robert said.

"There are a lot of ways for bodies to disappear," Joe reminded them.

"So," Leslie said, "you're looking for someone who has learned how to completely hide his crimes. He must be very bright." She turned to Joe. "Don't the profilers say that the usual age for a serial killer is between twenty-five and thirty-five?"

"Often," Joe agreed. "But not always."

Robert shook his head. "I'm glad you two have solved this thing."

They looked at each other sheepishly. "Sorry," Joe murmured.

"A dark sedan," Robert said. "That suggests middle class, probably white-collar. Maybe even someone who goes home after an abduction or murder to a wife and kids. Wouldn't be unusual."

"No," Joe agreed. "But let's not talk about murder over dinner, okay?"

The salads came and went. Leslie spoke enthusiastically about her time in Virginia, and Joe made them laugh with a few of the funnier details from his recent case in Las Vegas. But when coffee came, Robert returned to the subject of the disappearances.

"So . . . you both think our missing women are dead? And our one man, the Mimic, was a tranny. He liked to dress up and walk the streets with the girls. I guess he was good at what he did."

Leslie hesitated. "I'm afraid I do think they're dead. I assume you've had policewomen dressed up as prostitutes, working the same streets?"

"Nights on end. As soon as we pull them off, our guy knows. Apparently he can smell a policewoman a mile away."

"Then there's Genevieve. She wasn't a hooker, but she was close to them. Thing is, my witness says she went over to the car because she knew whoever was in it," Joe said.

"Presumably someone respectable," Leslie said.

"Great. In a city of millions, I'm now looking for someone respectable who drives a dark sedan," Robert said with a weary sigh. He frowned, looking at Joe. "So . . . now that you've spoken with Eileen Brideswell and looked into Genevieve's disappearance, you seem to think that it's connected to my hookers, as well."

"Yes, I do," Joe said.

Robert gazed over at Leslie thoughtfully. "Would you be willing to go to the street with me at night and see if . . . see if you get any hunches or vibes or whatever?"

"All right," Leslie said after a brief hesitation.

"No," Joe said flatly.

They both stared at him; Leslie was frowning.

"It would be better if she went with me. You're a nice cop, Robert, but you're still a cop. I'm not."

"You're a private investigator. Do hookers like investigators any better?" Robert asked.

"Frankly, yes, they do."

It was Robert's turn to frown.

Leslie leaned forward. "Robert, I'll help in any way I can, even though I honestly don't think I'm going to be able to help." If only he knew what led her to her discoveries, he wouldn't be so eager for her help, she thought. "But . . ."

"But?" Robert asked, curious.

"We need help, too."

"We?"

Robert stared across the table at them. Joe hoped he couldn't tell that he, too, had no idea what she was talking about.

"It was no accident."

"What are we talking about?" Robert asked.

Liar, she thought. He knew. "Hastings House," she said.

Robert groaned. "Don't you think I went over all the information we had with a fine-toothed comb?"

"And don't you think that explosion was pretty damn strange?" Leslie demanded.

"Accidents *are* strange. That's why they're accidents," Robert said testily. "Joe, you've been through the files. Everything points to—"

"It doesn't matter what everything points to. We both know that what's obvious is not necessarily the truth."

Robert groaned again. "You think some fanatic was trying to blow up the whole house? Why? Because he hates history and wants to see a skyscraper there?"

Leslie shook her head gravely. "No. If someone wanted the whole house blown up, it would have been."

Robert looked at Joe. "Did you instigate this?"

"Hey," he said gruffly, "Matt was my cousin. Don't ask me to accept something just because everyone else thinks it's obvious."

"Sometimes, when the sun is shining, it's daytime," Robert snapped.

"And sometimes, when it's dark, it's because there's an eclipse," Leslie snapped back.

"She's right," Joe said with a shrug.

"You two loved Matt. You don't want to accept that he died because of a stupid accident. I get it. But he's gone, and it *was* an accident. You have to learn to live with it."

"Matt wasn't the only one who died that night," Leslie said.

"But the thing is," Joe added, "I don't think it was an accident, and I can't help but think that Matt was targeted."

"Targeted?" Robert said. "Oh, come on!"

Joe was surprised when Leslie plunged in more quickly than he could. "Targeted. He was in the back room, and it was the back room that blew up."

"Because that's where the build-up in the line was," Robert said.

"You'll let me have the files again?" Joe demanded.

Robert threw up his hands. "I'll get you the files."

"That's not enough," Leslie said stubbornly. "If we need you to do something, you'll do it."

"You are . . . a mule," he told Leslie.

"Mule? Well, I've been called a cadaver dog before, so I guess mule is no worse."

Robert laughed. "Was I the one who called you that?"

"Maybe. I don't remember. But mule will do just fine."

He sighed. "More hopeless causes."

"Aren't they the best kind?" she teased.

Robert rolled his eyes, but he was smiling.

Leslie lifted her beer. "To us—and a solution to all our mysteries."

Joe felt a moment's unease. He didn't know why. Maybe because Leslie seemed so fearless.

"To us—and a solution to all our mysteries," Robert repeated. There was no skepticism in his voice, but there was no assurance, either.

"To us," Joe added simply.

Soon after, they left. Joe had left his car on the street near Hastings House. Robert offered them a lift, but it was only a few blocks back and the night was pleasant, so they opted to walk.

They walked in companionable silence for several

minutes. Then she turned to him with a smile, her eyes bright. "I have to know, just like you."

"We may never discover anything. Maybe it really was an accident."

"I just don't believe it," she said. "And you don't, either."

"Like Robert said, we both loved Matt," he reminded her.

"I know, but . . ."

Her words hung in the air. He was startled when, a moment later, she slipped her arm through his. Startled, and pleased, despite himself. She was counting on him as a friend, he thought.

Screw it, Matt. I can't help it. Damn, you were a lucky man.

He vowed to be the friend she needed without turning into a stinking lech. She had enough of those around her. She was strong. She could handle herself. But he still felt a sudden urge to smash Hank Smith's face.

Yeah, what about your own?

No way out of it. She was sheer seduction. Just by walking, talking . . . being.

"There's the house," he said, his voice husky as they turned a corner and Hastings House came into view.

"The house," she repeated softly, and she seemed distant for a minute.

When they reached the door, he knew that he didn't dare go in.

She didn't ask him.

In fact, it seemed that she changed a little, once they were there.

"That was a great dinner. Thank you."

"Sure. Nothing like discussing serial killers over a meal."

She smiled sadly at that. "They're out there."

"And it seems that there's one working this area. You be careful. Really careful."

"It's not like I actually go anywhere," she told him. "To work . . . and tonight I was out with you and Robert. I think I'm safe enough. . . . Well, good night, and thank you again."

" 'Night."

"When do you want to take a walk on the wild side?" she asked abruptly, surprising him.

"Whenever you're ready."

"Tomorrow night?"

"If your day isn't too exhausting," he told her.

"It won't be. Digging is fun, and luckily, the guys like to do the talking."

She stood on her toes and kissed his cheek.

"Good night. Set that alarm."

"Absolutely."

She went in. He listened, and could just hear her keying the alarm. Satisfied, he started down the walk, head bowed in thought as he turned onto the sidewalk and headed toward his car.

He heard the sudden revving of a motor.

He looked up just as a dark sedan shot past him on the quiet night street. He was in time to catch two numbers at the end of the license plate.

Six-three.

He looked back.

Where the hell had the car come from? The prostitutes' favorite corner wasn't far, only about four blocks down, one over.

He swore and raced toward his own car.

But he was too late, and he knew it. By the time he reached the corner of Broadway, there was nothing in sight but a Hummer and three taxis.

He stopped, irrationally tempted to go back to check on Leslie. In the rearview mirror, Hastings House seemed to look back at him like a living thing. Lights in the upstairs windows could have been eyes. The fanlight above the door could have been a mouth.

Upstairs, a light went out.

The alarm was on, he told himself. State-of-the-art. And the house wasn't far from One Police Plaza. She was safe. And he had to face it; she hadn't wanted to let him in.

Still, he drove back. He knew he should have been totally focused on finding Genevieve O'Brien, but he also knew he was doing all the right things, following the right leads.

Was the girl already dead?

There was no way to know. Not until he discovered the truth of where she had gone, and why.

Alone in the night, he swore out loud, drove around the block and parked again.

In front of Hastings House.

Where he spent the night, dozing in his car.

8

Matt didn't come to her that night.

Leslie lay awake for a long time, waiting, yearning for him to appear in the flesh.

Then she punched her pillows and made herself go to sleep, willing him into her dreams. But she woke early, all too aware that there had been no Matt—not even dreams of Matt—during the night. She rose, running her fingers through the tangles in her hair, and looked around.

"Please," she whispered. "I know you're here. Please . . . you have to let me see you."

Silence was her only answer.

Even though it was ridiculously early, she knew she wasn't going back to sleep, so she showered and dressed for the day, then went downstairs to make the coffee. It was when she was pouring water into the pot that she saw something with her peripheral vision. She held still for a moment, until she realized that the pot had overflowed and the water was running over her hands. She turned it off and looked toward the hearth.

Where she saw a woman apparently stirring something in a large pot hung over a ghostly fire.

Leslie remained silent, watching. The woman was young, pretty, wearing a mobcap over her soft blond hair.

After a long moment, Leslie spoke to her. "Please, don't leave," she said softly.

The woman froze; Leslie was sure she was about to fade away to nothing.

"Please," Leslie said very softly. "Who are you? Why are you here?"

The woman began to fade, then became more visible again.

"I was betrayed," she said. Her eyes became great pools of tears. "By one I trusted. One I loved," she whispered.

Suddenly she spasmed, arching slightly backward, then slumped forward and faded away completely.

Leslie inhaled, staring for a very long time at the spot where the woman had stood. But the woman was gone, and she knew it. Still, she felt a sense of elation. The apparition had not just appeared; it had spoken to her.

She turned, newly invigorated and wide awake, and finished making the coffee. A few minutes later, she heard a noise at the front door and Melissa came in. "You're up early."

"And you're at work early," Leslie replied.

Melissa nodded. "I have some paperwork to finish. I can't stop thinking about last night, though. I'm sure this house is haunted. I think a ghost put that missing money back on the table for me."

"Who knows?" Leslie said thoughtfully, then frowned suddenly. "Melissa, how long have you worked here?"

"Well, I was hired right before they had that party to open the place, but then they had to close it for a while because . . . well, you know."

"So what happened then?" Leslie asked.

"Greta—she insists we call her Greta—said she was sorry, but the society couldn't afford to keep us on while the house was being repaired, so I told her I'd just take a temporary job and come back here once it opened again. I love this house. I would never give up an opportunity to work here. And now that I know it's haunted . . ."

"Maybe."

Melissa pointed a finger at her. "You know it is."

"I do?"

Melissa gave her a smile as if to say it was okay that she was trying to pull the wool over her eyes. "You know it's haunted. You're special."

Leslie felt uneasy, as if she belonged in some carnival freak show. "Melissa . . ."

"If you see a ghost, you'll let me know, right?" Melissa implored.

"Sure. If we're standing here and a ghost appears, I'll let you know. And you let me know, too, right?"

"There was one here yesterday. That's why the books balanced."

"So we have a ghost who used to be a CPA, huh?"

Melissa frowned and looked hurt.

"I'm just teasing you," Leslie said quickly. "Who's to say a ghost didn't help you, right?" Leslie said, then went on to say, "If you still want to help with the dig, I'll arrange for you to come help on Saturday, how's that?"

Melissa looked as if she were experiencing pure rapture for the first time in her life.

"Great," Leslie said. "I'm going to head over there now."

"This early?"

"I like to get to the site ahead of the crowd."

Melissa nodded sagely. "Better for getting vibes, right?"

"Better for working."

"I brought doughnuts—you want one?"

"I'd love one, thank you."

"Actually, I keep eggs and bread and sandwich stuff in the fridge, too. You can help yourself."

Leslie helped herself to a doughnut. "Thanks. I owe you big time."

"It's my pleasure."

She wolfed down the doughnut, finished her coffee and thanked Melissa again. Then she headed out.

She was surprised to see Joe's car parked across the street. Frowning, she walked over to it. He looked up before she reached him, looking a little dismayed. But he had been sitting there going through files, and he didn't try to hide them.

"Hi," she said, her tone turning the simple word into a question.

"Hi," he said sheepishly.

"What are you doing out here?" she asked.

He lowered his lashes for a moment, then slid on a pair of dark glasses, effectively shielding whatever thoughts might have been evident in his eyes. He shrugged. "I saw a dark sedan leaving here last night. Just thought I should stick around."

She smiled slowly, a little irritated, but mostly grateful. "You've been here all night?" she asked him. "Thanks. I think. But, come on, you're a private investigator. How many dark sedans do you think there are in New York?"

"Okay, more than a few. Want a ride to work?"

"A couple of blocks?" she asked.

"Want a walk to work?" he asked.

"Sure."

He got out of the car. The sun was just beginning to come up over the southern tip of Manhattan. Skyscrapers reached up toward the heavens, bathed in a delicate pink light. There was no hustle and bustle yet. The muted pastels hid the sins of the city, cloaking the trash and decay.

She glanced over at Joe as they walked. He reminded her so much of Matt. She wanted to be close to him. Feel protected by his height and size. Touch his hair, stroke his shoulders.

Because he reminded her of Matt, she told herself. Which was a bad reason.

And it wasn't fair to him at all. He was a fine man in his own right.

"By the way, I'm sorry," she murmured.

"For what?"

"I know you lost someone, too. A girl . . ."

He gazed at her, offered a rueful smile, shrugged. "That was a long time ago."

"Do you ever really forget?" she asked.

"You don't forget, but you do go on. You learn to

laugh when you remember good things. A certain smile, a way of doing something. Oh, there's the guilt, too, of course. Why am I alive, when someone who deserved to live so much is gone? I've made my peace with the past." He was silent a minute. "Eventually, you will, too. It's harder when it's not the natural order of things, though. I still miss my parents, but they had a great life together. I honestly think my father died of loneliness after he lost my mother, but they were older and it was their time. But when it's someone young, cheated out of a natural life span, I guess we can't help but be bitter. But the truth is, long or short, life is a gift, and so long as we're alive, we need to appreciate that fact."

She grinned at him. "Trust me, I am grateful to be alive."

"Then you have to live your life to the fullest. Not just for yourself but for Matt. Follow your dreams. Look to the future."

She laughed. "Well, for me, that means digging for the past."

"Absolutely." He slipped his hand around hers and squeezed it.

A policewoman stationed on the corner near the dig gave them a pleasant nod. Leslie noticed that there was a greater police presence around the entire site than there had been previously. She stopped walking and looked around for a moment. So much that was new had been built on top of so much that was old, so much that was underground. Hastings House had been part of the Underground Railroad. She smiled ruefully to herself. She didn't know why that thought kept recurring to her. The word *underground* didn't always mean literally "under the ground," she reflected. Sometimes it meant below the scope of authority.

New York was definitely an underground city in every sense of the word.

"Where's the big excitement?" Joe asked.

"What?"

"You're staring awful hard at *something*."

"Sorry—just looking at the site and the buildings and . . . Just looking."

"New York. Gotta love it," Joe said.

"I do. Look at all the cops. I guess someone decided to step up security," she said.

"Your little 'accident' yesterday turned this into a major find," Joe reminded her.

At the gate, there were two guards. Leslie started to reach for her identification, but the taller one nodded at her and said, "We all know you, Miss MacIntyre. Come on in."

"Well, I'll leave you here," Joe said.

"And I'll see you tonight. If you're awake," she teased.

"I'll be awake," he promised her.

She walked on through the temporary wire gates that allowed entry to the site and carefully made her way through the grid, heading straight for the entry to the crypt.

Glow lights that couldn't possibly catch fire had

been set in two corners of the room. Leslie left them where they were and fumbled in her bag for her flashlight. Turning that on, she looked around.

Laymon, bless him, had already staked out his territory. Large signs propped against two niches in the wall read Do Not Touch!!!

But there was no such sign on the niche where Brad and Laymon had found the record book. She hoped it hadn't already been taken away to be preserved. She felt a little guilty, knowing that any touch might injure the old paper, but she had a feeling she might find a reference to the woman whose remains she had found, as well as to the child, Mary, and she was determined to find the little girl's remains so she could reunite mother and child.

Very carefully, she moved to the niche and found the book. Leather-bound, and protected for so many years in this sealed environment, it was in far better shape than she had dared to hope. Then again, she reminded herself, some books—well, scrolls—had survived for millennia.

A breath of cold air suddenly seemed to sweep around her. She frowned and looked over her shoulder. The place was in shadow, but she could tell she was alone. Even so . . .

"Hello?" she said softly.

She frowned. There could certainly be more ghosts here, of course, but she hadn't felt the sense that some disembodied being from a different time had joined her, even though surely there were at least a few here.

She was certain that some of the people interred in this earth had died violent or miserable deaths. No, she had felt a breeze. Movement. Not just the chill that some suggested accompanied ghosts, but a real breeze. As if someone or something had joined her in the crypt and disturbed the air by moving.

She shrugged. Strange. Even when she had first started seeing ghosts, she hadn't felt such a sudden chill. She had felt fear, but only the natural fear of the unknown. She had never felt the sense of unease that had ridden on that breeze, a feeling of something icy, like a warning trickle down her spine.

"Enough," she said aloud, then focused on the shadows. The room wasn't that big. She was obviously alone.

Gritting her teeth, she dismissed the strange sensation and returned her attention to the book.

As she had hoped, it was the parish register, filled with the dates of weddings, births and, of course, deaths.

She didn't run her fingers down the pages. She would never disrespect such a precious relic that way. But her eyes roamed. The book had been kept by a Father Browne, and his script was clear, with only a slight flourish. So many people. These were not the rich and famous, though she was sure there were a few rabble-rousers among them, since most of the entries were from the 1850s, when gang violence had been rampant. The *Times* had written about the desperate throngs, saying that the streets had been filled with ruffians, and there had been no promise of safety anywhere in the disorderly metropolis. May 1849 had brought the Astor Place riots, with many dying when a mob had protested the appearance of the aristocratic English actor William Macready, believing the role of Macbeth belonged to American luminary Edwin Forrest. Had a theatrical question really created such a stir, or had the true cause been the great chasm growing between the rich and poor of the city? Most people believed that the wretched living conditions of so many had lain behind the violence, fanned into action on the pretext of cultural controversy.

She went back and quickly noted that some of the earliest recorded deaths in the book were from May 1849. She wondered if any of the deceased had met their fates during the riots.

Next she went carefully, page by page, looking for a child named Mary.

She found ten of them. With a sigh, she knew she was going to have to find out Mary's surname before she could go any further.

Bit by bit she grew aware of a slight noise, like a muted shuffle. She had been so intent on the records, she realized, that she had forgotten her strange feeling of a few minutes earlier.

There really did seem to be something—someone?—hidden in the shadows behind her.

She straightened, determined that she wasn't about to start being afraid of the dark.

No good.

Closing the book, she turned, certain she had heard a noise. But no matter how intently she peered into the room's dark corners, there didn't seem to be anyone else there. Shifting earth, she thought. Or a breeze coming in through the hole in the wall where she had originally fallen through. They needed to shore up the place before they did much more work in it or allowed more people in, she decided.

She turned back to the niche where the book had lain, hoping more treasures might be stored there.

As she turned, she knew. *Knew.*

Someone was behind her.

Someone was there with her, unseen, hidden, but how? Where?

She started to turn.

Too late.

She felt a sudden, fierce pain knife through the back of her head. She staggered against the wall and fell.

Back at his car, Joe stared across the street to Hastings House and saw the door open. The woman in charge of ticketing came out, Melissa . . . something, he recalled. He'd talked to her in the course of investigating the explosion.

She looked up at the house, stretched and smiled. He felt as if he were interrupting a personal moment, her pleasure in just being there was so evident.

He walked over to her anyway. "Melissa, good morning."

For a moment she stared at him as if she were seeing

a ghost. "Oh, hi. Sorry. We've met . . . right? You're Joe Connolly, the P.I.? You look so much like your cousin. I talked to you after the explosion, right?"

"Right. And I'm friends with Leslie." He didn't see any reason to tell her that they'd just met a few days ago.

"Would you like some coffee?"

"Sure."

He followed her inside, wondering why he felt that just being in the house would somehow help him.

"Leslie is phenomenal," Melissa said as they reached the kitchen.

"Yes, she is."

"Doughnut?" she asked.

"I'd love one."

"Doughnuts get such a bad rap these days," she told him.

"Once in a while, they're good for the soul," he said.

Melissa looked around the kitchen. "I do love this house so much. Oh!" She blushed, realizing how she sounded. "I'm sorry. I know that your cousin . . . well, I'm sorry."

"It's not the fault of the house, Melissa," he said.

She leaned toward him, a slightly faraway look in her eyes. "Maybe it is."

"Pardon?"

"Maybe . . . I don't know. This house makes me feel . . . weird. Can a house be jinxed . . . or . . . evil?" she asked.

He arched a brow. "No," he said firmly.

"Sorry," she said quickly. "And it's not bad vibes I get here. In fact, I should get bad vibes, after what happened, but . . . I get good ones. If the place *is* haunted, though . . . it could be Revolutionary War ghosts, or Civil War ghosts, or Irish gang ghosts. . . ." She got a faraway look in her eyes, as if she'd traveled back in time herself.

Joe stared at her, feeling a strange creeping sensation along his nape. Hell. He was six foot three and two hundred and twenty pounds of muscle. He'd faced cold-blooded killers in his time, and he sure as hell wasn't afraid of the dark. So how the hell had this tiny woman given him the shivers? But it wasn't her, he realized.

It was the house.

Oh, like hell.

"You weren't at the party that night, were you?" he asked Melissa.

"Me? No. I'm just the hired help."

"You're far more than hired help," he told her, and watched her flush. She seemed to thrive on the least compliment. Earnest and sincere, and not homely but also not a raving beauty, she had probably worked hard for every achievement in her life. She deserved a few compliments, he decided.

"You weren't here, either, were you?"

"No, I wasn't." A strange sense of cold suddenly washed over him as he spoke. He looked around, thinking there had to be an air-conditioning vent somewhere near, but he didn't see one.

Then, inexplicably, while he was just standing there, he lost his balance and stumbled.

Disturbed, he frowned and strode past Melissa into the back servants' pantry, where the explosion had happened. Everything was perfectly restored now, but even so, he walked over and stood by the hearth, wondering exactly where Matt had been standing.

An odd sense of pressure filled his head.

Leslie . . .

He must be going crazy. He could have sworn he heard her name, but there was no one else in the room.

He felt torn between the urge to stay and discover what was going on here to spook him and the irrational urge to run back to the dig site to see Leslie, as if she were in danger.

He felt almost as if he were pushed to join her, as if a strange whisper in his head was urgently telling him to go to her.

Ridiculous. She was working and perfectly safe.

"What is it?" Melissa asked, looking at him from the doorway.

"Nothing. Nothing at all. Thanks for the doughnut. I'll be seeing you."

He was out of the house in a flash and found himself running down the street toward the dig.

She blinked. There was a blinding light shining in her eyes, and for a moment she thought she was staring at a monster, then realized it was a man.

Professor Laymon was staring down at her, the light

from his electric lantern reflected in the lenses of his glasses, his gaunt face made eerie by the play of light and shadow.

"She's fine," he announced to someone outside her field of vision. "She's fine."

A monster? Or a man? *Someone* had hit her.

She kept silent, suddenly suspicious.

"We need to call 911," she heard Brad announce worriedly.

"No, no," she said, waving a hand in the air, sitting up. The dark room swayed for a minute, but then her vision cleared almost instantly. She looked around and frowned. She definitely wasn't alone anymore. And she wasn't by the wall anymore, either. She was sitting in a pile of rubble, halfway across the room.

"I don't see—" she began.

"You got a good clunk on the head," Brad said.

"A clunk on the head?" she repeated.

"From the ceiling," Laymon explained. "A chunk of plaster fell on you. We need to install proper safety precautions in here."

There was a commotion just outside, and suddenly Joe Connolly was pushing through the entrance. He rushed over to her, looking like a fullback ready to face the opponent's starting line, and stared reproachfully at Brad and Laymon. She followed the direction of his accusing gaze to see Robert Adair standing nearby, looking acutely uncomfortable. And when she squinted toward the entrance, she saw a host of workers and more policemen, including Ken Dryer, looking in at her. Hank Smith was there, too, she noticed.

"What the hell happened?" Joe demanded gruffly.

"Time—and a weak chunk of ceiling," Brad explained. He stared at Joe and apparently decided that he had some influence over her. "She should see a doctor. She took a real bump to her head."

"I'll see to it," Joe agreed.

"No," she protested, gritting her teeth as she got to her feet. *Had she really been hit by a piece of the ceiling? Had she imagined the cold, and the sense of someone else being there?* Whatever had really happened, she wasn't about to protest their explanation. Not unless and until she had something to offer instead that wouldn't make her sound crazy. Even so . . . "No," she repeated. "I mean it." She could hear anxious voices from outside, and she forced herself to take a step on her own. "I'm fine," she insisted.

"You're not fine," Brad said.

"I *am* fine," she assured him.

"It's better to be safe than sorry," Joe warned. He looked seriously worried. What was he doing there? she wondered. He'd stayed in his car all night to keep an eye on her, not to mention he undoubtedly wanted a shower and a change of clothing. Plus, he had a missing woman to find.

"He's right, you know," Robert Adair said.

"It couldn't have been all that bad," Laymon put in. "She seems fine to me."

She looked at the professor. She knew that he cared

about her. She also knew that he cared more about his work than about any human being. If she'd been hurt badly enough to require a doctor, the city might insist on shutting down the dig until their safety inspectors okayed it. Laymon would be fit to be tied. The ceiling undoubtedly had to be shored up, but he would want to supervise, to be in charge. He wouldn't want his precious find contaminated in any way.

"The professor's right. I really am absolutely fine," she repeated firmly.

Robert shook his head. Laymon sighed. Brad stared at her.

Joe took her by the arm, turning her to face him. "Fine, huh? So *you* say. Let's take a little trip back to Hastings House, get some ice, keep you moving . . . and maybe stop by a doctor's, quietly, just so he can take a quick look at you, check you out."

Brad spoke up in support of Joe.

"Leslie, you were flat on your back, out cold, when we found you."

The light was blocked for a minute, and then she saw Ken Dryer—clearly not at all happy about what the dirt was doing to his clothing—slide carefully down to join them. "Leslie, what happened? Are you okay?"

She knew she should be grateful, but everyone's concern was starting to get on her nerves. And in the back of her mind was a question. *What had really happened?* Had she turned to look around, been hit on the head by a falling piece of plaster, and fallen this far away from where she'd been standing?

183

For a moment, she once again felt that strange sense of fear that had prickled at her nape when she'd been alone in the room. She wasn't accustomed to being afraid. The dark didn't usually hold any terrors for her.

After all, she didn't just see ghosts. She carried on conversations with them.

"I'll walk you home," Joe said gruffly. "And see you to the doctor."

"She needs her head examined," Brad said. Leslie looked at him, frowning. The way he'd said it, it sounded as if he thought more was wrong with her than a possible concussion.

"Guys . . ." she murmured uncomfortably.

"Leslie, the site isn't going anywhere," Laymon told her, his voice unusually gentle. Apparently there *was* a soul somewhere beneath that academic facade.

"You'll have to go out the back or else face the music out front," Brad said. He shrugged. "I don't know how, but the minute anything happens, we get a flock of reporters."

"Dryer can handle them, I'm sure," Robert Adair said.

Brad grinned at her. "I'll join him," he said with a rueful smile.

"Go to it," Leslie told him, smiling in return. "I'll see you all later."

"No, you won't. You'll take the day off," Laymon said firmly. Brad halted at the exit.

"Let's go," Joe said, equally firm.

Maybe they were right. But she didn't feel at death's

door. She had one hell of a headache, but she could handle that with aspirin. Mostly, she realized, she was angry at being unable to figure out what the hell had happened.

"Leslie, I'll bring in my own engineers, and I'll sit on top of them like a fly on roadkill," Laymon said.

"Leslie, let's go," Joe repeated quietly.

For a minute she was tempted to remind him that she wasn't a child, and that even though he looked like Matt, he *wasn't* Matt. They didn't have a relationship that stretched back forever. But she knew they were probably right. An exam or an X-ray wouldn't hurt. It would be the mature and sensible thing to do. As she headed for the exit, Robert set a hand on her shoulder. "I'll be in touch."

As she emerged from the crypt, a group of workers backed away in a single body. She smiled and waved. "I'm fine," she said reassuringly. "Go on back to work—we've got a lot to do."

With Joe holding her arm and Brad on the other side of her, they walked across the site in the direction of the back exit. Suddenly she stopped, pulling him to a halt with her.

"Wait!" she demanded.

"What?" Joe asked.

She looked around. "Who found me?" she asked quietly.

Brad frowned. "Laymon and I. You were flat on the ground, unconscious. We were really scared, Leslie."

"You were together?"

"Yes, why?" Brad asked.

"No one else was in there with me, right?"

"No. Why?" Brad asked, looking puzzled.

"Right. Of course." She forced a smile, said goodbye to Brad as he joined Dryer and started walking again.

Joe and Leslie departed via the rear and in a few minutes they were approaching Hastings House.

The morning rush was on and the sidewalks were full. Odd. Around the site, she couldn't move without someone stopping her. Here—even dirty and tousled—she was barely noticed. Serious, almost grim-faced businessmen and women were headed to their financial district offices. One man looked so depressed that she wanted to tell him to lighten up.

She looked at Joe, who wore a frown, as well. She smiled. "Well, I guess it's a good thing you didn't shower yet," she told him.

He glanced at her and seemed surprised by her easy grin. "What happened in there?" he asked.

She frowned. "A chunk of ceiling fell. Hey, that place has been buried for a century. Not even the Pyramids have survived without some damage, and this place was nowhere near that well built." She was trying to make him smile. No dice.

"I wonder if you should be working that dig."

"What are you talking about? It's what I do."

He shook his head.

"In fact," she said thoughtfully, staring at him, "how did *you* happen to be there?"

He stared straight ahead and didn't answer.

"Joe?"

"I don't know," he said at last, almost unwillingly.

"What do you mean, you don't know?"

"I mean, I don't know. I just . . ." He stopped speaking, shook his head again. "I just had a feeling I should go find you."

"Really?"

"Yeah, really. Instinct, fluke—I don't know."

"Well, that was really sweet of you," she said.

"Sweet?" He stared at her as if she'd lost her mind.

"Yes, it was very nice of you to worry."

He didn't reply to that, but his strides increased.

"Hey, slow down. I'm a fast walker, but I'm practically running to keep up with you," she said.

"Sorry."

Then they were at the house. It wasn't officially open yet, but the door was ajar and Melissa popped out just as they started up the steps.

"Leslie, are you all right?" she cried anxiously, hurrying out to greet her.

"Fine," Leslie said, frowning. "What—"

"The news announced that there had been an accident," Melissa said, then gave Joe a strange look. "You went from here to the site?"

"Yeah."

"Wow," Melissa said, looking at him in wonder.

"Hey there, is everyone all right?"

Leslie looked toward the entrance. Jeff Green, in complete Colonial grab, was standing in the doorway, his face wearing an expression of concern. Leslie had to smile. He could have been an eighteenth-century gentleman, standing on his porch to survey his domain. He reminded her a little bit of Ichabod Crane at that moment, rather than Washington, because, seen from below, he was so tall and lean.

"Everything's fine," she said as he, too, stepped outside. He ruined the impression of historical perfection when he reached into his Colonial jacket pocket and produced a pack of Marlboros. He lit up, still frowning. "Melissa and I had the TV in the office on and we heard what happened. That policeman—Dryer—came on to say that everything was all right, but that's what the cops always say. We couldn't help being worried."

"Thanks for your concern. I'm pretty dirty and I've got a headache, but that's about it," Leslie said.

"Well—" Joe began.

She stepped on his foot. He looked down at her, brows lowering. She stared at him, and he smiled in understanding. She was grateful, but growing weary of constantly saying that she was fine.

"Where's Tandy?" Leslie asked, changing the subject.

"Unless we have school groups or a major tour scheduled, she takes Wednesdays off and I have Thursdays, and we both take Sunday," he explained.

"We pull in our biggest crowds on Friday and Saturday," Melissa explained. "We *should* be open on Sundays, too."

"The Sabbath?" Jeff protested, sounding convincingly Colonial. Then he grinned. "Hey, I like my Sundays off."

"I could work them. And we could make big bucks," Melissa said.

"Well, if you guys don't mind, I'm going to go in and shower," Leslie said. She looked at Joe. He was dirty and covered in plaster dust, as well.

It occurred to her that, concealed in his strangely tinted shield of grime, he could pass for the ghost of his cousin.

"I'll wait," Joe said.

"You could go home and shower."

"I could, but I won't. I'll take you to my buddy, Dr. Granger, first."

"Doctor! What's wrong?" Melissa demanded, her voice full of concern.

"Joe will explain," Leslie said. He'd opened his mouth, so he could take care of telling them what had happened, she decided.

She entered the house and rushed up the stairs. In her room, she quickly shed her dirty clothing, turned on the water and stepped into the shower. The heat washed over her deliciously, and she turned up the force of the water. She always tried to conserve resources where she could. At that moment, though, she was grateful that the Historical Association had installed modern plumbing and a really good water heater. She let the steam roll around her and the water beat down. Washing her hair, she felt the bump on the top of her head. Not really all that bad, she told herself.

As she stood there, she began to feel the oddest sensation, as if she were being cradled by the steam and the water. Tenderly held.

She stood dead still. Was it her imagination? Or . . . ?

"Matt?" she said softly, her voice almost lost against the rushing of the water.

There was no reply.

Just the sensation.

So she stood, water and heat cascading all around her, barely breathing. Wondering. It was as if she were being held with such a gentle touch because she had just survived a great danger and returned home. As if she were a soldier who had been off to war and come home at last, despite the danger.

A loud knocking on her bedroom door broke the spell.

She realized that the water—no matter how good the heater was—had grown cold.

She turned it off quickly, wrapped herself in a towel and hurried out.

"Leslie?" Joe. And he sounded worried.

"I'm okay—sorry."

She heard him swear. "I was about to break the door down! I'd thought you'd passed out in the shower."

"No . . . I got carried away enjoying the steam and the heat," she replied. "I'm sorry, I'll be right out, I swear."

"Take your time. I was just worried."

She heard his footsteps recede down the hall.

Shaking, she sat at the foot of the bed.

"Matt?" she said aloud again.

Nothing, no sense that he was there, not even the hint of a breeze from beyond . . .

She was losing her mind. No. She knew better; she knew that sometimes, something remained after death. She knew that ghosts did exist.

But what about this particular ghost?

Was she inventing him, just because she so desperately wanted to see him?

"Matt?" she repeated softly.

But there was still nothing.

Nothing at all.

She dressed quickly, choosing good walking sandals and a black knit dress, not at all certain what the rest of the day—and the night—would bring.

She dried her hair and applied some makeup.

But when she was ready, she paused again. "Matt. I know you're here. You have to be here. And . . . I want you to know that Joe and I are going to find out exactly what happened. And, Matt, I know you know this, but . . . I love you so much."

Loved, she reminded herself. *Loved.* Matt was . . .

Dead.

"I *do* love you," she whispered aloud. "And I *will* discover the truth."

She started out the door . . . and was suddenly certain she felt a gentle touch at the base of her spine. She turned, but once again there was nothing.

She stood in the hallway, entirely alone.

9

The doctor's visit turned out to be a total waste of time, at least in Leslie's opinion. She'd insisted she was fine, and apparently she was right. She had a bump on her head but no concussion. Not unexpectedly, the doctor was concerned that she had blacked out, but she convinced him it had been for no more than a few seconds. He told her that she could check into a hospital for observation if she chose.

She didn't choose.

When they left the doctor's office, Joe, who'd cleaned up as best he could at Hastings House, decided that lunch would be a good option.

"Hungry?" he asked Leslie.

"Sure. I guess."

"Remember, any sign of an upset stomach could mean something more serious," he warned her.

"The skull is the hardest bone in the body," she told him. "Did you know that?"

"I know that *yours* is hard," he said.

"I'm willing to bet *yours* is granite," she returned. "Lunch sounds good. But should you be wasting all this time on me? You have a girl to rescue."

"Or a body to find," he said dully.

"You don't believe that Genevieve is still alive?"

"I want to. But usually, in a case like this . . ."

"I know."

"We'll pop in here," he said, opening the door to a pub.

She looked at him. "Are you sure you have time? You really are spending too much time on me."

"I don't think anyone could ever spend too much time on you," he told her. He said the words lightly, but he knew he meant every one of them.

"Very gallant," she said. "Still . . ."

"Don't worry, I'm working."

"Oh?"

"We're at O'Malley's."

"So I see."

"Eileen Brideswell's favorite place. Not ostentatious, real Irish owners . . . a family hangout for the O'Briens. I'm sure Genevieve hung around here, too, so I can ask some questions while we're eating."

"And do you think that will really help you any?"

"I think she disappeared in a dark sedan and she was taken by someone she knew. It sounded as if it was a decent car, so I need to learn who she was hanging around with, and this might be one of the places where they spent time."

"Aha."

A pretty woman with a broad Irish accent approached them with a smile of recognition for Joe and led them to a cozy booth.

"Special is Irish bacon and cabbage," she told them. "And, if I do say so myself, our potato soup is the best in New York." She grinned and added, "Maybe in all of the New World." With a wink, she left them.

"A friend?" Leslie asked.

"I've been here now and then," Joe said. "But I think

she saw me with Eileen Brideswell, and that makes all the difference."

Their waitress approached them. She had dark hair, brilliant green eyes and a definite accent. Her name was Bridget.

"What would you like?" Joe asked Leslie.

"What else? Potato soup and the bacon and cabbage," she said, with a light in her eyes.

"The same," Joe told Bridget.

"I'll bring the soup right out," Bridget promised with a bright smile and flashing eyes.

"Bridget, how long have you worked here?" Joe asked.

"Oh . . . well, since I came into the country. A bit over six months now, I'll be thinking."

Joe reached into his jacket and produced a picture of Genevieve O'Brien. "Did you know this girl?"

"Genevieve O'Brien?" A look of deep sorrow entered Bridget's eyes. "That I did," she said sadly. She stared at Joe. "Ah, you're the fellow looking for her, eh? For Mrs. Brideswell?"

He nodded. "Did she come in frequently?"

"Well, now, I can't say frequently. But you know, she was working sometimes not far from here, so she had the occasional lunch here, yes. A lovely girl, she was. My heart breaks to think what might've happened to her."

"Did she come in alone?"

A slow grin lifted Bridget's rosy cheeks. "Sometimes, yes. Sometimes she'd be bringing a woman in with her, and they'd be . . . well, all cleaned up. But I would kind of know when she would bring in a . . . well, I guess the term here would be 'working girl.' She tried to make life better for people."

Joe nodded, noticing the way Leslie was listening to Bridget, her own heart seeming to break for the girl she'd never known.

"You're in her booth, you know," Bridget said.

"We are?" Leslie asked.

"Oh, aye. She had the same booth—whenever it was free, of course. But Mrs. O'Malley . . ." She paused and indicated the hostess who had seated them. "She'd often hold it open, thinking Miss O'Brien might come by. The family was very supportive from the time her father-in-law, the elder Mr. O'Malley— he's retired now, left the place to his son—first opened here. So Mrs. O'Malley—"

"Was she dating anyone, do you know?"

"I'm just a waitress here," Bridget said.

He smiled. "That doesn't mean you might not have noticed if she had someone special. Did she ever come in here with a man?" Joe asked.

Bridget frowned. "Once or twice, I guess."

"Lunchtime? Cocktail hour? Dinner?"

"I saw her in here with a fellow once or twice. I think the one man was her boss. And the other . . . well, I guess she worked with him, too." She offered a quick smile. "The one fellow was quite a looker. The boss . . . well, he wasn't ugly as sin or anything, but he was a grump. You'll have to excuse me now,

195

please. I've got food that needs serving."

She smiled and left them.

"You think she was dating someone who turned out to be . . . bad?" Leslie asked Joe.

He shook his head thoughtfully, sipping the coffee Bridget had poured when she came to take their order. "No. I don't believe she was dating at all." He cocked his head, smiling ruefully. "I've done this a long time. I've been through all the basics. I've talked to her old friends, old flames. Her heaviest relationship was with a guy in college. He moved to Alaska to be a lumberjack and hasn't come back since. She had a hard time with her father, I know. He was the kind who demanded perfection. I think he spent most of his life trying to fight the 'lazy Irish' stereotype to show the world that the Irish were hardworking and intelligent, so much so that he never let her be a child."

Leslie stared back at him, sipping her own coffee.

He went on. "But she loved him anyway. I'm sure, when they had their last blowup and she walked away, she never imagined he would die before they made peace. She had a strong sense of family and really loved her aunt, too.

"So I'm pretty sure she plunged into work instead of taking time for a personal life—and I think she was trying so hard with those prostitutes because she had listened to her father so long. I think she felt that helping women get off the streets was like reaching back into the past." He met her eyes as he spoke. "A lot of Irish immigrants with nowhere else to turn

196

became prostitutes, and I think Genevieve felt she was helping to make that right by helping these women now."

"And you think, if she were able to, she would contact her aunt?"

He nodded.

The potato soup arrived.

He'd enjoyed it before and was irrationally glad when Leslie said, "It really *is* the best potato soup ever."

"You never came here before?" he asked her.

"Never. It's a big city, you know."

"Yeah, I do know. It's just that . . ."

"What?"

He shook his head.

"What?" she persisted.

"When we were kids, Matt loved this place."

"Ah." She shrugged. "We ate in Brooklyn a lot."

"I eat in Brooklyn a lot."

"And there you go—we never ran into each other."

"I haven't been in New York a lot the past few years."

Bridget brought their plates, her bright green eyes smiling. "So many people think they're going to get a pack of fatty bacon strips on their plates." She frowned. "I put the plates down and they say, 'Oh, goodness, the bacon—it's like pork.' What do they think bacon is?" she asked incredulously.

They both laughed politely.

Joe asked her, "Bridget, if I were to bring in pictures, do you think you'd be able to recognize the men Genevieve came here with?"

"I would, I think. Most probably. The one fellow . . . it was cocktail hour. Dark and busy in here. I'm not as sure about him, but I could try."

"Thanks."

"Delighted to help," she said.

When she left, Leslie asked him, "What pictures do you have?"

"At the moment, her boss's. A few old friends."

"So there really is a method to your madness—or at least your dining choices," Leslie said with a smile. He was glad to see she was eating well and really did seem to feel fine.

"Do you still have a headache?" he asked her.

"Only if I forget and touch my head," she told him, then stared at him seriously. "It's amazing that you showed up," she said.

He shrugged. "Maybe there is such a thing as ESP."

"You doubt it?"

"Of course. Why—do you believe you have it?"

"ESP? No. But there have been so many documented reports of it. I just read about one really sad situation. A mother woke up, sensing her daughter, who was serving in the army in the Middle East, was in danger. She called all over, trying to reach her daughter or at least find out how she was. It turned out she had been killed, just when her mother woke up, feeling so scared."

"Hmm," Joe murmured.

"And there have been dozens of cases involving identical twins. Sometimes one just knew when the other one needed help."

"Hmm," he repeated.

"So," she said, grinning, "you must have ESP."

He lifted his cup to her, studying her face. "You know, Robert Adair is certain you have some kind of psychic gift."

"Really?"

"Do you?"

"Who knows?" she said lightly. "Shall we go?"

"I'll get the check," he said.

It turned out that they didn't have one. Mrs. O'Malley insisted on picking up the lunches, so he left a hefty tip for Bridget and they left.

"I should go back to work," Leslie said.

"You were told not to. How about coming back out to my place for a while? I want to clean up and check my e-mail, and we can't look for Didi Dancer or any of the other girls until later."

For a moment she looked undecided. Then she shrugged. "Sure."

As they drove, Joe caught her looking pensively out the window. "What's so interesting?"

"City above the ground, city below the ground," she replied.

He frowned. She grinned ruefully.

"I can't get that thought out of my head, for some reason. Take the crypt we've discovered. So much had been built on top of it that no one had any idea it was even there. Look at the city we see from the car, then take the subway and you don't see any of it. You're traveling like a mole."

"Very true." He frowned, staring at her hard. "What happened this morning?"

She shrugged. She didn't know him that well yet. She had to keep reminding herself that he wasn't Matt. "A piece of the ceiling fell on me," she said.

"Are you sure?"

"They showed me where it caved in," she told him.

He lived in an old brownstone, the first floor and basement of which were his. He watched her examine the place as they entered. She looked around, smiling. He thought it was comfortable. He had a huge sofa and several armchairs in the living room, with an entertainment system in a polished oak cabinet facing it. There was an old hearth, and a display of the antique swords and rifles he had collected over the years. He had a surprisingly large kitchen, a nice dining area, a bedroom, an office and even an alcove that could function as a guest room. The basement hosted his pool table and some beat-up chairs.

"Well?" he inquired.

"Well, what?"

"Does it rate okay?"

She laughed. "Great bachelor quarters," she told him. With an amused grin, she added, "Very manly."

"Can I get you anything—I just want to check my e-mail and get cleaned up."

"I'm fine. I'll see if I approve of your music collection," she told him.

He left her, striding for his office. He'd sent out a number of inquiries to people who might have information on Genevieve, but he had a hunch so strong that he was willing to put money on it that finding Genevieve hinged on finding the right dark sedan— and the man driving it. Still, he had to go through the motions.

As he booted up the computer, hc picked up the sleazy magazine with the story about Genevieve. It was one of those articles that began by praising a person, then started tearing her down inch by inch. He'd never heard of the scandal before, but the article hinted of some affair around the time of Genevieve's birth, and talked about her father's coldly autocratic treatment of her. It was skillfully written, implying without directly saying anything that Genevieve might be the result of her mother's affair with another man. He leaned back. He'd read the article many timcs already, but he felt as if he were missing something. He started to read it one more time.

Joe's place was warm and inviting. The furniture was solid and the wood was polished. She had a feeling he enjoyed spending time at home, but also that he didn't fuss over it. She assumed he had someone in to clean—there wasn't much dust.

She wandered over to the cabinet and started going

through Joe's CDs. As she did, she noticed movement behind her and turned.

A man in a New York Regimental uniform was sitting on the sofa; he looked as if he had belonged to some kind of Irish brigade.

He was intent, frowning, concentrating, as he stared at her.

"You can see me," he said after a moment.

"Yes."

"You can see me," he repeated, almost in awe.

"Yes," she said again.

"And you're not scared? You're not going to start screaming?"

She smiled. "No. I mean, you don't intend me any harm, do you?"

"Harm to a lady?" He sounded outraged.

"I'm sorry, I meant no offense."

He was about thirty-five, she thought, gaunt, and his face was prematurely wrinkled; he looked old for his age. But then, she imagined, war could easily do that to a man. His hair was sandy, and he had a small mustache and neatly trimmed beard. His eyes were a soft brown, emphasized by flyaway brows.

He still seemed to be in awe. Then he rose, smiling. "Forgive me," he said anxiously. He looked a little uncomfortable and rubbed his leg. "Picked up some shell at Shiloh," he explained. "Please, sit."

She realized that he wouldn't sit again unless she did, so she perched on the edge of the chair, and he took a seat again. He continued to stare at her.

"All these years . . . kids coming, growing up, moving on . . . no one has ever seen me."

She hesitated, speaking carefully. She was becoming more comfortable with her gift, and thanks to Nikki and Adam Harrison, she knew that all apparitions were different, that they often interacted with the living in different ways. Most of them wanted, or needed, something.

"I see you," she said. Then she asked, "Why are you here?"

"I can't leave the music," he told her.

"Pardon?" He couldn't be talking about Joe's CD collection.

"I had a march published, just before the war. And then an étude. But . . . there was so much more. I didn't know if I was coming back or not—no man did." A frown creased his brow again. "You're from the South," he said suddenly.

"Originally. I've lived in New York many years." She didn't have an accent, or at least only a very slight one, so how had he known?

He was looking at her warily now.

"I'm glad to say that we're all one nation now," she said. How could she explain to him just how much had changed since the Civil War? Or that even now there were still remnants of that struggle that needed to be healed?

"Very glad," she continued earnestly. "As one nation, we're strong."

"I hid my music, but when I came back . . . I wanted

so badly to see more of it published. But I was always ill . . . my niece looked after me. When I died, she met a fine young lad. He'd lost a leg at Gettysburg, but he was still a fine man, a whole man, even minus a limb. I was glad to watch them here. To see their children grow." He stopped reminiscing and looked at her again. "May I tell you about my music?"

"Of course," she said.

Joe set the article down, thinking he would pick it up again later. Whatever it said that he hadn't seen before, he wasn't getting it now, either. He'd have to try again, with fresh eyes.

He ran through his e-mail, but as he'd expected, it didn't contain anything useful. He went into the bathroom that connected the office to his bedroom and quickly showered, shaved and threw on a change of clothes, then walked out to the living room.

Leslie didn't notice him at first. She had moved to the chair and was looking animatedly at the sofa. If he hadn't known it was empty, he would have sworn she was deep in conversation with someone sitting there.

"Leslie?"

"Oh!" Startled, she turned toward him.

"Are you all right?"

"Sure."

Puzzled, he pressed on. "Was . . . someone here?"

"Don't be ridiculous. I'd never let anyone into your house."

He took a seat on the sofa, directly opposite her. She

wasn't sitting back in the chair but was perched on the edge, the way she would have been if she'd been talking to someone sitting exactly where he was now. He reached for her hands. "Leslie . . ."

"I'm fine," she said very softly, then pulled one hand away and touched his cheek. He felt his heart flutter. She was close. Her scent was alluring. The light in her eyes was enchanting. The dip of her scoop-neck knit dress was arousing.

And she was Matt's woman.

But Matt was dead.

And she was touching him.

He caught her hand. It was a delicate hand, with long, elegant fingers, clean and soft despite the fact that she spent her days digging in old earth. He held her palm against his face, feeling the thunder of both his heart and his libido.

It would be easy, so easy, to draw her to him, hold her close. Kiss her lips, feel the silk of her tongue. Touch her. Know her naked flesh. He'd known his share of women over the years. If Nancy had lived, he would have stayed in love all his life, he thought. But she hadn't. There had been times after that when he would meet a woman, and he wouldn't really want to know her name, but he would learn it, anyway, just for the sake of decency. Then there had been the years when he hadn't been quite as much of an asshole, but there had never—until now—been a time when he had wanted someone the way he was discovering he wanted Leslie, wanted her with every carnal impulse he possessed, with a longing to know not just her face but her soul, the way she thought and everything she felt. . . .

He inhaled. She was close, and coming closer. Her fingers moved over his cheek.

He threaded his own fingers through her hair as they leaned closer, both of them perched on the edge of their seats. His lips touched hers. They were soft, pliant and molding. Her mouth was sweet fire. She knew how to kiss, how to move her lips, teeth . . . tongue. Hot, wet, closer . . . it was the kind of kiss that set the blood to raging, filling the mind with visions of each step that should follow.

And then . . .

They broke apart. Moved back. He didn't know which of them had realized first that they were going too fast.

She began to apologize. "I . . . wow, I'm sorry. I'm not ready—"

"No. *I'm* sorry. I look too much like Matt. But I'm not Matt. I'm Joe. And I want . . . but not . . . not until you're ready."

She rose abruptly, walking to the media cabinet. "What if . . . what if I'm never ready?" she whispered, and the words sounded so pained that he rose and, fighting every sexual instinct within himself, set his hands on her shoulders and drew her against him.

"You will be," he told her. "You will be. Although maybe it won't be with me." *Hell, it had better be with him.* He wasn't half as decent as he was trying to pretend, he thought, mocking himself. "Time . . . well, time has to pass."

"I've seen widows start dating again in less than a year," she murmured.

He pulled her more tightly against him. "Time and pain don't seem to pay much attention to the calendar," he told her. "You'll be okay."

She turned into him, leaning her head against his chest. He smelled the clean fragrance of her hair, felt it tease him. He prayed that she would move away.

She did.

She took a step back and looked at him. The tension in the air was palpable. She looked alarmed.

"Hey . . ." He lifted his hands.

"You . . . you're amazing, Joe," she murmured.

No, I'm a rat. And I know the only way I'll ever get to be close to you is to keep my distance. Wait. Bide my time. Pray.

"Leslie, it's all right."

"Okay."

They stared at each other for a moment longer. Then she cleared her throat and did her best to speak normally as she changed the subject. "Did you know that your house was once owned by a very talented composer?"

"Um . . . no."

She nodded. "His name was Zachary Duff. He had a few pieces published and performed before he was called up to fight in the Civil War."

"And just how do you happen to know this?" he

asked. "I mean," he joked, "the Civil War. That was a long time ago. He's not still hanging around, is he?"

She shrugged. "Well, you know, music lives forever."

"Seriously, where did you get your information? I've seen some of the records on this place . . . in fact, I think I remember seeing the name Duff. But in the late 1800s, the property was owned by a family named Norman. Duff must not have had children. Was he killed in the war?"

"He survived long enough to come home, then died from complications due to his injuries," she said.

"Is he haunting the house?" Matt teased.

She didn't smile.

His laughter faded, and he frowned.

"Leslie?"

"Check out the bricks by the fireplace in your basement," she said. "The left outside wall. Pull a few of them out, and you'll find a cache of his work. It would be great if you could get it to a music publisher."

He laughed then. "You *are* joking, right?"

"No, I'm serious. And I'm asking you to do this for me, as a special favor. Take the bricks out on the left side of the fireplace. You'll find you've been in possession of a treasure trove of old American music."

"How did you get this information? Seriously."

She pretended not to hear him, slipping past him, heading toward the door.

"Leslie."

He caught up with her, set his hands on her shoulders and spun her around to face him. Her expression was guileless.

"Leslie," he said very seriously, "you don't really believe in ghosts, do you?"

"I spend a lot of time in libraries," she said. "You know . . . we do tons of research on an area before we work it. A lot of Lower Manhattan—and some areas of Brooklyn, too—is a treasure trove, once you dig deep enough."

"And you just happened to research my house, and you know there's music stashed in a niche inside the bricks of my basement fireplace."

"Right," she said.

"Leslie—"

"I feel an urge for something stiff and fortifying before tonight. Let's head out, shall we?" she asked.

He had "fortifying" right there, in the apartment.

But they needed to get out. Being alone was . . .

Painful.

"Sure."

As he followed her out, locking up, he said, "Research, huh?"

"Check out your basement fireplace," she said.

Hastings House. His prison.

But she was all right; Leslie was all right. He had seen her . . . almost touched her. She had called out to him, and he had tried so hard to reply. Then she'd gone, and he'd known that she was all right, but he was still so . . .

Afraid.

It was laughable.

He was just the ghost of a man. Pathetic. Why was he here if he couldn't even help, couldn't stand against evil and injustice?

In dreams. There was a place for him in her dreams. Dreams filled with whispers and reminiscences. Poignant and sweet and surreal.

If he couldn't manage to summon enough of himself to be seen, to linger for more than a few seconds, to leave the confines of the house, how was it that he could pace—or seem to—endlessly and desperately?

Peace, rest in peace . . .

He couldn't. There was a reason for this pain of simultaneously being and not being, of needing to remain. It was fear. Fear for her. Strange warnings plagued his spectral soul. Somehow he knew she was in danger. He raged against it. What good did it do to feel this certainty that he should warn her, that the evil behind his death was still out there, when he was powerless to do anything about it? What had he ever done to deserve this wretched hell where he learned with more certainty each day that the greatest agony on earth didn't lie in the pain of living or the pain of death, but in the pain of separation that haunted the heart and soul?

It seemed, as he paced, that everything always came back to this room. The servants' pantry where he had died.

The dead room.

So often he stood here, reliving those last moments. Hearing the hum of a voice, trying to pretend he was paying attention, looking over others' heads and seeing her eyes. It had been a great party, swimming with all the right people, with money, power and politics. The perfect evening . . .

And then the very air had exploded. . . .

But she had been all right. Leslie had been all right. . . .

He found himself in the main kitchen.

Hastings House was closing down for the day. The tourists were gone. Jeff Green was there, doffing his wig, looking around, making sure Melissa was nowhere to be seen. He lit up a cigarette, inhaled deeply, still keeping an eye out. From his pocket, he drew a flask and took a long swig.

The cigarette suddenly flew from his hand. Jeff stared at the flask, then at the cigarette. He stared around the room, then, in a panic, swooped down to pick up the cigarette. He put it out at the sink, still looking around, and then he fled. Matt could hear the front door slam behind him.

And there she was. The Colonial woman who was always cooking over the fire. She smiled at him.

He smiled back.

"I was betrayed," she said.

"I know, but . . ."

"They never knew. They said I walked away. That I left everything . . . but I didn't. He killed me. Shot me in the back. And they never knew. They never knew."

Her face contorted. "How could they believe I would have left my child?" She looked hopelessly at him. "He bricked up my body."

"What?"

"I was working here in the kitchen, cooking. He was weary of me, you see, in love with another. My dowry made him rich, but he never really loved me. He killed me as I stood here, with a single shot. And then he told everyone I had left him, run away with another man. His mistress came to live here then, but she was not happy, either. He had betrayed me, and soon enough he betrayed her. But she caught the consumption. She died, but at least before she did she passed it to him, and he died, as well, choking on his own blood. But it was too late. It didn't change what he did to me, what he told everyone I did. I saw it all, and yet . . ."

"Yet you remain here."

"Yes . . . because I don't know how to clear my name."

"Where did he hide your body?"

"The basement. Beneath the pantry. The butler helped him. So I must stay."

She turned away from him.

Once again she began to work over the hearth. And then she began to fade, until she finally disappeared.

Just like the missing prostitutes, this woman had vanished two hundred years ago. Women continued to vanish. Life didn't change. Men didn't change. Cruelty could not be halted by time.

And now the danger was threatening Leslie. He knew it. Had it been his own determination to write

212

about the disappearances, to make the public aware, that had led to his death? And now Joe was searching for a missing woman, and he and Leslie were deter-mined to find the truth behind the explosion. Was that what was putting her into danger, too?

So many sins could be hidden and buried.

He found himself drawn to the dead room and simply stood there, wondering why. Why he had died there.

He found himself thinking about the secret door beneath the braided rug that led to the basement and the bones that lay bricked up down there.

He felt the impotent rage of his helplessness, and wondered if this was hell. The powerlessness, the watching . . . the fear.

He decided suddenly that if he couldn't help himself, at least maybe he could help the woman in the kitchen. For that, at least, there was a way.

As to Leslie . . .

How he loved her. But he had to let go, had to let her live. Perhaps he needed the answers in order to let go, in order to let her live. Maybe he was trapped here so he could protect her, and yet . . .

How?

10

There was glass and chrome everywhere. Leslie, though she loved old buildings, was thrilled to be in an atmosphere of the completely new.

She wasn't surprised to see Brad there, nor to see

that he was in the company of Ken Dryer—out of uniform—and that they were engaged in conversation at
the bar with a number of extremely attractive women.
They didn't see her enter with Joe, and she was glad
though not surprised, since the place was crowded,
having recently been listed as one of Downtown's
newest hot spots.

Joe looked amused as he caught her arm and whispered, "You're sure you want to be here?"

She grinned. "It's good to shake things up once in a
while. It's like . . . well, you know. You get too
involved in what you're doing and you can't see the
forest for the trees."

"Good point. I guess."

They made their way to the back of the bar. There
was one bar stool; Joe let her sit and stood by her side.
"What will it be? Sparkling soda?"

"No good beers on tap here?" she asked.

"You were conked on the head today, remember?"

"And the doctor said I'm fine."

"Not exactly. The doctor said you were conked on
the head," he corrected.

She liked his smile so much. *Of course she did. It
reminded her of Matt's.*

They both had the same way about them. A bit
rueful, as if they had learned early on not to take themselves too seriously. Not that they couldn't be serious,
because they could. They both cared about the world
around them, both had a quiet strength that demanded
respect. But there was one crucial difference.

Matt was dead.

And it was wrong for her to spend her time comparing Joe to him.

"What?" he asked.

"What about what?"

"You're smiling."

She took a breath, decided to be honest. "I'm sorry—there are just a lot of things about you that remind me so much of Matt."

He didn't seem offended. "Granny Rose," he said seriously.

"Who?"

He laughed. "Our grandmother. She was four foot eleven, in a stretch. A good eighty pounds. She was the toughest and sweetest—old bird I ever knew. She landed here, married Granddad, had her kids. Her respect for America was enormous, but her tales of the old country were full of her love for the place. She was as Catholic as the day was long, but in her own way. She loathed people who went to church every Sunday, then turned around and behaved badly. The true measure of a man, she'd always say, was the way he dealt with his fellow man. Of course, she was also fond of saying, 'Don't pee on me head and tell me it's raining.' She was quite an influence on us when we were boys. Our parents all worked, so we were with her a lot during our formative years."

"Matt mentioned her a few times. I wish I'd gotten to meet her."

The bartender came at last, staring at them with a

superior look. Joe glanced at her, arched a brow, then asked the man, "Any beer?"

The bartender looked at them as if they were utterly lacking in taste, but he shrugged and said that they carried one bottled beer. It was a new European brand, but Joe shrugged in return and ordered two. They arrived promptly.

Joe took a swallow, studying her. She looked back at him. "*Could* you meet her—if you wanted to?"

"Meet who?"

"My grandmother."

"She's dead."

"Yes, I know."

She didn't get a chance to answer, didn't even know if he'd been mocking her or if his question had been serious, because just then Brad spotted them.

"Leslie!" he called, walking over. "Uh . . . Joe," he added, with noticeably less enthusiasm.

"Hey, Brad," she said. Joe acknowledged him with a nod that matched Brad's lack of enthusiasm.

"Cool. You decided to check the place out," Brad said, then frowned at her. "Leslie, did you see a doctor? Are you all right? Should you be drinking?"

"I'm fine—I'm only having the one beer—but thanks for asking. And I can see why you like this place," she told him, smiling and indicating the bevy of very attractive women around the spot at the bar where Ken Dryer was still chatting. "It's a good pickup spot. You and Ken should do well. You're both gorgeous," she assured him.

Brad winked at Joe. "You can almost believe she thinks so." He grinned. "Dryer has been at the site a lot, and I thought he deserved a break. You know Laymon. He thinks the world lives to steal whatever it is he's looking for. He's bugging the cops constantly. He wants them to put out regular announcements that the police presence at the site is heavy."

"I don't think we're going to find buried treasure. It was a very poor area," Leslie said. She couldn't help glancing over toward Dryer. The guy was perfect at his job. Suddenly, though, noticing one of the girls, a tall redhead in a very short skirt, sporting a white fur ministole, she had an uncomfortable feeling. High-priced call girl? If so, did she know she was flirting with a police officer? Silly, she told herself, thinking anyone dressed that way had to be hooking. Half the women in town dressed like hookers and weren't. Since this one had it, she was certainly entitled to flaunt it.

Joe leaned in, resting an elbow on the bar. "Collectibles are big these days," he said, drawing Leslie's attention back to the conversation. "That includes artifacts that might not have been worth much when they were new but are antiques now," he pointed out.

Brad grimaced. "I still don't see the criminals of New York suddenly deciding to loot an archaeological dig. But, hey, Laymon lives for nothing but his work and probably thinks everyone else lives for it, too. Scary. If I ever start turning into him, hit me, Leslie."

"I don't see it happening," she assured him. Then

she frowned as a flash suddenly went off in her face and turned to see what was going on.

"Hey!" Brad protested.

"Sorry," the offending photographer said with complete insincerity. He looked young, maybe twenty-two, with slightly shaggy brown hair, a clean-shaven face and brown eyes. He was dressed attractively enough in casual slacks and a tweed jacket, but he wasn't quite up to the designer labels most people in the room were sporting. He grinned and turned to hurry out—only to be met by a couple of burly doormen.

"Hey, buddy, no hassling the customers," one of them said firmly.

"But the world wants to know," the photographer protested.

"Out!"

"The world wants to know," Joe repeated. To Leslie's surprise, he pushed away from the bar, heading after the receding bouncers and the photographer.

Brad stared at her blankly. "What the hell is he doing? What was that all about?"

"I guess we're the most important noncelebrities in the place, and he's from one of the tabloids," Leslie said.

"I got that much," Brad said. "But what got Joe going?"

"I'm not sure."

"He's not going to wrestle the camera away and

steal the film, is he?" Brad said worriedly.

"I don't think so." She smiled. Brad never tired of having his picture in the papers.

"Maybe I should go out there."

"Honestly, it's all right. Do you know what I think?"

"What?"

"I think you should head back to your position at the bar or Ken is going to steal the lady of your choice."

He stared at her, then laughed. "You know, you could be the love of my life. And then I wouldn't have to barhop."

"Brad, I don't think *any*one is going to be the love of your life, or at least not for a very long time, and you wouldn't want to ruin a great partnership, would you?"

"Maybe I'm ready to settle down."

"Like hell."

He grinned, then sobered, saying seriously, "Don't go falling head over heels just because . . . well, because you're trying to turn this guy into Matt. I mean, he seems fine. Dryer says he's really respected, that people are willing to fly him all over the world for help, it's just that . . . he isn't Matt, and you can't turn him into Matt. I just hope you're not setting yourself up for . . . well, I don't know what I'm saying. I care about you, that's all."

"Thank you. I care about you, too, and I'll be all right. Really. And you don't have to hang around until he comes back. I'm a big girl. I'm okay at a bar by myself."

"I don't want to desert you."

"It's okay."

"Besides, I want to know what he's doing out there."

"Aha! The truth is out."

"Hey, there are wolves in this place. I really don't think I should leave you alone."

"Brad, you *are* one of the wolves in this place."

"Yeah, but not to you."

"Okay. So how was work? Anything new?"

"Yeah, workmen shoring up the walls. Only guys Laymon approves of, and even then he spent half his day on top of them, driving them nuts."

Leslie grinned. Maybe it was a good thing she'd taken the day off. She looked toward the door, wondering herself just what had gotten into Joe.

The bouncers didn't take the camera, but when it looked like they were going to get a little rough, Joe stepped in.

"Hey, guys . . . you got rid of him. Let it go now."

The bouncers turned around. "Just trying to protect you and your lady friend, buddy," one of them said.

"And I appreciate it."

The kid stared at him, backing away. "Are you going to take my camera?" he demanded.

Joe shook his head. "No."

"I'm free to go?"

"No. Let's take a little walk."

"Down a dark alley?"

"No. You're from *The World Wants to Know*, right?"

"Yeah," the photographer said carefully.

"You're Phil Brynner, aren't you?" When the kid looked at him warily, he added, "I saw your picture next to your byline."

"Uh . . . what do you want?"

"To ask you a few questions."

"About what?"

"Your article on Genevieve O'Brien."

"Oh." His brown eyes widened. "I . . . uh . . . who are you?"

"My name is Connolly."

"Are you a cop?"

"No, a private investigator. I'd just like to know what *you* know about the scandal surrounding Genevieve's birth."

The kid still looked distrustful, but he wasn't ready to bolt anymore, and he wasn't cringing. "I never met her, you know."

"You're aware she's missing, though, right?"

He nodded, looking a little ill. "You can't blame me for that."

"Exactly what were you saying?"

"It wasn't right out there, huh? It made you think?"

"I'm not going to play twenty questions with you," Joe said.

Phil swallowed. "I went through a bunch of records. Public records," he said defensively. "I sifted through gossip columns and all kinds of stuff—I worked really hard on that, and it was a good article."

"It was a masterpiece," Joe said wearily. "I want to

know what you were saying. Genevieve couldn't have been another man's child. Have you seen her aunt's face? She's the spitting image of the woman, an O'Brien through and through."

Phil stared at him, then grinned broadly. "That's just it."

"What's it?"

"Eileen Brideswell isn't Genevieve's aunt." He stared triumphantly at Joe. "She's her mother."

Joe could feel his eyes widen in surprise.

"Hey," Phil said, "I found hospital records. I don't actually have proof per se, but that's why I danced around it. Eileen Brideswell wasn't married back then. Her upcoming engagement party was the talk of the city. I went through a million pictures, too. O'Brien's wife didn't look pregnant, then all of a sudden she looked like she had a pillow under her blouse. Eileen Brideswell was supposedly in New England when Genevieve was born, but I couldn't find a single piece of proof that she was actually there. And then all of a sudden she was home. And the O'Briens were all happy with their baby daughter and Eileen went on to marry a very rich man. You can come by and see my research, if you want. I'm in Midtown."

Joe accepted the card the kid produced, then handed over one of his own.

"This can't have anything to do with the fact that she's . . . missing," Phil said, but though he clearly meant it to be a statement, it came out as a question. A hopeful one.

222

"Honestly, I don't think so. But . . . who knows?"

The kid hesitated again. "Do you care if I print the picture? I won't write anything horrible about you and your friends, honestly. I just saw Miss MacIntyre at the table, and she's been on television lately, so I took the shot. I'll just say she had a nice night out with friends, including her partner and her deceased fiancé's . . . brother?"

"Cousin," Joe said flatly.

"Nothing bad, honest," Phil insisted. "Hey, do you think I'd be working where I am if I didn't have to get experience somewhere?"

"Print it. But I'd better like it. Let me put it this way—you'd better not say anything negative about Leslie MacIntyre, Brad or me—or Matt. I mean it."

"We still have freedom of the press, you know," Phil muttered a little resentfully. "Sorry, just kidding, I swear. I'm not out to hurt people."

"Right."

"Honestly. Come on, I have to write something titillating now and then. And I'd seen Genevieve O'Brien on the news, talking about society's lack of concern for the down and out. There she was, a socialite, gorgeous, and she was so passionate about working with the poor. Next thing I knew, I was delving into her past and—"

"Were you ever overseas?" Joe cut in irritably.

"Well . . . I was over in Staten Island. Sounds better to say overseas. Sounds far more exciting—and it is over water."

Joe shook his head in disgust, angry with himself for not having forced the issue with the man's rag magazine office. "All right," he said.

"All right?"

"You can go."

"You know where to find me."

"You bet."

Phil grinned, then cradled his camera to his chest and started at a leisurely pace down the street. A few seconds later, he started running.

Joe watched him go, then reentered the bar.

"So?" Leslie said, when they'd left the bar. "Spill the details."

He'd explained to her and Brad that he had seen an article the kid had written that interested him and assured Brad that his picture would make the paper, but he hadn't explained any further.

They'd wound up eating supper with Brad and Ken, though she'd been surprised when Ken had come by to suggest it, having figured he was having fun at the bar and would probably be going home with one of the women surrounding him. But he had assured her that he had an image to maintain. "I keep my *real* women a secret," he'd told her with a wink. She wasn't sure exactly what that meant, but she was glad she'd never fallen for the man. Not that there was anything really bad about him, but no way was she going to stand for being someone's secret.

She was glad when they spent the dinner arguing

about the next election—something different, for a change, she thought. Then Ken had talked about a new costume exhibit at the Metropolitan Museum of Art, and she found herself fascinated and anxious to see it. Then, at last, they left, ostensibly heading home.

"Details?" Joe asked her as he showed her into his car. "There are no details."

"Have it your way," she said, not seeing any point in trying to force him to talk if he didn't want to. "So we're going to see your prostitute, right?"

His brow furrowed. "She's not *my* prostitute," he said lightly.

"Sorry, I didn't mean it that way."

"I think you'll like her. There's something about her . . ."

"Don't worry. I have no intention of judging her," Leslie said.

They drove slowly along the street.

"There she is," Joe said. "I'm going to park."

"Let me out first, will you? I want to get a feel for the street."

He looked at her gravely. "Don't get into any trouble. I'll be right there."

"What trouble can I get into?" she asked.

He pulled over to the curb and she hopped out. She looked up and down the street. They were very near Hastings House. In fact, she could see the subway station she would have used if she'd needed to.

She was surprised by the number of women working the area. She never would have suspected it. By day, this was a business area. There were only a few hotels, and those median-range—*business range*—in price. Maybe not such a bad place to turn tricks after all, now that she thought about it.

She didn't look for Didi Dancer. She just stood on the street and closed her eyes, trying to get a feel for something.

"Honey, are you all right?"

She looked up at the tall woman in the very short skirt who had stopped to talk to her. *Definitely dressed for business.*

"Fine, thanks."

"I thought you were going to pass out there, for a minute. Well, if you're all right . . ." She hesitated, then shook her head. "Honey, you look as innocent as a lamb. Are you lost? You really shouldn't be out here alone at night. I mean . . . crime is down big time in the City, but still . . ."

"Are you Didi Dancer?" Leslie asked.

The woman stepped back, looking suspicious.

Just then Joe got out of the car and started walking in their direction. Didi took another step back.

"Didi," Joe said.

She just waited, keeping her distance, a frown furrowing her features.

Joe reached them. "I got you that job interview," he reminded her softly.

Didi looked at him. "And it's not till next week. Gotta eat till then," she murmured. "This the girlfriend? Looking for a three-way or something?" she demanded.

Leslie had the feeling the woman was just trying to be harsh. "I'm trying to help Joe find the women who've disappeared."

"You mean you're trying to find the rich girl," Didi said.

"Hey, what's the matter, Didi?" Joe asked. "You said you wanted to help."

Didi let out a sigh, but her eyes were still suspicious when she looked at Leslie. "There's something about her. . . ." she murmured.

"Will you show me where the car was—the dark sedan—when Genevieve O'Brien got into it? Please?" Leslie said.

"Right there." Didi pointed ten feet down the block. "I remember because of the fire hydrant. I knew when the guy pulled over that any idiot would know not to even pretend to park there."

Leslie walked over to the spot as Didi and Joe just watched her.

At first she felt nothing but the night air, heard nothing but the normal sounds of the city.

A cat meowed.

A dog barked.

A car backfired, and a horn blared.

Rap music shook the pavement as someone drove by with the radio cranked up.

What am I doing? she asked herself. *It's not like I have ESP.*

But she closed her eyes anyway, saw the picture of Genevieve O'Brien in her mind's eye.

The sounds of night faded. She imagined the street as it must have been that night. She could see Genevieve, passionate, urgent, trying to convince Didi that she had to get out of this life and help herself. And then . . .

She heard the car horn.

Genevieve turned. . . .

And recognized the person in the car.

Not a friend!

That sensation swept through Leslie fiercely. *Not a friend, but still someone she knew. Someone who bugged her, who compounded the headaches of the system, who didn't care about the work that needed to be done.*

Genevieve was irritated as she walked over to the car.

Leslie could almost hear the man's voice.

Get in and we'll talk about it. I'll even give you a ride home.

So Genevieve got in. She had no inkling of danger.

Not until they had been driving for several minutes. Then, with one hand on the wheel, he had turned to her while she was talking about the issue and snapped something with his free hand. She frowned, still not alarmed, until he pressed his hand over her mouth and a sickeningly sweet smell filled her nostrils. . . .

No! She struggled, tried to fight, tried to push away his hand. He was still driving, and there were people around, if she could just scream, fight, bang on the window. . . .

But she couldn't. She was losing consciousness. And she knew . . .

"Leslie!"

Leslie heard her own name and the spell was broken. The feelings, the vision, faded away.

The next thing she knew, Joe's arms were around her as she realized she had been about to crash to the pavement.

"I knew there was more to that bump on the head," he announced. "I'm getting you home."

"No, no. Please," she protested, somehow finding the strength to stand. "My head is fine."

What on earth had just happened? She'd never experienced anything like that before. And she'd thought talking to ghosts was weird?

Didi was staring at her as if she were an alien.

Leslie gave her what she hoped was a reassuring smile. "Sorry."

"You a psychic or something?"

"No," Leslie demurred, but the woman was still staring at her, as was Joe. "Well, kind of," she admitted uneasily. "Sometimes I get . . . sensations. You know, when someone is . . ."

"Dead?" Didi asked flatly.

Leslie shrugged. "I . . . I hope not. Genevieve did know whoever picked her up," she said with conviction, looking at Joe.

Didi sniffed. "I could have told you that. He had to be a friend."

"No, that's just it. He was someone she knew, but

not a friend. Someone she did business with, worked with somehow. She was annoyed when she saw him."

"She got right into the car," Didi said.

"Right—because she knew him. Because even though she didn't like him, he was respectable, someone people trusted, but she wanted something from him that she wasn't getting."

"Ain't that life," Didi murmured.

"Any chance you can tell where they went?" Joe asked.

Leslie hesitated, then shook her head. "All I know is that they drove for a while before he drugged her. That's what he did, he drugged her."

"Drugged her or killed her?" Joe asked quietly.

Leslie frowned then. "I . . ."

"What?" Joe asked anxiously.

"Listen, I'm not a psychic. I really—" She broke off. No way was she ready to explain that her real talent lay in talking to ghosts.

"What were you going to say?" Joe demanded.

Leslie stared at him, letting out a long sigh. "I . . . don't think she's dead. She was abducted, she was drugged . . . but I don't think she's dead."

Joe stared back at her. He didn't seem to doubt her, didn't question her. He looked thoughtful.

"I mean . . . I don't know anything," she said. "I just . . . I don't know. I can't help but think I would have . . . felt it if she'd died. I think she might be alive."

Joe folded his arms over his chest. "Then it's imperative that we find her. Quickly."

11

I am with you. All is well. . . .

Leslie didn't fall asleep easily that night, despite her desire to dream. She lay awake for hours, certain that the answer was there, but seeing it was like finding the proverbial needle in a haystack, the haystack being New York with its millions of denizens, and the needle being a single woman who was there somewhere.

So she had lain awake with the television on, keeping her company. Joe had somehow been loathe to leave her, despite the alarm system, and though she had absolutely insisted that he go home, she had the feeling he was sleeping in his car again. She should have suggested that he at least sleep in one of the other bedrooms, but she hadn't been able to bring herself to make the offer.

She wasn't afraid of her dreams. Quite the opposite: she welcomed them. She argued with herself that she had to be alone, that Matt was trying to reach her, and the presence of any other human being might keep him away.

That was true.

But equally true was the fact that she couldn't let go. Not yet . . .

And then, when she finally slept, he was there.

First, the tenderness.

The sensation that she wasn't alone, that the past hadn't been lost to tragedy, that what should have been forever hadn't been ripped away from her. The sweetness of lying down on a soft mattress after a long day, of being held, the comfort of another human being, loved and cherished, at her side. Then . . .

Flesh against flesh. The feathery brush of his lips on hers, the weight of him on top of her. Light, teasing kisses that quickly filled with passion. Blankets tossed and discarded. The slide of cotton against her body as the nightgown was tossed aside. The whisper of his breath against her skin, moving from the valley between her breasts, over her abdomen and down to her thighs.

I knew you would come, she said.

And his very simple answer.

I love you so much...

In her dreams she stroked his flesh, was seduced and aroused by the fire of his lips and tongue moving intimately and along the length of her. She looked into his eyes, blue like the sky. She saw his smile, the single dimple in his cheek. Caressed his jaw, hard and squared, almost as if it had been formed by the determination and sense of justice with which he had lived his life, rather than the lottery of genetics. She reached out and, with both hands, she cupped his face and drew his mouth to hers again. She initiated the ferocity of the kiss, so rapt herself that she needed to return each stroke and caress, needed to seduce as she was seduced, needed to tease and arouse.

She stroked the muscles of his shoulders and then, with the whisper-light touch of her fingertips,

232

caressed the length of his chest to the quickening muscles of his belly. In a fever she followed that touch with taunting kisses, pushing him back, straddling him, looking down at him until, smiling, she bent, her hair wickedly teasing his flesh as she played and stroked, lower and lower. At last his hoarse cry sounded, and she herself writhed and twisted and arced, desperate and hungry, almost wild, savagely in need of him, body and soul. Sensation coursed through her, and despite the volatile thunder and erotic friction of their lovemaking, beneath it flowed a subtle tenderness, a swell of emotion that elevated what was so simply human and physical and made of it something so much more.

She found herself beneath him, her breath frenzied, her heart in an uproar, and she lost the sense of being in her own body as he moved within her. All the while, his kisses fell on her breasts, her shoulders and then her lips. At last, locked to him by the joining of their flesh, she was rocked by the explosion of climax. Her limbs locked around him as she reveled in the cocoon of his embrace. Wonder filled her as she drifted back to earth, trembling in the aftermath of passion, her hot skin cooling, bathed in a fine sheen of sweat. He was damp at her side, their hair slick and tangled together on the pillow, and she marveled at how incredible it was to be so loved, so happy.

In dreams.

Because she knew she was dreaming, but she would not let the dream go. She entwined her fingers with his as she lay spooned against him, his hand resting on her belly. She felt the muscles of his chest where she rested her head.

This closeness was so familiar; they lay together just as they had so often when he'd come home late and slipped into bed. First had come lovemaking, then a few lazy words about the day, or their plans for the future.

I'm afraid for you, he whispered now.

Afraid for me? Matt, you were a reporter. You know what it feels like to see something wrong and feel obligated to set it right, and you know I have to discover the truth about what happened here.

He listened, considered her words, carefully formed his own answer before whispering it into the lush silk of the hair against her ear.

Yes, I know that, but I can't help it—I'm afraid for you. He was silent for a minute, almost as if it were painful to continue. *I can't be with you. Trust Joe.*

She started to tell him that she was constantly surrounded by people—including cops—so how could she be in danger, but then she stopped as she remembered the dig. As the day had passed, she'd convinced herself that the roof had caved in on her, but was that true? She had been focused on the niche in the wall where the record book had been, but she'd been sure she'd heard . . . something. Sensed . . . something. But she was certain no one else had entered after her, and she was sure no one had already been there when she came in. So . . .

I felt it this morning, a sense of fear for you, but there was nothing I could do. But Joe was here, and it was all right. Don't trust anyone else, do you hear me? Only Joe.

All right, she said slowly. *But why?*

"The basement."

Leslie woke with a start, certain someone had spoken the words aloud. She bolted up to a sitting position, the covers clutched to her chest. Her hair was a tangled, damp mess. Sometime in the night she had torn off her nightgown, and the sheets were hopelessly rumpled.

She groaned, feeling almost as if she had a hangover. She touched the top of her head, but the lump was almost gone.

"The basement?" she said aloud.

If she'd expected a reply, she didn't get one.

She rose and showered, then dressed in a T-shirt and khakis with a half-dozen pockets, three on each leg, and hurried downstairs. She was still early enough to have the place to herself. She put the coffee on, then went through to the servants' pantry.

She pulled back the braided rug and found the trap-door leading to the basement beneath. She'd been in the basement before, of course, long before the night of the gala. They'd hoped to find all kinds of treasures down there, especially because the simple cellar had changed very little since the house's early days, but in the end it wasn't a treasure trove as some basements and attics could be. Over the years, the owners of the house had cleaned out their own belongings, along with anything that had come before.

Now the hole in the floor gaped wide and dark, like the entrance to an abyss.

She left the trapdoor open and went back to the kitchen. The coffee was ready, so she poured herself a cup and sipped while rifling through the drawers, certain she would find a flashlight in one of them. Then she paused.

The spectral woman was back at the hearth, stirring her spectral pot. Finally she paused, turned and looked straight at Leslie.

"He wants you to help me," she said, a note of such poignant gratitude in her voice that empathy swept through Leslie with so much force that she nearly dropped her coffee cup.

"I would love to help you. Who are you?"

"Elizabeth Martin. Please. I never left my child."

Leslie stared back at her, noting that she could see right through the woman's spectral body.

"They're . . . all gone now, you know."

The woman looked agitated. "They have to know the truth. I never left my baby."

"Elizabeth Martin," Leslie said. "I'll do my very best."

The woman smiled. "The basement," she said.

Leslie *did* drop the cup then. It shattered on the floor just as Elizabeth Martin faded from view.

"She's gone crazy, but am I going to stop her? Not in this lifetime," Melissa said.

236

Joe stared at her blankly. She'd thrown open the door when he'd rung the bell, and those were the first words out of her mouth at the sight of him.

"I beg your pardon?"

"Leslie. She's down in the basement with a pickax!"

"Did you ask her why?"

"Of course."

"And?"

"She says that there's a body in the wall."

Joe frowned and hurried inside, along the hallway and straight to the back. When he entered the servants' pantry, he immediately shivered and realized he'd entered *the dead room,* then wondered where that thought had come from.

The braided rug that usually covered the floor had been pulled away, and the trapdoor to the basement was open. He could see light from a work lantern rising up the stairs going down to the basement, strong wooden steps added recently to cover the dangerous brick stairway that had been there originally.

He hurried down.

The vertical line of fireplaces throughout the house was in evidence here, as well. A brick fireplace and hearth were set into one wall, and Leslie was standing to the left. She had apparently finished with the pickax and was digging away at the brick with her hands. She scared him a little. Her beautiful face was intent, her movements almost frantic.

"Leslie?"

"Joe. Hey. Come help me."

"Leslie, what are you doing?"

"I . . . uh . . . found some old records. I think there's a body back here. Well, a skeleton, anyway. Come on."

He went to her side. One of the bricks was stuck. He had a Swiss Army knife in his pocket, so he pulled it out and chipped at the mortar to free the brick. She stepped back and took a deep breath.

"Are you sure you should be doing this?" he asked.

"Of course."

"Leslie, this property is owned by the Historical Society."

"If anyone is angry, I'll pay for repairs," she said. "Please, Joe?"

The brick fell away in his hand. He stepped back, stunned. Even in the weak light and through the grime and dust of the ages, he could see bone.

Shit!

He almost swore aloud.

Leslie didn't look surprised in any way.

"Well, there . . . all right. We can stop now. They're still shoring up the crypt at the site, I imagine. Laymon will be there, but Brad can come over and help me. Except," she said thoughtfully, "I'll have to get into the crypt . . . no, St. Paul's has been there since 1766, and the crypt we just discovered wouldn't have been completed then. Hmm. I need to find more records. Maybe the library . . . Hey." She stared at him with a sudden smile. "Did you check your basement wall yet?"

"Am I going to find bones, too?" he asked.

"I told you, you'll find music."

"And I guess I will," he murmured.

"I'd better start looking for those records," she said, suddenly decisive. She walked over to him and gave him a fierce hug and big kiss on the cheek. "Drop me off at the main library. I'm going to start there."

"Sure," he said, and then he couldn't help himself: He yawned.

She frowned. "You didn't go home last night, did you? I bet you just made sure you had a clean shirt in the car." She smiled. "You can't keep worrying about me, you know."

"Apparently, it's not a matter of can or can't. I simply do."

She started toward the stairs, then turned around, her eyes carefully assessing the basement. It correlated in size exactly to the servants' pantry—*the dead room,* he thought again—above it.

"What is it?" he asked her.

"Everything is uneven down here, have you noticed?"

"It's hundreds of years old. What would you expect?"

She was still studying the walls. Then she shivered suddenly, hugging her arms around herself. "The subway runs near here, right?"

He shrugged. "I guess. Probably much deeper, though."

"Right. But still, there are all kinds of shafts and tunnels."

"Want me to find an old subway map?" he teased.

"That would be great," she told him, completely serious. "Okay, I really have to get to work. What's your plan for the day?"

"I'm going to go back over the last-known movements of every prostitute who disappeared and see if I can find any connection to Genevieve O'Brien," he told her.

"That's a busy agenda. You'll still be able to find me some old maps?"

"You want maps? I'll get you maps," he assured her.

"Will you drop me at the library?"

"Sure. But you might want to shower and change again first. You're wearing a little too much brick dust to be fashionable."

She looked down at herself and laughed. "Okay. I'll hurry."

She was humming as she ran up the stairs.

Melissa and Tandy—who was leading the tours that day—were told about the discovery but sworn to secrecy. While Joe waited for Leslie, he found himself drawn to the main dining room, where Tandy was giving her speech to a group of college students from Columbia University.

"Imagine a very different place," she began. "When the story of New York first began, the action was here, downtown. Times Square was a distant and savage land where the Algonquin-speaking natives still reigned. New York was first taken by the Dutch. The

Dutch West India Company established a fur-trading post here in 1625. Peter Stuyvesant, the last Dutch colonial governor, was a tyrant. He closed the taverns at nine, for God's sake. When the English came in 1664, they easily ousted the Dutch without a fight and renamed the city—which had been called New Amsterdam—New York, after James, Duke of York, and brother of Charles II. We stand near the Five Points area of the Sixth Ward—the area roughly bounded now by Broadway, Canal Street, the Bowery and Park Row. Disease and death were a hallmark of the poorer, more densely populated areas. People used ponds and waterways to dump refuse and sewage. And with poverty came violence and finally rebellion.

"This city is one of the places where liberty began, where battles were fought and riots surged. When you walk out the door, you'll see the vital, high-stakes city of today. But I hope that by the time you leave Hastings House, you'll also have a better understanding of the city beneath and all the sins buried by time."

The city beneath.

Buried sins.

The words haunted Joe. How many people disappeared, simply vanished, as if they'd never been? The rivers were too iffy—sometimes bodies escaped whatever weights held them down and bobbed to the surface, and New York City wasn't an easy place to dig holes where they wouldn't be seen.

The city beneath.

But where to begin looking?

Leslie was grateful that her job allowed access to areas of the library where most people couldn't go, and that the records regarding Hastings House were in good order.

She waded through a lot of information on the many roles the house had played during the years, having been a school and an office building, among other things. So many facades and changes had been added over the years that the building's true contours had almost been forgotten. Only the threat of demolition ten years earlier had brought the true persona of the place to light. Additions, later ornamentation and other changes had been painstakingly researched and removed and the historic gem been brought back.

At last she reached the early history of the house. Built by a sea captain in the late 1700s, it had been left to his niece, Elizabeth, at his death.

Her heart quickened; she had never expected it to be this easy.

Elizabeth had married a merchant, Jacob Martin. Martin had remarried in 1803. The parish register commented that Elizabeth Martin, age twenty-one, was presumed dead. But there was also a notation left in the register by a priest who had not wanted to assume the task of remarrying Mr. Martin. "Jacob claimed earlier that his wife deserted him and their babe for Gordon Black, a sailor who often came to port but has not appeared since. In his haste to remarry, he has convinced the elders that Elizabeth must have perished on the journey, else she would have returned to take their babe, young Sarah. I fear that for a man to be so certain of his wife's death, he may have been witness to it. He appears, however, to be a pillar of our dear parish, and it is she, Elizabeth, who is scorned, dead or alive, by the men of character around us."

"Poor Elizabeth," she whispered, shaking her head sadly. She paused a minute, feeling as if her heart had suddenly become very heavy. *Matt, were you with me? Did you try to tell me first? I can see Elizabeth, talk to her. Why can't I see you, talk to you?*

"All right," she murmured aloud. "You wanted me to help Elizabeth, and I swear I'll do my best. Please, though . . . let me help you. And myself."

She shut up. She was alone and talking to herself. Time to get back to work.

She'd had access to all these records earlier. But at the time she'd been looking for old delft plates, silver . . . other treasures left behind.

She went still suddenly. She was in a private section of the library; she was alone. But she'd had the feeling of being watched. A creeping sensation teased the back of her neck. She looked up. It was the way she had felt in the crypt the other night. *Not at all as if she were being stalked by a ghostly presence.*

Ghosts were usually pale essences. They didn't want to hurt anyone; they wanted to be helped. Occasionally, they were bitter or liked to play pranks. Both Adam Harrison and Nikki Blackhawk had told her

243

that they'd never encountered a ghost that was actually vicious—except against whoever had caused them to become a ghost.

She groaned softly, laying her head on her arms on the table. She could just see the conversation with a therapist. *Am I paranoid? I don't think so. I'm not afraid of the dark, and I'm certainly not afraid of ghosts. Hell, some of my favorite people are ghosts. In fact, I may never date again. I have this spectacular ghost who comes to me at night . . . But the thing is, I feel like I'm being stalked, but not by a ghost, by . . . evil.*

She lifted her head, determined that she had far too much work ahead of her to fall prey to her imagination.

She dialed Brad's cell phone.

"Leslie?" he asked. "Where are you?"

"The library. Are the engineers still working at the site?"

"Yup. They think they'll finish around three."

"Can you meet me back at Hastings House? I've got something exciting to show you."

"When? I'll need a little time."

"Four o'clock?"

"Sure. What did you find?"

"I'll show you."

First things first. Joe put in a call to Genevieve's old office and, after only a few minutes of exasperation, got through to the voice menu and then to Alice. Bless her. She'd copied the files and agreed to meet him downstairs with them.

He took the files, giving her a big kiss on the cheek and promising her the best dinner the city of New York could offer. Flushed and pleased, she assured him it wasn't necessary but also that she would love it.

Then he hurried home. Time was of the essence—he felt that keenly. But he still had to shower, shave, change and get organized.

But the shower could wait another few minutes.

In the basement, he impatiently took a pickax to his wall. Dumb—it could have been done with much less damage—but he didn't have time.

What was it with people choosing to wall up their treasures—or their buried sins—in the fireplace wall?

At first he found nothing. Great. He had destroyed half his basement on a whim. But on what he had determined would be his last stroke, he hit a hollow spot.

And there, behind the bricks, was a little shelf. On the shelf was a single Civil War-era tobacco tin.

And in the tin were sheets of handwritten music.

He stared at the tin and its contents for several minutes, disbelieving at first, then uneasy. He looked around the house. *What? Was he suddenly going to start believing in ghosts?*

Was it all logic and research, as Leslie sometimes claimed?

"I'll get it to a music publisher," he said aloud. Then he was embarrassed. He was alone in his own house, talking to himself. Worse. Talking to someone who wasn't there. To someone who had been dead for more than a hundred years.

But he spoke aloud again. "I promise. I'll do it."

He took the tin and left the basement, still feeling that sense of urgency, that certainty that time was of the utmost importance. He headed straight to the copies of the files from Robert Adair's folders and those Alice had given him, and started cross-referencing. He found one name in both.

Heidi Arundsen.

Genevieve had worked with her.

The cops had interviewed her regarding a girl who had disappeared about a month before Genevieve O'Brien.

On his way to the door, he was waylaid by a phone call.

Didi Dancer.

"Joe?" she inquired almost hesitantly.

"Didi. How are you? Is everything okay?"

"I'm fine. I think I might have found someone who can help you out."

"Oh?"

"There's a Starbucks on my street. How about if we meet you there?" she added. "You know where."

"I'm on my way."

As he drove, he organized his mind, much as he organized his papers. Fact one: He was now con-vinced that Genevieve O'Brien had been kidnapped, and that she had been taken by the same person or persons responsible for the disappearances of the prostitutes. She had last been seen getting into a dark sedan.

She might still be alive somewhere.

Possibly beneath the city.

Buried sins.

Fact two: The explosion at Hastings House had not been an accident. Okay, that wasn't a proven fact, but it was a supposition so strong that he felt comfortable treating it as fact.

Fact three: Matt, who had died in that explosion, had written a number of articles on the disappearances.

Theory: All three things were related. Matt's death, the missing prostitutes, Genevieve O'Brien.

He felt a quickening in his heart. What had Matt known? What had he known that he hadn't realized he knew? Whatever it was, it had so disturbed a killer that he'd conceived and carried out the perfect plan, a targeted execution that appeared, even after a thorough investigation, to be an accident.

He reached for his cell phone. Robert Adair's assistant got him a number, and in moments he was talking with Greta Peterson.

She was surprised to hear from him, and he forced himself to chat with her a few minutes, explaining that yes, he was busy, yes, he was fine, yes, he'd seen Leslie, yes, they had a lot in common, yes . . .

She was more surprised when he asked her for list of everyone who had attended the gala, and for every caterer, police officer and private security person who had worked it. He also asked for a list of anyone who had recently done work at Hastings House.

"I'm sure I gave all those lists to the police." She paused, then said sadly, "It was an accident, Joe. You looked into it yourself. The file is closed."

It's been reopened, Joe thought. Aloud he said only, "Greta, you're a dear, but I can't let it go, not yet. Will you get the lists for me?"

"How could I refuse you?"

"Thanks. Can you messenger them over to Hastings House by this evening?"

She sighed. "Sure. If it will help you come to terms with what happened, go over it all you want."

As he hung up, he had the strange sensation that he wasn't alone. The feeling was so strong that he actually looked to his right, at the passenger seat. There was no one there. *Of course not, you fool. You would have known if someone had jumped in the car.*

But he looked in the rearview mirror, as well, feeling even more like a fool.

Suddenly he thought he heard a whisper. Something teasing in his ear, indistinct at first. It was the breeze, he told himself; he had the window rolled down. It was the sound of a radio on the street somewhere nearby. It was conversation coming at him from the crowded sidewalks of Manhattan.

Whatever it was, it seemed to form a name in his mind.

Leslie . . .

There was an urgency to the sound, which irritated him; common sense and logic were his bywords. Then again, ever since he had known Leslie, he had to admit that somehow what she saw was clearer, what she intuited was often real. . . .

"Screw it," he said aloud.

And then, despite his own plans, he headed to the library.

Leslie left the library with a roll of copies in her hands. She'd thought she would grab a taxi, but it was midday and the traffic was insane. Actually, she liked the subway, she thought as she headed for the nearest station. It was usually fast and rarely got hung up by traffic jams.

She hurried down the steps, finding her MetroCard as she went. The entry smelled only slightly of urine. There was an obviously handicapped man with a sign sitting by one wall, and she stopped to drop a dollar in his cap. Before she could reach the turnstile, she saw a skinny old woman with a skinny dog. That demanded another pause for a dollar.

Since she'd already opened her heart to the first two, she paused to give the twentysomething leaning against the yellow tiles and playing the flute a dollar, too.

As she dropped the bill into his flute case, she felt a sense of something again, a sense of being watched. This was the subway, for God's sake, she told herself. Full of people. Anyone could be watching her.

She paused. There was something in her head, a niggling piece of knowledge, but she couldn't quite get it to make sense. It nagged at her even more strongly as she stood at the top of the stairs leading down to the train platform. She was in the subway. Underground. There were miles and miles of subway tunnels. Maybe that was it. Over the years, subway workers had discovered any number of relics while digging new lines. And there were unused tunnels, too, so . . .

Great. The killer was probably burying his victims. Wow. Big break. But where?

Huge city. Huge underground.

She started. That strange feeling of being watched struck her again.

Sure, she was being watched. By the guy with the dull eyes in the corner. He wasn't really seeing anything, though.

It was just a feeling, she told herself.

But it wasn't that simple. It was . . . disturbing. She looked around. And saw a dozen people, none of whom seemed to be staring at her.

New Yorkers were busy people on the move.

Oh, Matt, I'm really becoming a total paranoid. If only . . .

If only you would speak to me. . . .

Matt was dead.

He lived only in her dreams.

With a mental shake of irritation, she moved on, heading down to the train platform.

People walked fast in New York. She joined the throng, people-watching as she went. There were the tourists, carrying guidebooks and looking around with wide eyes. There were the businessmen and women, looking crisp in their dark suits. There were punks with ski caps and students reading textbooks, oblivious to the world around them, their iPods all the company they needed.

A train had just left when she reached her track. She found her mind wandering as she waited for the next one to arrive.

She was happy, she realized, and she hoped desperately that she would be able to bring peace to Elizabeth Martin. Poor Elizabeth. She wanted to be vindicated so badly. The thing was, so many years had passed . . . who remained to know or care? It wasn't as if she could go to Elizabeth's loved ones and explain or ease their pain. But Joe had met a reporter the other night—heck, she knew dozens of reporters, she realized—she could get someone to do a story. She could see that Elizabeth received a proper burial.

She noticed a group of people coming down the stairs, crowding onto the platform, surging and jostling behind her. She staggered a bit but held her position behind the yellow line.

As she did, she felt a gust of fear again.

Cold at the nape of her neck.

Unease.

As if she were prey and something was stalking her.

She started to turn.

She was hit in the back by a heavy shove.

The next thing she knew, she was flying toward the track.

And she could hear the shrill cry of the approaching train, speeding along the rails.

12

Joe couldn't find a place to park his car. What had he expected? This was New York.

But the sense of danger was so real that he didn't care. Even knowing he would be towed, he pulled into the first empty space he found along Fifth Avenue. He raced up the stairs to the library, past the magnificent lions, and inside. A second's hesitation sent him to research, where an attractive young woman told him that he had just missed Leslie MacIntyre, who'd made the copies she wanted and headed out. "It's impossible to get a cab this time of day, so she probably took the subway. She said she was heading back to Hastings House."

Joe barely thanked her. He hadn't seen Leslie on the street, which meant he had already lost precious time. For all he knew, she could already be on a subway downtown.

A voice inside his head kept mocking him. *She's fine. She was at the library. You're acting like a madman. She's on her way home.*

But another thought kept plaguing him endlessly. *Buried sins.*

She wasn't heading down into a crypt, some dark

hollow in the earth. Well, not really. She was going to ride the New York City subway, used by thousands of commuters on an hourly basis.

Still . . .

He saw the entrance and ran down the stairs, scanning the signs for trains heading toward the downtown financial district. He leapt over the turnstile, again damning himself as a madman. Great. His car was going to be towed, and if the subway attendant yelling at him had his way, he would also be arrested.

As he rushed headlong through throngs of people on the stairs, he felt a sense of dread as he headed toward the platform.

Screams echoed from below, and he ran faster, shoving people out of his way and taking the steps two at a time.

Move!

In a split second, Leslie was aware of so many things. The vibration of the ground beneath her. The bruises forming on her flesh. The awkward way she was lying. The fear that she was going to be electrocuted. The squeak and scurrying of the subway rats . . .

And that voice.

Move!

She couldn't move; she was stunned, breathless and in agony.

Move!

Suddenly, arms were reaching for her, pulling her up.

Matt . . . ? Yes, it was Matt!

She blinked, and then she was up, moving with the speed of light. There were arms again, real arms, strong, powerful arms, grabbing her and dragging her up and . . .

She was lying on the platform. She heard the whistle of the train; felt the air rushing over her, the train so close that its passing rustled her hair, touched her face.

There were new sounds. People. Voices rising in indignation.

"Sweet Jesus—did you see that? She was nearly squashed like a bug!"

"Thank God someone got her out!"

"She got herself out."

"It's horrible, Harold. I'm always telling you, it's horrible—people pushing and shoving down here all the time."

"They should be arrested!"

"Who should be arrested? I couldn't tell who did it."

She just lay there, gasping for breath, staring up. Joe. Joe was there, hunkered down by her side. She tried to smile. He looked up as two policemen came running along the platform, calling for people to get back, to give her some air.

"The paramedics are on their way," a young uniformed cop said, squatting down by Joe.

She tried to rise up on her elbows, looking at Joe for help, wondering how in hell he had managed to be there. "I'm all right. I'm luckier than a lottery winner, but I'm all right."

"Sit tight," Joe said. He had the strangest expression on his face. "Did you break anything? Are you in pain?"

She didn't have a chance to answer, because just then there was a break in the crowd, and two young paramedics, a man and a woman, made their way to her side.

Joe and the officer backed off as the paramedics started gently questioning her. She explained as best she could that she was all right, that she was just bruised and the wind was knocked out of her. In a few seconds they determined that she had no broken bones, her back wasn't injured, and she could be moved.

The pulse of the city could keep thundering.

"What happened?" the second officer asked when it became clear that there was no immediate medical emergency.

"I don't know. It was really crowded down here," she said.

He looked fiercely concerned. "Were you pushed?"

"Well, of course I was pushed. But—"

"So you didn't . . . you didn't jump, did you?"

"Of course not!" she replied indignantly.

"Did you see anyone who looked like they wanted to hurt you? Did you see any gang members down here? Anyone out of the ordinary?"

She stared back blankly. "I don't come here every day. I didn't see any gang members. I think the platform was just very crowded, and people were getting

255

edgy and worried about getting on a train when it did come. Look—"

"Take it easy, Leslie," Joe said.

Then, while the paramedics continued to watch her gravely, the officer grilled Joe, who produced his ID and said that he'd known she was at the library, and that he'd come to find her, he hadn't just happened to be on the platform.

It was a nightmare.

And despite her protests, she was put into an ambulance to be taken to the hospital, where a doctor would officially ascertain the nature of her injuries. And though Joe rode in the ambulance with her, the police officer came, too, taking down her statement.

They both left her while the doctor on duty ordered X-rays and went through a long checklist of symptoms with her, and gave her a thorough physical exam. She had to explain that the little bump on her head was left over from an earlier accident. That seemed to concern him, which disturbed her. Did the man think she was suicidal?

Robert Adair showed up with Ken Dryer. Leslie was ready to pull her hair out. She wanted nothing more than to be alone, to try to remember those fateful seconds in the subway, to remember them exactly, to understand what had happened.

The voice.

Had it been Joe's voice? Had he been there, down on the platform, with her?

She didn't know. All she remembered for sure was

Joe being there, reaching for her, pulling her up off the track.

"You sure do like to create a lot of excitement," Ken Dryer teased, coming in once she was dressed and the doctor had moved on to his next patient.

Robert, who was right behind him, looked both irritated and anxious. "Are you sure you're all right?"

"No. I have a bruise on my thigh, and it hurts. Is it anything bad? No. Please, I'm desperate just to get out of here," she said.

"What happened?" Ken asked.

"It was crowded in the subway. People push and shove. I should have been more careful. I should have stayed farther back. It was an accident."

Even as she said the word, she thought it sounded hollow.

An accident?

The blast at Hastings House had been an accident.

The ceiling giving way in the crypt had been an accident.

Move!

Who had whispered the word to her? Had Matt somehow been with her in a time of mortal danger, or had she seen Joe's face in the crowd and imagined that her dead lover had reached out from the grave to help her?

Joe pushed past the others to get to her where she lay on the hospital bed. "You should stay here."

"Why?"

"Because I have work to do," he said ruefully.

She stared at the drawn, but still striking, contours of his face and longed to touch him. "How did you happen to be there?" she marveled.

"I was afraid for you."

"Why?"

"I don't know. But the doctor wants to keep you overnight for observation, and I think you should stay here."

She stared back at him. And lied.

"Okay. Sure."

He arched a skeptical brow. "Really?"

"Sure."

"All right," he said.

"My papers!" she exclaimed, sitting up suddenly.

"Your papers?"

"I had a bunch of copies from the library," she said with dismay.

"Stuff you had from the library, huh? I'll, uh, see if the paramedics collected your things," Robert said. She could tell that he was humoring her. They all thought she was either insane or ungrateful. She had survived a fall onto the tracks when a train had been coming, saved by no more than a few seconds from a hideous death, and she was worried about some papers.

But . . .

It mattered. Somehow, it all mattered. And the "accidents" wouldn't stop happening until she figured out why.

"Thank you, Robert," she called after him as he left the exam room.

"Looks like I'll be warning people to be careful on the subways tonight." Ken Dryer squeezed her hand. "You sure you're okay, kid? I know it's my job, but I'm getting to be a regular on the news, and you seem to have a lot to do with it."

"Thank God you're good on TV," she told him. "I'm fine."

He left. Joe was still tarrying, but before he could say anything, Robert returned to the room. "Some kind citizen apparently gathered your purse and whatever papers they could find. The nurses will see that your things are returned." He stared at her, then at Joe, then at her again. "You know . . . I'd been anxious to see you myself. I thought maybe you could help with the missing hookers. But now . . . I think you ought to leave town."

"Leave town? I'm in the middle of a project," Leslie protested.

Robert shook his head. "I don't like it."

"I'm not leaving town," she said firmly. "Robert, please. This is ridiculous. If it hadn't been me, it would have been someone else. The subway was a zoo. That's it. That's all. Okay?"

He looked at her, shook his head, started out, then turned back. "Stay safe," he said firmly. He shot Joe a look that seemed to blame him, then left.

She noticed that Joe looked thoughtful as he watched the other man leave. "What is it?"

"I don't know." He turned back to her, leaning over her, arms braced on either side of the mattress. "I need to know. I need to know a lot. You *are* going to stay here, right?"

"You bet. As soon as they find me a room, I'll catch a nice nap. Some nice candy striper will bring me tea and lunch. It will be great."

"It had better be," he warned. And then, at last, he left her.

To Joe's amazement, Didi was still waiting for him at Starbucks. She was with another woman.

"Joe!" Didi called when he entered, and stood, smiling.

"You waited all this time," he said.

"I knew you'd come."

"And who is this?" Joe asked politely.

She was tiny, blond and blue-eyed. She looked a little edgy, though.

"Do you want some coffee?" he asked, trying to put her at ease.

"Heidi wants a cigarette," Didi said.

Joe's eyes riveted on the woman. "You're Heidi Arundsen?"

She nodded nervously. Her size and delicate bone structure made her look young. But there was a tension about her, a strain, that showed her age.

"Go ahead. There are some tables outside. I'm going to get myself some coffee. Can I get you ladies something while I'm at it?"

He expected an answer of "Just regular coffee." Maybe with cream or sugar. But Heidi wanted a double latte with a shot of sugar-free vanilla syrup and fat-free milk. Didi was into a grande mocha, two pumps only, no whipped cream, and a piece of coffee cake.

In line, he chafed. But he had no intention of scaring Heidi away from spilling whatever she might be able to tell him. So he waited. And he was careful to get the order right. When he joined the two women at the table, he sat down casually, asked if he'd gotten everything right, then waited.

"Heidi saw the car, too," Didi informed him.

"The dark sedan?" he asked.

Heidi looked at Didi, as if for reassurance. Then she turned back to Joe. "It wasn't just dark, it was black. Tinted windows. Like Betty Olsen."

It took him a second to shift gears. Then the name registered as one he'd seen in the files about the missing prostitutes. Betty Olsen had disappeared approximately a month before Genevieve O'Brien. Betty hadn't been listed in Genevieve's case folders, but Heidi had been interviewed after Betty was reported missing.

"Betty was a friend of yours?"

"Betty lived in my building. I was out with her, chatting on the street, you know. And I saw her get into the black sedan. And that was the last time I saw her. Black," she repeated. "I know it was black."

"You don't remember the make or model?"

Heidi shook her head. "It was sleek-looking."

"Sleek . . . clean, in good shape, that kind of thing?"

"Yes."

"Like some kind of official car?"

"Maybe," she said, but she sounded uncertain. "I've seen hundreds of cars like it on the street. To tell you the truth, a couple things ran through my mind. I was thinking the dude probably had money. And I was thinking Betty might have known him, 'cuz she didn't stand by the window negotiating, just got right in."

Joe leaned back, puzzled. Who would have been driving around in a black sedan who knew both Genevieve O'Brien and a prostitute so well that they would both just jump in the car with him?

"I wish I could tell you more," Heidi said.

"Tell me more about Betty," he said.

Heidi looked sad and shook her head. "Well, for one thing, her name wasn't really Betty. She was in the country illegally. She couldn't get a regular job because . . . she doesn't have a social security number, and she doesn't pay taxes." She sniffed. "She lives in my building because the landlord is an asshole who doesn't ask questions 'cuz it's a roach motel. Half the tenants just name the rats and pretend they're pets. Genevieve talked to her one time about a way for her to get the right papers so she could stay in the country." She hesitated, looking at Didi again. "I'm the one who called the police. I called from the pay phone down the street. But they wanted me to fill out a lot of forms, and . . . anyway, they didn't do nothing. But I got Maria Rodriguez from my building to go down and file a report. She even took a day off work to do it. Didi and I made the time up for her, though. She scrubs floors." She hesitated, a strange look on her face. "Are you thinking Didi and I should scrub floors, too? That anything would be better than what we do? Maria has a scar and she's self-conscious, otherwise she'd be out here, too. Don't fool yourself that there aren't a lot of women out there tired of scrubbing and more than willing to hit the streets."

"Heidi, I wasn't about to judge you, I swear. I'm grateful for whatever you can tell me."

Heidi leaned back, not looking quite so friendly. "Right. 'Cuz this time a rich girl disappeared."

"Heidi, I was hired because a rich girl disappeared. I hope I can stop whatever is happening so no more girls disappear, rich *or* poor."

"Don't forget the Mimic," Didi said.

Heidi waved a hand in the air. "When he dressed up, the Mimic was the prettiest girl I've ever seen. He was taken by accident, I bet." She stared hard at Joe. "And they're dead, aren't they? They're all dead. And you know what? I told the cops Betty disappeared in a black sedan, a *nice* sedan, but *they* think she disappeared *after* that. Even though they never found anyone who saw her after me. Why don't people ever want to believe that rich people can be perverts? Those assholes are looking for a bum, a dealer . . . some low-life creep."

"Heidi, believe me, the cops aren't fools. They put policewomen out on the streets for a while, right?"

Heidi let out a sigh and nodded. "Yeah, they did. But

I never saw that car when those girls were around. Though . . . hey!" She sat back suddenly, staring at him. "I know you."

"You do?"

"You're dead." Her mouth opened in an O. "I saw your picture in the paper."

"You saw my cousin's picture in the paper. He was in the paper a lot. He wrote a column. He was killed last year in an explosion at Hastings House."

"Hastings House?" Heidi murmured.

"Do you know something about Hastings House?"

Heidi shrugged sadly. "No . . . but I remember Betty saying how Genevieve wanted to go to that party thing there last year—the one that ended up with that explosion. She told Betty some snooty society friend of her aunt's was in charge but she wasn't going to beg to be invited. She used to walk by the place all the time, though."

Those words stunned him into silence. He wasn't sure what this new information meant, if anything, but it was a link. A tenuous link.

A "link" that might mean nothing.

Lots of people walked past historic sites. Some people walked by them every day, hurrying to work, never noticing them. But others loved the fact that they could walk by places that had a history, that meant something.

"I see," he said at last. What the hell did he see?

"Heidi, is there anything else?" Didi asked for him.

"I don't think so. . . ." She brightened suddenly. "I

have Betty's things. That bastard landlord just dumped them in the hall, so I took them. Just in case she came back, you know? You can see them. I mean, if you're interested."

"I would love to go through Betty's things."

"I told you—I live in a roach motel."

"I'll see if I can kill a few for you. Lead the way."

Leslie did stay at the hospital. She stayed for two hours. Then she checked herself out, collected her belonging and discovered that she had a dozen messages on her cell phone. One of them was from Brad, and she hastily called him as soon as she reached the street—determined to catch a cab and not ride the subway again, at least not that day.

He answered his phone immediately and went off on a tirade. What had happened to her? Why hadn't she made sure someone called him? Was she all right? He was furious that he'd had to hear about what happened on the news. How could she do this to him?

"Brad, you're being dramatic."

"Really? Do you remember calling me, asking me to meet you this afternoon?" he demanded.

"And I still want to meet you. At Hastings House."

"Don't be an idiot. You almost died today."

"But I didn't. And I'm fine. I'm on my way to Hastings House now. Are you coming?"

"All right. I'll beat you there."

He did.

He was lounging on the porch with Melissa when the cab dropped her off.

They both rushed to the curb to help her from the cab. It took her twenty minutes and more energy than she had to spare to convince Melissa that she was all right. Then she led Brad down to the basement, where she showed him the wall and the bones, and the records she had copied from the library, then told him what she wanted him to do.

He stared at her. He almost looked as if he were frightened of her.

"Shit. This is getting uncanny."

"Brad, I've studied the history of this house. It will work."

He shook his head. "You want me to pretend that I just walked into Hastings House and started on the basement wall with a pickax because I knew that I'd find bones?"

She took a step back from him, frowning. *Actually, yes, that was exactly what she wanted.*

"Um . . ."

"You're too good at this, and it's getting scary," he informed her.

"Brad, please?"

He crossed his arms over his chest. "What does Wonder Boy think about all this?"

"Wonder Boy?"

"Joe."

"Don't be an idiot," she said.

"Sorry. I guess I'm jealous."

"He's been a very good friend."

"So have I."

"I know that, Brad."

"Sorry. But what does he think? I mean, is he getting a little freaked out, too?"

"What are you getting at?"

"I can't keep pretending to be in on all your discoveries—especially not when someone else knows the truth."

She started to laugh. "I think you don't mind doing it, you just don't want to get caught."

"Something like that," he admitted, laughing suddenly. "Okay, I'm pathetic. I love to get the credit. But it's not mine."

"I don't want any credit. I just want things . . . taken care of. Look, I know who this woman is. Her husband murdered her and told the world she'd left him. We need to bring the truth to light."

He was silent for a moment, his head lowered. "All right. You read the records, got me to do the same. We shared some logic and a hunch. We'll prove who she is when we make the announcement, and we'll get her a nice burial with all the right . . . whatever. Like I'm sure it makes a difference, all these years later."

"It makes a difference," Leslie insisted.

He sighed. "All right. Tomorrow we'll make the announcement and arrange to have the bones removed. I'll find a reporter and a priest—Episcopalian? Do we know that?"

"We'll assume. New York at the time . . . mostly Episcopalian."

He shook his head. "The crypt you discovered is shored up now. Laymon is going to be going insane to move in that direction, too. And now you're going to be more famous than ever—she has second sight, and she survived a cave-in *and* a subway accident. People will be talking."

"Brad, come on."

"That's not me, Leslie. That's just what people are going to say."

She let out a soft sigh. "Just help me, okay?"

"I'll do my best. Hey, if you get any better at this ESP thing, maybe you can pick us some winning lottery numbers."

"I've discovered bones, Brad. Not riches."

"Yeah, so work on that, will you?" He looked exasperated, then pulled her to him and gave her a kiss on the forehead. "Leslie . . . shit. I like you, but you really have gotten . . . *eerie.*"

"Thanks a lot, Brad."

"I don't mean anything bad by that, honestly."

"Right. I'm creepy, but that's not bad."

He grinned. "No, you're creepy good," he assured her. "All right, I'm going to get out of here. Get the ball rolling."

"Thanks." She hesitated. "Brad . . . at the site, when you found me, unconscious . . ."

"Yeah?" he asked.

"You and Laymon arrived at the exact same time?"

"Yeah, why?"

She shook her head. "No reason."

Brad suddenly frowned deeply. "Are you going to ask where I was today?" he demanded.

She stared back at him, stunned.

"Nowhere near the subway," he said curtly.

"Oh, Brad! I'm sorry, I didn't mean . . . actually, I was hoping you'd seen someone," she murmured.

"No. There was no other way in, no other way out. No one suspicious, and guards all over the site, Leslie. You know that."

"I'm sorry."

"I'd die before I'd hurt you, Leslie," he said. "And I'm a coward," he added ruefully.

She stepped forward, kissing his cheek. "Thank you."

"Well, I'd better get going. I'm supposed to meet Laymon for dinner."

"Where are you going?"

"Anthony's, just down the street. He doesn't like to leave the area. You know Laymon. He's always convinced someone is after his discovery."

"And he can catch them from a restaurant?" she asked, amused.

Brad shrugged. "I guess he figures he can get back to the site quickly if he has to."

"Think I should go with you?"

"If you want. Or I can tell him you're sore from the subway thing."

"No . . . I'll run up and take a shower. And call and invite Joe."

"Joe. Yeah. Sure."

"Hey, he's helping."

Brad took a deep breath. "Helping? Or reminding you of Matt every single second?"

"They're two very different people, and I know that, Brad."

"Are you sure of that?" Brad persisted gently.

"Joe is helping."

"Joe's convinced the explosion here was intentional," Brad said wearily.

"Maybe it was."

"Who the hell would gain from it?" Brad said.

She wondered if she should be dead honest when she was alone with him in a small underground room, then told herself not to be ridiculous. Melissa knew where they were, not to mention she had worked with Brad for years.

"Maybe someone was trying to kill Matt."

"And didn't care about hurting a houseful of other people?"

"A lot of people couldn't care less about who gets in the way when they have a goal in mind."

"Why kill Matt?"

"Because his voice mattered."

Brad looked down for a minute, then took a step toward her. To her amazement, he almost lost his balance and nearly fell face forward on top of her. She jumped, and he swore. "Where the hell did that box come from?" he demanded irritably.

She reached out, steadied him, gave him a quick kiss

on the cheek and retreated. "Let's go on up." She hurried toward the stairs, suddenly afraid that he was going to drag her back.

He didn't. He followed her up, asking, "So you're coming to dinner?"

"I think so. If I change my mind, I'll call your cell."

"Not from down there, I hope," he told her, pointing back down the stairs. "I doubt you'll get a signal down in your basement."

"I'm not going back to the basement," she said. "Do me a favor? Tell Melissa I'm going up to take a shower and not to worry about me, just to lock up when she leaves, okay?"

"Sure," he said, studying her. "You need a vacation, you know."

"We've just started."

"You still need a vacation."

She smiled. "Do you really want to miss your chance to be famous? Or infamous? One or the other, anyway." She laughed. "Now, get out of here. I'll see you later."

She waited until he was gone, listening as he talked to Melissa at the exit and then, when she was sure he was out the door, headed back down to the basement. She felt a desire so strong it was beyond resisting to go back to the basement.

Where the hell had the box that Brad had tripped over come from?

"Matt?" she whispered, then shook her head. Was there a *feel* to the room?

She had discovered the remains of a murdered woman, she told herself. It was natural that the basement would feel . . . haunted. But as she looked around, she could see various items that had been used to renovate the house. A few rolls of wallpaper, some paint cans, stirrers, boxes of nails and tools. She didn't feel as if it were a tomb, even though it had been exactly that for the poor woman in the wall. But there was something here that drew her, kept her from leaving. She needed to call Joe, she realized, and let him know that she'd left the hospital, in case he was planning to go visit her, and invite him to dinner. She reached in her pocket for her cell phone, making a tour of the room as she did so.

It was exactly the size of the servants' pantry above. There was another basement beneath the main house; this area had been used strictly for food and kitchen storage.

From the hearth, she walked around the perimeter of the room, her phone forgotten in her hand. The wall was entirely bricked. She tried to estimate her whereabouts. If she were able to tunnel through the earth and went north, then a bit to the east, she would reach the dig. The crypt she'd found there was quite a bit deeper than this basement, though. If she were to head further east, she realized, she would come to City Hall.

Curious, she laid out the subway construction records she had copied alongside those of the house. By the late 1900s, there had been elevated trains, or els, in Lower Manhattan. At the very beginning of the twentieth century, the first subway lines had gone in. The very first had run from City Hall to 145th Street. By 1910, there had been several lines. On a later map, she could see how many of the original tunnels had been abandoned. There were also work shafts that had once aided the subway workmen, and many of those had been abandoned, as well.

Okay, so there were a lot of holes in the Manhattan earth. What did that mean?

She hesitated, wondering if she was imagining the rush of air and looked around.

"Matt?" she said softly, hopefully. "I know . . . oh, Matt, there's something of you here, I know it," she whispered.

It seemed, she thought, that she felt a touch. A caress, soft and tender, against her cheek. And then a whisper.

Leave . . . please, leave.

"I can't."

You must.

"Let me see you, touch you. I know you're here."

She waited.

Nothing.

"Leave the basement?" she wondered aloud.

Go!

There was an urgency in the voice this time.

"Leave the basement? Leave the house? Leave New York?" Again, she spoke aloud. Again, all she felt in return was a movement of the air.

Or was it a cruel trick of her imagination?

"Matt . . . in the subway, I saw you. I know Joe was there, too, and he pulled me out. But at the beginning . . . it was your face. Your voice."

Go. Go!

"All right!"

She started to roll up her maps, and that was when she heard the sobbing.

13

The place really was a rat hole. Joe wondered if there was an agency in the city that looked into situations like this. Probably. It would mean a lot of red tape, he was certain. Still, it was worth checking into, he decided.

Space was at a premium in New York, that was a given. But he knew there were laws to protect tenants against these kinds of situations. But since most of the inhabitants were either in the country illegally or made their living in a doubtful manner, he doubted their complaints drew much response, if they even dared to make them.

Still, Heidi Arundsen was a good hostess. She had a studio with a tiny kitchen, separated by a counter from the main room, and a screen that separated the main room from the little bedroom area she had created. She kept the place spotlessly clean, but that couldn't help the leakage marks on the ceiling and walls, or hide the fact that the plaster was peeling and that some of the wires weren't properly installed.

"I'm sorry," Heidi said as they entered. "I'm really sorry."

"You keep a lovely home," he told her. "Under the worst circumstances."

"Well . . . thanks. Can I get you anything? I keep everything in the fridge. No bug eggs in my stuff."

"No, honestly, I'm just fine."

Didi had joined them. She strode across the room. "Here are the boxes with Betty's things. The cops looked for a diary and didn't find one," she said.

"There's not much there, but I kept it all anyway. Just in case," Heidi said.

Her words seemed to linger on the air. *Just in case.* None of them believed Betty was ever coming back.

"Mind if I just dig in?" he asked.

"Go ahead," Heidi said. "I'll go make some coffee."

Joe heard the women turn on a little television in the kitchen and talk softly to each other while he dug into the boxes. He didn't know what he expected to find. The first box was clothing. Washed, smelling pleasantly of fabric softener, neatly folded. Betty must have been tiny. She had skirts that would have served as a handkerchief for him.

He opened the second box and found pictures. Betty, looking young and innocent, hopeful, a brilliant smile on her face as she cradled a baby. People who might have been her parents. There was a picture of several women, Betty among them, playing softball in Central Park. There was a picture of a beautiful greyhound; on it, Betty had written, *Someday!* There were more pic-

275

tures of Betty with friends in front of the sagging old tenement, at the zoo.

Then he found a picture that arrested his attention. It was of Betty and Genevieve O'Brien—and there was a man with them. He was turned away from the camera, but his stance spoke of assurance, and he was wearing a suit that looked to have been expensively tailored.

"Heidi?" he called.

"Yeah?" she asked, hurrying over to where he was, Didi on her heels.

"Who is that?"

"That's Betty. And Genevieve. I thought you were hired to find her?"

"No, the man. Who's the man with them?"

"I . . . I don't know."

"Didi?"

"I have no idea," she said. "Hey!" she said, her attention caught by the television. "Hey, Joe, your girlfriend is on the news."

He set the box down quickly and strode into the kitchen to join them. The mayor himself was on, sternly warning people to be careful in the subway.

Ken Dryer was at his side. He went on to announce that it was Leslie MacIntyre, the archaeologist who'd been in the news recently, who had fallen and been pulled up just ahead of a speeding train. She had been taken to the hospital, but she was all right. There was a shot of Leslie, grimy and a bit tousled, smiling up at him as he walked beside the stretcher as the paramedics carried her up from the subway.

The anchorwoman went on to mention that in addition to her archaeological career, Leslie MacIntyre had been of help to the police on occasion.

"The girl must have special instincts," the co-anchor said, shaking his head. "Think ghosts are coming out of the walls to give her a hand?"

"We'll have to have her on the show," the anchorwoman said, then turned to face a different camera. "In late-breaking news from the Middle East . . ."

"Is she psychic?" Heidi asked.

"Maybe *she* should go through Betty's things, huh?" Didi asked.

Joe was already dialing the hospital on his cell, pacing the room as he was forwarded from extension to extension.

At last a nurse informed him that Miss MacIntyre had checked herself out a few hours after being admitted to the ER.

"Damn!" he swore violently, then turned to the two women. "I've got to go. Listen . . ." He wanted to throttle Leslie. He really needed to work on Genevieve's disappearance, but he was growing more and more afraid to leave Leslie alone for a minute. "Do you think I could hire the two of you?"

They looked at each other in surprise.

"I didn't think you—" Didi began, but he cut her off.

"No . . . no. I mean as assistants."

"Assistants?" Didi murmured.

"Does he mean . . . a threesome?" Heidi asked.

"I mean, to work for me." He picked up the picture of Betty, Genevieve and the mystery man. "I need to get this picture to a man named Harry Barton, up in Soho. If I give you an address, can you get it to him for me? And tell him that I need the man in the picture enhanced as much as he can. I'll pay you for being messengers, of course."

"That's a relief," Heidi muttered. "Sorry—I guess I didn't want you to turn out to be a weirdo. I can still dream, you know."

"And you don't have to pay us," Didi told him.

"I'm going to pay you because you work for a living and I'm using your time, plus *I'm* being paid, okay?"

They looked at each other again.

"It's a rich lady's money," he said. "You might as well get your piece of it."

"Done deal. Give us the address. And if you think of anything else . . . ?" Didi said, a question in her tone as her voice trailed off.

"Actually, yes. I want you both on the streets tonight," Joe said.

"He's a real reformer, isn't he?" Heidi asked Didi.

"*Not* taking tricks. I want you to keep an eye out all night."

"For a black sedan," Didi said.

"You got it. Okay, address . . . and I'll be in touch."

Joe ran down the six flights of stairs, thinking again that something needed to be done about the place. He hoped he knew the right people to do it.

If Matt were alive, he would write a column that

would have the landlord all but boiled in oil by enraged citizens.

But Matt wasn't alive.

When he reached the street, he paused. Strange. This morning it had been as if he was being warned to get to Leslie. Now . . .

Now, nothing. Where the hell had she gone? Back to Hastings House. He was sure of it.

The crying had faded. ·

Leslie walked around and around, listening for it, but it was gone. She sat on the box Brad had tripped over, frustrated. Then, suddenly, she heard it again.

She leapt up, trying to determine where the sound was coming from. At first, as she neared the hearth, she thought she had zeroed in on it. But when she got there, it seemed to be coming from the other side of the room. She walked around the small room, one hand on the wall as she went. It was all brick, and it all looked as if it had been there, getting grimy, forever.

The sound faded away again, and she went back to sitting on the box. Okay, so she was hearing ghostly tears. But she'd dug the woman out of the wall. She was doing all she could. "You know," she said aloud, "if you would all just show yourselves, I could be much more helpful."

She began to walk around the room again, this time pressing on the bricks, looking for . . . something.

She couldn't help thinking that there was more here

than met the eye. She thought about the underground railroad. And here, it might really have been underground. There were so many tunnels nearby. Underground tunnels, underground chambers. A city beneath the city.

"Leslie!"

She froze, stepping away from the wall, stunned.

The voice had come from above, from the servants' pantry.

"Leslie?"

Someone was coming down the stairs. Instinctively, she backed away, looking toward the stairs and the man coming toward her.

"Leslie?"

It was Hank Smith.

"Hey," he greeted her. "What are you doing down here? I saw the open hatch and came to check, but Brad said you were going to shower and meet him for dinner," he said, coming toward her, looking concerned. "You know, you're scaring the hell out of us. I can't believe you didn't hurt yourself with that kind of a fall."

"A few bruises, that's all. I was lucky," she said. He'd closed the hatch behind him, she realized. It had gotten darker, with only artificial light around them. Corners became deep shadows.

Hank was, as usual, handsomely dressed, but his attire was *GQ* casual. White cotton shirt, beige jacket, jeans, Dockers. Hair clean and slick, smelling of a subtle aftershave.

"So . . . what are you doing here?" she asked.

"I came to check on you, of course."

"Well, that was sweet of you. Thanks."

He looked around the basement. Shuddered. "Dark and creepy down here, huh?"

She laughed, aware that she sounded a little uneasy. The whole house seemed to be silent now. And she felt . . . unnerved to be alone down in the bowels of the earth with him.

I felt safer down here alone listening to ghostly tears, she thought.

"Not at all, not to me," she said, forcing a bright tone. Was it overly bright? Did he know that she was suddenly afraid to be with him?

He looked past her then and walked over to the wall, then turned to look at her. "You found more bones here?" he said incredulously.

"Brad found them, actually," she said. The room was too small. There was no way to put enough distance between them. Why the hell was she suddenly afraid of him? Or was it just being alone here with him? Even being alone with Brad had felt frightening, especially when he'd tripped and she'd momentarily thought he was attacking her.

Why not be scared? a voice in her mind taunted. *I was in the crypt and the ceiling fell. I was in the subway and someone pushed me onto the tracks. Sure, accidents. Like the accidental explosion right here at Hastings House.*

Hank was staring at her as if she had just turned emerald-green.

"Hank, you've got an engineering degree, and I'll bet you know when you're going to encounter an old post or wall or . . . whatever."

He lifted his shoulders, let them fall. "When there are old building plans, I can read them," he told her. "But . . . how the hell did you—and don't tell me it wasn't you, it was Brad, 'cuz I know that's bullshit—find bones here?"

"The same thing—I can read. You know how it is. When something doesn't jive, you have to look for whatever the truth might be."

"So . . . who is this?" he asked her.

"A Colonial housewife. Supposedly she left her husband and child, quite a scandal in those days. But women seldom desert their infants."

"Oh, yeah?" he said, and he sounded a little weary, a little jaded. "Look at recent history. There are women who *kill* their own infants."

"But, honestly, it's not the norm."

"Ah, yes, women are the fairer sex," he said.

Did he sound bitter, or was he just teasing her?

"In this case," she said, "it didn't ring true to me."

"So how did you know right where to look for the body?"

"Brad and I talked about a situation, about a time and place . . . a basement tends to be a good place, and because of the way a hearth is constructed, it's easier to remove bricks there than from a wall."

"Well, there you go," Hank said. "Has Laymon seen this yet?"

"No."

"But Brad has?"

"Of course. I just told you—"

"Yeah, yeah. Brad was in on the find."

"He knows it's here, knows I'm always poking around down here," she said.

"Oh, really?" He smiled at her. She didn't like that smile at all. Maybe it was the light. Maybe it was the irrational panic that began to assail her when she was alone in an enclosed space with anyone larger than she was.

She opened her mouth to reply.

She didn't need to.

He was standing by a stack of boxes. One suddenly teetered and fell, right by his side.

He jumped like a jack rabbit. A wrench bounced from the box and caught him on the knee. He howled with surprise and pain.

"It's not safe down here!" he exploded.

"Right. We should go up."

As she spoke, the hatch above them swung open. "Leslie?"

It was Joe, and he sounded deeply irritated.

"Joe!" she called in relief.

"You little liar! You said you were going to stay at the hospital." He was walking down the stairs as he spoke, then came to a dead stop when he saw Hank Smith. "Hank, I didn't know you were into archaeology," he said, his tone skeptical.

"I came to see how Leslie's doing—same as you, I suppose," Hank said.

Joe ignored that. He looked as if he wanted to throw Hank across the room. She set an arm on his shoulder. "I did stay for a few hours, and I'm sorry, I meant to call you right away when I left. I felt fine, and I wanted to get back. I'd made an appointment with Brad earlier, and I didn't want to break it."

"I guess you were going to show Brad the discovery the two of you made together, right?" Hank inquired politely.

"No, I had to make some plans with him," she said.

"Do you have a problem, Hank?" Joe inquired.

"You know, it's getting really musty down here," Leslie cut in quickly. "I'm going up. Oh, and Joe, we're going to meet Laymon and Brad for dinner. Mind waiting while I grab a shower?" She was up the stairs as she spoke. Joe followed on her heels, his eyes narrowed thoughtfully. As soon as Hank reached the top, she quickly closed the hatch, throwing the rug back over it. "Hank, it was very nice of you to come by, but I'm fine. I'll see you over at the dig in the next few days, I imagine."

"Sure. Take care of yourself."

"I'll see you out," Joe told him.

"I know the way."

"I've got to key in the alarm," Joe said.

They left the pantry, and Leslie followed them. Joe looked at her after he'd closed the door. "That was a lie, you know. I don't know the alarm code."

She smiled, walked over to him and set the alarm. Then she reached into her pocket for a pen, pushed up his sleeve and wrote down the numbers. "Now you do."

He was silent for a minute. "I wonder who else has these numbers?"

"Any of the big muckety-mucks in the Historical Society, I imagine, plus Melissa, Jeff and Tandy," she said.

"That's a lot of people."

"Yes, but—"

"A friend tells a friend, who tells a friend . . ."

"Joe, stop. I'm not leaving this house."

He caught her shoulders and looked earnestly into her eyes. "Come and stay with me in Brooklyn. I won't touch you—not unless you want me to. You know that."

"Joe, you are . . ." She broke off, laughing. "You're walking testosterone. You're also courteous, compassionate . . . cute as the devil. And I'm so grateful to have you on my side. But . . . there's something here. Something that has to be solved."

"Right. So that explains why I tell you not to leave a hospital and you leave it anyway. You don't call me. I come looking for you—and you're in a dark basement with an asshole who should never be trusted."

"I'm sorry. I didn't invite him down."

"My point exactly."

"I need a shower. And, um, I didn't mean to presume or anything, but would you mind having dinner with Brad and Laymon?"

"No, at the moment I only mind when I don't know exactly where you are."

"Joe, you don't have to be so responsible for me just because . . . because of Matt."

"Matt is in my mind constantly," he told her quietly. "But, honestly, I'm feeling responsible for you because you're scaring me to death. You're an accident waiting to happen."

"Either that," she murmured, "or . . ."

"Or," he said bluntly, "someone *did* murder Matt. And that someone may feel you're too close to figuring out the truth."

She was startled by the wickedly stabbing trickle of pure ice that snaked down her spine. She prayed she wouldn't betray herself.

She hesitated. "Joe, are you really seeing a connection between Hastings House, Matt, the prostitutes . . . and Genevieve O'Brien?"

"Well, I did learn today that Genevieve wanted an invitation to the gala. Does that mean anything? Maybe not. Half the city probably wanted an invitation, if not for the history, for the media exposure and the all-star attendance. Matt was writing about the prostitutes. Genevieve was trying to help the prostitutes. That's what I know. So . . . is a connection a long shot? Probably. But I haven't got a hell of a lot more to go on, other than a black sedan. And," he added very softly, his gaze probing as he met her eyes, "your belief that Genevieve is still alive."

She was tempted to go to him. To feel the real, live, flesh-and-blood assurance of his arms around her, breathe in his scent. He was a good man. True, he wasn't Matt, but if she'd met him on the street, at lunch, at a friend's house . . . she would have been attracted to him. If . . .

If there had never been Matt.

She nodded. "I'm going to shower. I'll be right down."

He nodded. "I'll be in the dead room."

"What?"

"Sorry. The servants' pantry."

Leslie hurried on up the stairs. In her room, she leaned against the door, closing her eyes. "Matt," she whispered. "I know you're here. I know . . . I know you're looking after me. If only . . . oh, Matt . . ."

She hadn't cried in so long, but tears welled up in her eyes now.

And then . . .

She felt something brush against her face. The slightest caress. Just a touch . . . that wiped away her tears. She opened her eyes.

But she was alone.

Dinner was . . . boring.

Professor Laymon spent all of two seconds assuring himself that Leslie was really okay. There was only one love in that man's life, and that was his work.

Then he spent a good half hour talking about the work done in "Leslie's crypt," as he called it. Then he started on the find in the basement, and that turned into an argument, because Leslie was absolutely insistent. Those particular bones were not going to become a spectacle. She was going to contact a friend of Matt's from the paper to see that the story was written up properly, and then she was going to find an Episcopal priest who would see to it that the woman was given a decent burial.

She was a tigress when she wanted to be. Joe watched with admiration as, in the end, she bested Laymon, who finally agreed to her plans.

But in return she swore that she would be back to work in the crypt the following day.

Joe decided he liked Brad better that night. He was willing to throw his weight Leslie's way when it came to the burial for the woman in the basement at Hastings House. He was also irritated that Laymon wasn't more considerate regarding Leslie's health.

Laymon didn't even seem to realize he was there until they got to dessert.

"You don't write?" he asked.

"No, Matt was the journalist."

"You were a cop?"

"For a few years."

Joe never felt the need to explain himself. He certainly wasn't going to do so now.

He was surprised when Brad chose to do it for him.

"Joe has a degree from Columbia in criminology. Police departments all over the country fly him in when they hit a dead end."

"Oh?" Laymon looked at him with a new respect.

Joe lifted a hand. "Fresh eyes see new things sometimes," he said.

"Don't let him fool you. He solved a big cocaine thing out in Vegas recently. The casinos didn't know how the dealers were getting the goods through their private security systems. They were doing it with coffee cups," Joe said.

"Thanks," he told Brad. "But don't go being too impressed. To tell you the truth, I got the idea because of a plot I'd seen on a television show once. They'd probably seen it, too, so there you go."

Laymon stared at Leslie. "Well, I guess it doesn't much matter where an inspiration comes from when it pans out, hmm?"

Delicate little Italian cookies arrived at the table just then, along with Laymon's espresso, Leslie's cappuccino, and the plain old coffee he and Brad had ordered.

"I understand you're convinced that the explosion at Hastings House was no accident," Laymon said, his eyes surprisingly sharp as they met Joe's.

"Hey, Matt was my cousin. Can't blame me if I question what happened," Joe said lightly.

"Where did you get the idea that Joe was still investigating the house?" Leslie asked.

"Well, hell." Laymon was clearly annoyed at being asked to explain himself. "Brad and Ken have gotten to be drinking buddies. Ken knows what you're up to."

"I'm not exactly 'up to' anything," Joe said.

"How are you doing on your quest for that young woman?" Laymon demanded.

"Hopefully, I'm getting a little closer every day."

"Does it matter now?" Laymon asked.

"I beg your pardon?"

"She's been gone a long time. She's undoubtedly dead."

"One way or the other, I'll find her," Joe said. He wasn't sure why, but the tension was growing around the table.

"Pass a cookie, Brad, please?" Leslie said lightly. Joe lowered his head. She was always determined to defuse a tense situation. Smart. He should have held his temper better with Hank Smith that afternoon. He didn't want to find himself persona non grata at the site or anywhere else Leslie might be.

"It's sad," Laymon murmured. "The aunt—Eileen Brideswell—she's a major contributor to the Historical Society."

"I imagine she's a major contributor to many charities," Leslie said.

Laymon nodded, leaning back, crossing his arms over his chest. "Strange woman, Eileen. She still loves all the musty little pubs of her youth. But, I'll tell you one thing. Genevieve O'Brien's grandfather was a tough old hickory stick. He wouldn't have approved much of Genevieve. He didn't feel that a bum in the street—or a prostitute—should ever be helped with a red cent. He gave to charities, all right, but he picked them carefully. He wasn't about to give a dime to anyone he felt wasn't helping themselves. The old fellow is long dead and gone, or else I'd say there was a good chance he'd walled his own niece up some-where himself."

"But he *is* dead. Long dead, as you say," Joe said.

Laymon shrugged. "Funny thing, I'd see the girl now and then. She loved to come and look at the house."

"She appreciated history?" Brad said.

"I guess. But it was strange. She'd walk around and around it. It was as if . . . it was as if she wasn't looking at the house, exactly, but at something more."

"Why didn't she come to the gala?" Joe asked. "I mean, you knew her, knew she was interested in the place. You could have given her an invitation."

"It never occurred to me," Laymon said with a shrug. "All she had to do was ask her aunt if she wanted to go."

But she wouldn't have done that, Joe thought.

"You don't think Genevieve O'Brien blew the place up out of some kind of bitterness, do you?" Brad asked.

"No," Joe said.

"Then she must have known something about the house that intrigued her," Leslie mused.

"Suspected, anyway," Joe said.

"Don't you think this is all getting a bit farfetched?" Laymon said. "The blast was over a year ago." He looked at Joe. "Genevieve has been missing . . . what? About two months?"

"Right around that," Joe agreed.

"Well, then, at least you can be pretty sure that no

one was trying to blow *her* up," Laymon said cheerfully. "She disappeared months later."

He realized they were all staring at him. "Sorry, but you three are the ones putting a lot of the truth of the matter that the blast was an accident. Some sicko is picking up hookers, and Genevieve just wound up in the mix. One day the bodies will turn up. Maybe they'll get the guy, maybe they won't. Sad, but that's the way it is."

Joe shook his head, staring at Laymon. "That's the way it *can* be, but not this time. Trust me. This guy is going down."

Dinner had ended. Laymon offered to pick up the tab, and Joe let him. He thanked him for the meal, pulling back Leslie's chair for her. "I'll see you home." He forced himself not to look at the other two men with real warning in his eyes. "And I'll be on guard. All through the night."

Leslie felt guilty. Horribly guilty.

Joe would sit in his car all night again. She knew it.

But she just couldn't ask him into the house for the night. Not yet.

She tried to talk him into going home, and he assured her that he would do so in the morning, when Hastings House was filled with people, when the bones in the basement were being gently removed— when she wouldn't be alone with anyone. He made her swear to that last point.

If he thought she should have the decency to suggest

that he sleep in the house, he didn't say so. It wasn't that there wasn't something about him, his touch, his scent, the sound of his voice.

There were just . . . things that needed to be solved. Leslie couldn't begin to voice what was going on in her heart and mind, and she was grateful that he didn't seem to expect her to.

Before he left her to return to his car, however, he asked her to look around for the list that Greta was supposed to have sent over that day. She found it on the kitchen counter and gave it to him. He told her not only to key in the alarm, but to lock her bedroom door, as well.

At the very least, she could do that for him. Upstairs, she locked herself in her bedroom and went to bed.

As usual, she lay awake, longing for something real. Longing to see Matt . . .

As she saw so many others.

But he didn't appear.

Not until she dreamed.

That night, he lay by her side, watching her. In her dream, she opened her eyes and saw him. His expression was grave. Only the slightest hint of a rueful smile curled his lips. He stroked her cheek, curled his fingers around hers.

"You were there, in the subway," she told him. "You saved me."

"Joe pulled you out."

"But you gave me the strength I needed to move, to save myself. And both of you were pretty fierce in that basement tonight."

Matt pressed a kiss against her fingers. "I keep trying. . . . I guess it takes time and practice, and then . . . maybe the heart or the soul or essence or whatever we are . . . maybe there are fragments of this being that have life of a sort. I can only find anything real in me when it comes to you, when I'm afraid for you. Leslie, I really want you to leave this house."

"I will. Soon."

His smile broadened. "Joe was right. You *are* a little liar."

"Matt . . . I can't live without knowing the truth."

"I just hope you can live with it," he murmured, then shook his head, his expression growing pained. "Leslie . . . I love you. You have to move on."

"But I have my dreams. *We* have my dreams."

"Leslie, I had my time. No one knows the rhyme or reason. No one knows . . . well, except maybe me, now."

"What do you mean?"

"I know that I'm here for you," he said.

"Poor Brad," she told him with amusement. "You made him trip, didn't you?"

"I'm afraid of all of them," he said.

"Why?"

He was quiet. She thought that she had lost him, except she still felt his arms around her. "Say they *were* after me when they set the explosion and just didn't care that three other people died." There was anger in his voice, anger that others might have died because of him. "Say that it did have to do with my writing about the prostitutes. That would mean that, whoever the killer is, the abductor . . ."

"Do you know if the girls are dead?"

"No, but . . . say there is something out there, very clever, obviously sick, a pervert, but a clever one . . . then I'd say that person was here that night."

"Matt, so many people were here that night."

"The killer is hardly going to be a Broadway star," he murmured.

"Well, unlikely, but—"

"Who's still in this vicinity on a regular basis? Who knows the area? David Laymon, Brad Verdun—"

"Brad's been in Virginia until now," she reminded him.

"Is that really so far away?" he queried. "Four or five hours by car, less by plane."

"I can't believe—"

"But you were afraid of him this afternoon, weren't you? And I'm not saying it's Brad. There's Greta, but she would die before doing anything to hurt this place, and anyway, it's not a woman taking the prostitutes."

"How do you know?"

"Something would have been said, someone would have noticed. That kind of thing . . . the girls on the street, the other girls, would have taken a closer look if it had been a woman. The place was teeming with cops, including our good friend Robert Adair, and the ever-in-front-of-the-camera Ken Dryer. And then there's Hank Smith."

He really didn't like Hank Smith, she thought, burrowing deeper into his arms.

"Did you ever meet Genevieve O'Brien?" she asked sleepily.

"Yes."

"Is she everything they say? Passionate, selfless, generous?"

"I met her at the paper once. She was being interviewed by one of our reporters for the local section— she was furious with the slumlords. She was lovely, vivacious, charming . . . and, yes, passionate. She really did care about other people. You think she's alive, don't you?"

"I do."

"Maybe," he murmured. She heard such a terrible note of frustration in his voice. *If I could just change something,* she heard beneath his words. *If I could just* make *life right for someone else, then . . . then it would make sense.*

She turned and held him fiercely. "I love you so much."

He was quiet.

"Don't go," she pleaded, then spoke no more. She didn't want to awaken; she didn't want to interrupt the vision that came to her by night.

In her dream, she drifted and, half asleep, felt him again. She turned in his arms. God, the dream was so vivid. She could feel his heat, the dampness of sweat on his skin, the strength of his muscles beneath her hands, the hardness of his body and his erection. The hot-lava stroke of his tongue over her flesh. Inside and out . . . his being, his essence, around her, within her.

Lips on her breasts, intimately between her thighs. The pulse and beat and hunger of melding together, striving and writhing . . . climbing, rising, exploding into the moment of climax with a strange mixture of tenderness and violence, all so vividly real . . .

She felt his touch on her hair, his cheek against hers. "Leslie, I'm afraid for you. I try, and sometimes, I find the strength to actually touch this world. But then I'm drained and you're alone, and I'm so afraid for you. . . ."

"It's all right," she assured him, then cuddled close and fell asleep in his arms.

She awoke suddenly, certain she could hear the sound of sobs coming from below, from the basement below the dead room.

14

Alone and awake in his car, parked just far enough away not to be conspicuous, Joe read over the list. He wished he'd been there that night, and he tried to envision the scene in his mind's eye.

He kept coming back to a place where he froze, afraid.

For Leslie.

Accident in the crypt, accident in the subway . . . accident in this house?

Like hell.

So if the first two weren't accidents and everything was connected, then he needed to look at the people around them now and compare those names to the list from the night of the gala. Professor Laymon? Absurd. He had no interest in anything but his work. Still, tomorrow he would assure himself that Laymon had been at the site all day.

Brad? But why?

Jealousy?

Robert Adair had been the one to put him on the case, which seemed to rule him out. Hank Smith? He hated the guy, but that was no reason to suspect him.

And no reason not to.

Was Genevieve the connecting factor?

Or was it Leslie herself? What if someone had actually been trying to kill Leslie, not Matt?

It made no sense. But the idea continued to plague him.

What about Ken Dryer? He was at the site far more often than a police spokesman needed to be, even with Laymon making demands and everyone trying to bow to his wishes, since the women behind him and the Historical Society were some of the wealthiest in the state.

Hank Smith. Ken Dryer. Brad Verdun. Laymon. Robert Adair. They'd all been at the gala. and now they were all revolving in the same social circle again.

He set down his list, startled, as he saw lights go on in the house. He sat for a moment, then hurriedly turned off his dome light and exited his car. As he did so, he noticed something that he hadn't seen before.

A man.

He had blended with a lamppost at first. But now, with the car light off . . .

The guy had been standing there all along, watching the house.

He'd thought himself completely hidden. Maybe he'd seen the lights go on, too, and shifted his position, the movement attracting Joe's attention.

Joe raced toward the lamppost, but the man heard him coming and shot down the street like greased lightning. Joe could run, but the guy had a head start on him. Joe chased him down one street, around the block and toward the site, where he saw a uniformed cop striding along the fence.

"Hey!" he called out.

"Yes?" the officer said, watching calmly as Joe headed toward him.

"I just chased a guy around this way. Did you see him? Did you see anyone running?"

The officer looked him up and down. "I didn't see anyone running, but who are you? And what are you doing chasing people at this time of night?"

Joe produced his ID.

"Oh, hell, you're him."

"Yeah, Matt Connolly's cousin."

"Huh?" The guy looked confused. "I just saw your picture with a story about a sting in Vegas. Good work."

"Thanks. Are you sure you didn't see anything?"

"Mr. Connolly, I swear to you, no one went by here."

"All right, thanks. Keep an eye out for anything suspicious, will you?"

"That's what they pay me to do."

Joe just nodded. He'd lost the guy, plain and simple, and he was irritated with himself. He was also growing alarmed. He'd left the house. He'd left Leslie.

He turned and headed back toward the house, running full speed as soon as he was out of the cop's sight. As he ran, he blessed whatever random bit of luck had caused Leslie to give him the alarm code that day.

As soon as he reached the door, he punched it in quickly, terrified of what he might find on the other side.

There were no doubt plenty of people who would certify her as stark raving mad without question. She was in a reputedly haunted house, all alone, in the dead of night. And she wasn't content to stay safely in her room.

No, she just had to head down to the basement, where there were still bones interred in the wall.

Wide awake, wearing slippers and a robe, she took one of the lanterns from the kitchen table and went back to the servants' pantry. She lifted the braid rug, then the hatch door.

For a moment, even she hesitated. The stairs looked as if they led to a giant and eternal black abyss.

But she was certain that she had heard sobbing, a sobbing that tore at her heart.

She held the lantern out before her and started down

the steps. The room began to fill with a diffuse light as she approached the bottom of the steps.

She could see Elizabeth's bones in the wall, but they didn't frighten her at all. She knew in her heart that she was doing everything she could for Elizabeth.

She wasn't afraid of ghosts, she realized.

She was afraid of the living.

She reached the bottom of the steps and walked into the center of the room. There was silence for the longest time, but then she heard it again. Sobbing. But try as she might, she couldn't ascertain where it was coming from. The sound faded before she could figure it out.

Then, to her astonishment, she heard something else. Footsteps, then two bangs. A door being opened and closed?

And then . . .

Silence.

She waited, not breathing. But still, she could hear nothing at all.

Elizabeth's empty-eyed skull stared at her in the strange lamplight.

Then she heard footsteps above her and froze.

"Leslie?"

She exhaled at last. It was Joe.

"Down here!" she called to him.

"You're back in the basement?" He sound incredulous. In a moment, he joined her.

"Joe, what are you doing here?" she asked, trembling.

"I saw the lights go on."

She smiled. "God, I'm sorry. I never meant to alarm you."

"What are you doing in the basement—*now?*"

"I heard crying."

"Crying?"

She opened her mouth, suddenly not knowing what to say. She didn't want him to know that she was convinced she was hearing the heartfelt sobs of a ghost. He was beginning to trust in her, but . . .

"I thought I heard something."

"So you came down here alone?" His tone was harsh, but he seemed to be trembling a little himself.

"I'm sorry."

"What the hell am I going to do with you?" he demanded.

He walked forward, grabbed her shoulders and pulled her against his chest. "What am I going to do?"

"Joe, it's okay. You can't get to the basement except through the house."

He was silent.

"Joe?" She pulled slightly away.

He looked down at her. "Leslie, someone was out there watching the house," he told her.

She looked up at him in alarm.

"I chased him, but he got away."

"Who was it?"

"If I knew, I'd have every cop in the city on his tail."

She had to smile at that. "Joe, I'm not sure we can have someone arrested for watching the house."

"Let's get out of here, shall we?" he asked.

She nodded, heading up the stairs, with him in her wake. There was no sense in trying to get him to stay down there with her. Whatever she had been hearing, it had stopped, at least for now.

She didn't want to stay in the servants' pantry, either. She quickly walked back into the main kitchen. Joe followed her.

"What time is it, anyway?" she asked. "Honestly, I'm so sorry. You're sleeping in your car to begin with, and then this. You must think I'm trying to torture you."

"It's okay."

"Actually, it's not," she murmured. "It's five . . . pretty early, huh?" It was, and she was exhausted.

"Joe, there's another room upstairs that they keep for the Historical Society workers—it doesn't open to the public. It's all made up. Why don't you try to grab a few hours' sleep? I'll do the same."

He arched a brow. "You're sure?"

"Yes." She smiled. "I promise I won't run out on you."

He hesitated. "All right. I guess it's going to be a long day tomorrow. Today. Whatever."

He followed her up to the second level, where she pointed out the door to the extra bedroom. He nodded, a smile on his lips. "Good night. And lock your door."

"But you're here now."

"Precisely," he teased. Then, "Seriously, lock your bedroom door whenever you go to sleep, okay? Please."

"All right," she agreed. "Good night."

"Good night."

They went into their separate rooms. Leslie didn't think she would be able to sleep. Then she prayed that she would.

She did.

Sadly, she didn't dream. And she only woke up a few hours later because the morning light was streaming in on her face and there was activity below.

She flew out of bed. Wrapped in her robe, barefoot, she walked out to the landing. Melissa was there, along with Professor Laymon, Brad and several grad students walking in carrying wooden crates.

"Hey there, sleepyhead," Brad called up at her cheerfully.

"I'll be right down."

"Good morning," Melissa said. She winked, then hurried halfway up the stairs as the others returned to the task of taking equipment toward the back of the house. "He's gone," she whispered.

"What?"

Melissa winked again. "Don't worry—your secret is safe with me. I looked for his car, and he's gone."

"Oh . . . you mean Joe?"

"Of course."

"Melissa, he was in the extra bedroom."

"Sure. But it's okay. My lips are sealed, I swear." She mimed zipping her lips.

Leslie rolled her eyes, then headed back to her room to shower and dress.

By the time she headed downstairs, she was greeted by an astounding surprise. For a moment she couldn't imagine who the tall white-haired man and slim blond woman talking to Professor Laymon might be. Then, while she was still halfway up the stairs, she recognized them. "Adam! Nikki!" she cried with pleasure.

Nikki turned, her delicate features forming an instant smile. Adam had his calm, fatherly look in place.

She didn't know who to hug first. "I can't believe you're here. *Why* are you here?" she demanded, hugging them each twice for good measure.

"I guess you three really *are* old friends," Professor Laymon said dryly. "I've been telling them about the remains in the basement," he went on, then looked pointedly at his watch. "You *are* working today, aren't you?"

"Of course," she assured him. "You're not just dropping by and leaving, are you?" she asked, looking from Adam to Nikki. "And where's Brent?" she asked Nikki.

"He couldn't come. He's out in Los Angeles at the moment. Adam told me he was coming up here, so I decided to join him," Nikki said. "I'm meeting Brent out west, but I have tonight."

"I'm leaving in the morning for London, but I'm here tonight, too," Adam assured her.

"Great."

"You didn't call, so I assume things are going well," Nikki said.

"Going well? She's incredible," Laymon said. "She found a crypt that could have taken us forever to uncover. I've been champing at the bit to explore it, quite honestly. A ceiling came down almost immediately, but the workmen have shored everything up now. But, leave it to Leslie, she's gone and found more bones here."

"Every discovery is an important one," Nikki said.

"Well, in this case, I'm trying very hard to see that the lady is given a proper Episcopalian burial," Leslie said.

"Have you done anything in that direction yet?" Adam asked.

"No, but I'm sure we won't have any problems."

"I have an old friend in the church," Adam said. "I can cut through some of the red tape for you, since I take it you don't want her sent out of the city?"

Leslie smiled at Adam. The man was a veritable miracle worker.

"Hey, maybe we could move this along some," Brad said, walking over to join the conversation.

As the introductions were made, Brad kept looking at the two newcomers strangely. "I've met you before," he told Adam. "You were at the hospital last year, when Leslie . . ."

"Yes, I was. Good to actually meet you," Adam said, shaking Brad's hand.

"Why don't you guys take a tour of this place this morning, then grab some lunch, and I'll be back by late afternoon," Leslie suggested to Adam and Nikki.

"I love tours," Nikki said.

"She gives ghost tours in New Orleans," Leslie explained.

"I thought she worked for Mr. Harrison," Brad said.

"I do research. Adam has researchers working all over the country," Nikki said.

Brad continued to look suspicious, and Leslie decided that he must be feeling proprietorial. A half hour earlier, he would have been certain he knew all her friends, and she suspected he wasn't enjoying knowing he'd been wrong.

That guess proved to be correct. Down in the basement, the crates were ready, the tool boxes were open, and work had begun. Time had taken its bitter toll on the remains. Laymon had already given her a speech about how the removal of the bones should have been videotaped, but out of respect for her feelings, he had decided not to allow filming in the basement until after the remains had been taken away. After Nikki thanked him, he left to go back to the work he considered important, exploring the crypt. Leslie and Brad were busy at the delicate work of preparing the skeleton for removal. Down here, conditions hadn't been kind. There were a few patches of hair on the skull and a few bits of fabric so blackened by time that they were barely identifiable as cotton.

"Are we test-tubing anything?" Brad asked her.

"No. Let's just get her a real burial. Please?"

"You know, someone with more power could step in on top of us."

"I have a feeling they won't."

"Because of your friend?"

"Adam, you mean?"

"Who is that guy?"

"An old friend." Well, Adam *was* old, even if she hadn't actually known him all that long.

"I see. He has that air about him."

"What air?"

"Like a guy who speaks softly but somehow everyone knows he's carrying a really big stick."

Leslie shrugged. "He owns his own company, and he's done work for the government."

Brad laughed. "He doesn't look like an assassin."

"That's because he's *not* an assassin."

"Then what does he do for the government?"

"Research."

"What kind of research?"

"Historical, of course. Hand me that brush, please."

"You're evading me."

"I'm telling you the honest-to-God truth," she vowed.

He held the brush for a minute, looking at her suspiciously, before finally handing it over.

A few minutes later, as they worked in silence, Brad gasped.

"What?"

"There—on the floor." He bent down to take a closer look. "I take it you won't mind if we have this tested?"

"What is it?" she asked.

"The shot that killed her," Brad said softly.

• • •

When Joe got to the site he was glad to find out that Laymon and Brad had already gone on to Hastings House to oversee the removal of the bones by the basement hearth. He didn't want to see either one of them.

One of the workers directed him to the guard who had been on duty at the gate the day before. He remembered seeing Laymon early in the morning and Brad late in the afternoon.

He went on to question the grad students. They, too, had seen Laymon early and Brad late.

"How about Hank Smith? Was he around yesterday?" Joe asked two of the students, a married couple in their early thirties who had met as undergrads on a dig. It had been a life of digging in the dirt for the two of them ever since.

"Calvin Klein, you mean?" the husband asked with a grin. "The guy with the suits?"

"Right. Him."

"He hangs around here a lot," the wife said. "Well, he hangs around for a while, goes to his trailer, comes out, hangs around . . . who knows what he does?"

"But was he around yesterday?" Joe asked.

They looked at each other, thinking. "I get busy with a dig, and . . ." The husband lifted his hands apologetically.

"No," the wife said decisively. "I know I didn't see him. I actually look for him every day."

"Wendy!" her husband said, surprised and hurt.

"It's his clothes, Cal. I love to see what he's going to wear next."

"Were any of the cops around yesterday?" Joe asked.

They both stared at him. Cal cleared his throat. "Take a look around. There are always a ton of cops."

"I'm thinking of Robert Adair, older guy, heavy, but all muscle. And the good-looking one who does the public speaking."

"Did you see either of them?" Wendy asked Cal.

"I don't think so," Cal said.

"I'm not sure about the older guy, but I didn't see the good-looking one."

"You're sure?" Joe asked.

"I would have noticed," Wendy said.

"Oh, so it's not just the clothes?" Cal asked wryly.

Joe left them to their friendly bickering and went on, still trying to put the pieces together in his mind.

Leslie was anxious about how Elizabeth's bones were being treated, but she was equally anxious to spend time alone with Adam and Nikki. For now, though, there was nothing more she could do for the evening. The bones were safely crated, and she and Brad had secured some of the fabric and surrounding earth for testing. In the morning, they would have to make a trip to the morgue, but once the remains were officially aged, Elizabeth could take her place in hallowed ground.

Leslie tried hard not to be rude to Brad, though she

was aware that he was angling for an invitation to join her and her friends. She gave him a quick hug. "Finish up with the tools, will you, please? I want to spend as much time as I can in with Adam and Nikki, and they both have to leave tomorrow."

"Sure. You guys going barhopping?"

"No, we're a sedate crowd."

"She's pretty cute to be sedate."

"She's married. Happily."

"Damn," he said. Then, "I'm teasing!" he added when she stared at him. He let out a sigh. "Go on. Have fun. I'll finish here."

She ran up the stairs, realizing that the basement had held no eerie mysteries all during the day. She hadn't heard or felt anything. Did that simply mean that she had been letting her imagination run wild? Was she inventing half of what she had been told was a "talent"? Or maybe her mind had been so filled with the present today that she hadn't had time to dwell on the past.

She could hear two tours going on. Tandy was in the parlor, while Jeff had moved on to the dining room. She quickly popped her head into each room to see if Adam and Nikki were there, but there was no sign of them. She headed upstairs to her room. As she got ready to hit the shower, she remembered that she hadn't spoken with Joe all day. She hesitated. She desperately wanted to speak with Nikki alone; she needed to ask her why she couldn't communicate with Matt when she was awake. But she also felt she had to call

Joe, given his concern for her welfare. And, whether it was because he was Matt's cousin or not, she felt an affinity for him, as if she had known him, been close to him, for years, rather than just days.

She called Joe, but he didn't pick up. She left him a hasty message, telling him friends had unexpectedly showed up in town and she would be out with them, but to please call her cell when he could. She tried Nikki then, and Nikki did pick up. "We're just down by City Hall, but we'll head back now. Oh, and Adam saw his friend Father Behan. Burial is all set, just as soon as the remains are cleared."

"Perfect, thanks. See you soon."

She jumped into shower, then paused. The house seemed so . . . empty. There had to be at least fifty people downstairs, and yet she felt . . .

As if the house was quiet. As if it were silent, watching, waiting. . . .

"Matt?" she whispered. He wouldn't leave her. He would trust her. If he could, he would come to her. But she had no sensation of him being near.

Thank God she would be able to explain some of what was going on with her now, and to people who wouldn't immediately jump to the conclusion that she had become delusional in the wake of her loss.

The thought made her feel cheerful as she dressed in heels and a knit halter dress, then threw an embroidered shawl over her shoulders. When she went to transfer her essentials into a dressier handbag than she usually used, she saw that there was a message on her phone.

It was Joe. He wanted her to call and tell him where they would be, and said he would join them at some point during the evening.

By the time she went downstairs, the tours were gone, Melissa was getting ready to leave, and Adam and Nikki were waiting in the hall.

Melissa, like Brad, looked as if she would like an invitation to hang around. Normally, Leslie would have asked her to join them at least for a drink, but not tonight. She was too desperate to spill her guts to her friends. "I'll get the doughnuts tomorrow morning," she told Melissa in answer to her hopeful look.

"Okay . . . cool. I'll be in early, like usual. Will I see you two again?" she asked Adam and Nikki, trying to hide her disappointment at being excluded.

"I don't have to be at the airport until around ten or eleven," Adam said, smiling. "I'm sure I'll see you in the morning. Good night."

At last Melissa was gone, and the alarm had been set, and Leslie spun around on the stairs to face her friends. "I'm so glad to see you guys!" she exploded.

"Was it a mistake to come back here?" Nikki asked gently.

"No . . . no, I would never say that, but . . ."

"Is Matt here?" Adam asked.

"Yes. And no."

"Why don't we find a place to eat and you can tell us all about it?" Nikki asked.

"There's a great pub around the corner, O'Malley's.

It's been there since before I first came to New York,"
Adam said.

"Sounds good to me. There's . . . a lot to tell," Leslie
said.

"We've got all night," Nikki said.

"I don't even know where to begin," Leslie said.

"Start with your arrival," Adam said. "We can talk
as we walk."

On the way back to his car, Joe realized with a touch
of anxiety that there were no messages on his phone.
He'd thought he'd simply missed Leslie's call while
he was out of cell range down in the crypt, but it
looked as if she hadn't called him back at all.

His association with her had apparently given him
free access to the site, so he'd decided it wouldn't be
a bad idea to check out the work being done in the
crypt for himself, just to make sure there wouldn't be
any more "accidents" of any kind down there. He
wondered how happy Laymon would have been to
find out that the people working the find considered it
to be far more Leslie's dig than his. He was certain
Laymon wouldn't appreciate the fact that he was
prowling around on his own.

The crypt yielded no clues to anything, though he
stood there just looking around for a long time. While
he stood there, he found himself talking aloud to his
dead cousin again. "What's going on here, Matt?
What the hell am I looking for?"

Damn it, Joe, don't you think I'd be doing more if I

knew? It's a mystery to me, too. It has something to do with what's happening underground, I know that much. I mean, that room where I died is right over the basement, and there are bones in the basement . . . Watch out for her, Joe.

Was that his own wishful thinking talking? Yeah, Matt, give me your blessing. She was the love of your life, and she's still in love with you, but I've got to be near her, at least. And I hope to God I'm helping.

After a while he decided he'd spent too much time by himself in a hole in the earth carrying on an imaginary conversation with his dead cousin, so he left and headed for his car. Once there, he looked at his watch, thought about what traffic was going to be like, swore and decided on the subway. As he was waiting on the platform, he found himself deep in thought again. He couldn't guarantee yesterday's whereabouts of any of the men who were becoming suspects in his mind. To imagine that any one of them could be an unbelievably crafty killer was beyond imagination. And yet, he was convinced that the missing hookers, the missing heiress and the explosion were all connected and that all he had to do was get the dots connected in the right order. He considered the possibilities as he stepped onto the train and grabbed the pole for support. The cops: Ken Dryer and Robert Adair. He'd known Robert forever, and it was Robert who'd connected him with Eileen Brideswell. Robert was a good old nose-to-the-pavement detective. Dryer was a peacock. Good at his job, though, a job that took him all over the city. The others: Hank Smith . . . the builder. He would know a lot about basements. Laymon. Seriously, did the man ever think about anything other than his work? Then again, maybe still waters ran deep, as the saying went. Laymon was so dedicated during his working hours that maybe he went off like dynamite when he wasn't digging. And Brad. Both Brad and Laymon had been working in Virginia when several of the disappearances had occurred. But the distance from New York wasn't that great.

The subway rattled on, the lights occasionally blinking off, then back on. They were deep underground. You had to love Manhattan. What it couldn't supply above—speedy transportation—it did beneath. Dark, damp and deserted, the tunnels down here seemed to stretch forever.

Had it been an accident when Leslie was pitched onto the tracks? It was actually surprising that things like that didn't happen more often than they did. So many people, a wave of humanity. The only way it could have been intentional was if someone had been following her. And he hadn't been able to clear any of his suspects; none of them had been at the dig.

So Leslie was very likely a target now, he thought.

What if she'd been the actual target all along, not Matt?

But why?

Because she had an eerie ability to find human remains.

He reached his stop and made his way up through

the crowds to the street, then the photo shop on Christopher Street. The storefront was simple, with cameras on display. It was narrow and looked like a hole-in-the-wall, but it stretched back forever. Cops and P.I.s used Harry constantly; he had a unique way with photos, no matter what their source.

"Hey," Harry said, seeing him when he entered. He had been helping an elderly lady with her cat photos, and while she was busy oohing and aahing, Harry was able to excuse himself. "Joe. How are you?"

Harry pumped his hand. Harry always reminded Joe of Dr. Bunsen Honeydew from the Muppets. He had a thatch of white hair that stood straight out to all sides, huge glasses, and was impossibly tall and thin. And he always wore a lab coat.

"Did you find anything?"

"Maybe. It would've been easier with a digital image, but I've been playing with it. Come on back and I'll show you what I've got."

Harry led Joe along a narrow hallway to the rooms behind the public area. They entered an office to the left.

"I've run off a few copies for you," Harry explained, sitting down at his computer. "But I thought you might want to see it on screen."

"Thanks."

Harry hit a button, and the photo popped up. There was Genevieve, her beautiful eyes wide and her arm around Betty.

The man was a bit to the side. Had he actually been

with them? Or had he simply been caught in the photo?

No photographic manipulation in the world could change the fact that he hadn't been facing the camera. But with the shot blown up and enhanced, Joe was able to get a sense of the man's profile. He stared for a minute, sensing that he should know who it was but unable to make an ID.

Then he swore softly.

"Did I help?" Harry asked.

"You bet," Joe told him, his heart racing. "Son of a bitch, you bet."

15

Even though she was the one who might be in trouble, Leslie had to find out how Nikki and Adam were doing—she couldn't help it. She was curious about her friends. But Nikki, sensing that Leslie had something on her mind, quickly steered her back to her own situation. But though she loved Adam, she realized that she just couldn't quite explain everything that had been happening, not to him. She merely said that Matt had been coming into her dreams, even though he hadn't made contact in any other way. She also talked about the "accidents," and she tried to explain Joe and the fact that he was so much like Matt . . . and yet not like Matt at all.

The hardest thing to explain, actually, was the incident on the subway platform. She'd been so certain that she'd seen Matt there at first, urging her to move, and yet, it had been Joe who pulled her out.

"Accidents," Adam murmured.

"Perhaps you should get out of here," Nikki said.

"I'm not afraid of ghosts."

Nikki smiled. "Well, we've both had the opportunity to learn that it's the living who are the most dangerous."

Leslie nodded; Nikki had voiced her own thoughts.

"And then," Leslie said, "there are the prostitutes who've gone missing, along with a young social worker who knew some of them and is also missing. Plus there's a good possibility that the explosion that killed Matt and almost killed me may not have been an accident."

"Another good reason for you to leave," Adam said.

"And another good reason for me to stay."

"Because . . . ?" Nikki prompted.

"Because I think I may be here because I can somehow help. There are ghosts in the house. I saw and spoke with Elizabeth—and Matt was the one who told me she needed help."

"There's a Civil War soldier in the entry, too," Nikki said.

"You've seen him?" Leslie asked.

"Briefly. He seemed like quite the gentleman," Nikki informed her.

"Really? I would love to meet him," Leslie said.

Nikki smiled. "I've been at this a little longer than you. The first time I realized I was actually seeing a ghost . . . I thought I'd die of shock."

"I pretty much thought I should be locked up," Leslie murmured. "Except that . . . well, I think I was with Matt. That I almost stayed with him."

"That was when you really had to admit that you see what others can't," Adam said gently. "What even *I* can't," he added wistfully.

Nikki set a hand on Leslie's arm. "Should you really be staying at that house alone?" she asked.

"Wild horses wouldn't drag me out of it," Leslie said. "And last night Joe stayed in the extra room. It was just for the one night, but I can ask him to stay from now on. You know . . . you guys should stay tonight. Please? You may . . . see something I can't. I guess you checked into a hotel, but . . ."

Adam waved a dismissive hand. "We can check out."

"There's also something I'd love your help with tomorrow if you have time before your flights," she said. She went on to describe the little girl at the dig. "Her name is Mary, but I don't know her last name, and there are so many Marys listed in the church register. I haven't seen her again, but I feel that it's urgent to reunite her with her mother."

"I'll do my best," Nikki told her. "I wish Brent was here."

"You and Leslie can fix things," Adam said reassuringly.

Leslie started to speak, but then she realized that she'd been staring at a woman sitting alone in a booth across the room from them. Apparently the waitresses all knew her. Whenever they stopped by to refill her coffee cup, they all had something to say.

"Do you see someone you know? Have you been here before?" Nikki asked her.

"No. And, yes. I came here once with Joe."

Nikki and Adam subtly checked out the woman Leslie had been studying. "That's Eileen Brideswell," he said.

"Of course," Leslie murmured, wondering why she hadn't recognized the woman. Not only had she seen her before, she'd even met her. Eileen Brideswell had been at the Hastings House gala the night of the explosion.

She looked exceedingly sad, though she tried to smile when waitresses talked to her. As soon as they left, though, the smile faded.

"You know her?" Leslie asked Adam.

"I've met her over the years. In fact, excuse me, if you will."

He left them, joining Eileen, who brightened at his appearance. He sat down opposite her, and they began to talk.

Leslie looked at Nikki. "I think I really am going crazy."

"We've all felt that way," Nikki assured her.

"It's not that I'm seeing ghosts. It's . . ." She hesitated. "I'm sorry, I love Adam like a father, but I couldn't talk about this in front of him. Nikki, Matt doesn't just talk to me in my dreams. It's as if we're together again.

Nikki, I'm having this wild sex life . . . with a ghost."

Nikki twirled her swizzle stick in her Irish coffee. Then she looked at Leslie. "We see ghosts," she said softly. "Do we really know anything about them? No. Josh, Adam's son . . . you know he died at eighteen. He immediately appeared to his best friend, who told Adam. And even though Adam can't see him, Josh often travels with him, and he speaks to a lot of people. I think maybe being a ghost is . . . well, not that different from being alive, in a way. If we're energy, then for a ghost, that energy remains and is like a brand-new life. Perhaps most people do just go on to whatever the afterlife is. But some stay for months or years, even centuries, because they feel they have to remain on earth for some reason, that they have a function here. So take a man like Matt. From what you've told me, he was someone who believed in what he could see and touch. So I bet it's difficult for him to learn the ropes, so to speak. Even more difficult than it is for most ghosts. Maybe he figured out how to enter your dreams, while it's still difficult for him to . . . well, materialize, for want of a better word."

"So . . . when I see him in my dreams, it may not just be what I want more than anything in the world?" Leslie asked.

"I wish I had all the answers, but I don't." She smiled. "I could be way off. Like I said, none of us has all the answers, and we're all surprised on a daily basis. But think about all the examples of ESP you've heard about. A mother knowing when her child is in danger. A wife knowing suddenly that her husband has been killed. Maybe, living or dead, we all have the power to connect with that energy somehow. We just have to learn to use it. Maybe, sometimes, people live when they should have died, and maybe, sometimes, people have died when they should have lived, but there's still a trail of communication. You and I both know other people who see ghosts, but think about it—this is New York, home to millions of people. And how many of those do you think see ghosts? Then again, ghosts can come in different ways. I had a friend who lost her dad when she was really young, and it nearly destroyed her. Then she had a dream about him, and he kept telling her how well he was doing, and how she needed to be happy, move on. And after that, she felt the pain, but she . . . adjusted, I guess. Who's to say she didn't see a ghost, that her dad didn't find a way to make life livable again for her?"

"Actually, that's a nice thought," Leslie murmured. "I just wish I knew what to do from here."

"I'm not sure exactly how you mean that, but I don't think you *can* do anything, not emotionally, until . . . well, until whatever is going on is solved. I think Adam is about to cancel his trip to stay with you. He's worried."

"I'm all right."

"That incident in the crypt? That fall in the subway? Do you really think those were accidents?"

"But I'll be careful now," Leslie vowed. "And I'll

have Joe stay at Hastings House." She hesitated. "Nikki, I'm certain that I'm on to something. I keep thinking about tunnels."

"And have you found a tunnel—or a solution?"

"No, not yet."

Nikki studied her. "Leslie, Adam and I think you're in danger."

"I'm around people all day, and Joe is around, too, even at night. Just not exactly with me."

Nikki lowered her head, then looked up at her again, a twinkle in her eye. "Face it. You don't want Joe to stay—even though I can tell you really like him, because you're afraid that if he's there, Matt won't show up."

"Maybe," Leslie admitted.

Nikki squeezed her hand. "Matt loved and trusted you. He trusted and loved his cousin. I'm willing to bet Matt would be a happier man if he knew you were safe."

Leslie's cell phone suddenly started ringing. Saved by the bell, she thought wryly, and excused herself to answer it, knowing from caller ID that it was Joe.

"Where are you?"

"O'Malley's."

"Who are you with?" He sounded tense.

"Adam and Nikki. Why? What is it?"

"I'm on my way," Joe said, and hung up. She closed her phone just as Adam came back to their booth, leading Eileen Brideswell.

"Hello," Eileen said shyly.

"Mrs. Brideswell, how are you?" Leslie asked. Bad question. The woman obviously wasn't doing well. But it was the polite thing to say.

"I gather you've met Leslie MacIntyre, Eileen," Adam said.

"Of course," Eileen replied, smiling.

"And this is my colleague, Nikki Blackhawk," Adam continued.

"How do you do," Nikki said, smiling warmly.

"Thank you for inviting me to join you," Eileen said. The words were sincere. Given her power and position, Eileen could have dinner with the city's most elite residents, but Leslie thought she understood the other woman. She didn't want to be surrounded by the wealthy and powerful, forced to smile and nod and talk about the important events of the day. She wanted to be alone with her thoughts. But joining them was different.

"I think we share a friend," Eileen said, sliding into the booth across from Leslie.

"Joe? I know he's working for you," Leslie said.

Eileen nodded.

"He *will* find out what happened to Genevieve, you know." Leslie reached across the table and laid her hand over Eileen's in a gesture of assurance as she spoke.

She wasn't prepared for what happened next.

Her vision seemed to disappear, not in darkness, but in a flash of light. She didn't see Eileen's inner soul or her past; she saw Genevieve.

The other woman was standing in a black abyss, and it was damp and cold.

Like a grave.

But she wasn't dead.

Her hair was twisted away from her face, knotted at her nape. She was thin and haggard-looking, but she was at work, her hands busy as she tore at something unseen. She worked and worked and worked. . . .

And then gave way to exhaustion, falling to her knees, sobbing.

Leslie drew her hand back as the vision faded to total blackness.

"Are you all right, dear?" Eileen Brideswell asked. "You look as if you've seen a ghost."

Leslie forced a smile. Not a ghost. A living woman. *Genevieve.*

She couldn't say that. Eileen would think that she was insane. Worse. That she was offering her false hope, playing on her emotions.

"I'm fine. Sorry."

"Maybe you should see a doctor," Eileen said. "I saw on the news that you were in an accident at the dig when the roof gave way, and then I heard about that dreadful incident on the subway."

"I'm fine. Honestly," Leslie said. "But thank you so much for your concern." She saw the pub door open and Joe walk in. He was scanning the room, looking for her. She could see the light reflect off his hair. Light, but not as blond as Matt's. No, he was darker. His eyes were a quicksilver shade between blue and green. Matt's had been such a piercing color; they had seemed to go from the color of the sky to indigo.

What the hell was she doing?

He strode over to the table, seeming to note without surprise that Eileen was there, too, before he reached them. Leslie quickly introduced Joe to Nikki and Adam, who rose to shake his hand. She knew that Joe was assessing them warily, and that he would remain wary until he had spent more time with them.

"Mrs. Brideswell," he said.

"Joe, I'm glad to see you." She tried to be casual, but her voice was anxious.

Joe looked unhappy. Leslie knew he was desperately wishing he had something concrete to tell her, even though she wouldn't come right out in this company and ask him how he was progressing. She tilted her head questioningly, and there was so much hope in that small gesture.

"I think we're coming along," Joe said softly.

"Really? Can you come see me tomorrow morning and tell me how things are going?" she asked him.

He hesitated.

Adam said, "Nikki and I will be with Leslie tonight, and we'll be with her tomorrow morning at the dig."

"Sure. How about nine?" Joe suggested.

"Right here," Eileen said. She smiled self-consciously. "This place is my comfort zone. And it's the only pub I know that opens for breakfast. Good business, though, with everyone who works down-town."

Joe slid into the booth next to Leslie. She could feel the tension in his body.

"What is it?" she asked.

He shook his head, forcing a smile. "Later," he murmured. Then, louder, "It's great to meet some of Leslie's friends. Are you both archaeologists, too?"

"Historian," Adam said.

"And I run a company that leads ghost tours in New Orleans," Nikki said.

"Ghost tours?" Joe said. "Interesting. How's the city doing? I've heard a lot of people still haven't moved back."

Joe, Leslie realized, intended to talk about anything *but* what was going on. Eileen Brideswell was watching him, a slight frown creasing her brow, but she seemed equally glad not to be discussing matters that tore at her heart.

Joe, however casual he pretended to be, remained tense throughout the meal, watching the door.

"Are we being joined by anyone else?" he asked Leslie at one point.

She shook her head.

"Your work buddies are elsewhere?"

"Brad and I finished in the basement, and I don't know where anyone went after that. Actually, I was in a hurry to leave. Nikki and Adam aren't here for very long." She gave him a broad smile. "At least tonight you can go home and get some sleep. I won't be alone."

He accepted that, though he didn't seem to be much

happier. He went on to ask Adam if he was also from New Orleans.

"Adam owns a company in Virginia called Harrison Investigations," Eileen inserted.

Leslie fought hard to keep her eyebrows from shooting up. Did Eileen know exactly what Adam did?

"I see. Historical investigations?" Joe asked.

Leslie lowered her head, smiling. She was coming to know Joe. By tomorrow, he would know everything about Adam, Nikki and Harrison Investigations.

At last the evening ended. They waited on the sidewalk with Eileen while her driver brought the car around, and then they started walking back to Hastings House. Leslie pulled back a bit, linking her arm through Joe's.

"What's going on?" she asked him.

He looked down at her. "Tell me more about what you were doing in Virginia."

"What?"

"Virginia. When you were working down there. You left New York City after you were released from the hospital, and you started working in Virginia. Were you working with Laymon and Brad from the beginning?"

"Yes. It was Laymon's project. He approached Brad, and Brad approached me. Where is this going, Joe?"

"The work was intense?"

"We worked fairly intensely, yes, but it was that kind of dig, a major project. An entire burial ground, an old churchyard. We made all kinds of finds. Civil War weapons and bullets, canteens . . . and Revolutionary artifacts, as well. It was slow-going, because there were so many separate layers to sift through. Which we'll find here, too, but—"

"Did you take days off?"

"Of course. No one works endlessly."

"Did you have weekends off?"

"Depending on what was going on. Joe, please, what are you getting at?"

They had reached the house; Adam and Nikki were waiting politely ahead on the sidewalk.

"You can say anything in front of them," Leslie said. "Trust me, Adam has had government contracts that far outweigh our problems."

Joe stared at her for a minute, then reached into his jacket pocket. He unfolded a large color photograph.

She frowned at him, then looked at the photo. She instantly recognized Genevieve O'Brien, and her heart fluttered. She hadn't said anything to Eileen or anyone else about the image that had sprung into her mind when she had touched Eileen's hand, but now . . . seeing Genevieve's face, she felt a swell of empathy. *She's alive and she's suffering, but she's fighting. She'll never give up, never.*

"It's Genevieve," she said. "I don't know who the other woman is."

"A prostitute—one of the women who disappeared."

"And who is the man?"

"Look closely, Leslie."

She couldn't complain that the light wasn't good, because they were standing directly under a street lamp. She stared at the photo, then gasped. She stared back at Joe.

"It's Brad."

"Yes."

"I'm sure there's an explanation."

"Whatever it is, I intend to get it from him," he said firmly.

She shook her head uncomfortably, suddenly aware that Adam and Nikki had walked over to stand by them and were looking at the photo, too. "This is Eileen's niece."

"Genevieve, yes," Adam said.

"And she's with your partner," Nikki added, having apparently recognized Brad more readily than Leslie herself had.

"There has to be an explanation. I mean, you can't assume someone is guilty of something just because he's in a photograph," Nikki said.

"It's enough for me to get the police to bring him in for questioning," Joe said.

"Joe, don't do that. Talk to Brad yourself first, please. It's just ridiculous to assume that he's been abducting women just because of a photograph, and even more ridiculous to think he blew up Hastings House. Or that he'd try to hurt me or Matt. He's not like that, Joe. He's a good guy. Really."

Joe clearly wasn't convinced. Adam and Nikki kept silent on the subject.

Leslie set a hand on Joe's arm. "Please, go slowly with this. Don't . . . I don't want to create a problem while the dig is going on."

"The dig. Right," Joe said disgustedly. "Amazing that a chunk of ceiling fell down just when you were there. Was Brad around when it happened?"

"I've told everyone. I had been in the crypt alone," Leslie said.

"Had been. Who exactly was there *after* the collapse?" Joe demanded.

She looked at him, blinking. She thought back, remembering.

"A number of people—including you," she said meaningfully.

"I arrived later, I had to shove through a crowd to get to you. Who was there when you opened your eyes?"

"Laymon, Dryer, Adair . . . and Brad," she said wearily. "But that doesn't mean anything," she added quickly. "There were dozens of workers around, too. Dozens of grad students, some of the development company people . . . tons of people."

He just stared at her. "All right. I'm not going to bring this to the attention of the police until I have a chance to speak with Brad myself." He looked up at Adam. "I'm assuming you have a lot of connections in the area where Leslie, Laymon and Brad were last working. Do you think you could have some of them look into Brad Verdun's movements while he was working down there?"

"I think I can manage that, yes," Adam said. There was a strange smile curving his lip. Joe might have startled him with the question, but he didn't bat an eye. Leslie could tell that he did think it ironic that Joe had apparently weighed and judged him so quickly, and that he was glad he had been approved.

"So for the moment, you're not going to turn Brad in, and you won't strong-arm him, you'll just talk to him, okay?" Leslie asked.

Joe arched a brow. "Okay."

"But you'd like to, right?"

"Yes," Joe admitted.

"Then how about driving Adam and Nikki to their hotel so they can check out and come stay with me instead?"

"What about you? Where will you be while I'm playing chauffeur?"

"I can just wait here, at Hastings House."

"No way am I leaving you alone."

She smiled. "Okay, I'll come, too."

The drive was nice. The windows were down as they shot up Sixth Avenue, making for a nice breeze, and the city was beautiful by night. At the hotel, Joe left his car right in front, after tipping a young man heavily to see that it went around the block a few times and then came back.

Adam was fond of old places, so they had intended to stay at the Algonquin. Joe and Leslie sat in the comfortable lounge while they were waiting for the other two to repack and check out. He smiled at her ruefully.

"So . . . do you see Dorothy Parker or any of her circle anywhere?" he asked lightly.

"Look over there."

"Who is it?"

"Lori Newman, the new Broadway sensation," Leslie said, smiling. But then she grew serious. "Joe . . . I know this sounds strange, but I'm absolutely convinced Genevieve O'Brien is alive."

"I feel it, too. That's exactly why I'm so frustrated. I don't believe that she's going to stay alive much longer. That's why I've got to find her soon, before he . . ." His voice trailed off as he considered the cost of failure.

"It isn't Brad. Trust me, along with everything else, he really isn't clever enough to pull something like this off."

Joe actually smiled.

Leslie hesitated. "I saw her, Joe. Tonight."

"What are you talking about?"

"It was strange. When I touched Eileen's hand tonight . . ." She stopped, wincing. "I saw her . . . in a vision, I guess you'd say. She was alive. But she was desperately trying to do something . . . escape, maybe. She had to give up. She didn't have the strength to keep going."

He just stared at her. "You . . . had a vision?"

She shook her head. "I don't know what it was, exactly. But tonight, when I touched Eileen, it was almost as if I could reach out and touch Genevieve."

"If only you could," he mused softly.

"May I take that picture? The one you showed me

with her—and Brad—in it?" Leslie asked. "I'm sure you have other copies."

He nodded. "Sure."

Adam and Nikki reappeared, and they headed outside as a group.

"Think that kid is coming back with your car?" Nikki teased Joe.

"Sure hope so."

But the young man, who in fact worked for the hotel, returned the car in less than two minutes. Traffic was light, and the drive back to Hastings House was quick.

Despite Adam and Nikki's presence, Joe came inside with them. Leslie was surprised when he walked through the house, upstairs and downstairs, then went back to the servants' pantry and down to the basement.

Adam and Nikki had already gone upstairs to get settled. Leslie waited for him in the servants' pantry. As she did, she looked around. It was amazing. If she hadn't been here herself when the room exploded into fire and splinters, she would never suspect now that any such thing had ever happened.

Joe came back up the stairs.

"Empty?"

"To my eyes," he said quietly.

Hands on his hips, he turned away from her, staring thoughtfully at the hatch. She stood behind him, slipping her arms around him, leaning her head against his back.

"Thank you."

"Hey, ma'am, anything I can do," he murmured.

He turned. His eyes searched hers out as he lifted her chin with his thumb and forefinger. His head bent.

She thought he was going to kiss her full on the lips. She didn't know what she felt, what she would do.

But his lips landed lightly on her forehead, instead. "Leslie, I'm begging you, for the love of God, be careful." He backed away and looked at her. "I don't get visions, but I do get hunches. And I feel nervous as hell right now."

"I swear to you, I'll be careful. And don't forget, Nikki and Adam are here tonight," she said.

At last, with a last brush of his lips against her forehead, he left for the night. She keyed in the alarm after he left and headed upstairs.

Adam was in the room where Joe had slept the night before. Nikki was in her room, in a big cotton nightgown, sitting up in the queen-size bed, playing with the remote control. "You must be a real celebrity," she said. "You've just been on the news," she told Leslie.

Leslie groaned. "I guess it's out that we found bones in the basement here," she said.

Nikki nodded. "There was just a shot of you and Matt dressed up for some kind of social event, then the story. Pretty low key, actually."

"I'm glad." Leslie went into the bathroom to change for the night and brush her teeth. When she emerged and crawled beneath the covers, she couldn't help but think, *Matt won't come tonight. I know he won't.*

"You all right?" Nikki asked.

"Of course. I'm thrilled you're here."

Nikki smiled. "It's just for one night. And . . ."

"And?"

"Joe is alive."

"Have you seen or felt Matt in any way?" Leslie asked, feeling desperate.

"No, I'm sorry. I get hazy visions of others . . . but not Matt." Nikki smiled again. "Remember what I said earlier. Entering your dreams might be Matt's only way to contact you. And he might want you to move on."

"I keep hearing that," Leslie said.

"Because it's what you have to do."

"I do go on. I love my work. And when I can do something like bring out the truth about Elizabeth, it's wonderful."

Nikki nodded, then yawned. "The world is a mystery. That's for certain." She yawned again.

Leslie turned off the bedside lamp. "Mind if I watch TV?" she asked Nikki. "It takes my mind off . . . things."

"Go right ahead."

Despite the TV, after a little while Leslie's eyes began to fall shut.

She slept.

Someone was out there. Watching the house.

Matt felt that he should have been able to get out there. He was actually becoming more and more con-

vinced that eventually he would be able to. When he had sensed with such certainty that Leslie was in mortal danger, the desperation of sheer will had propelled him to her. Yes, he had been there. Yes, she had seen his face. She had felt him, helping her up from the tracks.

Joe had been there, too. Joe, with his powerful, living arms. Arms that were probably the only ones he could trust her to himself. Matt couldn't stand her being alone with anyone anymore.

And soon he would be able to leave the house at will. He would reach the street lamp.

And he would see the watcher's face.

But tonight . . .

Tonight he was upstairs in the bedroom, watching the women sleep, quiet, beautiful. Two blondes, angelic-looking. He touched Leslie's hair with a rush of nostalgia and tenderness, and then he moved to sit on the floor, leaning against the wall, still watching.

He would stay through the night.

Leslie woke with a start.

She didn't know what had roused her. Frowning, she saw that Nikki was still sleeping peacefully by her side.

It must have been something on the TV, she told herself.

She aimed the remote at the television and pushed the Off button, then lay back down and smiled wistfully.

"Matt? Are you here?" she breathed almost silently.

There was no answer. She thought she saw the curtain rustle; perhaps she felt a breeze. Maybe it was only because she was tired and so desperately hopeful, but in that whisper of movement she felt enfolded by love. Tenderness.

Then she bolted up to a sitting position again.

What she'd heard hadn't been the television.

She heard it clearly now, the sound of sobbing.

Heart-wrenching tears.

Tears . . .

Just as she had heard them earlier . . . when she had seen that vision of Genevieve O'Brien.

16

It had been a hell of a long day. Joe knew damned well that there were things Leslie hadn't told him about her friends Adam and Nikki, just as he was sure there were plenty of things she thought and felt that she didn't say to him. But she trusted him. And that was enough for the moment. Though he ached to hold her—and more—he kept his distance. He had to.

As soon as he got home, he looked up Harrison Investigations on the Web. The official site was bare bones, giving little but contact information, but he did find several articles. He read them all, wondering whether to be amazed, amused or irritated at the allusions to the supernatural, including several strange situations that had required the government's intervention; situations that had been managed through Harrison Investigations. An apologetic call to a sheriff he'd worked with once in a town west of Richmond supplied him with far more of a response than he'd expected. His friend was friends with a fellow lawman, a Sheriff Stone, who was married to one of Harrison's associates and swore by the man.

At the least, Leslie was safe for the night, Joe thought. He could get some real sleep.

But he didn't.

He prowled back to his own basement, making a mental note to himself to make sure to do something with the music he'd found.

He went back upstairs and pulled out his copy of the picture of Betty, Genevieve and Brad, and studied it some more. When he'd first seen it, he'd been ready to drag Brad out of whatever watering hole he might have been frequenting and tear him to pieces. But Leslie had been right. He had nothing to go on here. Or not enough, anyway. No proof. He had to get a few more answers before going postal on the guy. No, before notifying the cops so they could arrest him.

He was still restless. He tried a long hot shower and lying down to watch the news, then a book. Nothing held his attention.

He was never going to sleep.

At last he rose. Hell, he'd gone several nights without sleep before in his life. He could do it again. He dressed, deciding that even though it was late, Didi and Heidi were probably still out on the streets.

Watching for a black sedan.

On his way out of the house, he paused. There, on a table by the door, was a picture of Matt. He'd been in the Middle East, reporting on the condition of the children there. He'd ridden with the Marines and had written a series of articles that chilled, tore at the heart and demanded thought. He had never been hesitant about going into danger. "Hell, Joe, if we can send our soldiers over there, you bet I'll go. It will be an honor to ride with them."

He'd been shot at, spat on and, his personal favorite, nearly run over by a mad camel. But the stories had been important to him. And as he'd said at the time, he'd been able to come home. Not all their countrymen would.

Joe picked up the picture of Matt with a host of children and stared hard at it, as if staring at the man himself.

"Why couldn't you have been an asshole?" he said aloud. A moment later, he put the picture down and headed out the door. As he did, it occurred to him that he had to forget the black sedan and tell Didi and Heidi to get off the streets for a while. Didi's job interview was coming up; he hoped that would change life for her.

But then there was Heidi. He wondered if Genevieve O'Brien would have been able to change the woman's life if she hadn't disappeared.

Leslie was convinced that she was alive.

But how long could she remain so?

· · ·

Sitting up in bed, Leslie remained still and listened. The sound had disappeared.

She waited, certain it had come from the basement, hoping it would come again. She glanced over at Nikki, who was still sleeping. Leslie hesitated, thinking that she had promised Joe to keep the door to her room locked.

But she wasn't alone in the house. Nikki was here, and so was Adam, who was sleeping just down the hall.

She crawled out of bed carefully, found her robe and slippers, and tiptoed to the door. For a moment she thought about waking Nikki, but she had the strange sense that the house wouldn't "speak" to her unless she was alone.

She must resemble a ghost herself, she thought, wafting down the staircase and heading to the foyer. She looked out to the street, almost expecting to see someone leaning on a lamppost, or to discover that Joe's car was parked across the street, despite the fact that she had friends in the house with her.

But the street was quiet.

In the shadows cast by the dim night-lights, she held very still for several seconds. Then she thought she heard it again and frowned. This time the sound was somehow different.

Muffled, faint, like an echo.

She went down the hallway to the kitchen, then into the servants' pantry, and hesitated again before lifting the hatch. As always at night, the basement entry loomed like an abyss.

She went for one of the lanterns and then carefully walked down the stairs.

The crates remained from their work that day, but Brad had carefully tended to their tools. The cold and empty hearth seemed all the more depressing because of the broken bricks along one side.

She stood still, waiting, until once again she heard the sound.

She moved to the wall to the right of the hearth, facing northeast, toward the dig and the old subway lines.

As she stood there, literally putting her ear against the brick, she became aware of something in the room. A presence. She turned.

Elizabeth was standing there, though not, as Leslie might have expected, hovering over the crate that contained her bones. She stood, watching Leslie, a sad smile on her face.

"Hello," Leslie said very softly.

The woman's smile deepened. "Thank you."

Leslie shook her head. "I couldn't have done it without your help." She hesitated for a moment. "Without Matt's help."

The apparition stood still for a minute, then said, "He loves you very much."

"I . . . Matt?" Leslie said, her heart skipping a beat.

But Elizabeth didn't reply. The strange sound of distant sobbing came again. Still muffled, like an echo of the past.

"She needs you, too," Elizabeth said.

"Who needs me? Can you help me?"

Elizabeth lifted a hand. She seemed uncertain. Then she pointed toward the wall. Leslie felt as if a shaft of ice had pierced straight through her.

"Is she buried there?"

Elizabeth looked uncertain. "She cries," she said.

"If I can just find her, get to her . . . can you help me?"

"I can try . . . it's not my time . . . I don't know . . . I can try." Elizabeth started to move, then stopped. She frowned suddenly, with a look of alarm.

"Go!" she cried, and she suddenly faded away.

Then Leslie heard what the ghost had heard.

Something that was not an echo of the past in any way. Something real.

Footsteps. Furtive, stealthy, and somewhere on the floor above.

"Hey!"

Joe saw Didi leaning on a shop window, smoking.

Her face lit into a smile, and she walked over to the car.

"Don't you ever sleep?" she asked him.

He shrugged. "Listen . . . I know I asked you to keep an eye out for that car, but I was wrong."

"I haven't seen a black sedan all night," Didi told him with a yawn.

"Where's Heidi?" he asked, suddenly anxious.

"Around the corner. She was restless, so she went for a walk."

"Find her. Find her, and go home for the night."

"Hey, Joe, you're a good guy, but you can't fix the whole world."

"Didi, it's occurred to me that this guy may know that we're on to the black sedan."

She frowned. "So?"

"So he could start using another car."

"Ooh." A shadow crossed her face as she realized the advantage that would give him.

"Find Heidi, huh?"

"All right, Joe," she said.

He pulled out a copy of the photograph. "One more favor. Do you recognize this guy?"

"That's Brad," Didi said flatly.

"You know him?" He sounded surprised. "Just how well do you know him?"

"That depends what you mean by 'well.'"

"In every way, Didi."

"Okay, I know him in every way. Do I know him well? No. But he treats us decent. He doesn't act like an asshole. Sometimes he brings us movie tickets. He doesn't come a lot, though, just now and then."

"How long has he been coming by?"

"For years," Didi assured him.

Joe felt the tension growing in him. "Didi, right now—just for right now—if he comes by, don't get in a car with him, okay?"

"I've never gotten in a car with him."

"Oh?"

"My place isn't as bad as Heidi's."

"Whatever. For right now, don't be alone with him. Got it?"

"Sure, Joe. Whatever you say." She shook her head, a rueful smile on her face. "Know what? You're the first man in ages who's ever cost *me* money."

"Didi . . ."

"Don't worry. I'll be careful. I want to make that job interview, you know. I'll find Heidi, and I'll go to bed for the night. Alone. Okay?"

"Good kid," he told her, and he watched her disappear out of sight around the corner before he drove away. He didn't intend to go far. He meant to park, and walk the area himself.

Matt knew Leslie had gone down to the basement because he'd followed her there. He'd tried so hard to touch her—hell, he wanted to shake her. She was supposed to be locked safely in her room.

And then . . .

He heard footsteps.

He hurried upstairs. The servants' pantry was empty; the footsteps were coming from elsewhere in the house. Matt moved along the hallway.

The intruder had just gained entry and was standing in the front hall. About six feet tall, and wearing a dark jacket and ski mask. He clearly meant not to be seen and, if seen, not to be recognized.

He was in the house. And there had been no alarm, no cracking of glass, no snapping of wood. He had gained entry despite the alarm.

And now he had paused, listening to the silence and the settling of the old house.

The intruder started down the hall, heading toward the servants' pantry . . . and the basement below—where Leslie would be trapped.

Matt rushed fiercely down the hallway, ready to tackle his adversary, as he had once tackled opposing players back in his football days. He was sure he would drive right through the intruder, making no impact, but . . .

The other man stopped. Staggered. Then he raised his arm to reveal that he was carrying a gleaming bowie knife, sharp and deadly.

Amazingly, he had felt Matt's attack.

Matt backed away, gathered all his force and raced forward again.

Again he made impact, and again the man swung the knife through empty air.

The sound of a siren suddenly penetrated from the street. The intruder seemed to feel a sense of deep panic. He turned, stumbling back toward the door, where he paused, as if regaining his senses. Matt got ready to gather all the strength he had left and attack again.

The intruder punched numbers into the alarm in seconds flat, solving one mystery and deepening another. Then he was out the door. Matt tried to follow. He had to go after the offender, rip off his mask, had to find out who had killed him. Who meant to kill Leslie.

He hit the door. Tried to get through it. Couldn't. He let out a groan of fury and despair.

Leslie knew she couldn't let the intruder corner her in the basement. She hurried up the stairs to the servants' pantry and stood there, listening. The house had grown silent. She waited, then silently shut the hatch, but still she hesitated, unsure whether to stay where she was or brave the return journey to the bedroom.

He might be out there. Standing dead still. Hovering in silence, as she was doing. Waiting, knowing he had been heard, biding his time . . .

Suddenly she heard the soft thudding of feminine footsteps on the stairs, followed by the sound of Nikki's voice. "Leslie?"

"Watch out!" Leslie cried. "Nikki, be careful!"

She rushed through the kitchen and along the hall toward the entryway, determined to keep any harm from coming to Nikki. But when she reached her friend, in sight of the front door, it was closed, the alarm blinking, and there was no sign of anyone having entered.

Stunned, she came to a complete standstill, staring wildly around.

"Leslie?" Nikki asked, flicking on the light.

"What's going on down here?" Adam called out firmly. He was already halfway down the stairs, and he was armed. It was just a small pistol, but Leslie had never seen him with a weapon before. She was sure, however, that he knew how to use it, and that he wasn't afraid to do so.

"I could have sworn there was someone in the house," Leslie said.

"Then we'd better take a look around," he said.

Nikki was still frowning. "What were you doing up?" she asked Leslie.

"I . . . I was looking for a ghost," she admitted. "Or something. I keep hearing the sound of sobbing."

"Make that a really good look around," Adam said.

Before they could take action, they heard the sound of a car pulling to a sudden halt outside.

"It's Joe," Leslie said in surprise, staring out the window. She saw him exit his car, looking at the house anxiously, and realized that he could see her staring out at him.

She walked over to the door, keyed in the alarm and threw it open. She was shivering, but she was also grateful to see him. She tried not to betray her sense of panic in her voice. "Didn't I tell you to go home to bed?" she said.

"What are you doing up?" he demanded worriedly, ignoring her question.

She waved a hand vaguely. "Um . . . noises."

He entered, looking from her to Nikki, and then to Adam, who somehow managed to look dignified despite being clad in a terry robe and scuffed slippers—perhaps because he was carrying a gun, Leslie thought half hysterically—and then back to Leslie. Before Joe could say anything, Adam told him, "Don't worry. I'm licensed, and I know what I'm doing."

Joe looked back at him. "I didn't doubt it for a minute. But . . . you thought that you had an intruder?" He was clearly worried by the possibility.

"I must have been mistaken," Leslie said.

"I say it won't hurt to make a thorough search of the place," Adam said. He was amazingly cheerful for someone whose sleep had been so rudely interrupted.

"We'll take the downstairs," Joe said, taking Leslie's hand.

"Upstairs for us, then," Adam said, nodding at Nikki. "You're armed?" he asked Joe.

"Always," Joe said quietly. Leslie gave him a shocked look, and he shrugged. "I'm always looking for the bad guys, remember?" he told her.

Adam and Nikki started back up the stairs, leaving Joe and Leslie alone in the front hall.

"Okay, what's going on?" Joe asked, staring intently into her eyes.

"Nothing. I'm sure I imagined it all," she said. "I mean . . . it's an old house. It creaks. And . . . Joe."

"Yeah?" He was opening doors as he led her down the hall, turning lights on as he went, chasing the shadows out of the corners.

"Joe, I think there's a shaft or a tunnel near here somewhere."

He paused, looking at her. "Yeah?"

"You don't think I'm crazy?"

He hesitated, and she felt as if he were holding something back. "I chased a man through this neighborhood the other night. He completely disappeared. So I wouldn't be surprised to hear that he found a bolt-hole like that somewhere around here. But what makes you think so?"

"I hear . . . noises. And I think they're coming from beyond the basement wall."

"We need to look into that, then," he said seriously.

They went through the whole of the downstairs. In the servants' pantry, Joe paused, looking question-ingly at Leslie, who ducked her head, unwilling to meet his eyes. Then he lifted the hatch. Light streamed up from below; she had forgotten to turn off her lantern earlier.

Joe didn't say anything, only started down the stairs. He waved a hand at her to stay where she was until he had made a circuit of the room.

"It's all right," he said.

She went down and found him studying the hearth and the wall beside it. He walked closer to the bricks and tapped them, pushed at them.

"What are you doing?" she asked at last.

"I don't know." He looked at her. "I thought maybe there might be a hidden latch, a secret door, a room behind the room. Sort of like your city beneath the city." He smiled.

"Oh." She walked over and stared at the wall with him. The grout was almost as dark as the brick. She tapped at one brick after another, but she couldn't tell if there was a hollow space behind it or not.

"You'd asked me for maps," he murmured.

"It's all right. I got them myself. At the library," she explained.

"And?"

"Well, the first subway ran north from City Hall to 145th Street," she said.

He nodded. "Something to think about. Anyway . . . the house is empty. I guess I should go."

Not really, she could have told him. But as for any flesh-and-blood danger . . .

"Adam is in the room you were in last night, and Nikki is with me. But please, don't sleep in your car again—and don't try to tell me that's not exactly what you're planning to do. The bed in the master chamber upstairs actually has a brand-new mattress on it. Stay here," she said.

"All right. It's going to be a busy morning."

"Right. You have your meeting with Eileen." She paused. "And you're going to speak to Brad, too, right?"

He took a deep breath. Exhaled. "Leslie, he's been a customer of the girls on the street for a long time now. Years."

She felt the blood drain from her face, but she refused to believe it. Brad? A kidnapper, even a murderer? No. No way.

"Lots of men hire prostitutes," she said.

He shrugged. "Hey, I'm not with the vice squad."

"Joe, if you get into a fight with him—"

"I have no intention of fighting with him. I'm just going to tell him what I've discovered and see how he reacts. But if I ever find out he was behind what happened to Matt, or what's been happening to you . . ." He didn't need to go on; the threat was obvious.

"I promise you, Brad would never hurt me. For one thing, I'm the one who makes him famous all the time."

"Let's call it a night, shall we?"

She nodded and started up the steps ahead of him. They met Nikki and Adam back in the main entry hall. "Clear?" Joe asked.

"Clear," Adam agreed.

"I'm sorry. I guess I heard the house creaking," Leslie said.

"There's nothing like a good tour of a historic house in the middle of the night, I say," Nikki said with a casual smile.

"All right, then . . . back to bed?" Adam suggested.

They all started back up the stairs. Leslie was surprised when Joe, who was bringing up the rear, paused on the top step, looking down.

"What is it?" Leslie asked.

"The house," he murmured. "Just the house."

On the upper landing, they split up.

"I promised Melissa that I'd buy the doughnuts tomorrow morning," Leslie murmured. "This morning, now."

"We'll still make it up early," Nikki promised.

"Your bed is in there—just step over the cords that hold the tourists back," Leslie told Joe, pointing.

"Cool," he said. "I get to cross the line." He gave her

a kiss on the forehead and said good night to Adam and Nikki. Adam gave Leslie a thumbs-up and headed for his room.

Nikki looked at Leslie and said, "This time, let's lock the bedroom door, too, huh?"

Leslie nodded. "I'm sorry I scared everyone, but I know I heard something. I swear there's someone sobbing down there," she said as they headed toward their room. "And it's so strange. Sometimes it sounds as if it's real, happening right now, but other times, it's like an echo of something that happened a long time ago."

"So is it real or ghostly?" Nikki asked, closing the bedroom door behind them and locking it herself.

"That's just it. I don't know." Leslie crawled into bed, then rolled over to face Nikki. "I could swear that there's a shaft . . . a room, a tunnel, something, near here. I have the subway maps, but . . . Anyway, we'll start searching tomorrow."

Nikki hiked herself up on an elbow. "At least Joe believes in you," she said.

"I've never actually told him I see ghosts."

"But he knows you have a special sense. And he believes in it. And if you don't plan on keeping him in this house with you, then neither Adam or I will leave."

Leslie laughed. "Don't worry, I'm starting to frighten myself. Joe is more than welcome to stay in this house."

Nikki grinned and plumped her pillow. "Good. Now, let's get some sleep. Doughnut time is near."

She rolled over, and Leslie sensed that she fell asleep almost instantly.

But she herself lay awake. She could sense that someone was in the room, and she was certain that . . .

That it was Matt.

She felt his warmth. She fell asleep at last, content in the sensation of being held in his arms.

The morning went surprisingly smoothly. By the time Leslie and Nikki headed downstairs, Adam and Joe had gone out to buy doughnuts and left coffee brewing. Melissa arrived and was delighted with the company. Then Tandy and Jeff came in, and Adam and Nikki admired their costumes before Nikki exchanged stories with them, New Orleans myth and legend vs New York.

But, inevitably, it came time to head to the dig. They circled the fence, said hello to the guards and were ushered through the gate. They were greeted by a number of the grad students, who seemed to know Joe as well as they knew her, Leslie thought.

She was dismayed to find, when they reached the crypt, that Professor Laymon and Brad were already there. She could feel the tension grip her when Joe greeted Brad, but apparently, whatever suspicion Joe was feeling, he hid it well. Brad clearly sensed nothing, and, true to his word, Joe kept from making a scene.

"Brad, I'd really like some time to talk later," Joe told him.

"Sure."

"Drinks after work? I'm buying," Joe told him.

"If you're buying, it's a deal," Brad said.

"Great. O'Malley's?"

"A fine place," Brad said, feigning a decent Irish accent.

"You staying here?" Joe asked Adam a little while later.

"Through the morning, at least," Adam said. "Longer, if you think it's necessary."

"I have to go meet Eileen Brideswell, but I'll be back later." Joe said, offering Laymon a hand. Then he kissed Nikki on the cheek. "I expect you'll be at the airport by the time I get back, but it's been a real pleasure."

"Likewise," Nikki assured him.

As Joe left, Leslie thought that Laymon couldn't be happy that she had brought Adam and Nikki, two "civilians," along, but he hadn't said anything. In fact, he had decided that so long as he was going to be burdened with extras at his site, they should work. Now Nikki was recording a list of their findings, while Adam had been handed a soft brush and told to carefully clear the etchings on the burial stones in the walls. She and Brad had already begun to carefully work on the stone tombs that littered the crypt.

Eventually, Laymon got a summons to come up to discuss something with a city official. Brad went along with him, anxious, as always, to make sure he was there if anything newsworthy came up.

While they were gone, Leslie showed Nikki and Adam the register with the births and deaths. "See? Mary . . . Mary . . . a few Kathleens . . . and more Marys," she said.

They were all facing the wall, but Nikki straightened suddenly. And turned.

Leslie did the same, while Adam just watched the two women and kept very still.

Mary was back.

She gazed at them solemnly.

"Mary?" Nikki said gently, walking toward her.

The spectral child edged away. To Leslie's surprise, she felt a tiny hand slip into hers. Like any shy child, Mary was hugging close to her.

"It's okay," Leslie told her gently, squeezing the hand that so trustingly enfolded in her own. "Nikki is my friend."

"And I'm so glad to meet you," Nikki said. "We think Leslie found your mother, and we can make sure you're together, but . . . Mary, what was your last name?"

"Mary."

"No, I mean . . . I'm Nikki Blackhawk, and Leslie is Leslie MacIntyre. What's *your* last name?"

The little girl whispered something.

"What?" Nikki asked.

Leslie dropped to her knees, praying not to be interrupted at this crucial moment. "Sherman. Mary Sherman," the little girl said at last.

Leslie stood, rumpling ghostly hair. "Miss Mary Sherman, please don't worry. I promise that I'm going to take good care of you and your mother. All I have to do now is find exactly where you are, and it's near here, right? Very near here?"

"I think so," Mary said.

Leslie smiled at Nikki, then at Adam, who was still just watching her and Nikki silently. "We're looking for a child's grave belonging to Mary Sherman. Let's get to work."

They began inspecting the crypt, Nikki using the register, Leslie and Adam covering the tombs on the floor and reading the plaques on the wall.

"Bingo," Adam said softly a little while later.

Leslie hurried over to him. He had dusted off a plaque on the wall. She read the old English carefully. There were six tiny coffins behind the slab; the children interred within had all died of a fever.

The last name was that of Mary Sherman. Leslie looked around, but the little girl was gone.

After the coffins had been discovered, Leslie kept staring at the walls, tapping them.

"Leslie?" Nikki said worriedly.

"There's another way in here," Leslie said. "I realized—as we found the coffins—that I was here when I was supposedly knocked out by the falling ceiling."

"All right."

They began a search together. Nothing. No secret door. At least, none that the ages would still allow them to find.

Nikki set an arm around Leslie's shoulders. "We did find Mary," she said.

Leslie sighed. It was true. Now all she had to do was convince Laymon that the bones in the crypt needed to be disinterred so those of the woman they had discovered in what would have been the churchyard could be carefully buried with those of her child.

"Mary?" she called softly. "Mary, I need your help. Is there another way in here? Please, Mary, I need to know."

One moment the child was nowhere to be seen and the next she appeared. But just as she did, there were loud noises from above. Laymon was returning.

Mary faded away, but just before she disappeared, it looked to Leslie as if a look of pure panic crossed the little girl's face.

Because of Laymon's interruption? Or because of Brad, who was right behind him?

17

"She's your child, isn't she, Eileen?"

Eileen Brideswell stared back at Joe for a long minute, her features giving away nothing. Then she lowered her head. He saw the tear she wasn't able to catch land on the hard wood of the table.

"I'm sorry," he murmured. "I didn't mean to upset you."

Eileen looked up, quickly wiping her eyes. "Yes. You don't understand. When I got pregnant . . . We were society. I couldn't marry her father. He was an immigrant, a bricklayer. In fact—" she looked sad again "—he died in an accident on the job before he ever knew about Genevieve. Back then . . . I was afraid that the stigma of her birth would follow her throughout her life. My brother and his wife wanted a child so badly . . . I was pressured by my parents . . . I had to give her up, and by letting Donald raise her, I at least got to be her aunt. I was supposed to marry well, and my marriage did turn out to be a good one. I don't expect you to understand . . . and I . . . I don't have to explain myself to you. Your job is to find Genevieve."

He'd learned over the years that defensive people could become angry and hostile. Still, he'd wanted— needed—the truth. From her own lips.

"Eileen, I'm not judging you. Not in any way. It's just that to find her, I needed the truth. I believe you're right—Genevieve wouldn't have disappeared without a word to you. I also believe she's alive." She was staring at him with wide, pain-racked eyes. He set a hand on hers. "I think we're close." He pulled out a manila envelope from his briefcase, producing a number of pictures, but not the one of Betty, Genevieve and Brad. He had found newspaper photos of the men who might have been involved in the case. "I need you tell me how well you know each of these men, and how well you think Genevieve might have known them."

She looked at him, startled when he showed her the first. "Well, that's Robert Adair, of course. I know him very well. And through her line of work, and through the family, Genevieve knew him well, too, of course. You're not suggesting that—"

"I'm not suggesting anything at the moment." He produced his second photo.

She stared across the table at him. "Ken Dryer. Everyone in the city knows him. He's on television every time anything happens and the police need to talk to the people of New York about it." She leaned back. "He's good at his job. He calms people down. He's not a personal friend, but I've met him. And Genevieve must have met him, too. He spoke at the opening of a day care center that was a pet project of hers."

"Here," he said, handing her the next.

Eileen stared at him, nodding. "Professor Laymon. Of course I know him. Greta is a dear friend, and I've been involved with the Historical Society forever. You know that."

"What about Genevieve?"

"I . . . I don't know. I know she was fascinated with Hastings House. As I told you, I knew too late that she'd wanted to attend the gala. If only I'd known . . . but maybe it's good that she didn't go. She might have been . . . although maybe that would have been better than . . ."

He gave her a moment to pull herself together, then showed her the next picture.

"Hank Smith," she said. "Yes, I know him and so did she. She wanted his company to start building affordable housing, rather than luxury highrises. She wanted to change the world."

Last, he produced the picture of Brad. Eileen looked at him. "That's Brad Verdun. Of course she knew Brad."

"Of course?"

"She met him when he was working on Hastings House."

"Oh?"

"He asked her out. She thought he was cute and fun, but far too immature. Still, I think they stayed casual friends." She sat back, shaking her head. "I don't understand where you're going with this. There's a lunatic out there killing girls, my niece may or may not be alive, and you're showing me pictures of upstanding citizens."

She was indignant. He wasn't surprised. "Can you think of anyone who might have read that tabloid article? Anyone who might have known that Genevieve was your biological child?"

"How on earth would I know who read what?" Eileen asked him. "And what does it matter, what someone read in some cheap rag?"

"They might have been taunting her with it. They might have lured her into a car to talk about it. Eileen, what I do know is this—the last time Genevieve was seen, she was getting into a black sedan. Just like the girls who disappeared before her."

The color drained from Eileen's face. "Then what makes you think she might still be alive?" she whispered.

"No girls have been taken in the same way since,"

he said. He glanced at his watch. Adam was due to leave for the airport any time now, and he didn't know how long Nikki was staying. He wanted to think that Leslie couldn't be in danger, not in broad daylight, and not at a well-populated dig, but then he remembered what had happened the other day in the crypt and realized that had already proved to be untrue.

"Eileen, I'll keep you posted," he promised her. "And if you think of anything at all that might be of help, tell me. Please."

"A black sedan, you said? A nice sedan?" she said.

"Yes. Why?"

"There are black sedans parked all over the financial district on a daily basis," she said dully.

"I'll be in touch," he promised.

He reached the dig right at eleven. Both Adam and Nikki were standing outside the grid tapes but near the crypt, waiting.

"What's going on?" he asked them.

"A minor argument," Nikki said, her eyes sparkling. "I think Leslie is winning. Somehow she's gotten Brad on her side."

"And you stayed to watch the fireworks? What about your flight?" he asked Adam.

"I've rebooked," Adam told him. "As has Nikki."

"Oh." Joe wasn't sure if he was relieved or a little dismayed. Would she still want him at the house if Adam and Nikki were there?

"I can put things off for a few days," Adam said.

"And I have a very understanding husband," Nikki told him.

They both sounded cheerful, but he had the feeling that if they were staying, it was because they were worried.

"That's great," he said, mostly meaning it. He had things he could be doing, and he wasn't meeting Brad until that evening.

"You're going to stick around the site, then?" he asked the other two.

"One of us will be with Leslie at all times," Nikki assured him.

He nodded again. "Great. So what's the argument about?"

"Leslie wants the remains of a woman and a child interred together. A mother and child."

"Laymon has a problem with that?"

"Laymon usually wants the bones he finds studied and cataloged, but this time, he doesn't want the graves in the crypt walls disturbed."

A moment later Leslie emerged from the crypt, looking triumphant. Brad was right behind her. She didn't notice Joe's arrival at first as she turned and flashed a giant smile Brad's way, squeezing his arm. "Thank you," she told him.

"My pleasure. But let's spend the day dusting and cataloguing and making the old ogre happy, huh? That was great, convincing him that you could make him out to be such a wonderful and compassionate man, not just digging into the past, but doing his best to lay it properly to rest."

"I shall enjoy every long and tedious moment of the day," she promised. "Hey, if you run over to the trailer, I bet you'll find Hank Smith. Fill him in on what we're doing. It will be good P.R. for Tyson, Smith and Tryon, as well."

"Where are those TV cameras when you need them?" Brad teased, running his fingers through his hair to smooth it back.

Leslie laughed, then saw Joe. She lifted her chin, clearly defying him to accuse Brad of anything as she walked over to where he was standing with Adam and Nikki.

"I hear you have another success story going," he said.

"I'm happy. I think we're doing the right thing," she said.

"Good. And Adam and Nikki are staying, so I've been told."

Leslie frowned at that, looking at the other two. "I don't like holding you guys back," she said.

"If it weren't fine, we wouldn't be doing it," Nikki said.

"Well, then, I'm off to see a man about a map—a bunch of maps, actually," Joe said. He didn't touch Leslie, not in that company, though he longed to. "I want to check out some public records," he added.

"I see. And you're meeting Brad for drinks this evening?" Leslie asked.

"Yes. Can I find you all for dinner after?"

"You've got my cell phone number," she reminded

him, studying his eyes. She was obviously still worried about his upcoming conversation with Brad.

"And you can call *me* if you need me. Anytime." He looked from Leslie to Nikki to Adam, then back to Leslie. She was smiling again. She appreciated his concern, he knew, and he thought she really did like having him around.

With a wave, he left.

His ultimate destination was the office of public records, but he didn't head straight there. Instead, despite the traffic, he found himself driving around the area, putting together a mental map that included the prostitutes' street, the position of the dig, Hastings House and the subway. There was a lot of ongoing construction in the area. There were cranes, scaffolding and temporary wire fences on several blocks. Finally he headed past the tenement where he had talked with Heidi Arundsen and Didi, then he continued on at last to his destination.

Leslie was pleased with the day's work, especially because Laymon had accepted the ongoing help of both Nikki and Adam with little question once he'd discovered that they knew how to move delicately and that Adamwas a whiz at deciphering records. Besides, they were free labor, the professor had said with a smile.

They never left the site for lunch but sat in the shade and ate sandwiches from the back of a truck. When five rolled around, they were exhausted.

"That really was a good day's work," Leslie murmured, stretching her back, ready to call it quits.

Laymon sniffed. "The first in several days," he commented.

Leslie grinned at Nikki and Adam as they all cleaned up as best they could in a hurry. Brad actually seemed eager to meet with Joe.

"Well . . . have fun," she told him, refraining from telling him that Joe suspected he might be a maniacal killer.

By the time she, Nikki and Adam walked back to Hastings House, it was closed to the public for the day, and the staff had all gone home. Adam excused himself, saying that he wanted to rest before dinner. Leslie and Nikki showered to rid themselves of the dust from their work in the crypt, and then Leslie said, "Want to go for a walk?"

"Sure. I'm up for whatever you think will help."

A few minutes later, they left the house.

"What?" Leslie demanded, seeing the troubled look that had suddenly come over Nikki's face.

"Nothing."

"What?" Leslie insisted.

"I . . . I might have seen Matt," the other woman said softly.

Leslie frowned, grabbing her arm. "Where? When? Why didn't I see him?"

She didn't realize what a death grip she had on her friend until Nikki gently removed her hand. "I . . . I've been at this longer, I guess. And I'm not certain at all. It was such a pale image."

"What was he doing?"

"It was as if . . . as if he was guarding the front door," Nikki said. "And . . ."

"And what?"

"He reached out for you as we were leaving."

Leslie stared at her, then went running back up the steps to the house. She opened the door, almost forgetting to turn off the alarm as she burst into the entry hall.

"Matt?"

Nikki waited outside, behind her.

"Matt, please!" Leslie said urgently as she walked farther into the room. Suddenly she thought she felt it. Something gentle against her cheek, her hair. She stood there, waiting. She couldn't leave.

Nikki came back inside, closing the door behind her.

"Do you see him?" Leslie whispered.

"No, I'm sorry."

Leslie couldn't see him, but she felt him. She was sure of it.

As she stood there, she suddenly heard the sobbing again. She spun around to stare at Nikki. "Do you hear it?"

Nikki frowned. "I'm . . . I'm not sure."

Leslie still couldn't see Matt, but she could hear him then.

Ignore whatever you think you hear, please. It's . . . it's dangerous for you. I'll find a way to help, I promise, but you have to get out. You have to leave. Dear, God, Leslie . . .

Ghosts were supposed to be accompanied by a chill, but all she felt was warmth. The warmth of his love. She shook her head. "I can't ignore it," she said aloud. "I can't, Matt."

She turned and started walking through the house, through the kitchen, to the servants' pantry. She lifted the hatch.

"Leslie, what are you doing?" Nikki demanded from behind her.

"Listening."

The crying sound floated faintly in the air, hollow, haunting.

"Are we going down?" Nikki asked.

Leslie spun around to face her. "Don't you hear it?"

Nikki looked back at her and sighed. "Yes, I hear something, like a keening. But it isn't real."

"Not this time," Leslie said. Then, decisively, "Come on. We're going for that walk."

She closed the hatch and started back toward the front of the house. Nikki followed her, questions in her eyes, but patient.

Leslie let Nikki leave first, then looked back into the house.

"Don't leave me," she whispered. "Matt . . . don't leave me."

She set the alarm, then closed and locked the door. "I want to go around the block, if that sounds okay to you."

"Wherever you want to go," Nikki assured her.

They started walking.

· · ·

There was no way out of the fact that a lot of investigative work was time-consuming and tedious. Such had been Joe's day.

But by the time he was due to meet with Brad, he had discovered several new links. For one thing, he now knew that Genevieve had almost certainly known Hank Smith well.

Furthermore, the building where Heidi Arundsen lived and Betty had once resided wasn't owned by a single man. It was managed by a drunkard with a record, a man named Sylvester Swanson. But Swanson was paid by something called the Jigger Land Corporation, which had been purchased by a megacompany two years ago.

Tyson, Smith and Tryon.

He had sifted through facts on the building and the facts on cars. Laymon drove a white Ford SUV. Brad had a refurbished classic Mustang. Hank owned a Mercedes, a Rolls and a Jaguar. Ken Dryer wheeled around in a beige Infiniti, and Robert Adair had a ten-year-old Buick. None of them owed a black sedan.

But as Eileen Brideswell had pointed out, there were hundreds of them parked in the financial district on a daily basis. He knew for a fact that both police officers, given their positions, would have access to city vehicles, plenty of which were black sedans. Hank could probably drive anything he wanted from the corporate motor pool.

Did that cut down on the possibility that Brad was the likeliest suspect?

With that information tempering the edge of his suspicions, he was able to meet Brad with a pleasant greeting. In a few minutes, they each had a Guinness and were seated in a corner booth. Joe had intentionally chosen the seat facing the door so he could see who else came and went.

"All right, why am I here?" Brad asked suddenly.

Good, Joe thought. No messing around.

"You were friends with Genevieve O'Brien," Joe said flatly.

Brad didn't seem thrown by the question. "Yes. I knew her."

"You dated her?"

He laughed. "She turned me down flat. No, wait, I can't say that. She was charming, but she still said no. Said she was too busy to spend time on a casual affair with a guy who liked too many casual affairs. I tried to convince her that I was actually the perfect guy for her—I wouldn't be too time consuming."

"Certainly not—especially since you were living in Virginia."

Brad waved a hand in the air. "It was a long time ago, a couple of years."

"And you haven't seen her since?"

"Oh, sure. Now and then. I'd, um, run into her."

Joe set the enhanced photo with Betty, Genevieve and Brad on the table.

"This you?"

"Sure looks like me."

"You do realize that the other girl in that photo is one of the prostitutes who disappeared."

"No!" Brad's jaw fell. He was either a hell of an actor or he was honestly surprised.

"Did you ever, shall we say, enjoy her services?"

Brad was studying the picture; he seemed distracted. "No . . . there were one or two girls, but not her." He looked up. "Hey, don't go judging me. I like the bar scene. I like women. Sometimes I'd rather find a good whore than play games at a bar. Cut and dried. Payment up front. Look, my career means everything to me. I'm not interested in getting involved at the moment. Who knows? I might have fallen in love with Leslie, but she was already in love with Matt from the time I first met her. She's still in love with him. Don't kid yourself."

"You can be connected to at least one of the missing hookers. You were friends of a sort with Genevieve. Some people might say that makes you look mighty damned suspicious."

"For hiring whores?"

"How often did you come up from Virginia?" Joe demanded.

"A few weekends, that's all."

"It would be interesting to know what weekends."

Brad stared at Joe, his jaw set. Then he shook his head. "You want my calendar? I'll get it for you."

"Do you want me to clear you? Get off your back?" Joe asked.

"Hell, yes, I want you to clear me. Maybe I should have offered you some of this information before, but, hell. You didn't exactly explain that in a city of millions—more than a few of them total loonies—you'd decided someone around Leslie had to be a murderer. Or kidnapper. Or whatever." He looked irritated. "Hey, you want to know who Genevieve had a beef with? Hank Smith."

"What was her beef with him about?"

"I don't know. I do know that one night when I was out for a stroll—looking to pick up a hooker, if you must know—I saw her with him in a coffee shop. I'd have said hello, but they didn't see me. They were too busy fighting."

Joe was glad he'd taken the seat facing the door when he saw Eileen Brideswell come in. She was with Robert Adair.

"You want some wings?" Joe asked.

"What?"

"Wings. Chicken wings. They call them clovers here. I'm starving."

"Yeah, sure. Get some wings."

"Unless that's all you have to say and you want me to get the hell away."

"Wings sound good," Brad said, sipping his Guinness.

Joe motioned to their waitress and put in the order. So far, neither Robert nor Eileen had noticed the two of them.

"So what's up with you and Leslie?" Brad asked, breaking into Joe's thoughts.

"Pardon?"

Brad leaned back. "You're not an old friend at all, are you? You may be Matt's cousin, but you just met Leslie recently, right?"

He stared at Brad. "I'll tell you this. I'd die for her. And I'd kill for her."

Brad was dead still for a minute. "See, here's what you don't understand about me. I wouldn't die for anyone. Les actually knows that about me, and she doesn't hate me for it. The whole world can't be as noble as Matt—and you. What is it with her and dead people, do you think? It works out great for me. I get all kinds of credit I don't deserve. But how does she do it?"

"She's a great researcher."

"Oh, bull. She was always good, but since the explosion . . . You know, she was actually more or less pronounced dead at the scene. They had her over with the corpses, but then one of the paramedics caught something . . . a pulse. They lost her, then zapped her back. Think she met a bunch of dead people and brought them back with her?"

Joe leaned forward. "Maybe she can smell out the dead. And maybe she can smell out the living—who create the dead."

"I'm telling you, you need to question Hank Smith. You don't believe me? Ask your buddy about it, Sergeant Adair. He knew about it. Genevieve complained to him about the guy. I honestly don't know what her problem with him was, other than something

374

to do with the company. But she wanted Robert's help—she wanted Hank arrested."

Brad sounded on the up-and-up. And with the information he'd recently gleaned, Joe knew exactly why Genevieve would have had a beef with Hank Smith—and all of Tyson, Smith and Tryon. He really didn't like Hank Smith. It would be easy—and convenient—to discover the man was guilty.

The wings came. "You're not seeing Leslie tonight?" Brad asked.

"Yeah, I am. I'll be staying at Hastings House."

Brad smirked. "It helps to look like the man she loved, huh?"

"Actually, it's none of your business."

Brad laughed. "All right. I suppose you're not sleeping with her. You're too noble for that, right? Or are you? Maybe you're just playing the good guy, strong and reliable, and when the time is right . . . You're a player, the same as any man. And don't go looking at me like that. She's never going to love me, so good luck to you." He shook his head. The wings had arrived, and he dipped one in hot sauce. "I'm not as big an asshole as you probably think. I love Leslie. She's a friend, one of my best friends. I was pretty nuts about Genevieve, too. I cared enough about her to respect her and *not* hit on her when she told me it wasn't happening." He chewed for a minute. "I felt sick when I heard she had disappeared. Did you know her?"

"No."

"She was beautiful. Absolutely beautiful. Huge eyes, hair like a deep auburn blanket of silk around her shoulders. And her voice . . . The main thing, though, what a fighter. When she thought something was right . . ."

"You're talking about her in the past tense."

"Do you really think she could still be alive?" he asked.

There was genuine hope in the guy's voice, Joe realized. He wasn't using the past tense because he knew for a fact that she was dead, only because he was afraid to think otherwise.

"Maybe. No one's proved she's dead, so . . ."

"No one's proved that any of those girls is dead, either," Brad said dully. "But I'll bet they are."

At that moment, Joe's cell phone began to ring.

He noticed that Robert Adair's phone had just started ringing, as well.

"What if I'm wrong?" Leslie murmured.

"What if you're right?" Nikki asked.

They had walked around the block. And around the block again. And each time, Leslie had slowed as they had got to a certain section of the sidewalk. The way she figured it, if she really had heard crying when she'd been in the basement, it had come from somewhere around here.

Because of construction, there was a wire mesh fence surrounding the corner building, with a barrier of narrow boards across a gap about ten feet wide between the building being worked on and the one next to it.

Leslie tried to figure distances. Hastings House was on the opposite side of the block. But beyond the boards and wire, this building's basement would abut the basement below the servants' pantry.

The cocktail hour was still in full swing. There were people everywhere. Down the street, Leslie knew, cops would be on duty all night, guarding the perimeters of the dig.

"We can slip behind those boards," Leslie mused.

"But we shouldn't. Why don't we call the cops?"

"What if I call the cops and they just laugh at me or, worse, tell me to mind my own business?"

"Call a cop you know, then. Call Joe."

Leslie hesitated. "He's with Brad right now. If we just slip behind the boards and check out what's down that alley . . . Come on. Let's just take a quick look. And then we'll call someone."

Nikki took a look around. There were people everywhere. "I guess we're safe. But it's pretty dark back there."

Leslie grinned. "Hey, you forget what I do for a living. I *always* have a flashlight." She reached into her purse, producing her slim but powerful flashlight.

"Okay, we take a quick look and then we call someone else."

"You heard the crying," Leslie reminded her firmly.

"Yes," Nikki admitted. "And I think we should call the cops."

Leslie grinned at her and ducked behind the barricade. Nikki swore, looked around, then followed her quickly.

A few feet along the alley, they hit what looked as if it had once been a shaft.

"Look," Leslie said excitedly to Nikki.

They could see where the opening had been covered and the cover nailed shut. "I think," Leslie said thoughtfully, "that this is an old subway entrance. In use sometime around 1915. See, you can just see a hint of tile there. . . ."

"Possibly," Nikki agreed.

Leslie started pulling at one of the boards that covered the opening. To her amazement, it came free instantly, so easily that she staggered backward. "Someone has pulled up that board before," she said.

"Leslie, we really need to call the police," Nikki said.

"Wait . . . just let me be sure."

She trained her flashlight into the opening. "There are stairs!" she said excitedly. "It *is* an abandoned subway entrance."

"Great, now let's go."

"Just let me get a better view," Leslie implored.

She knelt down and rested her left hand on one of the boards that was still in place, leaning down to get a better view. The board gave way, and she gasped and went careening forward.

"Leslie!" Nikki yelled as she made a grab to save her. Too late. Leslie hit the stairs and began to roll. When she reached the bottom, she bumped up against something that broke her fall.

"Leslie!" Nikki yelled again.

"I'm all right!" she shouted back. "I'm at the bottom of the stairs."

She trained her light over the wall. This area had been boarded up, as well, in an effort to keep anyone from getting onto the unused tracks. There were weeds growing here and there, and at some point people had managed to throw empty bottles and trash down the opening.

She trained her light on the barrier. It was old. She was sure that it had been put up decades ago. Shops, houses, the street itself, must have changed time and time again since the entrance had originally been abandoned and covered. Beyond the boards, she knew, there would be darkness. An old tunnel, dangerous, unused. She closed her eyes for a minute, trying to remember the old subway maps she had copied at the library. The tunnel was right where it should have been—and very close to the basement under the servants' pantry at Hastings House.

She started to rise, then remembered that her fall had been broken by something at the bottom of the steps.

Curious, she trained her light downward.

It appeared to be a bundle of old clothing.

Suddenly she realized that there was an unpleasant scent in the air.

The scent of decay . . .

She reached down, her light still trained on the bundle of clothing.

It was then that she realized she was looking at the body of a dead woman.

18

Joe's heart was in his throat when he arrived on the scene.

The street was crowded with police cars, the coroner's wagon and a dozen detectives. He arrived with Robert Adair, who immediately took charge. At first, Joe couldn't even find Leslie, there was so much commotion.

Then he saw her.

She was standing by one of the police cars, with Nikki beside her. She didn't appear to be hurt or even fazed. In fact, she looked incredibly calm.

He went over to her immediately, taking her by the arms, searching her eyes. "Okay," he said, and he cast a reproachful glance toward Nikki. "Explain to me how you happened to be down at the bottom of an abandoned subway entrance."

She stared at him, opened her mouth to speak, then paused as if to rephrase her answer. "I just . . . found it. The boards were loose, so I took a peek."

"Like hell," Joe muttered. "Excuse me. I need to see if they'll let me see the body."

Luckily, one of the cops guarding the entrance to the alley happened to be the guy Joe had talked to a few nights earlier. He sent Joe through to Robert Adair, who was down at the foot of the stairs. One of the detectives tried to stop him, but Robert shouted up that it was all right for Joe to come down.

The body was badly decayed, and insects and other scavengers had obviously been dining on it for a while.

The M.E. stood, dusting his gloved hands. "She's been down here a long time, probably four to eight weeks. Some of the flesh has been eaten entirely away. They've got a serious rat problem here."

"But it's definitely a woman?"

The M.E. nodded. "I'd say between the ages of twenty-five and thirty-five. She was about five and a half feet tall, maybe a hundred and twenty pounds."

One of the detectives nervously joked, "Hell of a way to lose weight, huh?"

"All right, all right," Robert said. "Cause of death? Can you tell me that yet?"

"Strangulation. Her own scarf."

"Is it one of the prostitutes?" another officer asked.

The M.E. shrugged. "Guys, as you can see, I don't have a lot to work with here. I'll get you facts as fast as I can."

"Right," Robert said, then swore. "Hell, we knew they had to be somewhere. Dead two months or so . . . has to be our last girl."

Or Genevieve O'Brien? Joe thought.

"Unless it's Genevieve O'Brien," someone said, voicing his own fears.

Except that, despite the state of the body, Joe knew it wasn't. There wasn't so much as a hint of red in the hair. It was Betty. He didn't need the M.E.'s report to settle that in his mind.

He prayed that whatever sixth sense Leslie had accessed during her "vision" was right and Genevieve was alive somewhere.

When he headed back toward the police car where Leslie was waiting, Joe discovered that she was giving a detailed report to one of the officers—and she was lying through her teeth. She had stepped behind the barricade to pull up her panty hose, stepped on the boards over the opening without realizing it, and they'd given way under her weight and she'd fallen down the steps. Then Nikki had dialed 911 and made certain Robert Adair was alerted.

Robert had followed Joe up to the surface and joined them over by the car. "Detective Langdon, are you done with these ladies?" he asked.

"Yes, sir."

"Take them home, Joe. As soon as I have anything on the body, I'll let you know."

Joe nodded. "Thanks. You know, this may not even be one of our girls."

"May not be," Robert said with a shrug. "But their street is only a block away. Anyway, I'll call you."

"All right, you two," Joe said to Leslie and Nikki. "Let's go."

"Joe, don't be angry," Leslie implored.

"I'm not angry."

"Yes, you are."

"No, you've just found a murder victim, maybe helped solved a puzzle the police haven't gotten a grip on in almost two years. Was it at great personal risk?

Yes. But am I angry? No. But, Leslie, why the hell didn't you call someone?"

"I was going to. I fell down the steps," she said. "Honest."

He sighed, setting an arm around her shoulders and staring at Nikki.

"We were going to call for help just as soon as we got a look," she said.

Joe groaned. "I'm getting you back to Hastings House, and we'll send out for pizza," he said, starting down the sidewalk.

Leslie looked at him, puzzled. "Uh, sure."

"I'd like to keep you off the streets and away from holes in the ground for a while. I've got to go back out, but you're staying in. I'm going to hire an off-duty cop to watch Hastings House tonight."

He was walking too quickly, he realized. Leslie and Nikki were both having to hurry to keep up. "Joe, why do we need a guard at the house? Adam will be there, Nikki will be there, and later on you'll be there."

"I don't know when I'll get there. And I want the code on the alarm changed—" why hadn't he taken care of that before? he berated himself "—and another bolt added to the door. Also, I want a steel bar for the hatch cover in the dead room."

"The dead room?" Nikki asked.

"The servants' pantry," Leslie explained.

When they reached the house, they didn't have to explain to Adam what had happened. They found him in the kitchen, watching the news. He ignored Joe and looked directly at Leslie. "You knew she was down there?"

"Not exactly," she said.

"Oh?" Adam persisted.

"But earlier, I heard crying," Leslie said.

"You heard a dead woman crying?" Joe asked in disbelief.

She stared at him, standing tall and straight, hands on her hips. "Yes."

"Nikki and Leslie can both . . . see things from beyond the grave," Adam said delicately.

"You see ghosts?" Joe accused Leslie.

"Sometimes."

He shook his head. "Matt? Do you see Matt?"

"No," she said, but her voice quavered.

"Adam, let's you and I go get some takeout," Nikki suggested.

"Come right back, please," Joe said, the words clearly an order, but his eyes stayed hard on Leslie's.

She was silent as they left.

"You actually see ghosts," he said at last.

"Sometimes," she repeated. "In this case . . . I heard crying. But, Joe—"

He waved a hand to cut her off.

"You don't believe me," she said.

"I *do* believe you. That's the problem," he told her.

"I don't understand."

"Leslie, you've got to get out of here. I mean it."

"But, Joe—"

"Leslie, I think you were the target on the night of

the gala, not Matt. I just don't know why. And now someone out there is kidnapping and killing women. And I think it's someone who knows you. Who knows you have a gift for finding the dead. For whatever reason—maybe for lots of reasons—someone sees you as a threat, don't you see that? And you're in danger here."

She was quiet. "How's Brad?"

Joe frowned, startled by the question. "He's fine."

"So you didn't . . . ?"

"I told you I wasn't going to hurt him and I didn't."

"But you still think . . . ?"

"I think he's a jackass, but one with a certain amount of integrity. Is he guilty? I still don't know. What I do know is that the area around here is honeycombed with underground passages. And there are a few things I have to do tonight, but I'm going to see to it that you're safe. I'm going to rejoin the police, and we're going to find the truth. Without you. Do you understand?"

"Joe," she said firmly. "Maybe things happen for a reason. Maybe I'm back here to help, to stop this bastard. For all I know, maybe I wasn't supposed to survive the explosion, but now I have a chance to try to help. You have to let me. Please."

"You *have* helped, Leslie. But now you have to let the pros take over."

He took her into his arms then and cradled her against him. Every male cell in his body wanted more. Every caution in his mind warned him that he could offer no more than his support right now, his friend-ship, his strength . . . his life.

He drew away, even though she wasn't fighting his hold. She was staring up into his eyes.

She touched his cheek, a smile slowly curving her lips. "I'll behave. Where are you going?"

"I want to get back to Robert. The rest of that tunnel needs to be checked out."

She frowned and backed away from him, her words suddenly urgent. "That's the most important thing you can do. She's down there somewhere, Joe. Genevieve is down there."

"How can you be so certain?"

"Because of the crying."

"But you said—"

"I heard the echo of the dead girl's tears, but I hear Genevieve crying, too, and her tears are real. And she's not far from this house. I know it."

He pulled out his cell phone. Then he hesitated. It was ridiculous to suspect Robert. But Robert had been on his list, and Robert was the one handling what was now no longer a missing persons case but a homicide.

Leslie didn't want to suspect Brad.

No one wanted to believe someone they knew and liked was capable of evil.

He realized he was going to have to head straight over to police HQ as soon as Adam and Nikki got back. To be professional, he had to work this as he would any other case, and that meant involving law enforcement. Luckily, it wasn't far. His feeling of urgency seemed to be increasing by the minute. Just then he heard the door open. "Pizza!" Nikki called out.

Leslie smiled. "It's okay, go."

He nodded. "And you be careful. When I get back, we have to talk."

She smiled, rose on her toes and kissed his cheek.

He left the kitchen just as Nikki and Adam entered carrying pizza boxes and a bag of sodas.

"You're not eating?" Nikki asked.

"Leslie will explain," he said. "Don't leave her," he ordered as he left.

"Not a chance," Nikki assured him.

After he left, Leslie ate pizza, drank soda and carried on what she thought was a calm conversation, but she felt as if she were going insane.

"Why don't we try it?" Nikki asked.

Leslie stared at Nikki blankly. Apparently she hadn't been managing the conversation as well as she'd thought. "Try what?"

"A seance."

"A seance?" She almost choked on her pizza. "A *seance?* Nikki, isn't that pretty silly for people like us?"

"Maybe not," Adam told her. "Maybe Matt has some learning to do and this will help."

She stared at them both. "Okay. If you think it can help."

Nikki shrugged. "The goal now is to find Genevieve alive. Whether any of the ghosts here can help with that or not, I don't know. But . . ."

"Okay, let's try it. If there's anything we can do, we should do it," Leslie said.

"Where?" Adam asked.

"Where else?" Leslie said. "The dead room."

After several frustrating minutes in which he was continually told that the man to talk to was Robert Adair, Joe was tempted to give up. It wasn't as if he didn't have other suspects. But Robert, Ken Dryer and Hank Smith were probably the only ones in his group to have access to a contemporary black sedan at a moment's notice. Tyson, Smith and Tryon would have a fleet of cars. And as high-ranking officers, both Dryer and Adair could use any car in the police motor pool.

He put through a call to Eileen Brideswell. "I need help. Now," he told her.

In a few minutes he was ushered through to the office of Lieutenant Grayson. Grayson was nearing sixty, thin and haggard. He lowered his head in thought as Joe laid out what he knew, which was, sadly, mostly hypothetical. He refrained from saying that he didn't want to take this evidence to Robert Adair because he was on the suspect list; he managed to make out that Robert was overworked and he didn't want to burden him any further.

Before Genevieve O'Brien was found as a rotting corpse, as well.

"I can give you three men," Grayson said. "And permission to enter the tunnels."

"That's all I need. Thanks."

"Thank Eileen Brideswell," Grayson said. It was obvious that he was feeling pressured into offering help. Why not? He already had a key officer on the case.

Grayson put through a call to a man in charge of the Metropolitan Transit Authority, and then Joe was on his way with three uniformed officers in tow. In a few minutes they were met at the functioning subway entrance nearest Hastings House by an MTA employee named Gregory Breen.

He offered Joe a map. "How good this is, I don't really know. Once you leave the main system, you're in no man's land. No one has used a lot of the old tunnels since . . . hell, the twenties, maybe."

Breen took them down, leading them through an employee route to a tiny station somewhere below Broadway, where they came to a locked door. He unlocked and opened it, and they came face-to-face with a wooden barricade.

"Told you," Breen said. "These tunnels have been blocked off for decades."

Joe reached toward the wooden barricade, which collapsed at his touch, the wood rotted and soft.

"Well, I'll be a monkey's uncle!" Breen exploded.

"Do we really need candles?" Leslie asked.

"Why not set the mood?" Adam replied cheerfully.

"Got any good wine?" Leslie asked dryly.

"Sit," Nikki told her.

They'd brought a table into the servants' pantry, and set three candles on it. Some light still filtered in from the main kitchen, but the small room itself was shrouded in shadow.

"What now?" Leslie asked.

"We hold hands," Adam said.

"And then . . . ?"

"Leave it to Nikki."

As they sat there, Leslie closed her eyes. Somehow it seemed like the right thing to do.

She waited, wondering what words Nikki would say to try to conjure the spirits. But there was no hoopla.

"Matt," Nikki said softly. "If you're there, we need help. We know that you've been trying to reach Leslie, that you *have* reached her, but we need more help from you. Please, if you can . . ."

Nikki was still speaking when Leslie first felt him. Somehow she knew he was by her side.

And when she turned, she could see him.

He was there, and yet he wasn't there. He was only the merest suggestion of a form in the air, but at the same time he was the man she had known, tall, handsome and, at that moment, serious. She forgot that Nikki and Adam were present and stood, slipping into his arms. He wasn't real, but somehow she could feel him, feel his touch on her hair, his strength as he pulled her against him. And she could hear him. *"Leslie, you've got to get out of here, all of you. He came in by the front door. He knows the combination."*

"Who?" Nikki's question was Leslie's first indication that she wasn't the only one hearing Matt.

"I don't know, but I know he's close. I fought him last time, but I couldn't stop him. Please . . . get out."

Suddenly the house was pitched into blackness, only the candles offering a respite from the all-encompassing darkness.

"Someone's here," Adam said.

And Leslie felt suddenly cold.

Matt had left her.

"What exactly are we looking for?" Officer Dale Nelson was young, just out of the academy. Joe didn't mind that fact. Nelson was willing and adventurous. He was just uncertain. Whether Nelson or O'Hara and Myers, the two older cops, believed in their quest or not, they had been told to listen to him and give him their best. He'd sent the two veteran cops down a northeastern tunnel, while he had chosen the more westerly one for himself and Nelson.

Closest to the prostitutes' street, Hastings House, the dig—and the site where they had found the body earlier. If Leslie really had heard sobbing from inside Hastings House, he had to be going in the right direction. If only the remains of the system didn't add up to such a labyrinth. Progress had left behind a bone structure that was now sad and dilapidated.

And dark.

"We're looking for a room of some kind. A room that might be used as a cell," Joe explained. "Look for anything that might be a door."

"Gotcha," Nelson said. Suddenly he let out a hoarse cry.

"What?" Joe demanded.

"Rat," Nelson said apologetically. "Sorry."

"Right."

They kept on trudging.

"Douse those," Adam said, and Nikki quickly put out the candles. They stood in the pitch dark, and Leslie nearly jumped a mile when she felt a hand on her shoulder. It was Adam. "I'm going for the gun."

"Upstairs?" she asked.

"Yes."

"No!"

"I have to."

"Adam—"

"I'll be careful."

He disappeared, but Leslie could hear Nikki breathing at her side. "We can't just stay here," she whispered.

"Do you have a better suggestion?" Nikki asked.

She did. Down in the basement. There were tools down there. Weapons with which they could fight back.

"Hey!" They heard a sudden cry from the parlor. "What's going on in here?"

Brad! Leslie didn't know whether to trust him or not. Had he cut off the electricity to take them by surprise? Or was someone else in the house, too?

She didn't know the answers to any of those questions.

She dragged the table aside and moved the braided rug.

"Come on," she whispered urgently to Nikki.

"No . . . you go down there. No one knows anything about me. You hide, and I'll cover the floor with the rug. Go!"

"Nikki, I can't leave you in danger."

"I'm not the one in danger. I'll hide, too, but if I don't put the rug back, it will be obvious where you are. Now get down there!"

Leslie did. She moved down the stairs blindly, trying to remember where she had left a lantern. She groped her way around the various boxes, until her fingers curled around a lantern at last. After more exploration she also found a scraping knife. Then she hesitated, listening, trying to see the room in her mind's eyes. A stack of boxes was piled to the right of the hearth. She slipped behind them, against the wall, the knife in one hand, the lantern in the other. She waited. And waited.

There was silence. Then . . .

Sobbing. She turned, staring in the direction of the sound, but the room was pitch black, and she couldn't hear a thing. She remembered the way Joe had been running his hands over the wall the other day. In the dark, she began to do the same thing herself.

She touched a brick, and it gave. Stunned, she paused for a moment. Then she fumbled in the darkness, found the uneven brick again and pushed until it gave even farther. Her hand met something cold and metallic. She felt it with her fingers, trying to picture what it was. Finally she pushed it, and the air itself seemed to fill with a loud, creaking sound.

The entire wall moved. She swallowed, blinked, still in darkness, aware of what had happened only because a gust of stale air struck her. The door, however, had made a sound loud enough to wake the dead. If there were indeed a killer in Hastings House, he had heard it, which meant there was no way she could go back upstairs.

There was only one way to go.

Forward.

Someone was in the house. Adam Harrison knew it even before he heard the voice call out from downstairs. When neither Leslie nor Nikki answered that call, he decided to play it safe and made his way along the upstairs hall as silently as possible, reached his gun quickly and started back toward the stairway. Then he heard a whisper in the darkness.

"Adam?"

It was Nikki.

Before he had a chance to reply, there was a commotion from below. He hurried down the stairs. He could just make out a single figure in the entry hall, but it seemed to be fighting with an unseen opponent.

"Stop or I'll shoot!" Adam shouted.

The figure stumbled out of the house, Adam in pursuit. "Stop, Adam!" Nikki called. "We'll call the police!"

"No! He'll be gone before they get here," Adam shouted without stopping.

As he tore out of the house, he realized that Nikki was right behind him.

"Shit!" Nelson yelled.

Joe spun around, wondering if he should have saddled himself with such a rookie.

But this time there was a look of agony on the young man's face.

"What?"

"My fucking ankle. I stepped into some kind of rut . . . there's a twisted rail here. Hell!"

"I can't walk. I'm sorry."

"All right. I'll get you out of here."

"No . . . hell, no. You go on."

"You want me to leave you in an abandoned tunnel?"

"I've got a light. My radio is shit down here, but the light is working. Just send help as soon as you can." He winced. "I'm serious. I'll be all right. Find that girl."

Joe nodded. "All right. I'll get someone back to you as soon as I can."

"It's a plan. Go on."

Joe nodded and left.

Leslie turned on the light; there was no reason not to. She could hear footsteps overhead. It could be Nikki or Adam, she supposed.

But maybe it wasn't.

She hurried through the doorway, checking out the door as she passed. It seemed to her that the latch and the hinges should have been far rustier. When the hell had the door been put in?

It must have been during the Civil War, when the house had been part of the Underground Railroad. She wasn't in a subway tunnel. This passage might lead to an old one, but . . .

She shoved at the door, closing it as best she could. Then she lifted her light. There was only one way to go.

She started walking, and then she froze.

"Leslie? Are you down here? What the hell is going on? The house was pitch dark and the door was open."

It was Brad, and he sounded truly baffled. But if Brad was in the basement behind her, where the hell were Nikki and Adam?

She kept silent. Then she heard the door opening and started running along the tunnel, quickly turning out the light. She heard the creaking of the door as Brad opened it.

"Leslie, it's me. Brad." He sounded indignant. "Dammit, Leslie, you've got me scared to death. Where the hell are you?"

She went still, barely daring to breathe. But she had to move, so she inched forward in the darkness, feeling her way along the wall. It was tile here, she thought. Then more brick followed concrete, before it turned to tile again.

"Leslie, it's dark in here!" Brad called.

She heard a cry in the dark, followed by a thud, like something heavy falling.

Brad?

Then nothing.

She hurried along, silent, desperate. Someone was behind her. She was sure of it. And something told her that it was no longer Brad.

Tile . . . concrete . . . damp and slick beneath her hand. Then . . . wood?

There was noise coming from the shaft ahead, but Joe couldn't tell what the hell it was. He drew his gun, holding his lantern high.

It seemed close . . . yet simultaneously far away.

Swearing, he paused to pull out the map again.

There was a tunnel that ran parallel to the one he was in. Apparently, it had never been part of the subway. There was a notation on it. *Old passageway, unusable, storage.*

Storage. That meant there had to be access to it somewhere. He strained to see the tunnel ahead. Was that something in the wall, about fifty feet ahead? He hurried forward to check it out.

There were bolts; she could feel them. A door! All too aware that someone was coming up behind her and with no idea how much distance there was between them, she felt for the bolts and began to work at them. She had no choice.

There was a snick as the first bolt gave. She moved faster, heedless of the noise she was making. Without meaning to, she began to scream. "Help!"

The sound came back to her as an echo as she slid the last bolt back and the door gave. Suddenly there was light. She blinked furiously against the abrupt brightness of it. She was in a room, a room that smelled of death. There was a cot in it, and a table by the cot that held a few bottles of water.

There was something piled on the far side of the room.

And there was a woman. She was dark-haired and blue-eyed, thin to the point of emaciation. Her ankles were chained together, but she was on her feet, pale and sickly but ready to do battle. Genevieve O'Brien.

"Get in! I can't believe you've found me, but he's right behind you."

Leslie turned. She screamed. He was almost on them.

"Get in!" Genevieve implored.

Leslie hurried into the room and quickly shut the door behind her. Both women laid their full weight against the door as someone pounded against it from the other side. Genevieve looked at her. "Who are you? How did you get here? Now he'll kill us both."

"But you're alive," Leslie gasped, fighting to hold the door. How long could they manage it? Who knew she was here? *Adam and Nikki.*

If they were still alive.

"Who is he?" Leslie demanded. "Who?"

Even as she asked, their enemy hit the door with staggering force and sent them flying backward.

And she knew.

Joe found the door. He thundered his weight against it time after time, trying to break through the rust of decades. Finally it gave.

He was in another tunnel. At one end, he could see a gaping doorway. Hastings House. If he had his bearings right, that was Hastings House. The crypt. And he had been right. There *was* a false wall, and it was open now.

He heard groaning and hurried forward, his light high. There was a body on the floor. He knelt down beside it and heard another groan.

Brad.

The man blinked. "What the hell . . . ? Why did you hit me like that? I swear, when I got to the house it was dark and the door was wide open. I started looking for someone . . . I went down to the basement and . . . Look, I wouldn't hurt Leslie, I swear!"

"Where the hell is she?"

"How should I know? You hit me."

"I didn't hit you."

It was then that he heard a bloodcurdling scream.

Robert Adair came in, a sad look on his face. "Leslie, I knew you were trouble."

"Robert," Genevieve said, bizarrely cheerful. "You're here. Please don't be angry. I think it will be wonderful to have Leslie with us."

Leslie shook her head, stunned, thinking as fast as she could, playing for time. Playing for her life. "Robert . . . think about what you're doing. I think you wanted to be found. You set Joe up with Eileen Brideswell. You're a good man. You don't want to hurt me."

His gun was drawn. She knew that he had killed before. She swallowed, suddenly realizing what the pile on the far side of the room was. One or more of the other girls. He had left their bodies here with Genevieve so she would know her inevitable fate. So she would behave. So he could bend her to his will.

"Leslie, why couldn't you have died in that blast? Then . . . you could have stayed away, but you didn't. Ask Genevieve—there's only one way to handle women. She had such a fit about those hookers going missing. She was going to do something. So she had to come here. She's been a delight, I have to say. But then, she wants to live."

"Leslie wants to live, too," Genevieve said.

"Robert," Leslie said, a shocked whisper of disbelief. "I just can't believe it's you."

"Who else?" he asked lightly. "Who else had access to sites and houses and cars, and who else could go all over the city, doing as he pleased? These tunnels are quite something, you know. You can get right into Hastings House. Of course, you figured that out, didn't you, Leslie? But did you know there's an entrance right into that crypt you discovered? I would have taken care of things the morning you were down there alone, but then Laymon had to show up before I could drag you away. No one would have known. But he showed up and I had to leave in a hurry. You're remarkably hard to kill, young lady. Not even a push onto the subway tracks could do it. You've got to understand. I never wanted to hurt you. But you know way too much. I don't know how you know, you just do. You would have discovered me eventually. You have some kind of a touch or a sight, and it got even stronger after you survived the explosion. A shame, that. Four people dead, but I missed the one I meant to kill. I'm really sorry, Leslie," he said softly.

She saw that his fingers were twitching on his gun.

He was going to shoot her. Then and there.

"Stop!" a voice roared. She heard running footsteps. Joe!

Robert turned and fired into the tunnel, but his arms jerked and the shot went wild. It looked as if he was fighting with himself—or an invisible opponent. Despite that, he kept pulling the trigger.

Again and again.

The blasts were horrendously loud in the confined space, and he was cursing and screaming even as he kept firing, the shots still going wild.

Suddenly he was slammed up against the door, his mouth an O of horror, but he wouldn't let go of the gun.

Matt! Leslie thought joyously as Robert twisted, struggling to aim his gun up the tunnel.

Suddenly Joe loomed out of the darkness, and it looked as if Robert couldn't possibly miss him. "No!" Leslie shouted.

She jumped on Robert Adair's back. Genevieve shouted, desperately trying her best to distract him. A shot rang out from the tunnel, and Robert was spun around by the force of it, staring straight at the two of them.

He smiled.

Leslie wondered why.

Then she knew.

He fired one last time, even as he died himself.

"No!"

She heard Joe scream out the single word. But she was falling. Genevieve tried to catch her as she fell, but the other woman had no strength. Leslie could only imagine what she had endured over the past weeks. They fell to the floor together as Joe raced toward them.

But she didn't see Joe.

She saw Matt.

He was down on his knees beside her, wrapping her in his arms.

There were tears in his eyes. "No, Leslie, no . . ."

"Leslie!" Dimly, she heard Joe shouting. He was desperately trying to staunch the flow of blood coming from her chest.

"Leslie, hang on, hang on. . . ."

She was dimly aware that the tunnels were alive with footsteps.

She smiled. She'd been blessed with good friends.

"Leslie," Matt whispered, cradling her. "Fight. *Fight.*"

She couldn't fight. And she knew it. She reached for Matt, saw his eyes, the tears. The love.

"Some things," she whispered, "are meant to be."

EPILOGUE

Joe sat on a concrete bench in the cemetery, staring at the newly tamped ground. He was alone; he needed to be. The funeral had been far too huge; he'd felt that he needed to take a step back, so this afternoon he'd come back on his own. So many good people had loved her. Adam. Nikki, who had been with Leslie when she'd discovered the street-level entrance to the tunnels, the route by which Robert had escaped the night Joe had chased him. Nikki and Adam had been there when the paramedics had desperately tried to save Leslie. They had been there when she was pronounced dead. They had suffered. As had Brad Verdun, who had cried like a baby. Even Dryer had broken down when he had to go on TV to talk about what had happened.

But that was over now. Just as the torture Robert Adair had inflicted on his victims was over. Genevieve had been able to shed some light on what had made the man crack, based on his lunatic ramblings when he came to visit her in her makeshift prison. He'd never had much of a social life, so he'd turned to hookers, then finally turned on them. In his opinion, prostitutes deserved whatever happened to them. Genevieve hadn't been alone there when he first grabbed her and he had hurt them all, she said. When he tired of a girl, when she angered him . . . he killed her. Joe was there when she stoically informed the police that she'd done what she had to do to live. She'd also informed them that she thought he'd gone psychotic because he was impotent. A powerful respected man with no one to come home to—because, in his way, he was powerless.

Joe's astonishment was fading. Despite the fact that he had listed the man as a suspect himself, he had never been on top of the list, even at the end. It was still almost inconceivable. And yet, and in retrospect, someone should have figured it out before. Except that Robert Adair had been the lead detective on the case.

The pain of Leslie's death seemed dulled now, but sometimes it struck him like a knife. He went over and over the series of events in his head, trying to create a scenario in which everything worked out differently. In which she lived.

He was carrying a single rose, and now he tossed it gently onto the grave. "I failed you," he said softly. She had no tombstone yet, but Matt's was there, a handsome, simple memorial in white marble. He'd chosen it himself. "I failed you, too," he said.

He closed his eyes. It had been an oddly beautiful day, pure blue sky, soft breeze. He had waited, though, until it was late afternoon to come back. A time when the sun was gentle, when the air was balmy, and he'd sat there until the colors of sunset had washed the sky, as if the pastel shades of the coming evening could somehow make sense of everything that had happened.

Why *had* he come?

Did he think one of them would talk to him? Maybe, he admitted.

He felt a hand on his shoulder. He turned.

Genevieve O'Brien stood there. She was almost shockingly beautiful, with her eyes the color of the sky, her hair a muted flame color that seemed to promise an inner wildness. She was slim and very pale—hell, she'd spent two months as a terrified prisoner in an underground cell—but other than that, she looked good. Her gaze was steady. But then, she'd been strong from the beginning. Strong enough to survive.

She'd spoken at the funeral. It had been an outstanding tribute to the woman who had died. For her. It had stirred every heart. For a while, at least, Joe had thought skeptically, it might improve man's behavior to his fellow man. Leslie had been a true heroine.

Earlier that day, Genevieve had been standing at the grave, ready to set her flowers on the casket, when a reporter had come up to her. That had been too much for Joe. He'd interposed himself between the two of them, and he wasn't exactly sure what he'd said, but the reporter had run, and Genevieve had looked at him with her immense blue eyes filled with tears, and she had said simply, "Thank you."

Now she joined him on the bench.

"How are you holding up?" she asked.

He stared at her. "I'm good. You . . . ?"

She stared down at the graves. "I'm good. Grateful. More determined than ever to make my life count."

She was amazing, he thought, then looked back at the graves. "I tried so hard," he murmured.

She set a hand on his shoulder. "You two saved my life. And you stopped a monster."

He shook his head. He hadn't been able to save Leslie.

"I could use a drink," she said.

"What?"

"Would you please take me somewhere— O'Malley's, maybe. I could really use a drink."

"I . . . yeah. Sure." What good did it do, sitting in a graveyard?

She stood first and offered him a hand. He accepted it, rising. They started out of the graveyard, down a gentle slope.

She stopped, turning back. "She's with him now," Genevieve said softly.

"Pardon?"

"Look."

He turned.

"Look over there. Right where we were sitting.

He did, and blinked. It was the fading sunlight. It was the wishful thinking of his numb and tangled mind.

And yet . . .

There they were. Matt. Tall, broad-shouldered, hair gleaming gold, smiling at the slender beauty standing beside him. Leslie. Leslie, elegant face lifted, eyes sparkling as she looked up at the man she loved. Matt caught her hand, laughed, took a seat on the bench and pulled her against him, cradling her there in the last rays of the setting sun.

Joe blinked. He looked at Genevieve, then back at the little rise. They were gone, of course. A cloud had dulled the brilliance of those last rays.

"Do you ever think that maybe, just maybe, she escaped death the first time because she was meant to do, because she was still needed here?" Genevieve asked softly. She squeezed his hand. "Maybe someday we'll see them again," she said pensively.

"What?"

"I'm just being whimsical," she murmured.

He couldn't help but look back again. The cloud was gone, but so was the last of the light. Maybe they were there, together, two wonderful beautiful people, impossibly in love with each other.

He looked at Genevieve.

"Did you really see . . . something?" he asked her. "Do you think it's possible . . . ?"

Genevieve laughed softly. "Know what I believe is possible now? Anything. Everything. Now come on. Buy me that drink."

She started toward the road. He followed.

Suddenly, he knew why he had come to the cemetery. To see a ghost. To ask a ghost to forgive him, to assure him everything was just as it was meant to be.

He groaned aloud. It wasn't going to become a *thing* now, was it? Was he going to see them all the time now, know where they were, what they wanted?

Hell.

Maybe he was.

He hurried, caught Genevieve's hand. She looked up at him and squeezed his hand as they walked into the neon light and vivid energy and sheer *life* of the New York City night.

Center Point Publishing
600 Brooks Road ● PO Box 1
Thorndike ME 04986-0001 USA

(207) 568-3717

US & Canada:
1 800 929-9108